Whisker of Evil

Whisker of Evil

RITA MAE BROWN

& SNEAKY PIE BROWN

ILLUSTRATIONS BY MICHAEL GELLATLY

DOUBLEDAY LARGE PRINT HOME LIBRARY EDITION

BANTAM BOOKS   NEW YORK • TORONTO • LONDON • SYDNEY • AUCKLAND

This Large Print Edition, prepared especially for Doubleday Large Print Home Library, contains the complete, unabridged text of the original Publisher's Edition.

WHISKER OF EVIL
A Bantam Book / April 2004

Published by
Bantam Dell
A Division of Random House, Inc.
New York, New York

ISBN 0-7394-4231-7

Manufactured in the United States of America

This Large Print Book carries the
Seal of Approval of N.A.V.H.

*Dedicated to
Judy Lynn Pastore.
Thank you for taking
in all those homeless
animals, including this stray.*

Acknowledgments

Not being a medical person, I relied heavily on my far more intelligent friends who are trained in the medical arts.

Martin Shulman, V.M.D., Christopher Middleton, D.V.M., and Lauren Keating, D.V.M., provided guidance and information about rabies in the animal kingdom.

Dr. Anne Bonda, along with keeping my horses healthy and happy, also provided rabies materials. "Dr. Anne" is both a gold mine of information and a godsend to humans and horses.

Dr. Mary T. O'Brien supplied facts, figures, and gruesome examples, bringing me up to speed concerning rabies in humans. It is, indeed, a dreadful disease and I am indebted to the good doctor for taking so much of her time to work with me.

Mrs. Jeanne Pitsenberger, a nurse with her own research firm, Foxdale Enterprises, piled folder upon folder on my desk. I have never worked with a researcher as organized, careful, or cheerful as Jeanne. No matter how absurd the question was I lobbed at her, shortly the answer was lobbed back.

Any mistakes in this book are due to my shortcomings and none of the above.

And concerning all of the above individuals, it is my privilege to know them. Apart from being good to me, these people cement together the communities in which we live. Our nation is filled with wonderful, giving people but it's the bums that get the headlines.

Cast of Characters

Mary Minor "Harry" Haristeen The postmistress of Crozet, Virginia, is curious, sometimes bull-headed, and often in the midst of trouble. Her life is changing and she's struggling to change with it.

Mrs. Murphy Harry's tiger cat accepts change better than her human does. She's tough, smart, and ready for action and she'll always take a little catnip, too.

Tee Tucker Harry's corgi bubbles with happiness and bravery in equal measure. She loves Harry as only a dog can love.

Pewter Harry's gray cat affects aloofness but underneath it all, she does care. What irritates her are comments about her plumpness and her hunting abilities.

Mrs. Miranda Hogendobber Miranda observes a great deal but keeps most of it to herself. A widow, she's a surrogate mother to Harry and the relationship means a great deal to both women.

Susan Tucker Harry's best friend has been putting up with her friend's curiosity and attraction to danger since they were children. They have their ups and downs like most friends but they stick together.

Fair Haristeen, D.V.M. Once Harry's childhood sweetheart and then her husband, he hopes to be her husband again. He has a good mind, a stout heart, and the patience to put up with her.

Olivia Craycroft "BoomBoom" Once Harry's nemesis, the two have settled into a slightly strained rapprochement. BoomBoom is quite beautiful, a fact never lost on men.

Alicia Palmer A former resident of Crozet, she keeps an estate there. She conquered Hollywood as an actress and now in her late fifties, she's coming home. She's retained all of her glamour while losing most of her illusions.

Rev. Herbert C. Jones Beloved, humorous, fond of fishing, all of Crozet knows that when the chips are down, "The Rev" will come through.

Marilyn Sanburne "Big Mim" The Queen of Crozet exerts her social power with whatever force is needed to accomplish her task. She can be a snob but she's fair in her own fashion and believes strongly in justice.

Jim Sanburne As the mayor of Crozet, he presides over the town, which is easier to do sometimes than to be Big Mim's husband.

Marilyn Sanburne, Jr. "Little Mim" She is emerging from her mother's influence. She's a contemporary of Harry, Susan, and BoomBoom but she's always been set apart by her family's wealth. She is the vice-mayor of Crozet and a Republican, which is quite interesting since her father is a Democrat.

Deputy Cynthia Cooper A young, bright officer in the Sheriff's Department, she likes law enforcement but wonders if it keeps romance at bay. She's become a buddy of Harry's and the cats and dog like her, too.

Sheriff Rick Shaw There are days now when Rick is tired of criminals, tired of their lies, tired of pressing the county commissioners for more funds. But when a murder occurs, he focuses his sharp mind to bring the pieces of the puzzle together—if only that damned Harry and her pets would get out of the way.

Tavener Heyward, D.V.M. A greatly respected equine veterinarian contemplating retirement. He's generous, hardworking, and often a mentor to young people in the horse industry.

Mary Patricia Reines Missing since 1974, she casts a lonely shadow over Crozet. She was wealthy, fun-loving, and strong-minded. She ran St. James Farm, breeding thoroughbreds for the track, and she was successful at it.

Tazio Chappars A young architect of mixed race, she gets men's hearts racing. She's a rather serious sort of woman but kind and considerate.

Paul de Silva Big Mim's new stable manager is handsome, efficient, and a little bit shy. He's crazy about Tazio.

Barry Monteith and Sugar Thierry Two young men, partners in the thoroughbred breeding and lay-up operation, have made some good bloodline choices but some shaky choices in women.

Carmen Gamble The young owner of Shear Heaven, a beauty parlor, exercises a sharp pair of scissors and a sharp tongue. She has energy to burn; if only she had money to burn.

Whisker of Evil

┌─────────┐
│   1   │
└─────────┘

Barry Monteith was still breathing when Harry found him. His throat had been ripped out.

Tee Tucker, a corgi, racing ahead of Mary Minor Haristeen as well as the two cats, Mrs. Murphy and Pewter, found him first.

Barry was on his back, eyes open, gasping and gurgling, life ebbing with each spasm. He did not recognize Tucker nor Harry when they reached him.

"Barry, Barry." Harry tried to comfort him, hoping he could hear her. "It will be all right," she said, knowing perfectly well he was dying.

The tiger cat, Mrs. Murphy, watched the blood jet upward.

"*Jugular*," fat, gray Pewter succinctly commented.

Gently, Harry took the young man's hand and prayed, "Dear Lord, receive into thy bosom the soul of Barry Monteith, a good man." Tears welled in her eyes.

Barry jerked, then his suffering ended.

Death, often so shocking to city dwellers, was part of life here in the country. A hawk would swoop down to carry away the chick while the biddy screamed useless defiance. A bull would break his hip and need to be put down. And one day an old farmer would slowly walk to his tractor only to discover he couldn't climb into the seat. The Angel of Death placed his hand on the stooping shoulder.

It appeared the Angel had offered little peaceful deliverance to Barry Monteith, thirty-four, fit, handsome with brown curly hair, and fun-loving. Barry had started his own business, breeding thoroughbreds, a year ago, with a business partner, Sugar Thierry.

"Sweet Jesus." Harry wiped away the tears.

That Saturday morning, crisp, clear, and beautiful, had held the alluring promise of a perfect May 29. The promise had just curdled.

Harry had finished her early-morning chores and, despite a list of projects, decided to take a walk for an hour. She followed Potlicker Creek to see if the beavers had built any new dams. Barry was sprawled at the creek's edge on a dirt road two miles from her farm that wound up over the mountains into adjoining Augusta County. It edged the vast land holdings of Tally Urquhart, who, well into her nineties and spry, loathed traffic. Three cars constituted traffic in her mind. The only time the road saw much use was during deer-hunting season in the fall.

"Tucker, Mrs. Murphy, and Pewter, stay. I'm going to run to Tally's and phone the sheriff."

If Harry hit a steady lope, crossed the fields and one set of woods, she figured she could reach the phone in Tally's stable within fifteen minutes, though the pitch and roll of the land including one steep ravine would cost time.

As she left her animals, they inspected Barry.

"What could rip his throat like that? A bear swipe?" Pewter's pupils widened.

"Perhaps." Mrs. Murphy, noncommittal, sniffed the gaping wound, as did Tucker.

The cat curled her upper lip to waft more scent into her nostrils. The dog, whose nose was much longer and nostrils larger, simply inhaled.

"I don't smell bear," Tucker declared. *"That's an overpowering scent, and on a morning like this it would stick."*

Pewter, who cherished luxury and beauty, found that Barry's corpse disturbed her equilibrium. *"Let's be grateful we found him today and not three days from now."*

"Stop jabbering, Pewter, and look around, will you? Look for tracks."

Grumbling, the gray cat daintily stepped down the dirt road. *"You mean like car tracks?"*

"Yes, or animal tracks," Mrs. Murphy directed, then returned her attention to Tucker. *"Even though coyote scent isn't as strong as bear, we'd still smell a whiff. Bobcat? I don't smell anything like that. Or dog. There are wild dogs and wild pigs back in the mountains. The humans don't even realize they're there."*

Tucker cocked her perfectly shaped head. *"No dirt around the wound. No saliva, either."*

"I don't see anything. Not even a birdie foot," Pewter, irritated, called out from a hundred yards down the road.

"Well, go across the creek then and look over there." Mrs. Murphy's patience wore thin.

"And get my paws wet?" Pewter's voice rose.

"It's a ford. Hop from rock to rock. Go on, Pewt, stop being a chicken."

Angrily, Pewter puffed up, tearing past them to launch herself over the ford. She almost made it, but a splash indicated she'd gotten her hind paws wet.

If circumstances had been different, Mrs. Murphy and Tucker would have laughed. Instead, they returned to Barry.

"I can't identify the animal that tore him up." The tiger shook her head.

"Well, the wound is jagged but clean. Like I said, no dirt." Tucker studied the folds of flesh laid back.

"He was killed lying down," the cat sagely noted. *"If he was standing up, don't you think blood would be everywhere?"*

"*Not necessarily,*" the dog replied, thinking how strong heartbeats sent blood straight out from the jugular. Tucker was puzzled by the odd calmness of the scene.

"*Pewter, have you found anything on that side?*"

"*Deer tracks. Big deer tracks.*"

"*Keep looking,*" Mrs. Murphy requested.

"*I hate it when you're bossy.*" Nonetheless, Pewter moved down the dirt road heading west.

"*Barry was such a nice man.*" Tucker mournfully looked at the square-jawed face, wide-open eyes staring at heaven.

Mrs. Murphy circled the body. "*Tucker, I'm climbing up that sycamore. If I look down maybe I'll see something.*"

Her claws, razor sharp, dug into the thin surface of the tree, strips of darker outer bark peeling, exposing the whitish under-bark. The odor of fresh water, of the tufted titmouse above her, all informed her. She scanned around for broken limbs, bent bushes, anything indicating Barry—other humans or large animals—had traveled to this spot avoiding the dirt road.

"*Pewter?*"

"*Big fat nothing.*" The gray kitty noted

that her hind paws were wet. She was getting little clods of dirt stuck between her toes. This bothered her more than Barry did. After all, he was dead. Nothing she could do for him. But the hardening brown earth between her toes, that was discomfiting.

"Well, come on back. We'll wait for Mom." Mrs. Murphy dropped her hind legs over the limb where she was sitting. Her hind paws reached for the trunk, the claws dug in, and she released her grip, swinging her front paws to the trunk. She backed down.

Tucker touched noses with Pewter, who had recrossed the creek more successfully this time.

Mrs. Murphy came up and sat beside them.

"Hope his face doesn't change colors while we're waiting for the humans. I hate that. They get all mottled." Pewter wrinkled her nose.

"I wouldn't worry." Tucker sighed.

In the distance they heard sirens.

"Bet they won't know what to make of this, either," Tucker said.

"It's peculiar." Mrs. Murphy turned her head in the direction of the sirens.

"Weird and creepy." Pewter pronounced judgment as she picked at her hind toes, and she was right.

2

Crozet was the last stop on the railroad before the locomotive disappeared into the first of the four tunnels Claudius Crozet had dug through the Blue Ridge Mountains. This feat, accomplished before dynamite, was considered one of the seven engineering wonders of the world in the mid–nineteenth century. At the beginning of the twenty-first century they were still wonders as two remained in use; the other two were closed but not filled in.

On the other side of the Blue Ridge Mountains reposed the fertile and long Shenandoah Valley, running from Winchester, Virginia, by the West Virginia line all the way to North Carolina. The Allegheny Mountains bordered the huge valley to the west.

But on the eastern slopes of the Blue Ridge Mountains the land, although not as fertile, could be quite good in patches.

Harry's tidy farm rested on one of those patches. Although lacking the thousands of acres of Tally Urquhart, she owned four hundred acres, give or take, plus she had kept her tobacco allotments current, allotments secured by her late father shortly after World War II. Still, like many a Southerner and especially a Virginian, Harry was land poor: good land, little cash.

Deputy Cynthia Cooper drove down the long drive with Harry in the front seat, her animals in the back of the squad car, stones crunching underneath her tires.

"House or barn?"

"House. Did my barn chores. Want coffee or tea?"

"Love coffee." Cooper stopped, cut the motor as Harry opened the car doors for Mrs. Murphy, Pewter, and Tucker. The animals raced ahead, ducking through the animal door on the side of the screened door and then through the second animal door in the kitchen door.

Harry and Cooper followed them.

"Ten-thirty. I hadn't paid attention to the time." She ground coffee beans in the electric grinder as she put up water for tea. Harry loved the smell of coffee but couldn't drink it, as it made her too jumpy. "There's corn bread in the fridge. Miranda made a mess of it yesterday."

Miranda Hogendobber, a lady in her sixties, worked with Harry at the tiny Crozet Post Office, where Harry was postmistress.

The light inside the refrigerator illuminated Cooper's badge. She pulled out the corn bread and some sweet butter.

"Applesauce?"

Harry nodded. "Church of the Holy Light."

Last fall the applesauce had been cooked up to perfection by the ladies of the small church to which Miranda belonged. Harry attended St. Luke's Lutheran Church, where her friend the Reverend Herbert Jones was the pastor. She sat on the Parish Guild, impressing other, older members with her organizational skills.

"Here." Harry refilled the cats' dried-food bowl, then reached into a large stoneware cookie jar to give Tucker a smoked pig's ear.

"*Thank you.*" The corgi solemnly took the tasty ear, remaining in the kitchen to chew it because she didn't want to miss anything.

"You okay?"

"Why wouldn't I be?"

"It's not every day you find a dead man."

"Dying. He was dying when we reached him. Yeah, I'm okay. I feel terrible for him, but I'm okay."

"*Gurgling.*" Pewter added the vivid detail.

"Right." Cooper opened a drawer, grabbed two blue and yellow linen napkins, placing them by the plates. A country person herself, Cooper understood that country people lived much closer to life and death than most urban or suburban people.

"It was good of Rick to allow you to take me home. I could have walked."

Rick Shaw was sheriff of Albemarle County, an elected position and one growing ever more difficult as more wealthy people moved to this most beautiful place. Wealthy people tend to be very demand-

ing. He was understaffed, underappreci-
ated, and underpaid, but he loved law enforcement and did the best with what he
had.

"Rick's more flexible than people realize," Cooper replied. "Once he'd inspected
the corpse, questioned you, no reason to
keep you. Another thing about Rick, he
doesn't miss much," she said. "I hope the
autopsy will reveal something. No sign of
struggle. No sign that he dragged himself
there." Cooper's blond eyebrows pointed
upward as her mind turned over events.

"I know."

"And no scent." Tucker spoke with her
mouth full.

"So handsome." Cooper sighed as she
sat down while Harry served her a big mug
of coffee, then took a striped creamer
from the fridge and poured some of the
rich eggshell-colored Devon cream into
Cooper's coffee.

"Every now and then a girl has to treat
herself to the best." Harry put the creamer
on the checkered tablecloth as she sat
down.

"Enemies—Barry?" Cooper knew Harry
would know.

"He used to run with a wild crowd, but when he and Sugar started the business over at St. James Farm he sobered up."

"Sex, drugs, and rock and roll." Cooper reached for more corn bread.

"He was so good-looking and easygoing that he got away with a lot. Course, when his father wrapped his Nissan truck around a tree and died, that started to sober up Barry. He hasn't any family left. When he started the breeding operation he really cleaned up his act."

"I recall he left a trail of broken hearts." Cooper sipped her delicious coffee. "The last one was, uh . . ."

"Carmen Gamble. She was mad enough to kill him six months ago."

"But not strong enough to bite his throat out," Cooper added. "For all we know a mad dog bit his throat."

"Maybe."

"Boy, what a way to go." Cooper thoughtfully paused a moment.

"If I came up on Susan breathing her last, I'd—" Harry paused. "I think I'd never be the same."

Susan Tucker was Harry's best friend, married to a successful lawyer. They had one son at Cornell and a daughter in high school.

"Makes you wonder about war. Fifty-one thousand dead at Gettysburg. People get used to it. Or the siege of St. Petersburg, Leningrad. You just get used to it."

"I don't know if I could ever get used to the smell."

"Yeah, that's worse than the sight, for sure. Helps if you don't breathe through your nose."

"Certainly makes you understand why soldiers smoke—kills the odor a little bit and soothes your nerves." Harry noticed a flaming red cardinal swoop by the kitchen window, heading for the large bird feeder hanging in the old tree by the kitchen.

"That's another thing: Humans will drink, take drugs, anything to feel better. If you knew how many little drug busts we do . . . I mean, they aren't exactly selling kilos of marijuana, but the law states it's a crime and so I bust these guys. I can't keep up with it and it doesn't work, but it sure has made me think about why so many people do stuff."

"Cooper, that's easy. It feels good. Their body chemistry is a little different from yours and mine. Booze makes me sick. But for someone else, it's heaven—temporarily."

"Well, I'm thinking about drugs and alcohol in a new way. You and I know we're going to die. Humans carry around all this anxiety that stems from that original anxiety: the knowledge of death. Hence drugs and drink. You don't see Mrs. Murphy lapping up rum."

"Tastes awful. But give me some catnip." Mrs. Murphy's green eyes brightened.

"I never thought about that. Coop, you're a philosopher."

"No, just a cop." She finished her third piece of corn bread. "I'm surprised you haven't called Susan or Miranda or Fair." Fair was Harry's ex-husband, who remained a dear friend. In fact, she was thinking how much a part of her life he was and, hopefully, would always be.

"Thought I'd wait until you left. Is anything off-limits?"

"No. We don't even know enough to hold back evidence." Cooper winked. "Not that Rick would ever do such a thing."

"Right." Harry smiled. "How's he doing?

I haven't seen him for a while except for to-day."

"He's been down at the courthouse en-gaged in the battle of the budget."

"No wonder I haven't seen him. Hey, to change the subject, have you heard any-thing about the new post office being built?"

"No more than you have. The population increase even out here in Crozet warrants a larger building."

"One of the gang called from Barracks Post Office and said a survey crew was coming out Monday. Miranda doesn't know anything about it, either. You'd think Pug Harper," Harry said, referring to the county postmaster, "would come down and talk to us."

"He will. Everyone's on overload. We're supposed to be in a recession, right? That's when businesses fire people and government won't hire. So everyone is do-ing his job and the job of the guy who got fired—or I should say let go."

"If they do build a bigger post office, the postal service has to hire new employees. Miranda and I can't handle it. We're strug-gling now. Every day, it seems, a new person comes through the door and needs a postbox or stamps or information. The only reason we get the mail in the boxes by nine every morning is that we're there by seven-thirty and so is Rob Collier." She mentioned the driver who dropped off mailbags from the main post office.

"Changes things, new people. Every time a new person comes on the job the composition of the team changes. Not necessarily bad or good. Just different."

"Hey, I'm the postmistress of Greater Crozet, so they do it my way." Harry smiled wryly.

"Do you want to manage people?"

This stopped Harry for a minute. "No."

"I thought so."

"What are you saying?"

"Change is gonna come."

"That's profound," Harry teased.

"Can you change?"

"I don't know. It depends. If there's a new and better bushog for my tractor, I'm happy to change. But if I personally have to change, I'd like to do it at my own speed. I suppose that's true of everybody."

"We all have different speeds. I find that I'm more innovative than Rick, but once he sees the benefit of a change, whether it's in technology or personnel, he accepts it."

"Is this a roundabout way of telling me you don't think I'm going to like the changes at work?"

"How do I know?"

Harry leaned back in her chair, tapping the side of her plate with her knife. "Actually, Cooper, I don't think I am going to like it. Miranda and I have a good system where we are; we can read each other's mind. It's so easy and, besides, we have such a good time together. The only fly in the ointment is, the volume of mail is increasing."

"Oh, I forgot to ask you. Back to Barry. Rick may have asked you this when I was back with the ambulance crew. Do you think he was conscious?"

"His eyes were open but, no, he was leaving life quickly. But I remember once someone telling me—maybe it was you or maybe it was Dr. Mary O'Brien—that hearing is the last sense to go, so I held his hand and told him everything would be all right. Maybe where he is now, it is."

3

After Sunday services, Harry slipped back to Herb's office. He was just removing his surplice, a rich green color embroidered with gold, signifying the season of Trinity in the ecclesiastical calendar.

"Rev." She often called him this.

"What can I do for you, honey? Here, sit down." He motioned to the Chesterfield sofa, and the long sleeve on his black robe, a design unchanged since the Middle Ages, swept with the motion.

"Thanks." She sank into the old, comfortable leather.

"Heard you had an upsetting day yesterday." He unzipped his robe from the front, exposing a Hawaiian shirt underneath.

"I can't believe you gave the sermon in a

Hawaiian shirt." Harry's brown eyes widened.

"Ned Tucker dared me to do it. Said I could use his new fly rod if I did. I'll collect after lunch." He hung his robe on a padded hanger, placing it in the closet. "But don't tell, now. It will offend some of"—he paused and winked—"the faithful." He sat opposite her. "Now tell me what's on your mind."

She launched right in. She'd known Herb all her life. He'd baptized her, confirmed her, and married her as well as consoled her during and after her divorce.

". . . not as tough as I thought."

"Oh, you're tough, all right." His deep voice filled the room. "When bad things occur, our minds are focused on what needs to be done. Afterward the emotions flow. Think of when old Mrs. Urquhart died." He mentioned Mim Sanburne's mother, Tally Urquhart's sister. "Mim bore up all through the illness, and that poor woman suffered. And even after the burial, Mim seemed fine, and then three months later she burst into tears at the stable and sobbed for a whole day. Scared Jim to death." Jim was Mim's husband and the mayor of Crozet.

"Funny."

"The mind protects itself. Some people are never strong enough to face emotions. They tuck them further and further in the recesses of their mind, and one day they freeze up. Prayer is a way to thaw out those frozen fears and pains. You thaw them out and the Good Lord gives you the strength to deal with them and the wit to be thankful. You don't grow up, Harry, until you thank God for your troubles as well as your joys."

"Mother used to say that."

"I know." He smiled broadly, for he highly regarded Harry's deceased mother.

Harry was like her mother in that she was well-organized and friendly, but she was more taciturn, more skeptical, more like her father in that respect.

"I feel terrible. I feel terrible for Barry."

Cazenovia and Elocution, Herb's two cats, had been lounging in the window, cruising the squadrons of robins on the verdant quad lawn. Hearing Harry's distress, they left their sightseeing to jump in her lap. She rubbed their ears.

"In the prime of life. I hear it was some sort of animal attack."

"I guess, but apart from his throat—not a mark on him. I could have missed something. I didn't examine him once he died. I just ran like hell for the phone in Tally's barn. Sorry to swear, Herb."

"You're upset." Herb waved away the apology. He, himself, could make the air blue on certain occasions.

"I am." Harry exhaled.

"Tally said she heard there were no animal tracks by the body—other than Mrs. Murphy, Pewter, and Tucker's paw prints."

"No tracks of him crawling, either," Harry said.

"And his feet weren't wet?" Herb inquired.

"No."

"Hmm." The older man rubbed his clean-shaven chin.

Herb, a very masculine man now in his early sixties with a rumbling bass voice, had been athletic and handsome in his youth, but over the years he'd allowed the pounds to accumulate until now he was portly. His and Harry's dear friend Miranda Hogendobber had also picked up tonnage over the years, but she'd gone on a sensible diet and in one year's time had lost thirty pounds. She was now the same size she'd been in high school and looked years younger in the bargain. But, then, Miranda had been inspired by the reappearance of her high-school sweetheart, Tracy Raz, all-state halfback during his years at Crozet High. Herb, on the other hand, had lost his wife and hadn't found anyone else, so he'd let himself go a bit.

"You'd think there'd be tracks from a heavy animal."

"Now, Mary Minor, I hear that tone in your voice. Hold your horses." He held up his hand to stop. "You let our esteemed sheriff and his deputy take care of this, and I bet when the autopsy report comes in this will all be explained. You are cool in a crisis, but under the circumstances you probably did miss things. I know I would, and you did the right thing running for the phone. You couldn't have done him any good by staying there or by searching the area. Rick did that once he got there."

"Now that I think about it, I should have recited the Last Rites. Maybe it would have eased him. In extremis, laymen can give the Last Rites, can't we?"

Herb nodded yes. "You did all you could

and you did the right thing. You usually do. Your downfall—well, downfall is too strong a word—your weak spot is curiosity. You're like Cazenovia and Elocution, just as curious as a cat and you can't stand not knowing something. Hepworth." He named her maternal family line, all of whom were known for their curiosity and bright minds.

"I'm glad I called on you." She smiled. "I guess I'm keeping you from borrowing that rod. It must be special."

"Special. You should see the reel. Ned paid over a thousand dollars for it." His forefinger flew to his lips. "Don't tell Susan. I mean how much it cost."

"She'll find out when she pays the bills."

"No, she won't. He paid cash. He's been squirreling away money. And you know she wants to paint the inside of the house. No point in rocking the boat. She's taking his run for the state senate in good stride."

"Been a tepid campaign."

"It will be until September, then the Democratic primary will heat up. Ned's campaigning hard on expanding the reservoir, environmental responsibility, and building the bypass, which would seem to be a contradiction but I've seen the plans he's got about the bypass. It's one of the alternative ones. I can't remember the number."

"This place has been fighting that bypass since I was in grade school."

"Well, sugarpie, it's got to happen. The question is: where?"

"Kind of like the new post office."

"Yes." He folded his hands together.

"I don't think I'm going to like that, any of it. The bypass or the post office."

"Tell you the truth, I don't think I'm going to like it, either. I hated it when they built I-64. Sliced in half some of the most beautiful farms in Albemarle County, and in all the counties from Tidewater to St. Louis, Missouri. More traffic. More pollution. More accidents, especially up on Afton Mountain. They can build the road straight as an arrow but they can't do squat about the fog. People ought to learn to live with nature instead of thinking they can control it. Damned fools." He stared down at his shining shoe tips for a moment, then looked up. "Now it's my turn to apologize for my language."

"I say worse."

"But you're not a pastor."

"The Very Reverend." She laughed back at him.

"Don't you forget it." He laughed back.

"*Poppy, we'd like some treats*," Elocution mewed.

"Either she's agreeing with you or it's a call for tuna." Harry ran her fingers along the young cat's cheek. "With my Pewter it's always tuna."

"Elo, just wait a minute. Now that you're here, Harry, I'd like to ask you something in confidence."

"Sure."

"Do you think the relationship between Blair Bainbridge and Little Mim Sanburne is becoming serious?"

"Yes."

Blair was Harry's nearest neighbor. Little Mim was the daughter of Jim and Mim Sanburne. She was also the vice-mayor of Crozet. Her father was a Democrat. Little Mim was a Republican. Table talk at Sunday dinners was never dull at the Sanburne house.

"Big Mim is coming around to it. Mim can't stand anything that isn't her idea. Jim's been working on her, wooing her, pitching to her ego. Why watch television when you can watch your friends?"

"That's why people watch television. They don't have friends."

"Harry, that's a big statement."

"Well, I mean it. If you're sitting around watching a simulation of life, you aren't living. If you've got work, friends, things you love to do, and people you love to do them with, you don't have time to watch TV. I watch the news and the Weather Channel, and half the time I don't even do that."

"You might have a point there."

"I got you off the track. I'm sorry."

"Well, here's what I'm turning over in my mind. If a marriage should result from this courtship, I can't imagine that Little Mim will move out to Blair's farm, can you?"

"I hadn't really thought about it."

"It's a lovely farm but not grand, and Little Mim, like her mother, has been raised in the grand tradition. He'll move over to Dalmally"—he named the Sanburne estate—"or Mim will buy them something close by, or, and here's what I think really will happen, they'll take over and restore Tally's estate."

"Tally will cane them to death." Harry

mentioned the cane Tally used for walking, an elegant ebony cane with a sleek silver hound's head for the handle. She used it to good effect to get her way as well as to find her way.

He shook his head and held up his fore-finger. "You watch: Mim will send her future son-in-law to inveigle Tally, and Tally may be in her nineties but she cannot refuse a handsome man. As it is, she adores Blair, and they'll work out some deal where the newlyweds live in one of the cottages or even in the big house with Tally."

"The house is in good shape."

"And so's the farm, but she's let the out-buildings go and the back pastures. I fore-see that Rose Hill will be restored to former glory and Little Mim will inherit her great-aunt's estate."

"But what about Dalmally? When Big Mim should be bumped Upstairs—not that I wish this to occur anytime soon—what happens?"

"First off, the Urquharts live a long time. Mim's mother died young for an Urquhart, at eighty. Mim will break one hundred, and she's not going to be moved from Dalmally any more than Tally would be moved from

Rose Hill. And when that day does occur, Stafford will come home." Stafford was Mim's son, currently living in New York City. Mother and son did not get along very well.

"Never."

"Oh, yes, he will."

"His wife is the highest-paid black model in America."

"She'll be in her sixties then and she'll come home with him, I'm telling you. And never forget, Virginia was the first state to elect an African-American governor, Doug Wilder. Stafford's wife will fit right with the black folks who are making a positive difference. You mark my words."

Harry didn't want to argue with Herb, but she couldn't imagine those two leaving the high life in New York. Then again, this was decades in the future. God willing.

"Having Little Mim and Blair at Rose Hill makes sense." Harry agreed with that part of Herb's scenario.

"My old family place will be put back on the market."

Blair's farm had originally been the old Jones homestead, a designation of some importance in these parts. No one ever wanted the homeplace to wind up in the hands of others, but more often than not such places did because the originating family couldn't afford the upkeep.

"Yes." Harry's voice dropped. A new neighbor was not necessarily an appetizing prospect, most particularly since she liked the old one.

"Well, I have a thought. I believe Blair would give you good terms."

"Oh, Herb, I'd love to have the land, but I can't afford all of it."

"I'd like to have the homeplace back, and my retirement isn't too far in the future. If, and I mean if, the time comes that you and I should approach Blair, I think we could work something out. I can't farm all that land, but you can. If you can buy the lion's share of the land, I'll keep, say, maybe twenty or fifty acres, whatever, with the cemetery. You take the rest."

She had one hand on each cat, and her hands rested on them. "That would be wonderful," she whispered. "Wonderful."

"Blair likes you very much."

"And I like him."

"And I think both Big Mim and Tally would help us all structure a deal that we could live with and perhaps even thrive on."

He smiled broadly. "Those women have two of the best business heads in the state of Virginia. If Tally had been a man she'd have run R. J. Reynolds or Liggett & Myers, I mean it. She was born in the wrong era. As it was she built her farm into something special and spread her risk. Tally played the stock market, too, and she taught Big Mim. As you know, Mim's mother was the society type. She didn't care about making money, only spending it."

"You know, I'm so excited by the idea that I can't breathe." Harry took a deep breath. "And I'd have a holy neighbor."

"I don't know about that." Herb laughed. "Well, let's you and I keep our ears to the ground, and don't tell Miranda or Susan. We've got to keep this just between us."

"Agreed." She petted the kitties. "Why don't I give them some goodies on the way out?"

"*Hooray*." The two vacated her lap and hurried toward the small kitchen.

Walking to the kitchen, Herb said, "This new carpet is the best thing. When you think of all the meetings the Parish Guild had about it—it was worth it."

"Like walking on air."

Driving back to her farm, the sunshine golden and fine, Harry wondered how she could get the money to buy that land. She'd get it somehow, if she had to work three jobs. The chance to buy land that you know doesn't come along but so often. Then she remembered describing to Herb where she'd found Barry, by the creek.

She needed to go back to the creek, but first she'd change her clothes and take along Mrs. Murphy, Pewter, and Tucker. Their senses were better than hers, and she had the good sense to know it.

4

A cool wind current snaked alongside Potlicker Creek. The wind flowed up and over a small hillock covered with mountain laurel, then dropped down to the lowland again.

Harry, a creature of the outdoors, felt it on her skin. She breathed deeply. Ofttimes she could smell deer scent or plant pollen odors on these currents. As the scent warmed, it would rise to her nostrils depending on the temperature during the day. There were days in winter when the scent stuck right on the ground. Even with the stronger aromas overhead, Tucker usually knew who and what had passed along the ground. The two cats did, as well, but since their sight was superior to either Harry's or

Tucker's, they usually relied on that sense first.

"Why are we back here? Wasn't once bad enough?" Pewter grumbled as she again examined the area where Barry Monteith had been discovered.

"Mom's got a notion." Tucker moved upstream, the clear water revealing rounded rocks underneath or pools of deep water where rockfish dozed in the early afternoon.

"Always means trouble." Pewter slapped at a mayfly zooming in front of her.

"Missed," Tucker, out of Pewter's range, said.

"As if you ever caught a bug." The gray cat turned her back on the dog, the feline version of the cold shoulder.

Mrs. Murphy walked alongside Harry. Like her human, she, too, overflowed with curiosity. Unlike her human, she had a much better sense of danger.

"You know, I didn't feel so bad at the time, but I feel bad now," Harry said to Mrs. Murphy. "What could have killed Barry? The only thing I can think of would be an eagle. There'd be no ground tracks, no fur, and one slash with those talons could open up any one of us, although it would have to hit him just right to slice the jugular. People don't realize how strong or how fast birds are. A bluejay going at top speed can hurt you. Of course, the question is, why would an eagle want to kill a human?"

"*I will kill that bluejay in the lilac bushes. I hate him,*" Pewter snarled, the vision of her nemesis arousing her ire.

"*He is pretty awful,*" Mrs. Murphy agreed as Pewter joined them.

"*Mom, there are eagles around now. Most of them are down along the James River, but bald eagles are making a comeback and they are scary.*" Tucker respected large raptors, and if she saw a shadow on the ground she looked up, prepared to fight.

"I don't even know what I'm looking for." Harry shook her head. "I'm wasting my time and yours."

"*I could be sleeping.*" Pewter agreed with her.

A snort through nostrils behind them, downwind, caused all four to wheel around.

"*You're on my turf,*" an old buck challenged them.

Mrs. Murphy and Pewter immediately huffed up, standing sideways. The tiger cat let out a ferocious growl.

"Pipsqueak." He lowered his head.

"Big enough to scratch your eyes out." Mrs. Murphy stood her ground.

"Damn." Harry simply exhaled.

Usually deer will flee from a human, but occasionally a buck or a doe with a fawn will become aggressive. They could do damage.

Tucker, flat on the ground, hind end bunched up ready to spring, bared her fangs.

The buck charged toward the cats, who spat and scratched. He was so nimble he soared clean over them as Tucker sprang toward him. The path was narrow; mountain laurel rolled down almost to the creek at this point. Harry leapt sideways into the creek, her shoes hitting the stones, rolling a large one. She lost her footing, falling into the water.

Tucker, furious, ran at the stag, leaping up at him. The large animal swung his head low at the dog, but the corgi had been bred to herd large animals. She dodged, then nipped the shiny cloven hooves. This upset

the stag. He kicked out, but the beautiful and brave little canine easily avoided the blow. She circled the stag, confusing him, then she nipped again and again. She was relentless and much faster than the stag anticipated.

"You leave us alone!" Tucker barked.

Mrs. Murphy stalked the stag, although Tucker had the situation under control.

"Climb a tree, Mom!" Pewter advised, taking her own advice.

Harry, wet, picked up a rock and aimed it at the enraged animal. She hit him hard on the side just as Tucker landed another painful nip. The stag leapt gracefully over the mountain laurel, flying away from Tucker, who chased the stag all the way to a meadow filled with buttercups.

She returned to cheers.

Harry, still standing in the creek, praised her. "You are the best dog in the world."

"Who does he think he is?" Tucker, adrenaline still pumping, puffed out her snowy chest.

"I'm glad you're my friend." Mrs. Murphy rushed up to the corgi and rubbed across her chest.

Pewter remained in the tree. A prudent

sort, she thought it best to wait for a few minutes just in case the stag decided to return.

Harry bent over to wash her hands, since the rock she'd plucked out had a muddy clump on the bottom. A shiny flash caught her eye. She reached down, but the water distorted her depth perception and she missed. She slowly reached again and grabbed it.

Pewter backed down the tree as Harry put a small gold school ring in her palm. A shield with a cross, an inscription in Latin underneath, the ring was distinctive.

"What the . . . ?" She peered but couldn't make out the inscription. The writing was reversed and quite tiny. She thought the first word started with a V. The shield looked like the shield for the Episcopal Church. Inside in larger script were the initials M. P. R. and, underneath, 1945. A 10K stamp rested to the left of the M, far enough away not to draw the eye from the prettily engraved letters and numbers.

"Must have been under the rock," Pewter opined.

"Gives me an idea." Mrs. Murphy, fur finally flattening down, paced alongside the

creek bank. She wanted Harry to come out of the water. If need be, Mrs. Murphy could and would swim, but she didn't like it. One hideously hot and humid day last summer she put her front paws in her water bowl, to everyone's amazement.

Harry stepped out of the creek, her work boots sloshing, her pant legs stuck to her calves. She bent down so her friends could see the ring. Living close to animals since birth, Harry naturally shared with them; more, she trusted them. These small predators, her dearest companions, had survived the millennia just as her species had. In her mind, they were all winners, and you learn from winners.

"Old," Pewter said.

"Strange. Strange to be here where we found Barry." Tucker could only smell watery smells on the ring.

"But it gives me an idea," Mrs. Murphy repeated.

"Which is?" Tucker's large brown eyes looked straight into Mrs. Murphy's electric green eyes.

"The creek. Whatever killed Barry could have carried him a distance, even a mile or two, just picked him up and carried him.

Barry wouldn't be wet or dirty, which he wasn't."

"Have to be strong." Pewter considered Mrs. Murphy's idea. "And if something carried him, there'd have been blood over his chest. He wasn't carried. Whatever attacked him hit him hard and he dropped and died. That's what I think."

"Lots of strong animals around here. Just chased one," Tucker replied.

"That's true, although deer don't kill and carry." Pewter knew enough to know that even prey animals could act out of character sometimes. One never knew, and best to be on guard.

"A bear could do it. A forty-pound bobcat could do it if he had to, or a coyote, or a big wild dog." Tucker thought out loud.

"Or a human." Mrs. Murphy was beginning to get a bad feeling about this.

5

Aunt Tally had been shrinking with age. As a young woman she towered over her female peers, but now in her nineties her five-foot-eight-inch frame had contracted to five feet four inches, the national average, and if there was one thing Aunt Tally hated it was being average.

Mim, her niece, sat next to her at the end of the sturdy kitchen table in Aunt Tally's wonderful old Virginia kitchen, the wood-burning cooking stove still in use as well as an expensive Aga, a convection stove known only to the cognoscenti. The Aga was the pride of Aunt Tally's cook, Loretta Young. Loretta affected the demeanor of the actress she was named for, which was quite a novelty in a cook.

As it was Sunday, Loretta was down at Big Mim's to assist with the Sunday dinner. Gretchen, the majordomo of that house, loathed Loretta. Jim had slyly placed a boxing bell on the side leg of the dining-room table. He intended to hit it with a small hammer, thereby amusing his family and guests and serving notice on the two battling broads, as he put it, to settle down, at least until dinner was served.

Big Mim had driven out to pick up her aunt, who didn't want to go to Dalmally until the last minute. She declared it took her all that extra time to just pull her face up off the floor.

Cynthia Cooper, Harry, Mrs. Murphy, Pewter, and Tucker arrived just as Tally had applied her peach lipstick. They hadn't known Aunt Tally was going to Dalmally. They were now all huddled around the table.

"I found this in the creek not far from where I found Barry." Harry reached into her pocket and removed the ring, which she'd wrapped in her handkerchief. She'd shown it to Cooper before, and both women decided to go straight to Aunt Tally.

"Mmm." Tally picked up her magnifying glass as Mim's face registered recognition.

"Holy Cross, Aunt Tally."

"I know that," Tally snapped. "I want to see what's inside. M.P.R. 1945."

Mim's face turned white. "Mary Patricia Reines."

"What?" The nonagenarian's light-blue eyes opened wide. "Mary Pat's been missing since 1974." She turned to Deputy Cooper. "You should know."

"That was before my time, Miss Urquhart. It must be an inactive file."

"Inactive? Unsolved is more like it." Aunt Tally's white eyebrows drew together.

"This is Mary Pat's high-school ring. She wore it on her left pinkie. I'd know it anywhere." Mim, hands shaking, put the ring down. "Exactly where did you find this?"

"In Potlicker Creek where the dirt road heads toward the mountains, the road that goes over to Augusta County 'cept no one uses it. Can't really get through anymore. Well, you could on a horse." Harry amended her statement.

"Potlicker Creek? Where you found Barry Monteith, you say?" Big Mim had heard about that because Sheriff Shaw called once the body had been removed. He notified the Sanburnes for two reasons. One, Jim was mayor of Crozet. Two, Big Mim ran this end of the county and it wouldn't do to get on her bad side.

"Downstream a little bit. I fell in the creek and picked up a rock to throw at a rogue stag. Tucker chased him off."

Aunt Tally plucked up the ring from the table where her niece had placed it as though it were a hot coal. "Worn. Wonder if it's been tumbling around in that creek for all this time."

"It was pretty much worn when she disappeared," Mim quietly said. "She wore it every day since her graduation in 1945 and it's ten-karat gold, thin as it is. Oh, dear, but this stirs up memories. Aunt Tally, if you will forgive me, I'm going to drink some roped coffee." Mim, slender and elegant, pushed away from the table and walked over to the counter where a huge, gleaming automatic coffeemaker, shipped over from Italy, kept a perfect brew steaming. "Can I fix anyone else a shot?"

"I'll have one." Aunt Tally leaned back in the ladderback chair.

"Just coffee for me, thanks," Cooper said.

"You aren't on duty, are you? No uniform," Big Mim noted.

"No, but I'll stick to coffee."

"Harry, tea for you?" Mim clicked on the electric teapot.

"Thank you."

Big Mim opened a cabinet, pulled out a bottle of Johnnie Walker Black, and poured a shot into two large mugs of coffee. No point in using single malt in coffee. Some folks used bourbon, others rum, or even a flavored brandy, but Mim and her aunt stuck to good scotch. She placed the mugs on the table along with sweet cream and brown sugar. She poured a plain mug for Cooper just as the teapot clicked off— perfect timing. Then she put down a few treats for the animals and sat down herself.

"I dimly remember Mary Pat's disappearance, but I was in grade school," Cooper commented.

"Me, too. She bred Ziggy Flame, a big flaming chestnut thoroughbred—beautifully bred, I remember that. The mare was one of the Aga Khan's best mares, a daughter of Almahoud. His sire was Tom

Fool, used to stand at Greentree Stud in Kentucky, one of the greats."

Big Mim smiled. "Harry, what a memory."

"If I could recite bloodlines my mother would give me a quarter," Harry replied. "But I don't remember much more than that."

"Mary Pat, a beautiful woman, inherited pots of money. Her parents were killed at the beginning of World War Two when the Germans sank a passenger ship that had left Lisbon. They'd been caught in Europe when war broke out and were trying to get home. Obviously, she was still a minor, so the executor of the will administered the estate. That was Randy Jenkins, and he did a good job. Mary Pat graduated from Holy Cross, studied at Hollins, graduated, and came back to run St. James Farm. She wanted to breed horses and she did. She disappeared in 1974 along with Ziggy Flame, not a trace of either one ever found until now," Big Mim recounted. "We'd been friends since childhood. She was older than I, but even when I was small she was a friend, like a big sister."

"No suspects?" Cooper knew she'd give up her Sunday. She would head right back to the station and search for Mary Patricia Reines's file.

"Oh, Marshall Kressenberg, a stable hand and exercise rider, was a suspect, but only because he was on the farm when she disappeared. They got along all right. Sam Berryhill, her farm manager, was a suspect, but he'd been in Middleburg so that ruled him out. Let's see, he died in '88. Her entire estate except for a couple of broodmares passed to Alicia Palmer, who became the prime suspect. They never could pin it on Alicia." Aunt Tally filled in details.

Cooper interrupted. "The actress?"

"Yes." Big Mim picked up the conversation. "She had a good career, married again and again and again. She lives in Santa Barbara and, as you know, occasionally comes back to St. James, which she maintains just as Mary Pat left it—except for renting out the stables and training track to Barry Monteith and Sugar Thierry. Alicia's not really a horse person."

"Graveyard of old movie stars, Santa Barbara," Aunt Tally giggled. She remembered Santa Barbara when Ronald and Benita Colman owned San Ysidro Ranch. Aunt Tally had spent many a lovely weekend there in her youth, and it was quite a wild youth, lasting well into her fifties.

"Her horses were sold at auction. A big breeder in Maryland bought most of them. I remember Humphrey Finney was the auctioneer. The progeny of her stable are still on the tracks today. Mary Pat knew what she was doing." Big Mim sighed, for she had loved Mary Pat. "And she bred back that mare to Tom Fool. Ziggy disappeared just as his career was burgeoning but, thank God, the bloodlines survived. When the broodmare band was dispersed, Ziggy's mother was bought by a breeder in Kentucky. Forget the name. Out of that breeding came Ziggy Dark Star, Flame's full brother, a year younger, who had a stud career. Never raced, or if he did I never heard about it. He was in Maryland. Of course, Mary Pat was gone by then, so she didn't know just how good her breeding program was."

"Don't forget Tavener Heyward."

"He was a suspect?" Harry was incredulous, since Tavener Heyward was one of the most respected equine veterinarians in the country.

"No, no. Mary Pat gave him four broodmares, daughters of Speak John, Raise a Native, Secretariat, and Buckpasser, and a sum for stud fees. She'd left instructions for their breeding, too. Tavener did quite handsomely with those mares. Course, he's made a bundle in the practice, too. He was one of the few people who stood by Alicia when she was under suspicion." Big Mim checked the large clock on the wall. "Aunt Tally, we need to leave soon."

"When I'm ready will be soon enough. I'm not ready," she resolutely replied. "Those broodmares put Tavener on the map. That's how he got into the racing world, but for him it's steeplechasing. As you know, he's behind one of the most successful chasing stables in the country and he took over her colors, green and gold. I think he was in love with Alicia."

"What a strange and sad story." Harry vaguely recalled her parents' distress when the popular Mary Pat disappeared.

"Strange, and now we know she's somewhere out there. I guess Ziggy is, too," Big Mim half-whispered.

"What do you mean, Mimsy?"

"Aunt Tally, she always wore this ring. Her remains have to be somewhere upstream; the ring would only wash downward," Big Mim replied.

"She could have lost it," Tally argued for the sake of arguing, but she knew if Mary Pat had lost her class ring everyone would have heard about it. Mary Pat always wore her ring.

"And just why did you bring it here?" Big Mim directed this to Cooper.

"If I turned it over to the sheriff, he'd put it in a tiny Ziploc bag and there it would languish. I wanted to find out whatever I could before turning it in."

"Well, you wouldn't have to even give it to Rick," Aunt Tally said. "Mary Pat's ring has nothing to do with Barry Monteith getting his throat ripped out, even if he did rent the stables on her old farm. It's just coincidence."

6

Fair Haristeen and Sugar Thierry turned out a lovely gray mare, which Fair had just vetted.

"Going to run her first. Then I'll breed her."

"Chaser?"

Sugar nodded. "Someone has to give Tavener Heyward competition."

"He's had a couple of great seasons." They walked back to Fair's truck. He tossed his clipboard on the front seat.

"Can you put this on account?" Sugar, muscles tight in his face, requested.

"No charge."

"Fair, you're good to me." Sugar's facial muscles relaxed.

"Starting out in the horse business is hard, really hard when you aren't rich."

"You can say that again."

"You doing okay?"

"I don't know." Sugar's eyelids closed, then opened slowly. "Shook up."

Fair's voice dropped. "A blow like that just blindsides you. You don't know what hit you, literally."

"Rick came here. Asked a lot of questions. It stung me." Sugar's voice grew louder.

"He has to do his job. You were Barry's partner."

"He acted as though I killed him!"

"Like I said, he has to ask uncomfortable questions. It's his job."

"Barry and I were a good team. Why would I cut off my right arm?"

"You wouldn't. We all know that. But like I said, Rick has to do his job, and the statistics show most people are killed by people close to them."

"Barry wasn't killed. I mean he wasn't murdered." Sugar's expression darkened as the grief cut him anew. "Poor Barry." He breathed in. "Is Harry okay?"

"Yeah," Fair replied. "She's tough."

"She was good to call me. You know, she called and asked if I needed help with the horses. No one else did that."

Fair stepped up into the truck. "She's a wonderful woman but she doesn't want anyone to know it." He smiled, then asked, "Do you need a hand here?"

"I can manage for a while." Sugar looked out over the white stables of St. James, Mary Pat's racing colors painted on each support post of the shed row barns. A one-foot band of emerald green with a thin band of gold was in the center, and an even thinner pinstripe of black in the gold enlivened the middle of each post.

"I'll keep my ears open for affordable help. But call me or Harry. You know we'll pitch in. We're all horsemen." He placed his hand on Sugar's shoulder.

"One of the reasons we were starting to break even was that we did all the work. Barry was a good hand with a horse."

"I know," Fair agreed. "Sugar, I'm really sorry."

Sugar squinted up at Fair, then shaded his eyes with his palm. "What's that saying, 'Life's a bitch. Then you die'?"

"Something like that." Fair cut on the motor. "You know where I am. Call if you need me, and, Sugar, it's okay to need people."

7

A long blue fingernail with tiny stars and a sliver of moon pointed in Sheriff Rick Shaw's face. "I didn't kill him, but I gave it a thought."

"Miss Gamble, when was the last time you saw Mr. Monteith?"

"You mean Shithead?" A streak of vulgarity ran through the undeniably pretty and petite Carmen Gamble. "And why are you on me like white on rice? An animal killed him. Leave me out of it."

Rick, a solid presence, leaned toward her. "Carmen, get over yourself."

He'd known her for years and decided that correct procedure as to proper address wasn't going to work with her.

She tossed her crimped curls. "Well, I don't like being a suspect."

"You just said you thought about killing him; now, calm down and answer my questions. I don't think you killed him. Does that make you feel better?"

"Why don't you think I killed him?"

"Because you would have castrated him." Rick pulled out a cigarette from his Camel pack, offered Carmen one, which she took.

He sat back down in the questioning room at headquarters.

"Okay, the last time I saw Shi—I mean, Barry, was at Georgetown Veterinary Clinic. I was taking Ruffie to see Mrs. Dr. Flynn." She said "Mrs. Dr." because Mrs. Virginia Flynn's husband was also a veterinarian, an equine vet, and one of the most respected men in his field nationally.

Dr. Dan Flynn was a contemporary of Tavener Heyward as well as a friend of Fair Haristeen. Fair was decades younger than the other two men, and he thought very highly of them.

"And what did Ginger Flynn have to say about Ruffie?"

"Oh, he just needed his rabies booster

shot, all his other boosters, and I got him a heartworm shot, too. They've got shots now so you don't have to remember to give them the heartworm pills each month. Ruffie hates pills." Like most pet owners, Carmen adored her wirehaired dachshund and assumed everyone else did, too, which in Crozet was a relatively safe assumption.

Rick, not a pet owner himself, thought animal lovers were all addled, but he nodded, feigning interest. "When was that?"

"Thursday."

"What did you say?"

"Hello, Shithead." She burst out laughing.

Rick couldn't help it, but he laughed, too. There was an insouciance about Carmen, a rowdy spiritedness, that made you like her even when she was crude.

"And what did he say?"

"Actually, he, um, he surprised me. I thought he'd say something ugly back, but he didn't. He nodded hello sort of and climbed into his Ford Harley-Davidson truck and drove off. Do you know how much he paid for that truck? Had to be the special issue Harley-Davidson. That truck broke us up."

"Uh-huh."

"Would you want to play second fiddle to a truck?"

"In my line of work, Carmen, playing second fiddle would be a step up." He inhaled then exhaled from his nostrils, two blue plumes curling over his upper lip.

"Yeah, you have to kiss ass a lot. I could never do it. That's why I opened my own beauty shop, Shear Heaven. I'm my own boss. They don't do it my way, it's the highway."

"Business is good?"

"Business is great. I specialize in color. A woman turns thirty and, Rick, she turns to me." She rubbed her forefinger and thumb together. "I've got no competition in Crozet. Well, I take that back. West Main, but they're in Charlottesville. They're good and we all get along. But other than that, no one can do color for squat. I even colored Barry's hair once. Gave him a magenta streak for sideburns. Cool."

"Who would want to kill Barry other than yourself?"

"I thought an animal killed Barry." Her eyes narrowed.

"Looks that way. But there's enough

that's unusual about his passing that makes me want to know more." He smiled. "And it's been a slow week. I might as well keep busy."

"Nothing's slow around Charlottesville anymore."

"Well, let's just say the weather's been good, hardly any accidents, the kids are out of school so that lightens the load, and there haven't been many break-ins. A slow week. Anyway, I might as well justify the trust you place in me."

"Oh, brother." She rolled her eyes, a dark shade of blue thanks to colored contacts. "What was unusual?"

"No marks on him. No tire tracks. No animal tracks. No struggle."

She held the cigarette at her lip, paused a long time, then took a deep, deep drag. "Yeah, that is pretty unusual. I mean, if Barry was going to get it, I figure a woman would just let him have it with a thirty-eight, you know? Or he'd piss off some boyfriend and die in a brawl, a tire iron wrapped 'round his neck. I never figured on anything like this." A wistful note crept into her voice.

"Maybe he wasn't all that bad?" Rick placed the cigarette pack on the table.

She tilted her chin upward. "He wasn't all that good." She pulled the ashtray toward her. "Oh, hell, he was just a man. Men think of themselves first."

"When we're young I think that's a fair assessment. But, Carmen, some men do grow up."

"Barry? Never. He was a big kid who wanted to play with his truck, dance, hang out, and have sex. I used to think he loved me, but I think I was just kind of there. I was convenient. That's when I walked. If I'm not special, I'm walking."

"Did he have enemies?"

"Nah. Oh, ex-girlfriends for a while, but most of them got over it. I guess I would have, too." She stared at the ashtray, then up at Rick for a minute. "I don't really want him dead."

"I didn't think so." Rick felt in his pocket for change. "I need a Co-Cola. How about I fetch you one?"

"Sure."

"While I'm down the hall, maybe something will come into your mind. Anything." He left and walked to the bank of food machines. The place was quiet. The dispatcher sat at her desk. Most of the force on this first Tuesday in June prowled around in their patrol cars. When he returned, Carmen had finished her cigarette and awaited him with her hands folded on the table.

"Here you go, girl."

"Thanks, Rick. I guess I should call you Sheriff, seeing as how this is an official visit."

"Better than calling me Shithead."

"I'd never call you that. I'd give your wife that privilege."

He smiled. "You won't believe this, but she has never called me that."

"I can believe it. She's such a lady." Carmen cut and colored Bettina Shaw's hair. Betts was an attractive forty-one, perhaps ten pounds overweight. Like most women she obsessed about her weight, but Rick thought she looked just fine. It was a strong marriage.

"Think of anything?"

"Nah."

"Do you know if he was dating anyone new?"

"He wanted to go out with Tazio

Chappars, but she was way above his head."

"He told you that?"

"No, but I could tell. Barry was transparent."

"Hmm. Carmen, you've been helpful and thanks for your time. If you think of anything, let me know."

"I will. Was it true he was still alive when Harry found him?"

"Yes."

"Funny."

"How so?"

"That was another one he had a crush on, but she was above his raisins, too."

"She know that?"

"No."

"I guess if I was with someone who looked around as much as Barry did, it would pluck my nerves, too," Rick said.

"I could just tell. He wouldn't do anything. Not while we were together. And if he did he would be singing soprano. You're right about that." She reached for another cigarette from his pack as Rick nodded that was fine. "Did think of one thing."

"Oh?"

"He said he sold a yearling. His share

gave him enough to buy that Ford model
Harley-Davidson truck."

"Yes."

"I never believed him."

8

Huge carpenter bees buzzed under the eaves of the barn.

"Talk about big butts." Pewter sniffed as a tiny thread of fresh-chewed wood sprinkled on her black nose.

"They make those holes up there and they're as round as if they had measured them." Mrs. Murphy, too, watched the bees, which could have been mistaken for bumblebees except that the carpenter bees' black bottoms weren't fuzzy.

Tuesday, the first of June, perfect, a light breeze, low seventies, grass as green as emeralds, produced a euphoria in the animals. Although six o'clock in the evening, the light gilded the weathervane, the barn, the outbuildings, and the neat clapboard house. The sun wouldn't set until around nine, and the summer twilights lingered, filling the sky with colors of surpassing beauty.

Harry's three horses, Poptart, Gin Fizz, and Tomahawk, dined on redbud clover, which enlivened the green pastures with dark pink dots. She mixed redbud clover, orchard grass, and a little rye in her fields. This year she experimented with some alfalfa down by the creek bottom, between her farm and that of Blair Bainbridge.

She was out on her old 1958 tractor, bushogging the sides of her long driveway. Once Harry fired up her tractor it was hard to get her to step down. The pop-pop-pop of the upright exhaust pipe thrilled her as much as a Brandenburg Concerto thrilled a music aficionado. Which was not to say that Harry didn't like Bach. She did. She just liked her tractor's pops and rumbles better.

Mrs. Murphy and Pewter hated the dust this chore stirred up. Furthermore, they'd worked diligently in the post office that day and felt they were entitled to a snooze amidst the lilies that Harry had planted in front of the low boxwoods by the barn. She

was going all out on her beautification program since BoomBoom Craycroft—a former adversary turned, if not friend, then
warm acquaintance—had gotten a whopping good price on all the stock of a nursery going out of business. The nursery
had specialized in only trees and shrubs,
no flowers. BoomBoom, Susan Tucker,
Miranda Hogendobber, and Harry bought
up maples, hickories, crepe myrtles, Italian
lilacs, redbuds, dogwoods, a new disease-
resistant chestnut, and even some red
oaks. The four women divided up the trees
and shrubs between them. Harry had lined
her drive and farm roads with her bounty.
Of course, the girls, as they called themselves, nearly broke their backs putting in
all this plant material, but Harry had a drill
on the back of her old tractor so she could
dig the holes. Then BoomBoom, operating
her new tractor, scooped up the trees, and
the huge root bundles in a ball of dirt were
perched on the front-end loader of her
tractor. And throughout March and April,
when weather permitted, they got the trees
and shrubs in the ground at each of their
houses.

As Harry bounced around on the tractor

seat covered with remnants of a sheepskin, she thought about how much she loved working outdoors. Even those raw days when the drizzle ran down the back of her neck and the temperature chilled at thirty-six degrees, she loved it.

When she wasn't puzzling over Barry, her mind returned to her present job—postmistress. Everybody trooped through the post office. She adored seeing everyone she knew, as well as the occasional stranger. But the threat of a new building, more employees, and more rules nagged at her. She and Miranda did as they pleased, and as long as they met the dispatcher in the morning and in the late afternoon, they were just fine. The building was as neat as a pin, the mail sorted and in the boxes by nine most days. And since they knew everyone, they knew who drove by on their way in to work in Charlottesville in the morning. Those people could always expect a wave, a smile. Best of all, Harry's three four-footed friends worked with her. What if a new post office and new people changed that? She would never work without her animals. It was unnatural. It would make her sick to just hang around with humans all the time.

A large rock outcropping near the drive necessitated a swerve. A groundhog nibbled grass to the side of the outcropping.

As she neared the dirt state road, she pulled over again, because Susan Tucker turned onto the gray stones, number five from the quarry in Staunton. Harry put a load down in April and complained for a month about the expense.

Stopping, Susan rolled down her window. "Looks good. Why don't you come up the other side—I know you hate to leave a job in the middle of it—and I'll make supper."

"You will?"

"I will. Brooks and her dad drove down to Sweet Briar this afternoon." She pointed to a bag of groceries on the passenger seat of her Audi station wagon. "Voilà."

"Susan, you are the best!" Harry, who rarely cooked, beamed.

"In fact, give yourself forty-five minutes. You ought to knock a mess of bushogging out by then."

"Roger." Harry touched the brim of her straw cowboy hat.

Each year she bought a new Shady Brady and wore it hard. By the end of the year that hat was tired, plus she'd invariably forget to bring it in the house and would leave it in the tack room, where the mice would chew on it.

Tucker, snoring next to the tack trunk in the barn, lifted her head when she heard Susan come down the drive. She roused herself, hoping that Susan had brought along Owen, her corgi brother.

As the two dogs played tag, the bemused cats watched.

"What's funny about those two is they have no idea they're shrimps." Pewter rested her head on her outstretched paw.

"Dwarfs." Mrs. Murphy accurately described the two corgis, large animals bred down to shortened legs but with the torso and head of larger dogs.

As corgis go, Tucker and Owen were on the large size of the breed. Tee Tucker weighed forty pounds and her brother weighed about forty-six, but he carried a little potbelly. Neither dog was terribly overweight, and both could turn on a dime and give you a nickel's change. Given that their function was herding cattle, their size

and demeanor were perfect for the task. A small dog like a miniature pinscher might not get the respect of the cattle, but a corgi with a stout bark and strong jaws could nip heels, duck or leap sideways, and drive those cattle down the road.

"Murphy, I've been thinking about Barry. No, we couldn't smell another animal, but he had the stench of fear on him. We didn't talk about that," Pewter said.

"Hmm." Mrs. Murphy sat up. "I attributed that to nature. He was afraid of what killed him."

"Me, too," Pewter replied.

"What's on your mind?"

"Well, let's say a bear grabs him or even takes a swipe so only his throat is touched."

"Yeah . . ." The tiger nodded, waiting.

"Wouldn't Barry have thrown his right arm up to protect his throat? That's the natural human reaction. They have no other defense in that situation and, God knows, the poor things can't outrun a rabbit."

"Pewter, you're right. And there wasn't a mark on him, at least not that we could see. No dirt on his right arm or bruises or blood. It's—"

"Unnatural." Pewter finished her thought for her.

"Even if a huge raptor swooped down on him, he'd still throw his arm up." Mrs. Murphy considered other possibilities.

"Okay, suppose the bird hit him from behind with his talons balled up. Barry stumbled and somehow fell faceup. Well, he'd have a big knot on the back of his head."

"Thought you didn't care much about humans except for Harry and a few of her friends." Mrs. Murphy taunted Pewter just a bit.

Pewter drawled, *"I don't. But I was thinking about what kind of animal would kill Barry without him having any time to defend himself at all."*

"You're it!" Tucker roared by, too close for comfort, as she chased her brother.

"Watch it!" Mrs. Murphy swiped at the white rear end.

The possum, Simon, awakened for a night's foraging, peered out of the hayloft door, open to let the breezes through the hay. *"Pipe down."*

The cats looked up at Simon, whom they liked well enough. *"Good luck. Tucker's about to go into her frenzy. Give her another minute and she'll chase the tail that isn't there.*"

Simon, half-domesticated, had endured every shot and test for EPM, a degenerative, complicated disease that would be passed to the horses, and emerged a remarkably healthy possum, if a disgruntled one.

"*I'm not coming down until those two are in the house. They'll chase me. Tucker forgets her manners when Owen's around,*" Simon grumbled.

As Susan stepped out back to ring the large bell hanging by the screen door, the dogs decided that the prospect of food was more alluring than chasing each other to exhaustion.

"*Simon, have a good evening.*" Pewter shook herself, then trotted to the screen door.

Pewter was never one to hang back when food was on the table.

Mrs. Murphy called up, "*Peppermints in Mom's barn coat. She forgot to give them to the horses.*"

"*Thanks!*" Simon could taste those candies already.

Harry, hungry, pulled her tractor into the

old shed the minute she heard the bell. Johnny Pop, the old John Deere, belched a few times, black puffs of exhaust rising like smoke signals from the exhaust pipe. Harry disengaged the PTO—the power takeoff— a rotating axle that powered attachments. Tomorrow before climbing back on she would dutifully check fluids on her old tractor. She had a mania for maintaining all equipment properly because she assumed she'd never be able to buy any more.

The two friends caught up on their own doings as well as everyone else's. The animals gratefully ate the chicken that Susan had made for them.

"Susan, no wonder Ned married you." Harry smiled as Susan put apple crisp before her for dessert.

"Bet he has days when he wonders," Susan laughed as she sat down to the apple crisp topped with vanilla ice cream. "Oh, ran into Fair, and he said he's off this coming weekend if we want to go to the furniture stores in Farmville."

"Do you want to go?"

"Can't make up my mind. If I go I'm afraid I'll buy that chest of drawers I keep dreaming about. My husband won't be happy about it." She sighed, then smiled as she delivered ice cream and apple crisp to her mouth.

"Let's wait until we get closer to the weekend. I don't want to be tempted, either." Harry savored the crunch of another mouthful of apple crisp. She changed the subject. "Is Mim going to Keeneland this year?"

"She's waiting for Saratoga."

"I'd love to go!" Harry adored Saratoga Springs, a beautiful city north of Albany, New York, and the center of the thoroughbred world in August.

"She's selling this year."

"She had those two yearlings by, uh, one's by Fred Astaire and the other is by J. C. Smells, the Pennsylvania horse. But the mares are granddaughters of Secretariat. Everyone wants that blood, especially from the mares."

"Mim is shrewd. Ran into her, too, and she said you had found Mary Patricia Reines's class ring. I can't believe you didn't call me."

"I'm sorry." And Harry was. "I've been on overload and I didn't know who it belonged to when I found it. Took it to Coop only because I found it not far from where I found Barry, poor guy. And she took it to Aunt Tally. It's a long story about why she took it there instead of to Rick, but, anyway, Big Mim knew. And Mary Pat's initials are inside the ring plus the date, 1945. Oh, Coop and I came back here after Aunt Tally's and used Mom's big magnifying glass. The inscription, which is reversed so you can use the ring for stamping, is *Victuri te salutamus*."

"We salute you, Victory?" Susan's Latin was rusty but serviceable. "Or, we who are about to be victorious salute you?"

"Close enough. The ring is worn but I think it's *Victuri*. Could have been Victoria, she who conquers."

"Victoria, -ae, is conquest, victory," Susan said. "Easy to remember since it's first declension. I forget fourth and, well, if you don't use it you lose it."

"Men say that, too."

They burst out laughing.

"Well, victory is feminine but victor is masculine. It's coming back. Victor, victoria." Susan polished off the apple crisp. "That's so good."

"Is there more?"

"Yes. I shouldn't, but, well, the thing about temptation is, if you can resist something it's because it's not tempting enough." She walked over to the counter. "What about you?"

"I'm full."

"I'm never full."

"Susan, you've always been like that. You burn it off."

"I burned it off until I turned thirty-five. Then my metabolism changed. I don't know why yours didn't."

"Farm work."

"Thank God you spend part of each day inside at the post office or you'd be rail thin." She cut another large helping, using Harry's spatula.

Harry needed more kitchen utensils. Susan made note of that for future presents.

"Didn't we have fun putting in all those trees?"

"Fun? I about broke my back."

"I loved it."

"Harry, you love anything with a motor in it, and you and BoomBoom were in hog heaven. It's so funny to see BoomBoom in the cab of that eighty-horsepower tractor. I

mean, she really is one of the most beautiful, feminine women, and she works at it,
too. But let her get in a car or a tractor and,
like you, she's as good as any gearhead.
She *is* a gearhead!"

"I've gained a new appreciation for
BoomBoom. I think that ordeal we survived
at the Clam turned me around." Harry
mentioned the big sports arena at University of Virginia, where they had been
pursued by two criminals.

They worked together, fought back, and
lived. The cats and dog helped, too.

"I'm glad. Before it slips my mind—
where is Mary Pat's ring?"

"Here." Harry removed it from her pinkie.

"Rick let you have it? I can't believe it."

"I found it. Cooper took it to him first
thing Monday morning. They dusted it and
examined it and, as you would suspect, my
prints, Aunt Tally's. Obviously, no one expected much, but Rick went through the
motions. Rick said I could have it. Coop
brought it by on her way home last night.
Finders keepers."

"That's good luck. Finding a ring is good
luck, even if in the end she had bad luck. I
guess we'll never know. Back to our Latin.

Finding a dismembered hand is good luck. It means power is coming to you. Victory." Susan pointed to the tiny inscription on the ring underneath the Episcopal shield.

"Vespasian was sitting in his tent after a battle and his dog brought him a hand. He knew he'd be emperor. 69 A.D., I think. It's amazing how that Latin does stick in there." She tapped her head. "That's why I made Danny and Brooks take it. Danny is still taking it up at Cornell, and, Harry, he called me this morning and says he still doesn't know what he wants to be. I thought he'd be a lawyer like his dad, but Brooks, you know, I think she's heading that way. Well, it's too early to tell. They have to find their own way."

"You're a good mother, Susan."

"Tosh." Susan waved away the compliment and handed back the ring to Harry. "What a lovely woman she was. Generous to a fault. I always thought she was brave because she never married, and in her generation you married even if you were as ugly as a mud fence."

"Never thought about it. We were in grade school when she disappeared. It amazes me how sensitive you were to other people even when we were kids."

"Mary Pat was an original. Remember the time she let us ride on her track? We were nine years old and we thought we were in the homestretch for the Preakness!" Susan glowed.

Harry, content after a full meal, lapsed into nostalgia, "I was on Silly Putty, that gray pony, and you were on Tickles. You won."

"Yes, I did."

"Wonder why Mary Pat didn't marry. She was beautiful and rich. Maybe she figured if she married she'd lose control of her money," Harry said. "Back then if you weren't careful or if the trusts weren't tied up, you did. I mean, women were chattel. And Mary Pat was making money from breeding horses. You could do that then. Maybe she didn't want to risk losing that money. You know," she sat upright, "I never did think about it. When you're a kid you mostly think of yourself and your peers. I thought the world began with me."

Susan laughed. "I think that's the way every generation feels until it matures.

Mary Pat didn't marry because she was gay."

"Mary Pat?"

"Yes."

"How do you know?"

"Big Mim told me. I mean in her own way. They were friends. Mim wasn't direct about it exactly, but I put two and two together."

"Mary Pat gay? Must have driven men wild. She was gorgeous," Harry exclaimed.

"So were the women around her. I guess Mary Pat had an eye for a good woman just as she did for a horse."

"To each her own."

"That ring looks good on you."

"I wonder if she was killed because she was gay." Harry reached for her teacup.

"You don't know that she was killed. She could have suffered a heart attack and never been found."

"Right. She and Ziggy Flame had simultaneous heart attacks." Harry mentioned the great stallion who disappeared along with Mary Pat.

"Ziggy—he was never found, either," Susan mused.

"Mim said something. You know how

smart she is. She said if I found the ring in the creek bed, then Mary Pat is somewhere upstream."

"Possibly." Susan cleared the table, walked over, and put her hand on Harry's shoulder. "When do you want to start looking?"

Harry touched Susan's hand. "Susan, you know me too well."

"Cradle friends."

"How about tomorrow after I get off work? And I'll ask Fair so he doesn't fuss."

"Tomorrow. Meet you here at five-thirty?"

"I'll burn the wind getting home." Harry got up to wash the dishes. "Oh, today a tourist all hot to get to Monticello somehow took a wrong turn and wound up at the post office. So Miranda gave her directions. And you know what this lady says as she leaves?"

"No."

"She says, 'Crozet's so ugly even Lot's wife wouldn't have looked back.' "

9

". . . Running through the barn as though chased by the avenging Furies themselves." Tavener Heyward slapped his thighs, laughing until the tears rolled down his cheeks.

Fair Haristeen laughed with him. "Paul will never live that down."

"I asked him what possessed him to do such a thing, and he said when he heard Big Mim coming toward the barn he got so flustered, because she has No Smoking signs posted about every two feet, that he stuck his cigarette in his back pocket. Never thought about putting it out. That's one derriere that will sit lightly in the saddle for the next week," Tavener, his hazel eyes merry, said.

Paul de Silva, Big Mim's new trainer, was a young, wiry, small-sized man with dreamy eyes and curly black hair. He spoke with a light Spanish accent, which added to his allure. He worked with Big Mim's hunters, those for the show ring and those for actual hunting, often the same horses. Big Mim believed in bringing along horses the old way: foxhunting them first, then introducing them to the show ring or steeplechasing. Paul appreciated the wisdom of this approach. He had a terrible crush on Tazio Chappars, an architect. He was trying to find the right approach to her, since he feared she wouldn't look at a horseman twice. Horsemen's prospects aren't as shining as those of architects, although miracles do happen.

The two vets met in front of the post office and, the morning being especially lush and fragrant, they stood outside and chatted for a while. At nine-thirty they'd both been up for five hours.

"Saw a lovely little fellow over at Albemarle Stud this morning," Fair reported. "Another one of Fred Astaire's babies out of an old Cool Virginian mare. As correct as they come."

Cool Virginian was a stallion, now deceased, who had enjoyed a solid career as a stud.

"Who bred him?"

"Dr. Mary O'Brien. I'm going to see if she'll sell him to me. I'd like to buy him for Harry. You know how good Harry is with a young horse. Five years from now he will be the best-looking horse in the hunt field. Just a balanced little guy."

"Ah, love." Tavener winked, for he meant both the love of a woman and the love of a horse.

"Makes the world go 'round." Fair, who at six feet five towered over Tavener, wrapped his arm around the older vet's shoulder. "We wouldn't be here without it."

"Well, my lad, you wouldn't have a business without it." Tavener laughed. "Neither would I, neither would I. But I tell you, equine matings are better planned than human ones."

"Frightening, isn't it?" Fair dropped his arm to open the door to the post office.

"Hello, gentlemen." Miranda leaned over the wide counter.

Harry, who was at the back table, put down the magazines she was collecting.

"Two good-for-nothing, good-looking men. I don't know, Miranda. I think we'd better call Rick Shaw and ask for protection."

"Heartless. Harry, you always were heartless." Tavener shook his head. "And what have you been up to this fine morning?"

"Sorting your bills."

He winced. "And have you noticed they always come faster than the money? It's one of those irrefutable laws of finance, just as Newton's laws are of physics. Ah, yes, what comes up must come down. The financial version of Newton's Law is, what comes in must go out."

"If we secede from the Union again and fight a limited war, we'll get war reparations and all be rich." Fair's deep voice filled the room.

Tucker had already barreled through the animal door in the divider between the public area and the work area. Tucker loved Fair.

The two cats, recumbent in a mail cart, loved Fair, too, but not enough to disturb their repose.

"Certainly didn't hurt Germany or Japan." Tavener nodded his head in agreement. "The United States gives away more money than any nation in history, and you know what? Those nations take our money and despise us. We really ought to keep some of it right here in Virginia. You've got a good idea there, Haristeen."

"Isn't life wonderful? Isn't life grand?" Tucker wiggled, then stood up on her hind legs, resting her front paws on Fair's shins.

"Miss Happy Camper," Pewter sarcastically said, and rolled to her other side, which meant she rolled into Mrs. Murphy since the canvas in the mail cart had no firm bottom.

"Miss Fatty Screwloose." Mrs. Murphy opened one jaundiced eye.

"I am not fat. I am round. It's the way I'm built."

"Doesn't explain the 'Screwloose.' " Mrs. Murphy gave a little laugh that sounded like a cackle.

"I'm leaving you, Hateful." Pewter lurched out of the mail cart, which further discomfited the tiger.

The cart rolled a little bit, the form of Mrs. Murphy clearly delineated on the bottom.

"Hello, Pewter." Fair leaned over the counter.

"Hello, Fair." The cat minded her manners. *"I am going on record: Mrs. Murphy is conceited and mean. She's mean because she doesn't eat enough. She thinks she's sleek and beautiful. She looks weedy and"*—a spiteful pause—*"wormy."*

That fast, Mrs. Murphy shot out of the mail cart. She erupted like a feline Old Faithful geyser, straight up and spewing, as she headed right for Pewter, who flattened herself to withstand the onslaught.

"You'll pay for that!" Mrs. Murphy pounced on Pewter, who rolled over so her powerful hind legs could bang into Mrs. Murphy's beige tummy.

They rolled, hissed, spat, and then Pewter broke free to give everyone the thrill of seeing her circle the interior of the post office three times at top speed before blasting out the back animal door, where she crossed the alley and headed into Miranda Hogendobber's beloved garden.

Mrs. Murphy was right on her tail.

"The energy." Miranda shook her head in wonderment.

"Life." Tavener smiled. "We'd do well to learn from them. To live in the moment."

"I don't mind their living in the moment. It's when the claws come out. I mind that a lot," said Tucker, who had been scratched on the nose a time or two.

"Harry, my girl, I left my key in my other coat pocket." Tavener put both elbows on the counter.

She reached into the back of the post-box, pulled out a handful of envelopes and two magazines, which she slid to him over the counter. Behind her a sign read, PLEASE DON'T FORGET YOUR KEY. MAIL CANNOT BE HANDED TO YOU OVER THE COUNTER. This was yet another federal regulation ignored because it made not a bit of sense in a small community. Most farmers and merchants in Crozet were responsible, hardworking people, who had the great good sense to set aside the morass of state and federal regulations whose only purpose was to drag down productivity and increase paperwork.

In fact, most Virginians went about their business minding their own business. If they absolutely had to do something like get a county sticker for their vehicle, they did. But the motto of residents of the Old Dominion was, "That government governs best which governs least." This was first uttered by another Virginian, Thomas Jefferson.

Of course, if Jefferson could return to see the mess of it, just the tax laws alone, he'd pass out. Then he'd wake up and get to work cutting the Gordian knot the rest of us have allowed to become entwined around ourselves.

When Tavener took the mail from Harry's hands, he blinked, then reached for her right hand. He held it, turned it back side up. "Holy Cross. Haven't seen one of those rings in years. Mary Pat wore one."

"This is Mary Pat's," Harry quietly replied.

Tavener gasped. "My God, where did you get it?"

"Found it in Potlicker Creek. Both Sheriff Shaw and Deputy Cooper examined it. Couldn't find anything. Didn't expect to, anyway, so they gave it back to me."

Tavener sagged and Fair caught him. "Tavener, are you all right?"

He nodded, then leaned his elbows and weight on the counter. "I never thought I'd see that ring again. She was good to me. I worshiped that woman. I worshiped the ground she walked on."

Fair patted Tavener's shoulder sympathetically while Miranda, the most expressive of the group, flipped up the divider and came around. She gave Tavener a good hug.

He hugged her back. "Not a day goes by I don't think of her and give thanks she walked into my life. I wouldn't be where I am today if it weren't for Mary Pat."

"She was a good soul."

"And beautiful. I was ten when she vanished, just old enough to begin to look at women but not old enough to know why I was looking at them." Fair remembered her honey brown hair, which had streaks of blond in it, hair so shining that light seemed to come from it instead of reflecting off it.

"Mary Pat was one of the great beauties of her generation." Tavener stood up straight, wiping his eyes with his forefinger knuckle. "Sorry. Shocked me—seeing her ring."

"Maybe one day we'll know what happened to her," Miranda said.

"I hope so, but I gave up on that years

ago." Tavener picked up his mail. "Harry, it would make her happy to know you wear her ring. You were just a sprite when she left us, but you could stick on a horse and Mary Pat liked that. Yes, it would make her happy." He opened the door and shut it softly behind him, too overcome to stay.

"I feel awful." Harry bit her lower lip.

"Honey, you didn't do anything," Fair comfortingly said.

"I had no idea." Harry turned as Mrs. Murphy and Pewter both came back in, the animal door flapping.

"That was very nice of him to say that Mary Pat would have liked you to have her ring. She never had any children and I think she regretted that. She liked you and Susan and BoomBoom. You were all such happy, feisty little things." What Miranda neglected to say was that she, too, regretted not having children. For whatever reason, she and George just hadn't had them. In those days, fertility studies hadn't progressed very far.

"How old was Mary Pat when she disappeared?" Fair asked Miranda.

"Mmm, late forties, maybe about forty-five or forty-seven. And still beautiful.

Maybe more beautiful," Miranda said. "The money. We always thought maybe she was killed for money, but Alicia Palmer, hot-blooded though she was and young as she was—in her middle twenties, I guess—just didn't seem the murdering kind."

"Women can lose their tempers and kill. I don't know if we don't kill as frequently as men or if we don't get caught."

"It was all so long ago, and now it's stirred up again and, really, we have a recent serious matter. What if whatever killed Barry is out there and kills again? I wouldn't rest too easy until we know more about that unfortunate young man's end." Miranda sighed.

"She's right," Tucker resolutely agreed. *"Brinkley!"* Tucker bounded to the front door as a handsome, well-groomed yellow Labrador retriever, tail wagging, waited on the other side of it. His human, Tazio Chappars, opened the door.

The two dogs rapturously greeted each other. The cats, on the divider now, liked Brinkley but thought it prudent not to be too effusive. That was dog stuff.

The humans chatted. Tazio, who was half Italian and half African-American, was warm, gentle, and very, very gifted. Young as she was, she was being sought out for large commercial commissions ever since her design won the competition for the new University of Virginia Sports Complex.

Just then Paul de Silva came in to pick up his mail.

"Paul, hear you went up in flames." Fair pointed to Paul's cute, tight rear end.

A small burn hole in his left back pocket was evident.

Paul, embarrassed, told his story and was delighted when Tazio laughed, too. They walked out together, his heart beating so hard in his chest he could barely breathe. He still couldn't work up the nerve to ask her out, but she smiled at him, giving him hope.

Miranda, observing this from inside the post office, said, "They make a cute couple."

Harry and Fair turned to look.

"They do." Fair smiled. He was much more romantic than Harry.

But even Harry agreed. "They do."

"Of course, not as good-looking as you and I."

"Fair." She punched his arm but was nonetheless pleased at the compliment.

Mrs. Murphy rolled her eyes. *"Another woman would have kissed him, but, no, Harry punches him."*

"She's dyslexic," Pewter said.

"She can read fine," Tucker opined.

"Emotionally dyslexic," the gray cat shrewdly said.

The other two remained silent but knew there was truth to Pewter's insight.

10

Potlicker Creek earned its name in the early nineteenth century. The runoff from the eastern slopes of the Blue Ridge Mountains, clear and cool, tumbled into Potlicker Creek and many others that ultimately rolled into the James River, the first river in the New World to nourish an English colony, which survived back in 1607.

The Native-American name of Potlicker Creek had been lost along the way. The strong-running waters took on a succession of names over the centuries depending upon who owned the land, but finally, after the War of 1812, Potlicker Creek stuck. The many stills tucked away in the hollows along the creek testified to the curative effects of the water when distilled.

Harry and Fair worked the western bank while Susan paralleled them on the eastern. The cats stayed with Harry, while Tucker and Owen assisted Susan.

The deep pools under the overhanging trees remained still, the current gentle underneath. Small schools of smallmouth bass called rockfish in these parts lazed there along with other fish.

Muskrats plied their trade, skippers darted on the glassy pools, while blue herons and green herons fished along the banks. Crayfish burrowed to get away from those long, lethal bills. Frogs croaked, turtles slept in the sun.

The late-afternoon warmth lulled everyone except the insects. As the humans would approach, small clouds of tiny black no-see-ums would flare up, occasionally aided by a hornet buzzing by to a football-size gray home hanging overhead from a sycamore limb.

The deer slept in small coverts, the squirrels dozed in their nests, and the groundhogs, already plump, waddled in the small meadows that dotted the woods like green jewels.

The goldfinches and purple finches

chirped and darted about along with blue-birds, indigo buntings, and nuthatches. Cultivation was close, and the birds made the most of having the best of both worlds. Then, too, finches are active little creatures with bright black eyes, missing nothing.

The cats ignored the chirping and chatter. Never let a bird know it's getting to you.

The humans diligently looked for any suspicious sign—a weathered rock pile, a beaten-down mound. Nothing presented itself except for the occasional faded beer can, a few old glass soda bottles from long before they were born. Susan could never resist that stuff and soon she was toting her treasures, begriming herself in the process.

They walked about three miles away from the borders of Aunt Tally's land before finally turning back.

Harry and Fair each took some of Susan's finds as she was tottering. They turned off the old path, walked up the narrow deer path, emerging on top of a rolling, low foothill about a mile from Harry's westernmost border. These three had grown up here. Dropped from a helicopter anywhere between the Afton Gap and Sugar Hollow, they could find their way home.

At the westernmost corner of Harry's land, where it touched both the land of Blair Bainbridge and Aunt Tally, stood Blair and Little Mim. An old quince tree marked the spot where the three pieces of land touched one another.

Harry waved, little bits of dirt falling on her hair from the brown bottle she carried in her right hand. In her left she had a cobalt-blue medicine bottle. Blair and Little Mim, surprised to see them all, waved back.

Within minutes they were at the old quince tree.

"What are you all doing back here?" Blair said.

"Look!" Susan put down her pop bottle. "Nehi. Now, when was the last time you saw that? Or Yoo-Hoo? And then I've got this old Pepsi bottle here. I mean, this one's even before Joan Crawford took over the company."

"Joan Crawford ran Pepsi?" Little Mim thought that was odd.

"Yes." Susan, who avidly read movie-star biographies, supplied the information.

"She married the president of Pepsi, and when he died she took over. And look at this blue. Have you ever seen such a blue?" She pointed to the flat-sided cobalt-blue bottle that Harry carried.

"Susan, what do you intend to do with all this?" Little Mim, smiling, wondered.

"Wash them out, put them on my windowsill, and I'll—"

"Move them because you won't be able to clean around them," Harry finished her sentence.

"No, I won't. I'll put stuff in to root."

"I know what this is about," Fair genially said. "Ned will get so tired of the clutter, he'll finally build you that little greenhouse you've always wanted."

"Hey, I never thought of that." Susan brightened, then her smile faded. "No, he won't. I'm getting the interior of the house painted. You can't believe how expensive it is. For just three rooms and the trim it's almost eight thousand dollars."

"Big rooms," Harry simply said.

"Hell, Harry, it's not the Hall of Mirrors at Versailles. They aren't that big."

"If it were the Hall of Mirrors, Susan, you wouldn't need to get much painted."

"Will you shut up." Susan playfully put her hand over Harry's mouth, which now had a dirt smear. "Oops."

"Maybe that's where the expression 'Eat dirt' came from." Blair laughed.

Harry wiped off her mouth, but a little of the grit lodged between her teeth. "Yuck."

"Are you checking your borders?" Fair asked Blair.

Little Mim answered for him. "He's trying to figure out how much land he really has, since this old place was always described as two hundred and thirty acres more or less."

"Surveying costs so much that folks just approximated and no one at the court-house much minded. It's such a nice piece of land." Harry picked up a blade of grass to chew to get the earthy taste out of her mouth.

"Remember Herbie's old uncle?" Little Mim recalled a slender gentleman, the last Jones to inhabit the farm.

"Bryson," Susan said. "He was so courtly."

"He used to sit up in the family grave-yard and read Greek. He had a wonderful faculty for languages but wasn't much of a farmer or businessman." Fair had liked the old gentleman.

"Used to drive the Rev crazy because he couldn't go to seminary and look after the farm, too. You keep the cemetery looking good for Herb," Harry complimented Blair.

"I enjoy it. I like being outside." Blair, although one of the highest-paid models in America, was growing weary of flying to locations over the world, dealing with the egos of photographers and other models.

"Harry, I haven't seen you since Saturday." Little Mim pushed a lock of hair from her eyes. "You okay?"

"Yeah." Harry shrugged. "I felt terrible for Barry."

"And they still don't know what killed him?" Blair put his arm around Little Mim's shoulders.

"Yancy performed the autopsy." Fair mentioned the coroner. "Sent off tissue samples to Richmond. I ran into him this afternoon and he hadn't heard anything back, but sometimes these things can take a month or longer depending on how backed up they are down there."

"Did he find anything on the body?" Blair, like everyone else, was curious.

"Not that he mentioned. He said Barry had no marks on him except for his throat. And here's the really strange part: The wound was clean. Clean as if it had been surgically created. No saliva. No bits of rust." Fair shook his head. "Yancy hopes that something will show up in the blood work."

"It's so clean it almost seems premeditated." Little Mim, intelligent like all the Urquhart clan, pursed her lips.

"By an animal?" Blair handed Harry his kerchief, since she hadn't removed all the dirt.

"The human animal," Mrs. Murphy quietly said.

11

A pair of brilliant turquoise eyes peered out of the passenger side of the car. Sissi, a gray tuxedo cat, was irritated that her human, Rose Marie Dunlap, was chatting at the gas pump at the Amoco station.

Sissi accompanied the always well-turned-out Rose Marie on her regular trips from Washington, D. C., to Crozet. She enjoyed riding in the car but she enjoyed arriving at their destination even more, the farm of Rose Marie's daughter, Beth Marcus.

"I haven't seen you in ages." Rose Marie smiled.

"You know it's been years since I've been back here." Marshall Kressenberg, florid, bent over to shake her hand. "I was coming back from Lexington, Kentucky, and thought I'd stop by to see some of my old running buddies. Course, I should have called first. Everyone's out and about." He accented "out and about" the Virginia way, which also sounds Canadian. "You're looking well."

And indeed, Rose Marie Dunlap's appearance—petite, fresh, and healthy—belied her eighty-six years.

"I keep busy. For one thing, Sissi keeps me busy."

At the sound of her name Sissi meowed, *"Let's go to Beth's now!"*

Marshall laughed as the cat continued to jabber. "Well, I'm so glad to see you." He opened the door to his truck.

"I read your name in the sports pages. I'm glad you've done so well."

He closed the door, window down. "It's a good thing the horses are running and not me. I wouldn't make it to the first pole." He laughed, cut on the motor, and drove off.

"We can go now," Sissi grumbled.

Rose Marie slid behind the wheel. "You can be so impatient."

Marshall switched on his cell phone, dialing Big Mim's barn number. Big Mim had a good breeding program, good but small. He wouldn't mind seeing what she had before the sales. The barn recording came on. He disconnected and headed out toward I-64. Tavener could tell him what Mim had on the ground. Maybe it was just as well no one was around. He'd get pulled into long conversations, and he needed to get back to Maryland.

Too much going on in the horse world right now.

12

A sample of Barry Monteith's brain tissues rested under the fluorescence microscope.

The gang at the lab examined a variety of Barry's tissue samples. Given the odd circumstances of Barry's death, a variety of tests had been ordered by the Albemarle County coroner, Tom Yancy, at Sheriff Shaw's request.

Georgette Renfrow, one of the best of the bunch, peered intently through the lens. She was performing a direct fluorescent antibody test, shortened to dFA. Round dots of varying size, a bright fluorescent apple-green color, jumped right out at her.

"Jesus." She whistled.

In all her years at the lab, Georgette had only seen this once before, and that was in the brain tissue of a prisoner who worked the road gangs and died mysteriously. The prison physician couldn't detect the cause of his intense suffering.

"Jake, take a look." She motioned for a twenty-seven-year-old assistant to look.

He came over, bending to put the eyepiece at just the right place. "I've never seen that."

"Remember it."

"What is it? I suppose I should know, but I don't think I've seen it and I don't remember it from school."

She peered into the microscope one more time, then tapped her index finger on the smooth desktop. "Rabies."

13

That's bizzare," Harry exclaimed when Cooper told her the report on Barry Monteith. The deputy also told her everyone who had contact with the body needed to get tested for rabies. She'd gotten Harry an appointment with Bill Langston, her family doctor, at eight the next morning.

Harry and Fair were in Miranda's garden when Cooper arrived, putting together a gazebo as promised. Tracy Raz, Miranda's high-school beau, was down in Charlotte, North Carolina, on business or he would have put his shoulder to the wheel, too.

Having chased one another to exhaustion, the animals had plopped under Miranda's sumptuous roses, which were every color imaginable. Pewter preferred the peach, a thin red outline tracing each petal. Mrs. Murphy dozed under pure white roses, while Tucker snored under hot coral. They awoke when Cooper walked up the hand-laid brick walkway this late Friday afternoon.

"Wouldn't we have known? Wouldn't he have been foaming at the mouth when Harry found him?" Miranda, shocked at the news, asked.

"Not necessarily." Fair knew a great deal about rabies. "Once the virus is in your nervous tissue it can take one to three months to present itself, for the victim to show clinical signs of infection," Fair said.

"Not in the blood?" Miranda asked.

Cooper, who had grilled Dr. Hayden McIntire the second the report came over her computer screen, said, "No. Rabies is only in nervous tissue. It's not going to show up in blood samples. Ideally you want brain tissue, which, of course, you can't get from a living victim. In Barry's case, we had samples."

"You suspected rabies?" Harry inquired.

"No. But given the manner in which he was found and that the cause of death might be an attack from a wild animal, Rick and Yancy of course asked for rabies tests."

"So it's not in the blood but it would show up if whatever killed him had infected him?" Harry asked.

"Rabies." Tucker's ears pricked right up, as did the two kitties' ears.

"That depends," Fair said, his voice reassuring just because it was so deep. "Rabies is in saliva. A human is bitten and the virus replicates fairly rapidly, but it has to travel to the brain. Actually, this disease is quite unique and terrifying, really. It's a bullet virus. It gets into the nerve tissue, and when it finally gets to the brain, you see the typical signs of rabies. Like I said, that usually takes between one and three months."

"That long?" Miranda was surprised.

"That long, but if you're bitten and you don't get the series of shots within a week, there's nothing that can be done. Rabies is always fatal."

"Fair, how would you know—I mean, how would you know that the animal that bit you was rabid?" Cooper thought she knew the answer but wanted to hear his reply.

"You don't. Let me back this up a minute. Usually the first person to identify rabies is a veterinarian or a hunter. Domestic animals like dogs, cats, and horses so rarely have rabies now that it's noteworthy if they do. The public is educated about inoculating their pets and stock. When we see rabies it's usually raccoons; that accounts for 40.6 percent of reported cases, with skunks coming in at around 29.4 percent."

"How do you remember all that?" Miranda was impressed.

He smiled genially. "It's my profession. How do you remember all your rose varieties? But the thing about rabies is, if someone is bitten by a raccoon or a skunk they know it."

"What about fox or coyote?" Harry asked.

"Negligible. Only 5.4 percent of reported cases are foxes and coyotes. And the numbers are going downward. Oddly enough, we've seen a spike upward in sheep and cattle. Not enough to be alarming, and it may just be that farmers and ranchers out west are becoming better at reporting symptoms. Also, I think in many

ways people are becoming more environ-
mentally responsible. In the old days if a
fellow had a sick cow he'd shoot it. If it was
found dead he'd not get an autopsy. Today
he might call the vet. It's one of the reasons
we've been able to slow this disease and
to just about stamp it out in pets."

"If Barry was bitten by a raccoon or a
skunk, wouldn't he notice? Wouldn't he go
to the doctor?" Harry's mind was whirring
along.

"Who said he knew he was bitten? It
could have been a bat, too, and those bites
are so tiny you don't see them most times
and you don't feel them, although a numb-
ness at the site of infection is often a sig-
nal." Fair laid down his hammer on the floor
of the gazebo. "Bats get a bad rap about
carrying rabies, but the percent of humans
bitten by rabid bats is tiny." Cooper started
to speak, but Harry jumped in.

"If the rabies was in Barry's brain tissue,
then he had it for at least thirty days,
right?" Harry jammed her hands in her
jeans pocket.

"That's a safe assumption. He displayed
no symptoms yet. Or did he?" Fair looked
at Cooper.

"Everyone we've questioned said he behaved normally. So he—I think the word is presented—he presented no symptoms."

"What are they? All I know is foaming at the mouth." Miranda was worried.

"That's the stereotype, but the progress for humans is that they feel flu-y, headachy. That might last for a couple of days. They run a fever, and this provokes anxiety, agitation, and confusion. By now, if you know the person, you know something is not right. They aren't acting normal. Finally they become delirious, completely abnormal. Some become enraged and others sink into a torpor. And some people and some animals do foam at the mouth, but that's because the virus leads to dehydration, and almost every animal foams at the mouth when it's hot and thirsty. That's why that's such a misleading concept."

"And it's *always* fatal?" Miranda said.

"Always. Once the symptoms appear, it kills you within two to ten days, and it's a hideous death. At least today we can somewhat comfort the person, knock them out with drugs. But," he blinked, "it's an ugly, ugly way to die."

"No one has ever survived. Really?" Cooper wondered.

"There are five reported cases, and in four of those the people had had the vaccine shots but not the treatments after exposure. Every veterinarian has the preventive vaccines but we all know, if we're bitten, we still need the shots. You might survive rabies infection if you've had the prophylactic series of shots. You're taking a chance, but you might survive."

"What about the other survivor?" Cooper sat on a gazebo step.

"I'm not sure, but I think it was early in the twentieth century, someone in Brazil. Which reminds me, rabies is epidemic in parts of Latin America and Asia. They don't vaccinate pets like we do and they also don't neuter like we do. If you're going to any places like that and you'll be outdoors a lot or on a farm, you should get the prophylactic shots."

"How many people died in the United States from rabies last year?" Harry liked facts.

"None." He smiled. "Thirty-two people were exposed, got the treatments, and were saved. It's been years since a human died of rabies from a bite in our country."

"Maybe." Harry was skeptical.

"What do you mean?" Cooper squinted into the sun.

"It's possible that someone died of it and was asymptomatic. Who would know?" Harry continued. "When an autopsy is performed, sending brain tissue for a rabies test isn't a regular occurrence."

"Could be. But even so, wouldn't be but one or two." Fair conceded her point.

"Maybe Barry was asymptomatic," Miranda said.

"I doubt it, Miranda." Fair felt sorry for the deceased man. "There was a case where a man was bitten and the presentation of symptoms did not occur for five years. But like I said, one to three months is the norm. He just hadn't had enough time."

"No bite marks on the body other than his throat?" Harry remembered only too well how he looked.

"No." Cooper shook her head. "And here's the scary part." They collectively held their breaths for a moment while she told them. "His throat was ripped out by short tongs or a jagged-edge knife. It wasn't a wild animal."

"What?" Fair couldn't believe it.

"Someone bites him and he doesn't fight back?" Harry was flat-out amazed. "That's not going to happen. Not with Barry Monteith."

"He was drugged. We asked Yancy to go over his corpse with a fine-tooth comb when we brought him in, and there were no marks, needle marks. He ingested Quaaludes. Whether he did this willingly or was purposefully drugged, we don't know. He would have been a limp noodle. Whoever wanted him dead wanted to make us think it was a wild animal."

"We've lost all this time and he's gotten away." Harry almost wailed. "The killer just dusted us!"

"Good God, who would even think of something like that?" Fair mopped his forehead with a red kerchief.

Harry collected herself. "It would be someone who didn't want to run away. I was wrong. He hasn't dusted us."

"He's sure gotten us all confused." Miranda noticed the three animals emerging from underneath her prized roses. "Do you have your rabies tags?"

"Mine's on my collar, as you well know," Tucker answered.

"We've had our shots. Mom has the paperwork and so does Dr. Shulman," Mrs. Murphy, very disturbed at this report, informed Miranda.

"They've had every shot and pill possible. Their medical records are better than mine." Harry smiled as Pewter rubbed against her leg.

"How do you know that Barry wasn't bitten by a bat?" Miranda asked Cooper.

"He was. The various strains of rabies can be identified. The strain identified was from a bat," Cooper simply stated. "They look in those microscopes, get gene sequences, and tell you if it's bat, a dog from Asia, or one from Latin America. They can tell just like they can tell different strains of influenza. I started to tell you that when Fair mentioned bats, but I got sidetracked." Cooper smiled, as she didn't want to say Harry more or less cut her off.

"So Barry would have died—no matter what. What a sad, sad thought." Miranda quoted scripture, First Corinthians, Chapter 15, Verse 22, "For as in Adam all die, so also in Christ shall all be made alive." She paused. "He's with the Lord. I know we should rejoice, but such a young man. It's hard to see him go."

"Yes, it is." Cooper agreed. "And knowing that he was murdered doesn't make it any easier."

"Okay, he was murdered." Harry reached for her nail gun. "It doesn't make a bit more sense than when I found him. No tracks. And Fair and Susan and I walked along Potlicker Creek for two and a half, maybe three miles, heading upstream. If there'd been footprints or tire prints we'd have seen them."

"You didn't tell me." Cooper narrowed her eyes, for Harry loved to stick her nose in a mystery.

"Oh, we're kind of looking around because of Mary Pat's ring. Big Mim said if it was in the creek, Mary Pat might have been upstream, you know."

"She could have lost that ring foxhunting, Harry, not when she went missing." Miranda thought of the number of ways that ring might have slipped off Mary Pat's finger.

"No. Mim says that if she'd lost this ring everyone would have known. She would have looked for it. She would have had the town looking for it, according to Mim. But we didn't find a thing," Harry said.

"Susan's bottles," Fair laconically added.

"Jeez, we carried out all these old bottles that Susan had to have"—Harry stopped a moment, then frowned—"but, Cooper, we didn't find a blessed thing."

"He really did come down the creek." Tucker wondered why someone wanted Barry Monteith dead.

"Yes, baby." Harry stooped down to pat her glossy head.

"I'd guess the killer came down the creek," Fair said.

"He understood." Pewter's whiskers swept forward.

"Lucky guess," Tucker replied.

"Not so lucky. It's obvious." Mrs. Murphy flicked the end of her tail up and down, a sign that she was thinking.

What wasn't obvious was what Tucker hadn't voiced: Why would anyone want to kill Barry Monteith, a cute guy who mucked out Mary Pat's wonderful old stables, who many hoped would succeed in the horse business?

14

The second Wednesday in June, Mim threw a supper party for her friends. Her late-blooming wisteria, in lavender as well as white, draped over the back porch of the beautiful white Georgian house. The southeast side of the barn was covered in lavender wisteria, and the old pump house, a massive stone building, was smothered in white wisteria, contrasting with the dark gray fieldstone.

Dalmally, the name of Big Mim's estate, was one of the gems of central Virginia. Fortunately, Mim inherited enough money to keep the place up. So many grand Virginia estates fell to rack and ruin after April 9, 1865. The ones that survived had been snapped up by Yankee carpetbaggers. A few survived because their original owners were both flexible and intelligent, and this certainly applied to the Urquharts, Mim's maiden name.

Aunt Tally Urquhart also lived on an historic estate, Rose Hill, but hers was much simpler: a white clapboard house of graceful proportions that lacked the conscious grandeur of Dalmally.

Aunt Tally sat at her niece's right hand, where she proceeded to direct people and events. Mim gave up reining her in and let her go, which pleased the elderly lady.

The other guests had been selected for conversation or for their equine connections, since Mim was preparing yearlings for the big Saratoga sale in August.

Her husband, Jim, sat at the head of the table. On his right sat Tavener Heyward and on his left was Miranda Hogendobber, whom Jim adored. The other guests— Fair Haristeen, Harry Haristeen, Tazio Chappars, Dr. Bill Langston, BoomBoom Craycroft, Little Mim, Blair Bainbridge, and Rev. Herb Jones—rounded out the party billed as "impromptu." Of course, nothing Big Mim did was impromptu, but the fiction was preserved, especially since the guests' various house pets played outside with Mim's English springer spaniels, two liver-and-white beauties.

Ever the Cupid, Mim thought that Bill Langston might find Tazio Chappars attractive. As she was brilliant and lovely, he did, but he found BoomBoom Craycroft even more attractive, although, being a gentleman, this was not apparent.

Few men could resist BoomBoom, the result being she toyed with them.

". . . Tom Fool blood." Tavener Heyward was holding forth about thoroughbred bloodlines.

"One can never study pedigrees to one's satisfaction," Herb said. "The Bible is full of pedigrees, starting with the sons of Adam and Eve, and everyone lived eight or nine hundred years."

"Doesn't really count until Noah's sons." Tavener, a keen reader, smiled. "Shem, Ham, and Japheth. They all lived to a ripe ole age, too. Noah made it to nine hundred and fifty."

"I don't know if my knees would hold out," Jim remarked, as the others laughed.

They talked about the computer programs to study thoroughbred bloodlines, then eased into Mim's plans for a new stable.

"I love walking through stables. You know, at Red Mile"—she mentioned a harness-racing track in Lexington, Kentucky—"there's a round barn, and it makes wonderful sense."

"There's a kind of round barn right up the road in Orange." Fair mentioned a town northeast of them by about thirty miles, give or take.

"A lot of Washington money moving into Orange," Herb said.

"And Madison and Greene counties. They come on down here and we're glad to see the bump up in the tax revenues, but they don't all ease into country life as we would like." Jim stated the problem succinctly.

"By the end of this century, we'll be lucky if anyone remembers country life," Harry predicted.

"Oh, Harry, don't say that. They can learn." Little Mim kept a positive attitude.

"Well, I hope so," Harry said. She was in a good mood since her tests had come back negative for exposure to rabies.

"I'm not a born country person but I'm

trying," Blair said, his warm hazel eyes solemn.

"No fair." Fair laughed at his little play on his name. "You live next to Harry, and you're being well trained by Little Mim. You're doing just fine."

"A thorn between two roses." Blair laughed.

"Or a rose between two thorns." Big Mim smiled.

"Tazio, you were raised in St. Louis; what do you think?" Bill politely asked the architect.

She blushed slightly. "It's like learning a new language. And I thank Brinkley for helping me." She named her yellow Lab. "He always knows where the deer are or the hawks. I find the quieter I am, the more I learn."

"Isn't that the truth!" Aunt Tally, who liked the young woman, said. "To live in the country you have to use all your senses. Can't just depend on one. So if you smoke," she cleared her throat and stared at Little Mim a moment, since her great-niece was known to puff sometimes, "you've already lost one sense. And speaking of senses—taste—Mim, dear, this has been the most delicious supper, and I am longing for dessert."

Big Mim cast her eyes down the table. Everyone had finished the main course, a pork tenderloin lightly brushed with a chutney. Fresh, large white asparagus and wild rice filled out the plate. Of course, she always had fresh breads, including corn bread. Couldn't have a Virginia dinner without corn bread or spoon bread.

Jim said, "Honey, just bring in the cherry cheesecake and put it in front of Tally. She'll eat the whole thing."

"I will. I'll drink what you put in front of me, too."

Big Mim tried to keep her aunt on sherry this evening. A crisp white wine during dinner was acceptable, too. If Aunt Tally got her hands on the clear spirits like gin or vodka, she became more animated than usual.

The rules of dining had relaxed considerably since Big Mim's youth. Not that Aunt Tally approved of any of this, but she adored company, so if one no longer dressed as was once proper, she'd pay that price.

The cheesecake, rich and covered with

the most delicious cherries, met with approval. Even Miranda, who had been very careful about her diet, couldn't resist.

After dinner, the small gathering repaired to the lovely back lawn, where small tables and chairs had been set up for this purpose. A portable bar was also there, along with a humidor of cigars: Cohiba, Tito, Macanudo, Romeo y Julieta, and Diplomatico.

Herb, eyes half closed with intense pleasure, puffed on a Tito. "This is new to me."

Tavener, who couldn't pass up an exorbitantly expensive Cohiba, said, "Perfect."

Jim, favoring a Diplomatico, answered Herb. "Tito. The tobacco store by Giant Food carries them. Don't know if the tobacco shop in Barracks Road has them. I'll have to check. Quite a good smoke, isn't it?"

"And I imagine expensive?" Herb admired the dark wrapper leaves on the Tito.

"Eight dollars and forty cents. Granted, that's not your White Owl"—he mentioned a very cheap cigar but a consistent one in that you always knew what you'd be getting—"but when you think of the inflated cost of these contraband Cuban cigars, the Tito is good. I think it's a spectacular cigar, myself."

Blair, not really a cigar smoker, bravely puffed away on a mild Macanudo and said, "How much is a Cuban cigar?"

"Depends on the size." Tavener held out the Cohiba with the distinctive yellow, white, and black band. "Depends on your source. Hazarding a guess, this cigar probably runs between seventy-five and one hundred dollars."

"That bad?" Fair had selected a Diplomatico, a cigar with an enticing flavor and also a Cuban.

"Well, I have my sources, which I will never ever tell, but I pay a little less," Jim responded. "Now, off the record, since I'm an elected official, this damned embargo is a crock. Hell, even when the embargo was first enacted, Jack Kennedy was sitting up there in the White House smoking Cuban cigars. For one thing I don't like paying way more than something is worth, and for another thing I don't like breaking the law."

"The same argument could be used for legalizing drugs," Tavener said.

"It could." Big Jim exhaled a tongue of

blue smoke. "Can't enforce the law, so what good is it?"

"Meaning you can't control human behavior." Herb watched the women walking among Big Mim's roses.

"Precisely," Tavener replied.

"Sets me to thinking of old man Noah again." Herb smiled at Blair, who was clearly not enjoying his too-strong cigar. "Son, put that thing down. We won't tell." He then returned to Noah. "The Lord put up a rainbow as a covenant and said He wouldn't send another flood to destroy mankind again. And He knew it wouldn't do but so much good."

"Meaning we were all at it soon enough." Fair nodded.

"Wickedness. What's interesting about wickedness is how it differs from century to century and from culture to culture," Herb said.

"Killing has always been regarded as wicked unless committed during war, and even then one is only to kill the uniformed enemy." Blair put the cigar in a big crystal ashtray.

"Well, what about religious killing? A Muslim fanatic kills Christians. He believes he'll go to Allah and also be rewarded with sixty or seventy virgins. I forget the number." Herb waved his cigar.

"One would be enough." Tavener laughed, as did the other men.

"All that responsibility!" Fair tapped ash into one of the large crystal ashtrays.

"Women are a responsibility whether virgin or slightly used." Tavener noticed the last rays of the sun washing the stable and outbuildings. "A woman can send you to heaven or consign you to hell."

"I wouldn't trade one minute of my life with my wife." Herb said this with feeling. His wife had succumbed to cancer a few years ago.

"I agree. I could kill Mim sometimes, but she made a man out of me," Jim said.

"Maybe you'll find someone again, Herb," Fair simply stated.

"Maybe," Herb said noncommittally. "But I think Blair's—well, Blair, you tell us."

The men focused on the handsome model.

He stammered a moment, then surprised even himself with his firm reply. "Any man who could spend a lifetime with Little

Mim would be a lucky man." He call Marilyn by her nickname, as did everyone.

"Indeed." Fair seconded this, as did the other men.

"She's spoiled." Her father smiled. "My fault."

"It's hard not to spoil a daughter." Bill Langston shrugged. "Just an observation. Hope I have a daughter someday."

"I'll do my best to spoil Marilyn even more." Blair smiled, a genuine one.

As Blair had not yet asked for Marilyn's hand in marriage, this declaration surely meant the time would be forthcoming.

Fair stepped in to save Blair an embarrassing question in case one of the gentlemen forgot himself. "You know I feel the same way about Harry. I sinned. I repented. I need you all to help me win her back, all the way back."

"Ah." Herb again closed his eyes from the pleasure of his cigar, then opened them wide. "The way to win back your ex-wife is to work with her on the farm. Other women are wooed by words and flowers, but Harry is wooed by work and, well, I suppose a few flowers wouldn't hurt."

"Do you really think so?" asked Bill Langston, new to the community as Hayden McIntire's new partner in family practice.

"Known her since she was born." Herb nodded.

"As have I," Jim said.

"And I." Tavener nodded, as well.

"Herb's right. Work is the way to Harry's heart."

"I think I knew that." Fair, too, noticed the incredibly beautiful gold and scarlet light. "But I'm working morning, noon, and night."

"It's time for you to take a business partner. I mean that." Jim held up his hand to silence Fair, who had started to speak. "The money. I know. And for the first year you will make less money, perhaps. But, Fair, you're killing yourself. If you took on one or two partners you could expand your practice beyond equine reproduction. All these new people that we've been talking about at dinner come here and, what's the first thing they want, a horse. There are only so many vets to go around, and you and Tavener are so specialized and at the top of your professions that you're going to miss the wave. What do you think, Tav?"

"You're one hundred percent right. I'm

close to retirement or I'd follow your advice."

"I've heard the retirement speech before." Fair smiled.

"Well, I mean it." Tavener reached for his glass of port.

"Fair, come talk to me," Jim advised.

"I will."

Jim stood up as the ladies were walking toward them. "Ladies, we need some uplift here."

Tally sassed, "Buy a bra."

Big Mim rolled her eyes as everyone giggled.

"Does he ever rest?" Tazio asked Big Mim, as she watched Paul de Silva walk out into a paddock to check on a mare and foal.

"My beloved niece is a slave driver." Tally said this without a scrap of self-consciousness.

"We're here!" all the dogs shouted as they raced around the lawn.

"I am not a slave driver. Paul loves his work." Big Mim turned to Tazio. "Would you be interested in designing a stable, or is that too small a commission?"

"I'd love to work with you," Tazio replied.

"I need to study equine behavior, though. I'm not a horsewoman."

"Well, that's fine." Big Mim smiled.

"I'll walk you down to Paul. Why not start right now? I know some of what Mother wants, and Paul knows the rest." Little Mim was anxious to escape her mother's grasp.

Brinkley happily tagged along with Tazio, his sun and moon.

Herb winked at Harry, which meant he had something to tell her and would at the first opportunity. He wanted to tell her what Blair had said. Perhaps the old farm could be purchased from Blair.

A few moments passed, then they heard one shot from behind the stables. The dogs started barking.

"Tucker, stay here," Harry commanded.

"I will, but I think you're being mean." Tucker resigned herself.

Little Mim and Tazio hurried up over the pastures and onto the lawn, Brinkley running alongside.

"Fair and Tavener, we need you!" Little Mim was flushed.

"What's going on?" Big Mim stood up.

Tazio breathlessly replied, "Paul shot a raccoon. He thinks it was rabid."

15

Fair had taken charge of the carcass, immediately returning to his clinic, where he removed the head and packed it in a plastic container of dry ice to ship out to Richmond in the morning. Then he called the home of the state veterinarian, a man he liked, Dr. Bruce Akey, informing him the raccoon head would be arriving tomorrow afternoon.

All that was needed was the head, since only brain tissue would be tested. But to satisfy himself, Fair pulled blood. As he hadn't observed the raccoon, he wasn't going to jump to conclusions. The animal could have been suffering from other maladies. Distemper can also produce strange behavior before the suffering creature dies.

An animal becomes disoriented or, in the case of a wild animal, lethargic, no longer frightened of humans.

Harry, latex gloves on, had been in the operating room with her ex. She hung up her lab coat while Fair was on the phone with Bruce.

She walked into the office as he hung up. "Well, it will be all over Crozet by the morning that we have a rabies epidemic, whether we do or don't."

"I know." He glanced down at Tucker, whose metallic rabies tag was fastened to her rolled leather collar. "What do you think, Sugar?"

"Glad I've got my vaccination."

"Think we could be seeing a surge in the disease?" Harry asked.

"We could. My experience is, rabies goes in cycles coming down from the north. Starts in Canada, moves into New York State, and about three years later it's here."

"Guess there's nothing the Canadian government can do about it with all that wildlife."

"And think how long our border is with Canada." Fair stooped down to scratch Tucker's ears. "Even if you put a ranger every hundred yards, the animals would still run through them. No, the only answer is a pill form of the vaccine."

"How do you know wild animals will take their pills?"

"If we had access to a pill and could afford it, we could put out thousands and thousands of pills in the various foods." He thought some more. "Corn; so many animals eat corn. And for the obligate carnivores I suppose we could grind up hamburger. It's a start."

"You always have good ideas." She smiled up at him, then checked her watch, an old Bulova that had been her father's. "Later than I think!"

"Remember how your mother used to say that time moved faster as she got older? It's the truth."

"I know. Kind of scares me."

He walked her out to her old 1978 truck, Tucker bringing up the rear. He opened the door, lifted up Tucker, then kissed Harry on the cheek. "Jim said something to me. Said I ought to take one or even two partners. I suppose I should, but I like running my own ship."

"You'd still run your own ship, but there'd be more money and more paperwork."

"And more personalities. All I have to worry about now is Alma." He mentioned his new secretary, as his former one had retired.

"Jim's right. First of all, honey, you'd be doing the hiring, and you're a good judge of character."

"Why, thank you."

"I guess it's kind of like marriage: You don't really know somebody until you live with them, but, still, you'd get a good sense of them and you could build in a trial period for both of you. And the other thing is, you aren't forty yet but we're both kind of closing in."

"I know." He smiled weakly. "Just a number."

"It is, but everyone sure makes a big damned deal out of it. If you had partners, the practice could expand and you'd make more money and hopefully have a little more time for yourself."

"Which I would like to spend with you."

She climbed into the truck, closed the door, then leaned out the open window to give him a kiss on the cheek. "If you're lucky."

16

Morning, ladies," Rob Collier sang out as he tossed up two large canvas mail sacks in the back. "Thursday and heating up!"

"Morning. I didn't hear you drive up." Miranda, who lived across the alleyway, usually heard the big mail truck when it rumbled to the back door.

She felt she had the perfect life, for all she had to do was walk through her garden, cross the gravel alleyway, and unlock the back door. She incurred no commuting costs, and the walk wasn't far enough to wear out shoe leather.

Harry, on the other hand, drove in from her farm at the base of Yellow Mountain, or, if the weather permitted, she might walk the four miles in just for the delight of it. This morning she drove.

"Any news from the other P.O.s?" Miranda asked.

"Page's Store closed in Batesville, but the P.O. still rents space there."

"Page's Store? Why, that's been open since 1913." Miranda gasped, for she enjoyed the store and the whole Page family.

"I know, but time's a movin' on. Time flies like an arrow," Rob said.

"And fruit flies like a banana," Harry said.

Both Miranda and Rob laughed and shook their heads.

"Mom's in one of her Looney Tunes moods." Tucker smiled.

Rob, never one to turn a deaf ear to gossip, announced, "I heard that Dr. Langston told Sugar and Carmen, too, to come in and get tested for rabies."

Harry, who thought she worked at the nerve center of Crozet, betrayed a flash of irritation. "Where'd you hear that?"

"Sister-in-law. Her best friend works in Dr. Langston's office." He enjoyed his scoop. "And Sugar said, 'The hell with it. He'd be too damned late to do anything.'

But I reckon Carmen will go. She'll have to emote over it for a time."

"Rob." Miranda had to stifle a laugh so her voice didn't truly carry censure.

"Carmen is all over the map." He had his hand on the doorknob. "I tell you, that girl is nine miles of bad road. She will get a man in trouble."

"Rob, I thought most girls could get a man in trouble—especially you." Harry raised an eyebrow.

"I wish." He winked and left, the rumble of the big mail truck audible even inside the building.

At eleven the tall, genial Pug Harper stopped by.

Miranda leaned over the counter when the county's postmaster came through the front door. "Mr. Postmaster, what can we do for you, or is this an inspection?"

Harry gathered up white rigid-plastic mail cartons into which she had folded the large mail sacks and placed them back on the floor, the wooden boards polished smooth from use. "Pug, how are you?"

"Just fine. And no, Miranda, this isn't an inspection. Crozet's post office is one of the best run in the county. Make that the state." He beamed.

Pewter, half asleep in a canvas mail cart, opened one eye. *"Laying it on thick."*

Mrs. Murphy, stretched out next to her, replied, *"Wonder what's up."*

Pug noticed the lump in the bottom of the mail cart sway ever so slightly. "Your coworkers are asleep on the job."

Tucker, dead to the world under the cart, didn't even lift her head.

"They sorted mail this morning at seven-thirty. You have no idea how productive they are." Harry laughed.

"And you know, Pug, they have an un-erring sense of which letters are bills and which are for real." Miranda walked to the small table in the rear and picked up a dish covered with a dish towel, returning to the front counter. She lifted up the corner of the dish towel. "Blueberry muffins and oat-meal cookies."

"Oh, my." He patted his stomach, bulging somewhat, then gave in, reaching for a blueberry muffin.

As he polished off the muffin, they chitchatted.

BoomBoom sailed in. "Pug, what happened? You couldn't stand the main post office any longer?"

"I like to come where the women are beautiful." He winked.

"Here we are. The Three Fates." Boom-Boom leaned against the counter as both Harry and Miranda leaned forward so they were a picture.

"I need my sunglasses," Pug joked.

BoomBoom retrieved her mail from the brass box. "Girls, guess what?"

"You won the lottery," Harry responded.

"No. Bill Langston asked me to play golf with him Friday morning."

"No grass under your feet."

BoomBoom shrugged. "I'll let you know what I think after eighteen holes. Bye." She blew kisses and left.

Pug's eyes followed her out the front door. He scanned the small parking lot. "Ladies, I'm actually here to tell you we are going to build a new post office right across the street. It's official." He pointed out the door, which had a large window in it.

"Where?" Harry flipped up the counter divider and walked to the front door, Miranda right with her.

"We'll clean all that off there, take the parking lot right up to the barber shop— well, what used to be the old barber shop—and at the back we'll put in a brand-new post office. Next to it the bank's building a new branch. As soon as I get the architect's plans, I'll bring them by."

Harry, hiding her lack of enthusiasm, said, "What will happen to this P.O.?"

"Well, I don't know. As you know, we don't own this building. I expect whoever rents the space will change the interior to suit."

"I expect." Harry didn't notice two kitty heads pop up out of the mail cart, paws on the side.

"*A brand-new building!*" Pewter exclaimed.

"*Might be nice. Might not. Sounds like too much traffic with the bank, and we'll be across the street with the elder-care high-rise.*" She mentioned the tallest building in town, at six stories.

"*Mother won't like it,*" Tucker, finally awake but still immobile, declared. "*She doesn't like change.*"

"*She's not that bad.*" But Mrs. Murphy

had her doubts about the new building, too.

"How big is the proposed post office?"

"Six thousand square feet." Pug thought this was wonderful.

"My word." Miranda's hand flew to her chest. "The two of us will rattle around in there like two peas in a large can."

"You won't be alone. We'll add more workers, plus we'll also have shifts. There will be three scales at the counter with computers, of course. So at any given time there will be two people in the back sorting, stacking, getting ready for the pickups. We have so many types of mail now, so many new services, which I know you know, and I just read in *The Daily Progress*"—he mentioned the county's daily newspaper—"that our growth rate right here in Albemarle County exceeds the population growth of India. Plan ahead!" He returned to the building. "There will be one large garage door in the rear so Rob can back in. It's going to be very efficient as well as attractive."

"Who's going to be the postmaster?" Harry got right to the point.

"I hope you," Pug said. "No doubt,

Harry, our federal government in their wisdom may wish for you to take some extra administrative tests. I think it's all pretty silly given that you've been the postmaster here—I mean, postmistress—ever since you graduated from college. But if there's any way I can waive some of the paperwork for you, I will."

"How long before you start building?"

"As soon as we get the permit through the county. August. Southwell Construction will be building it. Naturally we'll buy our cement and stone from Craycroft Industries, who I bet will give us the best bid. That BoomBoom is a genius at bidding jobs." BoomBoom's business had been started by her late husband.

As Pug left, it was as though backwash from a large ocean liner was tossing about a slender craft.

"Damn!" Harry cursed.

"This place is home. A new building might be larger, but it's going to be antiseptic." Miranda returned the blueberry muffins and oatmeal cookies to the table.

"I don't want to manage people."

"Harry, you'd be good at it."

"That's nice of you to say, but I don't

think that I would. I know I fell into this job. But I like it."

The summer that Harry graduated from Smith College, George Hogendobber, the postmaster in Crozet and Miranda's husband, died. Harry took the job thinking it would be temporary. The position had first been offered to Miranda, but she was too emotionally distraught to consider a regular job.

Fair breezed through the door. "Distemper." Then he noticed the expression on Harry and Miranda's faces. "What's wrong?"

They told him of Pug's visit.

". . . August. And you know what else?" Harry's voice rose. "He didn't say anything about Mrs. Murphy, Pewter, and Tucker."

"That doesn't necessarily mean anything," Fair evenly replied.

"I think it does. I think he'll wait until we're ready to move across the street and then tell me my friends can't work there. And if my cats and dog can't go where I go, I'm not going. I don't want any job without my pets."

"Now, honey, don't jump the gun," Fair said soothingly.

"He's right. Wait and see." Miranda also sounded comforting.

The two cats and dog said nothing. They observed this exchange with great interest.

"Sorry. I guess I did jump to conclusions." Harry exhaled deeply. "And I'm glad the raccoon only had distemper."

Fair held up his hand. " That he did, but that doesn't mean he didn't also have rabies. We still need the report from Richmond, and that can take days."

"Oh, great, half the town will be in a tizz." Harry threw her hands up in the air.

"Well, you see all the town, not just half. You can tell them the results of my own little lab work." Fair smiled.

"Where are you coming from, or maybe I should say where are you going?" Harry knew that Thursday mornings Fair operated at his clinic.

"Out to Big Mim's. She's culling her broodmares and wants my opinion. Then she'll make her annual pilgrimage to Lexington, Kentucky, and pick up a few more black-type broodmares. You know Big Mim. But I'll tell you, she really does have a gift for finding a good mare, and usually at an off time. I think even if Mim hadn't in-

herited money, she could have made it herself."

"Quite true," replied Miranda, who had
known Mim all her life.

"It's so hard to make money in the horse
business," Harry opined.

"That it is, but some people do—I mean,
some people apart from the people who
have tons of money made from something
else. Tavener has done well. Debbie Easter
runs a good operation up there at Albemarle Stud. There are a couple of good
folks out there with one or two well-bred
stallions. They manage but, you're right, it
is hard. Think of the heartbreak in Kentucky
in 2001 when all those foals died. First you
fight to save the poor little critter's life, then
lose him or her. You have very little to take
to the sales. It's desperate. I admire anyone who sticks with it in this business."

"Me, too," Miranda agreed. "I had no
idea it could be so difficult or I guess so
emotional."

Miranda was not a horse person, but in
working with Harry she'd learned a little bit.
Mostly she learned that Harry loved her
three horses and would be happy sleeping
out in the stable.

As Fair left to keep his appointment, Carmen Gamble, in her haircutting smock, picked up her mail. "Heard we've got rabies."

"No, we don't." Harry went on to explain.

"Well, I know that Barry had rabies." Carmen pressed her lips together. "And I have to go in and get a test, but Sugar says it won't do any good. No one bit me." A flicker of worry passed over her face.

Miranda, who liked Carmen, encouraged her. "Well, honey, it can't hurt. And since the paper reported that Barry had rabies, people will get all worried. Not that you have a thing to worry about."

"In a small little column. Like they don't want us to panic, you know." Carmen had jumped back to the newspaper report.

"There isn't any reason to panic. For one thing, Carmen, Barry showed no signs of the disease. I imagine he would have, but he was still normal, for lack of a better word." Harry wanted to head off a rabies scare.

"He would never listen to me." A pair of expensive scissors hung from a holder on her belt. "He'd go out and pick up dead things. He'd work without gloves. Like the time he nearly got killed with the old Massey-Ferguson tractor. He had on an old T-shirt and he leaned over the PTO. The only thing that saved him when the shirt got caught, it was so worn it ripped right off him instead of pulling him into the PTO, you know. I mean, people get killed with spreaders and all kinds of stuff. The PTO whirls and sends them right into the tractor attachment. He never listened to anything I ever said."

"He must have listened to some things, Carmen, as you are so pretty. Men tend to listen," Miranda warmly said, because she knew Carmen was more upset about Barry than she let on.

"Men think they know everything."

"Some do. Life usually takes care of them," Miranda again spoke.

"Took care of Barry."

"Who had it in for him?" Harry asked.

"Me." Carmen slapped her mail on the counter. "He must have irritated someone else. Someone more violent. All I ever did was throw a spray bottle at his head. But Barry could stick his nose in the wrong business. Kind of like you, Harry."

"Gee thanks, Carmen."

"Well, I didn't mean it that way. I mean, it came out backward."

"You're digging that hole deeper," Harry, somewhat offended, said.

"Barry would go through my mail. My drawers. He was nosy that way. He didn't respect privacy. You're not like that—except you do go through our mail, of course, but you don't open it." Carmen dumped junk mail in the trash can as she babbled on. "Barry would even open my glove compartment in the car. I don't know what he thought he would find."

"Love letters." Miranda smiled. "Like I said, you're very pretty. He was probably nervous."

"Barry?"

"Yes." Miranda nodded.

Harry asked, "Do you think he was nosy like that with other people? Like rooting around at St. James Farm?"

"Uh"—she thought a moment—"yeah, I expect he was."

After Carmen left, Harry said to Miranda, "I wonder what Barry found out."

"Now, Harry, you know what Fair said:

'Don't jump to conclusions,' " Miranda said sternly.

"Oh, that was about the new post office. This is about murder." Harry had already jumped to a conclusion, an accurate one.

17

Tazio Chappars, BoomBoom Craycroft, and Harry served on the Parish Guild of St. Luke's Lutheran Church. Last year, after exhaustive dickering, the board raised the money to install new carpeting. In the process, Harry, Tazio, and BoomBoom drew closer to one another. In the case of Harry and BoomBoom this was an important development, since it meant Harry had finally forgiven BoomBoom for having an affair with Fair after they had separated. Harry had also forgiven Fair. The more difficult emotional task was forgiving herself for hanging on to resentment and anger. And sometimes in the quiet of a country night she thought that maybe, just maybe, she wasn't the warmest, most loving woman God had ever put on earth. Maybe Fair had strayed because of that.

The three ladies, along with Susan Tucker, who'd served on the board before Harry was elected, met at Harry's farm. It was an impromptu gathering urged by Miranda Hogendobber, who reminded the ladies that July 17 would be the thirtieth anniversary of the Rev. Herbert Jones taking over the parish.

Outside, the late-afternoon light cast long golden shadows over the barn, the rolling pastures.

Harry had intended to shepherd the little group into the living room, but they all plopped down at the kitchen table. She opened the back door to the screened-in porch; all the windows were open and a fragrant breeze filled the house.

". . . never happen." BoomBoom rapped the table with the golden dolphin ring she wore on her right hand.

"Oh, Boom, don't be a cynic." Susan was at the kitchen counter helping Harry put together a plate of cold meats.

"I'm not a cynic, but this is Crozet and no one can keep a secret. I'm not even sure Claudius Crozet could keep one."

BoomBoom mentioned the famous engineer, a soldier in Napoleon's army, for whom the town was named.

"What a life. Fight with Napoleon. Get captured on the retreat from Moscow. Napoleon marched into Russia with about a million men and only one hundred thousand survived, give or take a few." Harry loved history. "Crozet must have been tough."

"Harry, let's not get off the track," Tazio gently chided her.

"You're right." Harry put the plate on the table. "Cold cuts, and you'll just have to make the sandwiches yourselves." She set a huge jar of mayonnaise on the table, a pot of country butter, and a smaller jar of imported mustard. "Notice the lovely crockery."

"First class, all the way." Susan laughed as she set out a plate of cheeses. "Everyone have what they want to drink? Good. I'm sitting down, Harry; you, too."

"Yeah, yeah." Harry looked out the kitchen window to watch Brinkley, Tucker, and the two kitties, ferociously puffed, taking turns chasing one another. "We've got a hot game of tag out there."

"I can never thank you enough for talking me into taking Brinkley." Tazio spread butter on whole-grain bread. "And can you believe how handsome he is?"

"Gorgeous," Susan agreed, as she well remembered the starved half-grown puppy Tazio had rescued as a terrible winter storm crept over the mountains.

BoomBoom got up and walked to the refrigerator.

"What did I forget?" Harry stood up.

"Pickles. I can get them. You forgot them so you wouldn't have to share."

"You put pickles on your sandwich?" Tazio feigned shock.

"On my good days. On my bad days I use olives." Jar in hand, BoomBoom rejoined them. "Plus, Harry loves pickles."

They chatted, teased one another, and devoured their sandwiches.

"I was hungrier than I realized." Susan patted her mouth with her napkin.

"Save some room, there's dessert." Harry had picked up a carrot cake as well as brownies on her way home.

"Well, let's get back to the subject at hand." BoomBoom dueled with Harry, both having their forks in the pickle jar.

"There is no way we can keep this thirtieth-anniversary bash a secret."

"She's right." Tazio seconded this opinion.

"We could try." Harry wanted to surprise her pastor and friend.

"But then it's half baked." Susan turned this over in her mind. "We probably should print up invitations. Do it properly. That'll let him prepare himself. He'd prefer being prepared, I think."

"Hmm, I hadn't thought of that." Harry hopped up to make another pot of coffee and to refill the creamer. "Tazio, you're missing a good one. Mrs. Murphy has Brinkley's tail and she won't let go."

Tazio couldn't resist. She walked over to the window and, sure enough, Mrs. Murphy was clutching the yellow Lab's considerable tail. He'd sat down to discourage her, but it wasn't working. Mrs. Murphy, eyes big, was thrilled silly with herself.

"Girls," Susan called them back.

Harry returned. "Do we know what we're going to do? And remember, we have to present this to the rest of the board."

"They'll go along with whatever we devise," BoomBoom said with assurance.

"We saved them a meeting by having this one."

"Picnic on the quad," Susan suggested.

Tazio added to Susan's suggestion. "The quad is a good idea, and lots of people will fit in there. Let's decorate with green and gold, St. Luke's colors."

"Mary Pat's racing colors," BoomBoom mused. "I still can't believe her ring showed up."

They batted ideas back and forth with a few digressions, finally agreeing on a huge picnic. Once everything was settled and the dishes washed, they all walked outside to pet the horses. Harry ran back into the kitchen for carrots.

Poptart delicately took a carrot from Susan's fingers.

Pewter watched this and said, *"I don't see how you can eat carrots."*

Gin Fizz, the older gray mare, replied, *"I don't see how you can eat mice."*

"She doesn't. She's too fat to catch them," Mrs. Murphy sassed.

"Die, peasant!" Pewter whirled and chased Mrs. Murphy under the lilac bushes, through the small rose garden, and into the barn.

The two dogs thought this looked like fun, so they joined in.

BoomBoom said, "Harry, while Tazio is here why don't you show her your old tractor shed?"

"Why? It's on its last legs."

"That's my point. Maybe she can design something or think of something better." BoomBoom headed in the direction of the tractor shed.

"Tazio, I can't afford you," Harry sheepishly said.

"You can if it's free." Tazio put her arm around Harry's waist for a moment.

As they headed for the shed, Deputy Cynthia Cooper drove down the long driveway in her squad car. The dogs rushed up to greet her as she disembarked.

"Hey, Coop, there's sandwich stuff left in the house." Harry hugged her.

"Are you going on duty or off?" Susan asked.

"Off." Cooper smiled. "But I thought I'd swing by to tell that we've been sifting through Barry's things over at St. James. We found a bound notebook of Mary Pat's." Everyone looked at her expectantly, and Cooper continued. "It's mostly her breeding ideas—what mare she took to whom. There's a few scribbles in there about farm-machinery purchases. Odd, isn't it?"

18

Looking good." Fair beamed as he watched the ultrasound image on the small screen early Friday morning, June 11.

"Finally." Sugar Thierry smiled.

Ultrasound helped determine whether a mare was in foal or not. A tiny little camera on a thin, flexible hose was inserted into the mare's vagina and gently pushed up into the womb. The other end, attached to a small box with a screen, allowed the veterinarian to see if a breeding had been successful. This was usually done fourteen days after the breeding took place.

Most mares allowed this intrusion without too much fuss. A gentle handler and a handful of hay, if needed, distracted her from whoever was fiddling around her nether regions. Danzig's Damsel endured this but sighed a long sigh once Fair had finished observing her womb.

Sugar walked Danzig's Damsel, whose barn name was Loopy, into her stall. As most thoroughbreds have long names often indicating their bloodlines for their Jockey Club registration, a barn name is a must. She was an old-fashioned thoroughbred of substance and good bone. Her great-granddam had been in Mary Pat's band of broodmares. Mary Pat favored distance runners as opposed to sprinters, which put her in the minority.

As Fair and Sugar walked out of the long white shed row barn into the early-morning sunshine, Fair admired the pignut hickories lining the gravel drive.

"How's Binky?" Fair mentioned another one of Sugar's mares, an old acquaintance.

"Out in the back pastures. She's enjoying her retirement."

"Binky's got to be twenty-five if she's a day." Fair smiled, remembering the light chestnut mare from her flaming youth. She could be a handful.

"Every bit." Sugar rubbed his temples.

"Pollen count must be up again. Been fighting this headache for two days now."

"This May was a record breaker. My truck was yellow. Couldn't see out the windshield for the pine pollen."

"Yeah." Sugar stopped at Fair's truck as the tall veterinarian put the ultrasound equipment in the special aluminum tool beds made for veterinarians. "Haven't seen Paul for a couple of weeks. How's he doing?"

"Pretty good. He gets along with Big Mim."

"That's half the battle, but at least she knows what she's talking about when it comes to horses. More than you can say for most of these rich folks."

"You're talking about the comeheres." Fair used the slang "come here" pronounced as one word, which meant someone who moved into the area.

"You're right. She was born to it."

"Nan Young's a good hand with a horse. She'd work part time if the money's right." Fair thought this was a good time to mention help.

"I'll talk to her." Sugar rubbed his head again. "All that paperwork Barry did with the Jockey Club—the insurance stuff and stallion shares—I never paid a bit of mind to that. My job was out here. Course, he did a lot of that, too."

"You two were a good team."

Sugar, in his late twenties, sported a winning grin. Although not classically handsome—he had a crooked nose—he had an appealing way about him. Lean, hardworking, he loved the thoroughbred business. "Got in a couple of lay-up mares yesterday, which will help the cash flow."

Lay-up mares or lay-up horses are placed at smaller farms with good care, usually by large farms or by private city owners who have an injured horse off the track or a broodmare and they can't or won't pay the expensive day rates charged by trainers, boarding tracks, and large racing operations. With careful management, a lay-up facility could provide a useful service to horse people and make a little bit of money.

"Might be able to find a few more for you." Fair liked Sugar.

"Fair, will you do me a favor?" Sugar's dark-blue eyes looked away, then back at Fair.

"If I can."

"After Barry was killed I made out a will. Kind of gave me the creeps, you know."

"I do." Fair smiled, since no one liked to consider one's own mortality, especially when in one's twenties.

"If anything happens to me, you get my horses, you and Harry. You've both been good to us. I know you'll do the right thing by my girls. I know you would never sell a horse to the knacker, and I got to thinking about old Binky. Knacker would just haul her out for meat price." His eyes misted over. "That's not right. Not right to do that to an animal that did right by you."

"I agree." Fair clapped his big hand on Sugar's shoulder. "Nothing's going to happen to you, but if it should, I'll make sure all your horses are happy."

Sugar smiled. "I know Harry won't sell any of them."

"You got that right." Fair laughed, for his ex-wife couldn't bear to part with any animal once she got to know him or her. "Have you talked to Harry?"

"No," he sheepishly replied. "Well, I don't know that anything will happen, and she'd get all upset. Easier to tell you."

Fair tried to think as Harry would. "Sugar, are you worried that you might be in danger? Barry's death was bizarre, and with each passing day it seems more, well, bizarre."

Sugar's voice rose. "What *did* he know? I can't think of anything. Barry worked hard. What could he have known? I go over it and over it. He just pissed someone off. Over a girl. That's what I think. So they rip out his throat and dump him. That's what I think."

"Kind of what I think, too. When there was no saliva found on the body, that was the tip-off. But I thought he was between romances and not between the sheets."

"Me, too, but he could have taken up with a married woman. He knew how to talk to women." Sugar said this with admiration.

"I'm starting to think it isn't about talking to women, it's about listening to them."

Sugar thought about this. "Might be right. I sure do listen to Carmen. That girl can talk. We're sort of going out."

"I've got new respect for Barry." Fair paused, then winked. "And you."

"Why?"

"Barry didn't talk to you about his conquests. He wasn't a braggart, even to his best friend. And you've been very circumspect about Carmen."

"A couple of times Barry said Carmen plucked his last nerve, but that was different. Barry was raised right."

To be raised right as a man in the South, regardless of class or color, meant you did not discuss women in disparaging terms and you never whined about a woman if she did wrong by you; you kept your mouth shut. Men suffered in silence.

Like most ideal behavior, many men tried to live up to the standard but fell short.

"Speaking of being raised right, these mares represent an investment of money and hard work. Your mother would have been proud."

Sugar beamed. "Thanks."

Sugar's father left his mother when Sugar was four, and the ne'er-do-well subsequently died in a bar in Baltimore, literally falling off the barstool dead drunk. His mother passed away three years ago of lung cancer.

"Well, I'd better push off. Got a couple of mares to check over at BoomBoom's."

"She do late breedings, too?"

"No. She's only got two mares left, the hunters. As luck would have it, the pretty refined bay, Keepsake, jumped the fence and checked around until she found someone she liked."

Sugar laughed. "Hope it wasn't a donkey."

"That's just it. We don't know. The closest intact horse"—meaning stallion—"lives down Whitehall Road at Phyllis Jones's place. Let's hope that's where that hussy visited. Called Phyllis. Her fences are just fine, but the mare might have jumped in and jumped out."

"No wonder Boom hunts that mare."

Fair nodded in agreement. "For Boom-Boom's sake let's hope it was one of Phyllis's stallions—because those are nice, nice horses—and not the donkey over at Short Shot Farm."

"I didn't know they had a donkey."

"Just bought it for their little girl."

Sugar started to laugh. "I want to see this one. If BoomBoom winds up with a mule, she'll pitch a fit and fall in it."

If a donkey breeds a horse, the offspring is a mule. Mules can't breed as they are sterile.

"Hey, Boom will fool you. If it's a mule, she'll keep it."

"No way."

"Five bucks says I'm right if it's a mule."

"Can't predispose her toward keeping the critter. Promise."

"Cross my heart and hope to die." Fair laughed as he repeated the childhood oath.

"Five bucks." Sugar shook Fair's hand.

As Fair climbed into the truck he called back, "Try one of those generic antihistamines. There are a couple that won't make you drowsy. Knock that headache right out."

"Okay."

19

Can't people just elope?" Harry grumbled as she sorted the unusually large number of envelopes Saturday morning.

Isabelle "Izzy" Stoltfus, a ripe twenty-three, worked the post office on Saturdays, but this Saturday, June 12, her first cousin was getting married over in Stuart's Draft, so Harry filled in.

Izzy's distant cousin, Jerome, was the animal-control officer. The two of them possessed literal temperaments. If something was written down, surely it was revealed wisdom. If it wasn't written down, they were paralyzed by indecision.

Fortunately, post-office procedures had changed little since the postal relays of ancient Rome. You delivered the mail, simple as that. What had changed was the speed with which it could be handed to you.

Once the mail sack was dropped at the Crozet Post Office, sorting the mail took time. Harry had to place each person's letters, magazines, and junk mail into their box. Packages too large for the box were set on industrial shelving, numbered by postbox rows. So the top shelf, since this was a small town, was one through fifty; the second shelf was fifty-one through one hundred, and so on.

"Why is she moaning about elopements? The wedding invitations went out and came in two months ago," Pewter logically said.

"She's not complaining about the volume of mail. She's complaining because Izzy's not here. She's ready to cut hay, and you know how she gets about that first cutting." Tucker loved the first haying, the sweet smell of the newly mown hay flat on the ground in rows that often curved as gracefully as the line on a Manet canvas.

"It really is a mess of mail." Pewter sauntered over to the pile on the sorting desk, the rest in the cart.

Mrs. Murphy, already on the white, blue,

pink, yellow, and even cerise envelopes, said, *"Party time. Flag Day parties. Fourth of July parties coming up. Bastille Day parties."*

This being Virginia, there were parties for every single human endeavor or lack of same. There were fishing parties, hunt club trail-clearing parties, the usual round of birthdays, retirement parties, let's-celebrate-death-to-chiggers parties (chiggers being a nasty little bug), and the ubiquitous informal parties. Now, these informal parties could be tricky. A lady didn't put on white gloves and party manners, but she couldn't show up in flip-flops, a tube top, and cutoff jeans. Despite protests to the contrary, there really were no informal parties. Dress might be relaxed, but folks pulled themselves together. Virginians take their public appearances seriously. This seriousness about personal display allows them to be wonderfully charming, funny, and entertaining at all the parties. When a person knows they are correctly turned out, even if the clothes aren't their favorites, they relax.

Every one of those invitations that Harry flicked into the back of the mailboxes specified the dress code. Not one of them said, "Come as you are." No one wanted to see you as you are. Much too scary. They wanted to see you at your best.

Harry, born and bred in these parts, from families that arrived here in the early seventeenth century, received almost every invitation possible. She loved parties, but the dress tortured her. Her limited funds were spent on her farm.

No one could hold a candle to Big Mim or BoomBoom in the turnout department, but Harry looked okay. Big Mim could and did pop over to Milan and Paris. She ran ahead of the fashion curve. BoomBoom preferred shopping in New York, knowing just where to find all the bargains south of Houston Street. Nor was she averse to tromping through Bergdorf Goodman.

When Harry began to look a little tatty, Susan Tucker would drag her to Tyson's Corner—not Milan, Paris, or New York, but Nordstrom's was at Tyson's Corner and that was a plus. The real reason Harry allowed herself to be yanked up to Occupied Virginia—as Crozians thought of northern Virginia—was so she could then drive over to Middleburg and visit her Smith College friends, a few of whom had settled there. It should be noted, those Smithies had also married quite well.

Alone, Harry had finally popped the last letter in the box when she noticed Big Mim's sleek Bentley Turbo R glide past the post office. Seated next to Mim was the unmistakable profile of one of the most beautiful women of her or any generation, Alicia Palmer.

Harry heard the deep motor purr as the Bentley rolled around the back of the post office. Big Mim was just as happy coming in the back door as the front. She rapped on the back door.

Federal regulations specified that this back door should be locked, but life in a small town and in a small post office challenges such restrictions. Harry usually kept the back door unlocked because Miranda came in that way. Rob Collier, if the day's drop was large, would pull in the back alley instead of the front. If she counted all the times she would need to open the back door, it just made more sense to keep it unlocked. Since the front-door parking lot was small and often full, friends just naturally came 'round the back way.

"Harry, dear," Big Mim cooed as she stepped through the door. "Alicia's home for a good long stay."

Alicia extended her hand to Harry. "It's been a long time between visits. You look as fresh and fit as ever."

Big Mim grumbled, "A summa cum laude from Smith sorting mail. Alicia, encourage her to better herself."

"Don't pay the least bit of attention to her, Harry. She always was a dictator." Alicia squeezed Harry's hand.

At this Mim laughed. Most people were scared to death of the powerful woman. When someone teased her as Alicia did, it actually delighted her.

"You look gorgeous, Miss Palmer. We wish you'd move back to St. James permanently."

"Must have had the world's best face-lift," Pewter cynically commented.

"She really is stunning," Mrs. Murphy said. *"Who cares how she does it?"*

"I think Mom looks stunning." The corgi stoutly stuck up for Harry.

"Oh, Tucker, that is so sweet, but Mom has all the fashion sense of a praying

mantis." Pewter hopped on the divider counter to be closer to the humans.

The corgi defiantly curled back her upper lip. *"You say! Well, she has a wonderful face and the best body. Not an ounce of fat on her, and if she wanted to wear expensive clothes she'd look better than anyone else."* Tucker then sat next to Harry's leg, refusing to even cast a glance at the fat gray cat.

". . . the most extraordinary thing." Big Mim finished her sentence on Harry finding Mary Pat's class ring. She reached for Harry's hand.

Harry held up her hand for Alicia, then thought it better to slip off the ring so the retired movie star could study it.

Alicia placed the gold ring in her palm. "She was so proud of her high school." She peered inside at the inscription, M.P.R., 1945.

"Would you like the ring, Miss Palmer?" Harry spontaneously offered it.

Alicia looked into Harry's eyes, her own violet eyes filling with tears. "You're very kind." She took a deep breath. "You keep it, Harry. Mary Pat bestowed upon me wealth worth a raj's ransom—that and a wealth of wisdom. I learned so much from that woman." She gently handed the ring back to Harry. "She died much too young."

"Do you have any idea who might have wished her dead?" Harry inquired.

"No. I was the prime suspect. Obviously, I didn't kill her. I never would have killed her. God, what an awful, awful time." Alicia noticed Pewter and Mrs. Murphy on the counter. "Still working at the post office, I see."

"Yes, couldn't do it without them. Tucker, too," Harry answered.

Alicia looked down at two bright eyes looking back up. "If dogs can fetch the paper, why not deliver the mail?" She laughed.

"Harry, dear, come over tonight. I'm giving an impromptu dinner party for Alicia. I browbeat her into it."

"Now, Mim, you didn't have to browbeat."

"Harry, it's a hen party." Big Mim smiled. "Wear something cool." The elegant small woman then said to Alicia in a stage whisper, "If Harry presses her jeans and white T-shirt, that's formal."

Harry laughed at her as well as at herself. "Oh, I'll tart myself up."

The two left by the back door just as Sugar Thierry lurched through the front door. He walked to his mailbox but kept inserting his key into the box to the left of his. "Harry, Harry, this damned key won't work."

Harry leaned over the counter and noticed sweat running down Sugar's face. "One box to the right."

He slipped his key in, turned it, and the heavy brass door with the glass front flipped open. "Right." He pulled out his mail, dropping some of it, then he bent over, picked it up. He walked to the long table in the middle of the entry area to sort his mail. He'd study an envelope, throw it in the trash, then retrieve it.

"He's not right," Mrs. Murphy observed.

"Maybe he's hung over," Pewter opined.

"We'd smell it," Tucker sagely noted. *"I smell his scent, though. It's heavy because he's sweating."*

Then Sugar gave up on sorting his mail, glanced up at Harry, and realized she was staring at him. He burst into sobs. "Harry, Harry, I can't stop thinking about Barry.

There's evil in this world. Terrible evil." He choked back another wrenching sob. "Nureyev, Nijinsky, Fred Astaire." He rattled off the names of three thoroughbred sires.

"Sugar, are you all right?" asked Harry, who knew perfectly well he wasn't. "Let me get you a Coke, or how about tea?"

His eyes, glazed, widened. "No, I'm fine. I'm fine." He bolted out the front door.

Harry hurried to the phone, dialing Dr. Hayden McIntire in the office.

The receptionist, Frances, picked up the phone. "Oh, hi, Harry." Harry had a distinctive alto voice. Once heard it was not forgotten. "What's up?"

"Is Doc there?"

"If you mean Hayden, no. He's out on the golf course with David Wheeler, Cindy Chandler, and BoomBoom. He's got Cindy as his partner. He just might keep that money in his pocket." Frances laughed. "What do you need?"

"It's not me. It's Sugar Thierry. I think he's sick. Bad sick."

"Oh, Bill's here. Let me page him."

A few moments passed and Bill picked up the phone. "Hello, Harry. Frances said you were concerned about Sugar Thierry."

"Yes. He was Barry Monteith's business partner." She clearly identified Sugar because Bill was new to the community. He hadn't been in Crozet a year yet.

"What seems to be the problem?"

"He's sweating; he must have a terrible fever. And he's, well, I don't know how to say this—he's acting loopy, looney. He's not a drinker."

"Where is he?"

Harry looked out the front door. Sugar was trying to open the door to his truck. He slid down to his knees. "Bill, he's out front. He's really sick. He can't get in his truck."

Bill, his office just a short distance away, said, "I'll be right there."

20

Are you sure?" Fair sternly questioned Harry.

She sat next to him in his truck, with Mrs. Murphy, Pewter, and Tucker cuddled around her as they rolled down Route 250 heading west.

The post office closed at noon on Saturdays.

"I told you." A note of irritation crept into her voice, a note reserved for husbands and ex-husbands. "Sugar acted weird. He fell down at his truck. I called Bill. I ran out to help Sugar, but he was kind of rolling around. He scared me. I mean, he didn't intend that but he was just—sick. So I didn't touch him."

"Did he spit on you?"

"No." She stared out the window as they passed the middle school and Western Albemarle High School. "Bill Langston knows what he's doing. I was impressed with how he handled the situation. He arrived at the same time as the rescue squad. Everyone wore gloves. AIDS has changed everything, hasn't it?"

"Harry, nature is cooking up diseases we can't even imagine. A new virus from the heart of Africa can reach here in twenty-four hours thanks to air travel, and we live within two hours of a huge international airport, Dulles."

"Hadn't thought of that."

"Few people do." He checked his speedometer and slowed to fifty-five.

"Where are we going?"

"Mary O'Brien. She came in to the clinic just for you."

"Why?" Harry liked the good doctor but wondered why Fair was whisking her over to Staunton.

"You're getting the rabies vaccine."

Harry turned toward him. "Fair, those are awful. My tests came back negative."

"You need them."

"They shoot the needle in your stomach!"

"Not anymore. I'm not saying this is the most pleasant experience you'll ever have, but you're outside, you're around wild animals, and I just have a bad feeling about recent events. You need the prophylactic shots. Better safe than sorry. That's it." He was firm.

"Can't we wait?" Harry's heart was sinking.

"No." His deep voice was firm. "I don't think you've been exposed to rabies. You can only contract the disease through saliva. You'd need to be bitten, although you could also contract it through corneal transplants. Well, I'm getting off track. But you're going to get the vaccine the same way I've been protected or Mrs. Murphy, Tucker, and Pewter are protected."

"The series is very expensive."

"About two thousand dollars."

"Fair!"

He kept his eyes on the road. "What's your life worth?"

"Uh—a lot," she sighed. "To me."

"And to me. I'm willing to bet Sugar's got rabies." He sighed. "When I was out at the farm he thought he was allergic to pollen—so much of it now. I should have been thinking that perhaps whatever bit Barry bit him." He paused for a second. "But I'm really confused about Barry's situation. Still, I should have been more alert."

"What!"

"Every vet sees this film about rabies. Can't get through school without viewing it, and there's old footage of a man dying from rabies. It tends to stay in your mind, that old grainy footage."

"I didn't touch Sugar, and all I did was hold Barry's hand."

"I know that. I know you're fine. Bill Langston said you're fine, but you're getting the vaccine, Harry. Just shut up."

Harry rubbed her temples. She'd endure the series of shots. She wasn't that big of a chicken. "What's going on?"

"I don't know."

"Barry and Sugar," she half-whispered. "Could it be that one of the horses is rabid?"

"Harry, I gave every animal on that farm shots. I've got all my records. Sugar must have records for the lay-up horses. I'm going to have to go through everything in his files. I don't know if he's mentally clear enough to give me permission. I hope so. But I'll do it anyway."

"If a horse had rabies, you'd know it."

"Eventually, yes. I'm not worried about any animal on the farm now. I'd see the symptoms. I want to go through the records to see what lay-up horses have passed through the farm in the last four months. If Sugar or Barry were exposed via a horse, it would have been in that time frame. Remember, it takes rabies one to three months to incubate. The symptoms don't present themselves until the virus reaches the brain."

Within forty minutes, they pulled into the parking lot of the red brick medical building. Dr. O'Brien, a tall, slender woman with gorgeous silver hair and an engaging manner, had been a close friend of Fair's for twenty years. Harry liked her, too, although she couldn't participate in the scientific discussions Fair and Mary enjoyed. Both were people who loved medicine, who loved learning.

"Harry, come on in here." Mary pointed to an examining room. "Fair, you can come in, too."

Harry dragged in, plopped on the examining table. "Is this going to hurt?"

"Yes," Mary forthrightly said, "but for less than a second. How's that?"

"Not so bad. Will it make me sick later?"

"That I don't know. Different people have differing reactions. I think of each person as their own specific chemical cocktail." She smiled. "But to be on the safe side, take it easy today and tonight. What I'm doing is introducing the killed virus into your system. You'll fight back, create antibodies. Some people don't feel it. Others do, find themselves tired, off feed. This is your first shot." Mary hit her so quickly with the needle that Harry hardly knew she'd been stuck. "I'll see you in two weeks for the second. And if you don't mind, Harry, let me take blood then. So come first thing in the morning, don't eat or drink after midnight. You can have a big breakfast when I'm done with you." She wiped Harry's arm once more with the antiseptic pad. "Told you it would take less than a second."

"You're amazing."

"Thank you." Mary smiled.

"Why are you taking blood next time if this is a disease of the nervous system?"

"Because, my dear, I want to check your cholesterol. You haven't had blood pulled in four years. I reviewed your records. And, Harry, when you go out, stop at the receptionist's desk and pick up your papers for a mammogram. I signed them. All you have to do is make the appointment."

"Mary!"

Smiling, the tall doctor held up her hand. "Save your breath. I know you're not forty. I know you're a strong girl. But I know a checkup *is* in order. Don't argue with me."

Fair laughed. "Mary, I need to take lessons from you."

"Thought your patients didn't talk."

"I mean Harry. You can handle Miss Bullhead."

"I just love that you two are having a laugh at my expense."

"You poor thing." Mary's voice registered false pity, then she winked. She walked to the door, put her hand on the knob, then paused. "Called Bill just before you arrived. Sugar's hallucinating." She took a deep breath. "Not much doubt."

"Jesus." Fair whistled. "I'd hoped against hope, you know."

"Bill questioned him when he could.

Couldn't get much out of him, but Sugar did swear he hadn't been bitten. You know, if someone comes to me after they've been bitten or think they've been exposed, the shots will save them if they come in time. But two men working at the same place," she shrugged, "what's there?"

"Barry was murdered. He didn't die from rabies and he sure didn't die a natural death, although at first it looked like it." Fair's jaw tightened.

"Disturbing—very." Mary knew all the horse people, being one herself, so she'd heard all about it. "But he still had rabies. It's not impossible that both Barry and Sugar were bitten by a bat and didn't know it. Anything else, they'd know."

"But that's what makes Barry's death so disturbing," said Harry. "His throat. The killer wanted to pin it on an animal. He wasn't sick—I mean, he wasn't sick when I found him. No one would have known he had rabies if the pathologists in Richmond hadn't run a dFA test on a brain-tissue sample."

Mary's blue eyes clouded over. "Well, there might be a connection. You can't assume there is, but you can't assume there isn't."

Driving back down Route 250, Harry noticed the rich green of the leaves, a green that would deepen throughout the summer. "Fair, I'll help you go through the files."

"Thought you might."

"May I use your cell phone?"

"Sure."

She called Big Mim, explaining why she couldn't attend the hen party and hoped that Alicia would understand. Big Mim, horrified to hear that Sugar had rabies, told Harry to take care of herself.

Harry hit the End button. The phone was in a cradle, and a speaker was fastened to the roof of the cab so the driver need not hold the phone. "There. I really want to talk to Alicia Palmer."

"There's something else I need to tell you."

"What?" Harry's face registered worry.

"Kind of odd. I was at Sugar's yesterday. Ultrasound on his big mare. And he said the strangest thing. He asked me if he should die, would you and I take over his mares. He has no family, and he knows we'll do right by the mares."

"Good Lord." The tears rolled down Harry's cheeks.

21

This silver's more valuable than the gross national product of Ecuador."

Big Mim, Little Mim, Aunt Tally, and Alicia stood in front of the huge trophy case in the large paneled tack room of the main barn.

Silver glistened. Loving cups, large inscribed plates, small bowls, and one enormous bowl festooned with carved grapes filled the case. Ribbons covered the back of the case, their blue and red reflecting on the silver. Mim never threw away a ribbon, but she displayed only the Championship, Reserve, First- and Second-place ribbons. The others she carefully laid flat in heavy cardboard boxes, putting them in her attic for safekeeping.

Usually Big Mim's dogs and Little Mim's dog—an offspring of her mother's English springer spaniel named Carbon Copy—would accompany them, but today, Sunday, they decided to surround a groundhog hole. The groundhog turned a deaf ear to their entreaties to come out.

"I remember when you won that one. Mary Pat nearly died. She wanted that trophy." Alicia indicated a large loving cup with two graceful handles.

The cup was inscribed, Virginia Hunter Champion, 1970. Horse: Interest Rate, Rider: Mrs. James Sanburne.

"She was a good sport about it." Big Mim relished that triumph.

"Mary Pat *was* a good sport." Aunt Tally leaned on her cane. "She came right back and beat you at the Washington International that year."

The Washington International was one of the premier horse shows in the mid-Atlantic.

"She fussed at me because I wouldn't show." Alicia smiled. "I told her people looked at me enough. I needed time off."

"You foxhunted. That's what really counts." Big Mim had her priorities straight.

Brinkley entered the barn from the opposite end, bounding into the tack room.

"Where did you come from, big boy?" Little Mim thought the yellow Lab one of the loveliest dogs she had ever encountered.

"Tazio must be here." Big Mim introduced Alicia to Brinkley, who, being a gentleman, offered his paw.

Little Mim stuck her head out of the tack room. "She's with Paul."

"Ah." A twinkle lit up the eye of Aunt Tally, who thought romance should be promoted enthusiastically and regularly.

"Don't start," Big Mim admonished her aunt.

"Oh, la," Aunt Tally insouciantly replied.

When Paul and Tazio entered the tack room, Big Mim introduced Tazio to Alicia. Paul had already met her.

"We've walked over the two possible sites for the new barn," Paul said.

"And with your permission, I thought Paul and I could drive over to Morven to look at the barns there. Both the old ones and the ones that Mr. Kluge commissioned."

"Excellent idea." Aunt Tally beamed.

Big Mim cut her eyes at Aunt Tally but agreed that it would be a good idea.

"I called the hospital about Sugar. Just in case." Paul liked Sugar.

"Yes, I did, too." Big Mim shook her head. "Miracles happen, but I don't think one will happen for Sugar."

"Mother, how long can this go on?"

Big Mim shrugged. "Possibly a week. Hopefully less. Bill said Sugar started thrashing around, so they've heavily medicated him to alleviate some of the suffering. And by the by, I had my reservations about this new doctor, but the way he's handling this, I think we're lucky to have him."

"It's such a terrible thing. One rarely hears of rabies today. When you told me yesterday, I thought surely there must be a mistake." Alicia couldn't imagine a worse death.

"Barry Monteith, too," Little Mim grimly added.

"Fortunately, he didn't know it and neither did we." Big Mim spoke in her perfectly modulated voice.

"What about the raccoon?" Little Mim wondered.

"No results yet." Paul answered, since he'd kept in touch with Fair Haristeen. "Fair is pretty sure the raccoon had distemper, but he's still waiting on word from Richmond."

"They take too long," Aunt Tally grumbled.

"Well, the state of Virginia in its wisdom will squander millions on a road going to a state senator's house in the backwoods but will not add more people to the agencies that actually serve the people," Big Mim complained.

"That could be said of any administration, anywhere, anytime." Alicia laughed, having abandoned the idea of a just government decades ago.

"I should rule the world," Aunt Tally simply stated.

"Well," Big Mim took a deep breath, "we'd all know exactly where we stand." She turned to Tazio and Paul. "Teatime. Please come up and join us. Brinkley, too."

Paul, like most single men, was never one to pass up food. Tazio was delighted to be invited, also.

Once they were all settled on the summer porch, an array of scones, cookies, biscuits, jams, marmalades, jellies, cream, and butter appeared. Black teas and green teas were served. Aunt Tally, under the glaring eye of Mim, drank a shot of straight vodka, chased by a bracing cup of tea. The others chose to wait until later for spirits.

They chatted about the upcoming yearling sales, summer horse shows, and garden shows, about Tazio's plans for a new shed for Harry, about new building materials, round barns from the eighteenth century, and about design in general, whether for buildings or gardens.

After the impromptu gathering broke up, Little Mim drove Aunt Tally back to her farm. Big Mim and Alicia were alone, watching the long slanting rays of the sun, about a half hour before sunset.

The two had stayed in touch after Alicia moved to Los Angeles, and then Santa Barbara.

Mim, who adored traveling, would visit Alicia at her California home or on the set at least once a year. Alicia would return to Crozet for short visits, to recharge her batteries, to check on St. James. Fortunately, the farm manager and his wife were honest and hard workers.

"Little Mim is the spitting image of you. It's funny to see the two of you together."

"Well, I wish she'd find direction. Something."

"She has her boyfriend." Alicia defended Little Mim. "And she is vice-mayor of Crozet. You're hard on her."

"We both know that's not enough. As for her first husband, the less said about him the better. But this Blair," Mim shifted in her seat, "what do you think of male models?"

"That anyone who lives by their looks is doomed to disappointment. I should know." Alicia said this genially.

"Hmm." Mim's voice dropped. "He seems normal enough."

"You mean that he's not gay?"

"In so many words."

"You'd know. I mean, sooner or later you'd know. He probably has the sense to know that his days are numbered in his business. You said he had another business."

"He owns land in the northwestern part of the county, which has a great deal of underground water. This will probably become very important in the near future, especially since we've had a series of droughts, not horrible but bad enough to wake us up. He's not stupid or vapid."

"Isn't that a prejudice? That terribly attractive people are stupid or vapid?"

"Yes and no. My experience is that the divinely beautiful or handsome have so many things done for them, doors opened, that they aren't aware of how much easier life is for them. They sometimes don't develop the skills other people learn early in life. One thinks immediately of Elizabeth Taylor."

"You coped."

"Aren't you flattering." Big Mim smiled. "But I'm not beautiful." She held up her hand. "I take good care of myself and I'm attractive, but the kind of beauty you have—or, say, a Clark Gable had—is some kind of radiance. That's very, very special."

"Thank you, Mim. But remember, beauty can be a curse, too." She stared pensively for a moment at the huge summer bouquet on the coffee table. "Do you think Blair loves her?"

"I'm not sure."

"Does she love him?"

"Yes. She has the sense not to tell him,

but I know Marilyn. She's in love and he's good to her, attentive, kind."

"What can you do but wait?"

"I know, but I hope she doesn't make another big mistake. It's all so messy and painful."

"I expect that's a working definition of life." Alicia laughed. "Along with a lot of happiness woven throughout the mess and pain. Somehow it all works out."

"It has for you."

"Ha," she laughed. "Once I realized I didn't have to marry every man I slept with it became easier."

"I always thought you were in love with Mary Pat. She certainly was in love with you. Not that we ever spoke of those things then, but now we can. I hope—I mean, I hope I haven't offended you." Big Mim was genuine in her concern.

"You have not. I did love Mary Pat and I think she loved me, but she was spoiled, as the very rich can be. Forgive me, Mim, I know you fall into the very rich category."

"I'll admit I've been spoiled in many ways."

"Mary Pat had to be the center of my attention. I was much younger than she, twenty years her junior, and I suppose, truth be told, that I wanted to be the center of attention, too. Actors usually do." She laughed. "I wanted a career. She didn't resist that but she was diffident. And she wanted to live here, not Los Angeles."

"Do you ever regret putting your career first?"

"No. Not once."

"What about your marriages? Wasn't it hard to go against your basic nature?" Mim innocently asked.

Alicia paused for a long time, the marquise diamond on her left hand catching the light. "Yes. It was, especially when I was younger. Oh, I know I could have had affairs with women. Hollywood is accused of being sin city, but that kind of behavior goes on everywhere, even here in Crozet."

"Amen."

"But you know, I took my vows seriously. Each time I married I really wanted the marriage to work. Of course, in retrospect, how could they work? I was not where I was supposed to be, too afraid to look inside and, worse, in a grueling business where one is discarded sooner or later. It has taken me until now, until my fifties, to understand who and what I really am—and to be grateful for what God has given me. And eventually I'll find love. I hope so, anyway, and if I'm fortunate enough to find a life partner I'm not going to hide or lie about her. I'm going to be grateful and proud."

"In some ways I envy you. You proved yourself," Big Mim said.

"So have you."

Mim twirled her earring. "Oh, I like to meddle. I like to run the show. Turns out I'm good at it, but I never had to go out into the world. You did. I admire that."

"Thank you, but don't you think, somehow, some way, we all wind up just where we are supposed to be, doing what we're supposed to be doing?"

Mim smiled. "If we have any brains at all, yes."

"Discipline," Alicia said. "That's the key to everything."

"Apparently few people have it. I think of it as a WASP virtue."

Alicia's eyes widened. "I don't. You either have it or you don't. Being raised a WASP isn't going to help you. Think of all the lazy sods we know who are white Anglo-Saxon Protestants."

"It's funny, Alicia, but the older I get the more I wonder if I know anything, and then there's Aunt Tally, who truly believes she could run the world."

"She could."

They both laughed.

"I'm so glad you've come back, for a long stay, I hope." Big Mim meant that.

"Mary Pat's school ring." Alicia inhaled. "She's calling me back. I came back to rest, to enjoy St. James. It's all so wonderful and restorative, but now she's calling me back."

"Harry went back to Potlicker Creek. Later. She had Susan Tucker with her—you remember her, Gregory was her maiden name—and Fair Haristeen. They combed the woods and the creek bed, but after all these years they found nothing. Harry fancies herself an amateur sleuth."

"I don't think there's anything left of Mary Pat except the love she gave to all of us."

"I always thought someone killed her, took the horse, and shipped him off to Ireland or South America or wherever. If they'd both been killed you think we'd find one or the other. But no trace of Mary Pat or Ziggy was ever found."

"And I'd just left for L.A. for my first screen test the day before she disappeared. It didn't look good, did it?"

"No."

"I came back immediately, of course. The papers couldn't accuse me of being her lover, thanks to the libel laws. And the police couldn't accuse me of murder. No proof. But a pall hung over me. Hell. Sheer hell. As soon as I could put everything in order I left again. I was glad to go. And the gods were with me. I had a great career." She paused. "I never could come up with a motive as to why someone would kill Mary Pat."

"There is one. There always is."

Alicia sighed. "Done is done. It seems Crozet has other problems right now."

22

Sugar Thierry's suffering ended at 4:36 P.M., Monday, June 14. Harry and Miranda received a phone call at the post office from Bill Langston.

Miranda placed the phone in its cradle. "Be thou faithful unto death, and I will give thee a crown of life." She quoted Revelation, Chapter 2, Verse 10.

Harry looked at her. "Sugar?"

"Yes."

"Poor Sugar. I don't know if it's a sin to pray for someone's death, but surely it isn't a sin to pray that he's not in pain."

Miranda's warm features relaxed. "The Good Lord hears your prayers and knows your spirit. Harry, I think everyone in Crozet has prayed for that young man."

Blair Bainbridge walked through the door. "Hello, ladies."

"Blair, Sugar just died," Harry sorrowfully told her neighbor.

"Good God." Blair walked to the counter, leaning his elbows on it. "Never really had a chance, did he?"

"I need your help." Harry walked to the counter directly across from the gorgeous man. "Sugar's mares will be coming to my farm. May I borrow your tractor and the posthole digger? I can keep them in the upper paddock for a week maybe, but I'll need to fence in those back acres. I wanted to do it, anyway—just put it off because of time and money."

"You can have those fence posts I never used. I'll drop them by your old shed and I'll leave the tractor there, too."

"I don't want to put you out. And you're too generous."

"You've done plenty for me, Harry; let me do something for you—and Sugar."

Harry opened her mouth to protest, but Miranda said, "Harry, he's right. You can be too self-sufficient, dear."

"Thank you, Miranda," Pewter, stretched

on the halfway shelf behind the postboxes, agreed.

"Humans are funny about favors." Tucker thought Blair was fine, but some people would hold the favor to your face ever after bestowing it upon you.

"Humans are funny, period," Pewter, resident cynic, said.

Mrs. Murphy, who had been behind the post office prowling through Miranda's garden, burst through the animal door. *"Cop!"*

A loud knock on the back door was followed by an even louder knock.

"Just a moment," Miranda called.

"Jerome Stoltfus. Animal control!"

Miranda opened the door, and Jerome, all one hundred twenty pounds of him, stepped through. "Where's that cat?"

"She's not here," Mrs. Murphy called from under the mail cart.

"I want to see her papers," Jerome, who had a large, drooping mustache, demanded.

"What papers?" Harry endured Jerome rather than liked him. This seemed to be the town consensus.

"Rabies vaccination." He folded his arms

across his scrawny chest. "And I want them for the fat cat and that tailless dog, too."

"Who are you calling fat?" said she who was.

"First of all, Jerome, as you can see, Tucker is wearing her rabies tag. If you'll bend down and examine it you'll note it's correctly dated."

Jerome knelt down as Tucker glanced sideways at him. Being a good girl, she did not curl her lip, but she wanted to because she didn't like strangers reaching for her. She thought it was rude, and the corgi could never understand why so few humans bothered to learn canine manners.

"Okay." He stood back up. "But what about those two cats? Animals are here in a public place. Shouldn't be here, Harry. Shouldn't be here. Could be passing diseases. Allergies."

"I've had my animals here since I first took this job, Jerome. It's a little late to complain." Harry's face reddened.

Blair's pleasant voice carried authority. "You know Harry takes excellent care of her pets."

"I want the paperwork," Jerome spat.

While he was laying down the law,

Miranda called Martin Shulman, D.V.M. When he came on the line she quietly explained what was afoot, then handed the phone to Jerome.

"Yes." Jerome sounded very important.

"Mr. Stoltfus," Martin Shulman cleverly addressed Jerome by his last name, "I have the records for both Mrs. Murphy and Pewter, and they had their booster shots last February. Where would you like me to fax these so you need not trouble yourself to come to the clinic?"

"Well, uh, the county office." Jerome gave the number. "Thanks." He hung up the phone, glared at the two cats as Mrs. Murphy joined Pewter on the ledge. "Spoiled rotten cats."

"Dimwit," Pewter sassed.

"Wienie," Mrs. Murphy added her two cents.

Jerome, hand on the back doorknob, turned and said, "I'm going to protest to Pug Harper about these animals. It's not sanitary. And Blair Bainbridge, I'll be at your farm to check your paperwork in"—he checked his digital watch—"twenty minutes, and that means the cattle, too. Harry, I want to see the paperwork on your horses."

"I'll have Fair fax it to you." Harry had written down Jerome's office number when he gave it to Dr. Shulman.

"You do that." Jerome opened the door, then pointed to the animal door and said, "Got to close that up. Dangerous. Rabid animals or terrorists could use this to gain entry." With that jump of logic he left.

"Mr. Personality," Blair dryly commented. "Well, I guess I have work to do." He rapped the counter. "Harry, if you need it, you can use my adjoining pasture, the cemetery pasture. There's plenty of water in that pasture, too, and the fencing is good. Oh—I'd keep my eye out for terrorists crawling through the animal door if I were you."

"Right." Harry half-smiled, for she was doubly unhappy. She was upset about Jerome and just miserable over Sugar.

"Bye, ladies."

As Blair walked outside into the sunshine, Harry gritted her teeth. "I will kill Jerome Stoltfus, that idiot!"

"A little man with a little power is much worse than a big man with big power," Miranda sagely noted.

"Oh, Miranda." Harry threw up her

hands, then sat down at the small table covered in a checkered tablecloth. Tears filled her eyes.

"Honey, what's the matter?" Miranda, motherly and kind, put her arm around Harry's shoulders.

Mrs. Murphy and Tucker hurried over to comfort Harry. Pewter walked over, but slowly. It wouldn't do to be too obvious in her devotion.

"I don't know." Harry reached for a napkin to dab her eyes.

"Sugar is with the Lord. 'Have mercy upon me, O God, according to thy loving kindness: according unto the multitude of thy tender mercies blot out my transgressions.' Sugar is forgiven and in a better place." She had quoted Psalm 51, First Verse. "And as for Jerome, well, he will make trouble, so the way to head him off is to draw up a petition. Ned Tucker can do that for us and have every single postal patron sign it."

"What?"

"A petition that declares Mrs. Murphy, Pewter, and Tucker are valuable members of our community and the post office can't function without them." Miranda smiled down at the three faces looking up at her. It was uncanny, but sometimes Miranda thought they understood.

"She's come a long way. Remember when she didn't like cats and dogs?" Tucker recalled.

"A lot of people are like that until they get to know us." Mrs. Murphy rubbed against Miranda's leg.

"Miranda, that's a wonderful idea." Harry cried a little harder.

"Now, you don't worry about a thing. I'll take care of it." Miranda patted her on the back.

"I feel like I'm slipping." Harry wiped her eyes.

"What do you mean?"

"I don't know exactly. I'm stalled out and I don't know where I'm going. I feel terrible about Sugar and Barry, too. And I'm sitting in the post office getting cussed out by Jerome Stoltfus, whose IQ hovers at his body temperature. You know?" Her voice lifted up, lilting. "And Pug Harper is going to come on down here and be nice, but it won't be nice for us." She reached down to stroke Tucker's glossy head.

"That's why this petition is going on Pug's desk."

Harry, more composed, leaned back in the chair. "Miranda, I don't say but so much, but I know how things work. Pug will acquiesce to the petition and be all smiles. Jerome will slow down once this rabies scare is over, plus he will irritate so many people in the pursuit of his duties that Jim Sanburne will haul him on the carpet. What will happen to me is when the new post office is built, that's when the boom will be lowered. No cats and dogs."

Miranda sat opposite Harry. "We can hope that won't happen, but I think you're right. It seems nothing is particular anymore." She used the Virginia word for individual, special, distinctive. "New buildings mean new rules, and those rules don't take into account people's feelings, traditions, or ways. Americans confuse things with progress. Progress is really of the spirit. Material progress is secondary."

Harry lifted Mrs. Murphy onto her lap, so Pewter, not to be outdone, jumped up. "What can we do?"

"Keep the old ways."

"But some of the old ways meant racial

oppression, women treated as second-class citizens . . . you know."

Miranda nodded that, indeed, she did know. "Harry, you're much younger than I am and you lost your parents in your early twenties, too young for that. Maybe you've missed out on their perspective. Perhaps I can supply a little of it. Honey, all your life things will change. You have to decide what is important to you and stick to that. I decided a long time ago, before you were born, that what was important to me was love: love of God, love of friends and family, and, of course, the love of a good man. George was a good man. Now, to someone walking down the street I probably seem like I have a little life, but it's a full life. I don't need all that stuff that's advertised in magazines and on television. I still drive my Falcon and it gets me where I want to go. I have a rich, rich life. You have to decide what is important to you."

Harry realized she'd held her breath when Miranda was speaking. She exhaled, then inhaled. "My babies!" She meant her cats and dog. "My farm. The whole swing and sway of country life and country values. My horses. The sunrise shining on the mountains and the sunset glowing behind them. My friends. St. Luke's. Miranda, I'm babbling."

"But you know what's important."

"Our way of life. I guess it does come down to love. I don't know that I'm as faithful as you are, Miranda. I have so many questions that the church doesn't answer."

"Church doctrine is one thing." Miranda belonged to the Church of the Holy Light, whereas Harry was high church, meaning she followed a liturgy, a catechism, a strict protocol. Miranda, on the other hand, didn't have much truck with doctrine, for her spiritual experience was emotional, not intellectual. "Follow your heart."

"The funny thing is, I know that."

"We all do. We just need to be reminded."

"Miranda, when the new post office gets built and if Pug jams a bunch of new rules and new people down our throats, what are you going to do?"

"Wish them all well and dig in my garden." Miranda stood up because Carmen Gamble walked into the post office, and she looked peaked.

"Hello, Carmen."

"Poor Sugar. I feel awful for him. He was such a nice guy. I'm just shook up. I mean, I guess, well," she stammered, "we dated a little. Nothing major. I guess I lost interest because he was too nice a guy." Her lower lip trembled.

Miranda flipped up the counter divider, walked over to Carmen, and put her arms around her. "I'm sorry, honey. Put your faith in the Lord."

Tears cascaded over Carmen's cheeks. "I do put my faith in the Lord. I just don't have any faith in Rick Shaw or Cynthia Cooper."

Harry quietly said, "Carmen, they'll figure this out. They will."

Carmen sobbed as Miranda hugged her. "And I keep thinking I kissed both Barry and Sugar. I know my tests came back okay, but what if the lab made a mistake?"

Harry, who had grilled Fair over rabies, reassured her. "You can only get rabies if the saliva enters your body from a bite, gets into the muscle tissue, and travels up your nerve highway. It takes one to three months. So the virus won't be in the infected person's saliva until they show the symptoms, until the virus has reached their brain. You're fine."

This calmed Carmen a lot. She hugged Miranda, then walked to the counter divider. "Dr. Langston did tell me that rabies in humans is extremely rare." She wiped her eyes. "But I wonder—I mean, I wonder about Barry most of all. He had a kind of sly streak. I used to get on him about some of his horse sales, you know? He'd say he was an entrepreneur. I said I saw it differently."

"How?" Harry asked, as three pairs of animal eyes focused on Carmen.

"Whenever money passes hands, it sticks to someone's fingers. He was doing pretty good for a guy starting his own business, and you know what else?" She paused as Harry and Miranda leaned toward her. "There was a lot he didn't tell Sugar. He'd tell me. Bragging."

"Do you think he cheated Sugar?" Miranda hated this idea.

"Not exactly. I think he made side deals and just kept them to himself. Sugar wouldn't even think to question Barry. Sugar was, well, you know, he lived up to his name." The tears rolled afresh.

23

Jesus Christ, what are you, jet-propelled?" Tavener exploded.

"We got a situation," Jerome glumly pronounced.

"You're damned right we do. We have an animal-control officer who's a few bricks shy of a full load," the veterinarian rancorously said.

The sun, brilliant today, illuminated the tiny broken veins in Tavener's face, testimony that he'd lived a convivial life. Declaring every day a celebration, he delighted in bending his elbow.

"Paperwork."

Tavener—called by Fair, who had been called by Harry—expected Jerome to show up at his office door, but not two hours af-

ter harassing Harry and then Blair Bainbridge. Fortunately for Tavener, his office
manager, Tim Fornay, was equal to the
challenge and had assembled the paperwork on every stallion and mare at Dr.
Heywood's breeding establishment. As an
extra caution, Tim had also printed out rabies documentation on every equine patient.

Tim rose from his command station, a
long and high desk to the left of the front
door. He watched out the front window as
the two men spoke. Then he called Ramon
in the breeding shed, warning him that
Jerome Stoltfus might stick his nose in
their business. That meant, get your green
card out and ready because, although
Jerome had nothing to do with the Immi-
gration and Naturalization Service, he was
an official of Albemarle County and lived to
throw his weight around.

Ramon told Tim, "No problem," and returned to the business of packaging sperm
straws in blue plastic cylinders crammed
with dry ice. These would be picked up by
FedEx and would arrive at their destina-
tions by ten the next morning.

Those thoroughbreds to be registered

by the Jockey Club had to be bred by a live cover, meaning the stallion literally covered the mare. However, those people breeding for hunters, eventers, steeplechasers, fox-hunters, or even dressage saved the time and worry, to say nothing of the expense, of hauling their mares from Colorado or New Hampshire to Virginia. This way they could inseminate their mares without all that hassle and without the risk always attending a live cover. Stallions could get their legs broken by mares who found them singularly unattractive. By the same token, stallions could savage mares. Fortunately, such incidents were rare, but anyone who had ever been in the breeding shed when they occurred never wanted to see one again and often counted themselves lucky to get out in one piece.

Recently the technology had advanced so that, instead of pulling blood for blood-typing, a saliva swatch from the horse would do to prove the validity of the breeding. The Jockey Club instituted blood-typing in 1977, which was superseded by DNA testing in 2001. Before 1977, the true reason for a live cover was it was too easy to cheat, particularly those people green to the horse business. An unsuspecting owner would send his or her best mare to a good stallion without someone to watch the breeding, and would pay a whopping fee, only to have her bred to a lesser stallion. Even though a live cover was supposed to guarantee the legitimacy of the mating, unscrupulous people took advantage of the situation until 1977. After blood-typing was demanded, cheating became more difficult.

The racing industry spawned blood-stock research companies, often using different criteria, which would present you with the best match for your mares. One paid for this expertise. Some people have a breeding gift; by watching horses, by reading pedigrees, they come up with good breeding matches. No amount of computer research could substitute for that "feel."

Jerome Stoltfus, to his credit, knew that. He'd broken up enough puppy mills, saved enough mistreated horses to recognize a good animal from a sorry one. Nine times out of ten, it was the ill-bred animal that suffered.

He also knew that Tavener Heyward kept

excellent records. But he wasn't going to back down in front of Tavener. The distinguished and successful veterinarian would roll right over county officials. Jerome wasn't going to be one of them.

"Tim's got all the paperwork ready for you. Jerome, I've got to get up to Fox Glen Farm." He reached into the open window of his truck, pulling out a leather notebook with a zipper around the outside. He unzipped it, sliding out a business card from the side flap. "Here. My cell-phone number is on there, as well as my pager. If it's an emergency, call. If you see any equine you think might have rabies, call."

"You think we got an epidemic?"

"I think we should all err on the side of caution."

"Right." Jerome squinted as Tavener hopped in his truck and drove off. Then he walked into the office.

"Mr. Stoltfus. Here you be." Tim jovially walked out from around the desk, his arms filled with four huge manila folders closed with thin string.

"Great day." Jerome held out his arms.

"Dr. Heyward thought you should have the records of every horse we have inoculated. The dates are clearly marked, as is the batch number of the vaccine. If, for any reason, you need a vaccine traced, we can get right back to the pharmaceutical company."

"Right." Jerome couldn't think of anything else to say. He walked back out the door when Tim opened it. He placed the bulging large folders on the hood of the white county car, a Jeep, the county emblem emblazoned on the side. He opened the door to put everything on the passenger seat, already full. He decided to put the materials on the floor.

The sun glistened on the running-horse weather vane on Heyward's stable, which shifted ever so slightly, indicating wind was coming up from the southwest.

"Hmm." Jerome watched the arrow point of the weather vane sway back and forth gently. "Hmm."

A wind from the southwest usually meant fierce, soaking storms.

Ramon walked out of the breeding shed.

Jerome closed the door of the car, sauntered over, and demanded to see Ramon's green card, which the Mexican happily produced. Ramon, smart and hardworking, smiled as Jerome read the card and handed it back to him.

Without another word, Jerome Stoltfus got in the car and drove to the next farm.

Jerome, irritating and not the most intel-ligent man, had two things going for him. He knew he wasn't the brightest bulb on the Christmas tree. He knew that in first grade, so he studied harder. And he re-tained everything he ever learned or ever saw. It would take him nights of labor to go through every single file from every barn he visited. He would write down batch num-bers, he would cross-reference, he would use his computer, too. But he would make certain things were as they should be. And that was the other thing Jerome had going for him: He truly wanted to do a good job. He wanted to be the best animal-control officer in the great state of Virginia.

24

Four black-type mares in foal to four very good mid-Atlantic stallions—Fred Astaire, Corporate Report, Wayne County, and Allen's Prospect—along with the redoubtable Binky, grazed in Harry's upper paddock. Black-type didn't mean the mares were black but referred to heavier black type printed on their papers, signifying graded stakes winners in their pedigrees. The more black type, the better the pedigree, on paper, anyway.

Poptart, Tomahawk, and Gin Fizz leaned over the fence, wildly curious about the newcomers.

"Pretty well-made mares." Tomahawk judged the looks of Loopy.

"Pretty is as pretty does," said Gin Fizz,

a foxhunter admired by all who saw him in the field.

"Well, all these girls have to do is produce good foals." Poptart winked. *"Guess not Binky. She's ancient."*

"We will," called out Countess Cool, a 16.1-hand liver chestnut, a very eye-catching girl.

"Who are you calling ancient?" Binky snorted.

Harry and Fair sat on the fence line, watching the horses. With Paul de Silva's help, they'd loaded the mares that represented all of Barry and Sugar's worldly investments. The cost of the mares plus the stud fees totaled $62,000, a modest sum by the standards of Lane's End Farm in Lexington, Kentucky, but quite a lot for two young start-ups in Crozet, Virginia.

Paul also packed up blankets, tack, bandages, meds, and even a set of jockey silks. Since Fair and Harry worked all day and Paul's hours could be somewhat flexible, he'd asked Big Mim if he could go over and pack up. She readily agreed and was touched that he wanted to help. She was beginning to realize that Paul was a good man as well as a good horseman.

Harry would tackle unpacking everything and finding a place for Barry and Sugar's equipment tomorrow after work.

This evening, the fireflies darting over the creek, she sat on the fence, her arm around Fair's waist. Emotionally worn, she said nothing, nor did he. Mrs. Murphy and Tucker sat below them. Harry wasn't one to discuss her emotions, so the silence was natural.

Pewter's fascination with the new mares lasted for ten minutes, and then she trooped back into the kitchen and stuck her face in a bowl of crunchies, tuna-flavored, her fave. She then curled up on the old club chair in the living room. She had to wedge next to *The Decline and Fall of the Roman Empire* by Edward Gibbon, Volume I, which Harry was rereading. Harry loved to read well-written history, and Gibbon's prose filled her with awe. Pewter could not have cared less about what happened to the Romans. As far as she was concerned, it was cats that kept the empire thriving for a thousand years. Cats guarded those grain shipments from Egypt. Yes, cats were responsible for the rise of all civilizations.

Mrs. Murphy leaned next to Tucker. The two friends loved each other dearly.

The corgi said, *"Think she'll ever figure it out?"*

"What happened to Mary Pat or who killed Barry?"

"No. That she belongs back with Fair."

"Oh, that." The tiger rubbed her left paw over her whiskers. *"Humans are singularly stupid about love."*

25

The cool damp of the dew tingled underneath Mrs. Murphy's paws. The Big Dipper, high overhead at two in the morning, sparkled against the night sky.

The tiger cat left everyone asleep in the house. Pewter's snoring kept her awake, but she probably would have gone outside for a brief prowl, anyway. The scent of rabbits, possums, even the steady slick trails of earthworms in their ceaseless toil beckoned her. She was, after all, a nocturnal creature who had altered her habits to work with her human.

Simon, the possum, shuffled out of the tack room as Mrs. Murphy entered the center aisle.

"Tootsie Rolls." He triumphantly chewed on the delicacy.

"You're as bad as Mom. How can you eat that sugary junk?" Mrs. Murphy preferred—craved—meat, raw or cooked, although occasionally she would eat the tender tip of asparagus.

"It's so-o-o good." His eyes closed in gustatory pleasure.

The sounds of merriment floated out from the tack room. Mrs. Murphy's pupils now expanded to give her a terrifying appearance. She tore into the tack room. A convention of mice played with Tootsie Roll wrappers and bits of grain.

Screaming, they scurried for their hole, cleverly hidden behind a small aluminum tack trunk.

"Mass murderer!"

Mrs. Murphy growled at their opening, *"Death to all mice!"* She sat down and in a more reasonable tone instructed, *"Now, listen, you worthless mammals. You promised me you wouldn't make messes here or in the feed room. Look at this. This is shameful. I'm going to have to kill a few of you and leave your corpses on Harry's desk here. Otherwise, I'll be out of a job."*

"You surprised us," answered the head mouse, Arthur. *"We always clean up. And furthermore, we didn't throw the wrappers around. Simon did."*

"I did," Simon confessed as he joined the tiger cat. *"But I don't have to clean up, because the mice do it. Anyway, I leave some Tootsie Rolls. I keep up the deal."*

Excited chatter wafted out from behind the tack trunk. A little nose stuck out, tiny black whiskers swept forward, followed by a pair of jet-black eyes. Arthur, an older fellow, spoke. *"Mrs. Murphy, there won't be one wrapper on the floor tomorrow morning, nor will there be a single kernel of grain. Not one."*

"You can start cleaning now."

He looked up at the beautiful cat staring down at him. *"What do you take me for? A perfect fool?"*

"I've kept my end of the bargain," Mrs. Murphy protested her innocence.

"That's true. You haven't killed one of us in years, but you've wreaked havoc among the field mice. If their population drops, you'll be in here slaughtering us."

"Don't be such a drama queen." She feigned indifference, then with lightning re-

flexes swept her paw down and snagged Arthur, hauling him up on the tack trunk. *"Worm."*

Although terrified, he wasn't going to beg for his life. Great consternation could be heard from behind the walls.

Simon, not much for killing since he preferred sweets and grain, opened his mouth. Only a squeak escaped.

Mrs. Murphy cackled with glee.

Arthur's wife, a plump little mouse, hopped up on the tack trunk. *"If he's going, I'm going!"*

"Martha, think of the children," he pleaded.

"You have so many of them, which brings me to my next demand. Slow down, will you? If there are too many relatives here, I'm going to have to cut down the numbers. Harry doesn't have the money to feed every mouse in the county. My job is to see that she doesn't waste money feeding the likes of you. You get the gleanings, but show some sense."

Martha defiantly scolded, *"We do not breed beyond the food supply. That's more than I can say for humans!"*

"Harry is the exception that proves the

rule." Arthur hoped to soften Martha's words, as Mrs. Murphy fiercely loved Harry.

Mrs. Murphy batted Arthur with her other paw. Martha valiantly charged the larger predator.

"You bully!"

That fast, Mrs. Murphy pinned down Martha. To her great satisfaction she had a mouse underneath each paw. *"I'll let you go if you promise a complete cleanup, including the dust balls behind this tack trunk. I don't care if you made them or not."*

"Agreed." Arthur wriggled.

"No more babies this year, and no chewing tack!"

"We have never chewed tack!" Martha, indignant, spat.

"See that your good behavior continues." Mrs. Murphy swatted them off the tack trunk like two hockey pucks. Then she left, Simon waddling after her.

"You are so fast. I don't think there's another creature as fast as yourself that isn't in the cat family." The gray possum with his hairless pink tail was anything but quick.

"Foxes are fast, but we hunt the same game. That's why we don't get along."

"There's plenty for everyone."

"Now. But in bad years we have to fight for our territory."

"But, Murphy, you don't need a hunting range. You have good food in the house and at work, too."

"It's a matter of principle." Mrs. Murphy walked out onto the pea-rock drive.

"Where are you going?"

"To the fox's den."

"Oh, is there going to be a fight? I don't want to get in a fight."

"Simon, go eat your Tootsie Rolls and make sure those mice get to work." Mrs. Murphy burst into a flat-out run from a standstill.

Simon watched. He wished he could do that. Any human with that ability would be signed as a halfback by a professional football team for millions of dollars. Of course, Mrs. Murphy would still outrun the player.

The cat ran for the sheer joy of running. Her long, fluid strides covered the ground, her paws barely touching the slick grass. Within five minutes she stood outside the fox den, secure in the stone base ruins of what had been the old spring house.

Since gray foxes keep a modest entrance, the large mound in front of the den announced the presence of the red fox.

The vixen, with characteristic intelligence, had selected a den on high ground, secure from the weather and within a leisurely walk to the strong-running creek dividing Blair Bainbridge's and Harry's property. This was the west side of Harry's property. A family of gray foxes lived near the eastern boundary, so the two types of foxes rarely conversed and never competed against each other. It was a good working arrangement.

A young cub peeped out at Mrs. Murphy. *"Momma, a tiger!"*

Mrs. Murphy laughed to herself, then called out, *"It's Mrs. Murphy."*

The sleek vixen, shedding her undercoat, came outside. Four little red heads popped up to listen, their luminous eyes wide in wonder at this exotic, striped creature.

"How are you?" The vixen minded her manners.

"Well, and yourself?"

"Healthy, thank you."

Mrs. Murphy used to spit and fuss whenever a fox was near, until one cold

night years back, when a bloodthirsty bobcat had come down off the mountain since
game was scarce. This terror chased Mrs.
Murphy, and the cat only escaped death
thanks to this fox den. Even Tucker had
ducked in, squeezing herself next to the
fox. That night she was as close to a bobcat as Mrs. Murphy ever wanted to be.
Since the truce was in effect, Mrs. Murphy
dutifully informed both the reds and the
grays when the hunt club would be leaving
from Harry's farm. This usually happened
twice during hunt season, mid-September
to mid-March. The foxes could decide
whether to give the hounds a run for their
money or to snooze inside.

*"I was wondering if you'd heard any re-
ports of rabies among the foxes?"*

The vixen shook her head. *"No. Oh,
Lord, I hope another epidemic isn't sweeping over us. It's been a good time. No
mange or rabies."* She cast a fearful eye at
her children.

*"If you haven't heard of anything, then
we're all right. Now, you're eating the kibble Harry puts out from time to time?"*

Harry, as a dutiful hunt-club member,
once a month put out kibble with wormer

dripped over it. This knocked the parasite load right out of the foxes. She also would trap the cubs just before the fall and take them to Dr. Shulman for their first rabies shot. Getting the booster into them three years later was a lot harder.

News of an oral rabies vaccine, used extensively in France, had Harry and other foxhunters hopeful it would soon be allowed here in the States. Feeding foxes their vaccine would be much easier then.

"Yes. I'm grateful. Why do you ask about rabies?"

"Two humans have had it. Both dead, although one was killed outright. They discovered the rabies later, after the autopsy."

"Two humans. That's very strange."

"What about the raccoons or the beaver? You all talk."

"Everyone here is fine." She looked lovingly at her litter. *"They're too young for their distemper shots or their rabies. Early fall."* She let out a long sigh. *"Means I'll have to get in the cage. They'll come in it if I do, but, oh, Mrs. Murphy, those cages scare me."*

"I know. They scare me, too, but a little

fear is better than a lot of rabies," the cat sensibly said.

"I know."

"Foxes have long memories. Ask some of the old ones if their grandmothers or great-grandfathers ever spoke of Mary Patricia Reines."

"She was buried up in the high pastures behind St. James under the stone wall. That's the story I always heard. But whoever dragged her up there didn't do a good job. That's how come her arm was dug out. That's what I was told by my grandfather."

"Why didn't anyone see the killer?"

"Grandpa said it was a wicked rainy night. No one with any sense was out. And that was one of the reasons the human got away with it. Not only were no other humans out, the pouring rains washed out all his tracks. You'd be surprised how many human remains we've found over time, all the way back to murders from the colonial era. One of those men is under the Clam parking lot down at UVA. That's what my grandfather told me. Someone killed back in 1781. But these things are always troublesome when they come to light. Best to keep silent."

"Did your grandfather say anything about a horse? Ziggy Flame, Mary Pat's great stallion, disappeared when she did."

"Ziggy was in the high pastures. He lived."

"Hmm." Mrs. Murphy tilted her head to look directly down at one of the cubs, who shrank closer to his mother.

"Is Harry off on one of her toots?" The fox knew Harry could get obsessed.

"Yes." Mrs. Murphy nodded. *"She has more curiosity than I do."*

At that they both laughed, then Mrs. Murphy headed back toward the house. She was disturbed by the thought that some of Mary Pat's bones had been scattered over time. A crow or some small predator must have taken the hand or a finger and dropped it near or in Potlicker Creek, and year after year the ring, finally off the bone, must have inched its way down to where Harry found it. Unless Barry had it. Dropped it. That was equally disquieting.

Being a feline, her senses were much sharper than Harry's, although Mrs. Murphy knew Harry possessed remarkable hearing for a human and was able to hear into some of the cat range. She also possessed a decent nose. But what Harry could never possess was that extrasensory perception that even the lowliest feline had. And that sixth sense was warning Mrs. Murphy that danger was coming closer, closer in a fashion that not even she could suspect.

A startling swoosh overhead sent her crouching, eyes upward.

"Hoo, hoo, HA!" The great owl laughed as she landed.

"Flatface." Mrs. Murphy breathed a sigh of relief.

Flatface lived in the cupola in Harry's barn. She wasn't especially social, but she was more social than the giant black snake who lived up there and had recently taken to interrupting her hunting circle to steal some of Simon's treasures. Simon had saved a perfect little robin's egg, which the black snake took right off his special towel.

But Flatface, like Mrs. Murphy and the vixen, was a predator. It was easy for predators to talk to one another honestly.

They discussed Barry Monteith and Sugar Thierry both having rabies.

"Something over there," Flatface said.

"And if it's over there it may well spread throughout the county."

"That's just it. I asked the red vixen if there were any reports among the foxes. She said no, and same for the raccoons and beaver."

"What about the skunks?"

"It's difficult to ask them." Mrs. Murphy laughed.

"I'll perch in a tree and ask next time I see one." Flatface, true to the myths, was very wise. *"And Sugar had no memory of being bitten?"*

"No."

"The silver-haired bat can bite you and you'd never know it."

"Fair, Paul, and Tavener helped at St. James when the health department went into the cottages, barns, and outbuildings to look for bats and catch them to test them, but I heard—and this is really strange—there were none."

Flatface turned her head almost upside down, then right side up. *"Ah, that gets the kinks out."*

"There are all those caves in the Shenandoah Valley. I mean not just the Luray Caverns but caves all over. Just right up

over these mountains. I know they're full of bats. If you have any friends over there, maybe they could ask the bats if they know about rabies among them."

"No owl will go into those caves. Fetid. Why humans do it is beyond me. The air's not fit to breathe."

"I thought some of them had fresh air piped in."

"Mrs. Murphy, never breathe where there are bat rookeries. This is something every owl learns as an owlet. I pass it on to you." Flatface walked along with Mrs. Murphy for a few paces, her side-to-side rolling gait amusing to the cat, who nonetheless respected how fear-inducing Flatface was in her natural element, the air.

The cat told her about Mary Pat's remains.

"Ah, well, ashes to ashes and dust to dust. That was a long time ago. Before my time or yours." Flatface lifted her head, opening her beak. "Storm. Be here within the hour."

No sooner had she spoken than a light breeze tumbled down the mountains, ruffling Flatface's feathers and lifting up Mrs. Murphy's fur.

"If you do hear anything, tell me." The tiger cat watched as the owl stood to her full height, opening her wings.

Just as Flatface lifted up, she said, *"I will. Now, see if you can't keep Harry from playing detective."*

"I'd be a miracle worker," Mrs. Murphy called up.

"Hoo, hoo, HA."

26

Emotions are messengers." Carmen, her own nails buffed to a high luster, filed down BoomBoom's. "And I realized that the anger I felt was just covering up the sorrow and the loss. Which meant I had a lot of love, and I can love. I just have to get through this."

"What are you going to do?" Boom-Boom leaned back in the comfortable chair, the light jazz music in the background competing with hair dryers and conversation.

"Review my relationships. Not just the last one but all of my relationships with men. My father. My brothers. I have un-realistic expectations." She breathed in through her nose, as a thin, colored cigarette was firmly clamped between her lips. "And I like bad boys. I'll like a nice guy for a while and then I get bored."

Since this was Carmen's beauty parlor, she would damned well smoke if she wanted to and she defied the "health Nazis," as she called them, to stop her.

"Don't we all?" BoomBoom laughed, her bosom, and the reason she endured her nickname, heaving upward.

"I suppose. And I suppose they have some pretty stupid ideas about us." Carmen put BoomBoom's left hand in a slanted bowl so her fingertips would be washed in emollients.

"I know." BoomBoom, born and raised in the country, did know. Having graduated from the University of North Carolina, Chapel Hill, with honors, she was well educated and intelligent. Her major had been English, so if she had not married very well, she could have been taught to do just about anything. However, women as beautiful as BoomBoom always marry well unless they are stone stupid.

Carmen hopped to a variant of her topic: men. "Well, that Dr. Langston is as cute as a bug's ear. He said these days very few doctors can diagnose rabies or even Lyme disease because they mimic other diseases, and he said another hard one is syphilis. He said they all have some things in common, but I said I was a lot more worried about AIDS, and he said he was, too. These little dots of whatever a virus is can evolve quickly. It's like they have intelligence."

"It is strange and frightening." Boom-Boom closed her eyes, her long lashes dark against her suntanned skin.

"Boom," Carmen's voice rose.

"What?"

"Want me to shut up? I can go on, I know. And I'm upset over Sugar dying, so I'm blabbing more than usual. I just open my mouth and whatever I'm thinking pops out."

"I'm thinking, too."

"Boom," Carmen lowered her voice to a whisper, "have you ever been truly in love?"

"In high school." BoomBoom laughed, opening her eyes.

"Who?"

"Charlie Ashcraft. That lasted two months."

"He was gorgeous, though. Died the death he deserved." Carmen snapped her mouth shut like a turtle, for Charlie had seduced and abandoned women for all of his thirty-seven years until it finally caught up with him in the men's locker room at Farmington Country Club. "One has few defenses against such male beauty. People say that about you."

"Oh, that I have male beauty?" Boom-Boom giggled.

"Hey, hold still." Carmen squeezed BoomBoom's right hand tighter. "You know what I mean. Men can't resist you."

"Men are easy. Now, seducing women, that would be a challenge."

"Boom!" Carmen pretended to be scandalized, then lowered her voice again. "Would you?"

"I don't know. All I know is I'm very, very happy alone. Do you know, Carmen, I haven't been alone since I graduated from college? Even after Kelly died, I had one affair after another. This New Year's I made a resolution to take a year off. I might go out, I might date someone steadily, but I am not sleeping with him. I'm not making any promises until I arrive at next New Year's."

A long, long pause followed, then Carmen dipped BoomBoom's right hand into another slanting bowl. She reached for a terry-cloth towel, removed BoomBoom's left hand, rubbed it vigorously. "I don't think I could do it."

"Be alone for a year?"

"I'm too scared."

"Didn't you just say that emotions are messengers?"

"Yes."

"Fear is a big, big messenger. Pay attention. If you listen, fear will bring you courage."

Carmen slathered BoomBoom's left hand in a thick pink cream. "But when I'm alone, things rattle around in my head. I need someone to love me."

"You need *you* to love you. And you know who taught me that without trying?" BoomBoom said as Carmen shook her head. "Harry."

"Harry?"

"When her marriage broke up, she put her head down and kept working. She didn't run out and grab the first man who winked at her. And she's been alone for years now. And she kept her mouth shut. Still does."

"But he still loves her."

"She didn't know that for a good, long year, and that doesn't mean she'll take him back, although he's worked hard at—well, at himself."

"How many years have they been divorced?"

"Umm, four, I think."

"Four years is a long time to be alone."

"Maybe, but you certainly get used to your own company. And while I'm hardly Harry's closest confidant, I think she's learned a lot. I think she has forgiven him and she realizes how much he means to her. Are you putting me in the heated mittens again?"

"I am. While you're sitting there waiting for the color to work"—Carmen had added some lightener to BoomBoom's blond hair—"we might as well go the whole nine yards. I'm going to do your feet, too."

"Full service." BoomBoom wriggled her toes in her sandals. "I'm not in the advice business, but time alone won't hurt you."

"The thing is, if only Barry hadn't gotten himself killed. I kind of thought the relationship was over. But we'd screamed and hollered and thrown things at each other before, and then time would go by and there'd be a full moon." She sighed.

"So you thought maybe you'd find him again during the full moon?" A wry smile played on BoomBoom's full lips.

Carmen shrugged. "Who knows, but now I'll always wonder."

"You're doing the smart thing, reviewing your relationships with men. Everything will sort out; it always does."

The door opened and Tavener Heyward came in for his haircut.

"I don't believe I've ever seen you quite this way." Tavener chuckled as he sat next to BoomBoom.

"Be careful." BoomBoom narrowed her eyes, feigning revenge.

"Oh, I am. We're all careful around you. Beautiful women must be obeyed."

They both laughed, as did Carmen, now slathering BoomBoom's right hand in pink goo. The mittens, plugged in, were just reaching the right temperature.

"Are you going up to Timonium?" Boom-Boom mentioned a regional thoroughbred sale held at the Maryland State Fairgrounds. She didn't discuss Sugar's passing with Tavener, as they'd spoken on the phone early that morning. She'd called about Keepsake, the mare in foal, and the conversation got around to Sugar.

"Thought I'd go take a look at Orion's Sword's babies. I've been tracking this stallion, and if I like the babies, I'm going to try to bring him back to my place. He's a Mr. Prospector grandson, and you can't go wrong there."

"That will give you six stallions. Not that you shouldn't get some Mr. Prospector blood, but, Tavener, you'll need more staff."

"Oh, I know it." He turned his head from BoomBoom to stare in the mirror as Henry Dickie snipped, the silver hairs falling to the ground. "Still, I'll never live down that I didn't buy Ziggy Dark Star when Marshall Kressenberg found him in Kentucky. A full brother to Ziggy Flame, and I foolishly let him get away. Oh, how I have repented my economies."

"You've certainly got some good stallions."

"Well, Captain Kieje put me on the map." Tavener mentioned the stallion, sire of many graded stakes winners. "And, at least, I bought a share in Dark Star. That was something."

The Captain had lived to the ripe old age of twenty-five. His son, Kieje's Crown, was as potent and successful as his sire.

"Tavener, I hope our state fairgrounds, being constructed even as we speak, will look better than Maryland's."

"It will," Tavener said with confidence.

"All the money in the state of Maryland and they build that bland thing in Timonium." She would have thrown up her hands but the mittens were plugged in to an outlet restricting her movement.

"Well, we can tease our Maryland friends all we want about Timonium, but they've got the Maryland Hunt Cup, the Preakness, and some damned good horses."

"Chalk it up to being a border state during the War Between the States." Boom-Boom smiled. "That's when Virginia lost our equine hegemony."

The thoroughbreds, often called blooded horses, led by grooms and women, had walked through two mountain ranges and forded deep, swift rivers to another border state, Kentucky. Given the economic devastation as well as the appalling loss of human and equine life after the war ended, those animals that had managed to avoid consumption never returned. Many were hidden so they wouldn't go to the war.

One could barely even find a mule or donkey after 1865 in Virginia, much less a man between the ages of twelve and seventy who had all his limbs and mind intact.

"We've done precious little to get it back." Tavener, a stalwart on every thoroughbred and racing commission in the state, had fought the good fight for over two decades. When Virginia finally voted to allow racing, they put the track outside of Williamsburg, not the best place at that time. However, the buildings were lovely and the turf track was one of the best in the country. Perhaps in time the population would grow south of Richmond to support the track. It sure was a long haul for horsemen, though, most of whom were in central or northern Virginia.

"Now, you've spearheaded every group, you really led us to racing. And, Tavener, you can't blame yourself for the location of Colonial Downs. No, it isn't convenient to the largest population in our state, which clogs up every artery in northern Virginia."

She smacked her lips. "Occupied Virginia." They laughed and she continued, as Carmen soaked BoomBoom's feet in soothing oil. "But you've done your share."

"If we don't get more Off Track Betting sites, BoomBoom, you can kiss it all goodbye. And I am just tired of fighting these entrenched interests who think gambling will lead us to the devil. The equine industry pumps one billion dollars into our state economy, and if we can expand racing and Off Track Betting, I guarantee another billion in two years' time. I mean it, I'd bet my life on it."

"Now, don't you think foxhunting brings money into the state?"

"I do." His eyes opened wide. "I do, but wagering, BoomBoom, hundreds of thousands of dollars of handle on race days— all to the public good." He used "handle," which meant the money flowing through the betting windows.

"Dr. Heyward, sit still." Henry rapped him on the shoulder with the scissors.

"Sorry. I get hot about this."

"And other things." BoomBoom blew him a kiss just to torment him.

"Whooee." Carmen fanned herself,

adding to the merriment. "Dr. Heyward, Barry always said you ran a tight ship. He said he was going to give you a run for *your* money someday."

"Oh, he did, did he?" Tavener smiled broadly.

"Said he was going to get good stallions, and he already had those mares. He and Sugar—" She stopped. "They had big dreams. He read everything. He said he studied what Mary Pat did, too. He asked questions about her and looked for notes and stuff." She smiled. "But he said you were really, really smart."

"I'm flattered. It's hard to believe they're gone." He snapped his fingers. "You never know."

A silence followed this, then Carmen said, "Barry wanted to know everything. He used to watch you. He said he learned a lot from Fair about reproduction, but he said you knew the blood, knew it in your sleep."

"You watch a lot of horses, you study a lot of pedigrees."

"A little luck never hurts." BoomBoom smiled. "And you had the good fortune to see Mary Pat's organization when you started out."

"Impeccable. Tell you another one I studied: Peggy Augustus. Her mother was good, and Peggy—what an eye, I tell you." He folded his hands under his smock. "Paul Mellon. Any chance I had to drive up there to Upperville, I took it. Another great breeder and a great man. Learn from the best."

The door opened as Little Mim came in, and Pewter scooted right between her legs.

"What the—"

"Pewter, what do you have?" Boom-Boom called out.

"Mine. All mine!" The gray cat dropped a fried chicken wing, then picked it up, hurrying to the supply closet, door open.

Just then Harry pushed through the door, her face red. "Pewter."

"She's not here," Pewter called from the closet.

Carmen pointed to the closet, as did the others.

"Your lunch?" Tavener laughed jovially.

"Worse. Herbie's."

"It's half a block from the post office to here. That's a long haul for such a tubby pussycat." Tavener thought this was pretty funny.

"The Rev is back in the post office blessing her this very minute." Harry strode to the closet. "I see you in there." She stooped down, scooped up the cat, who would not release the chicken wing from her jaws. "God will get you for this, Pewter."

The cat refused to open her mouth.

As Harry left, Tavener laughed and laughed. "Would you like to hear Herb right now? The air is blue. Then he'll remember himself and apologize profusely."

"It's amazing how strong a little animal can be when it's defending itself or wants something." BoomBoom loved all animals.

"That's what upsets me about Barry." Carmen looked up at BoomBoom. "His throat was ripped out. Why didn't he fight? I think there's *something* out there."

"Now, Carmen, don't let your imagination get the better of you," Tavener said soothingly.

27

The old wood from the shed, neatly stacked, bore testimony to Harry's hard work and essential frugality. She wasn't cheap but she saved anything that might be useful, and the boards could repair breaks in the fence line.

Blair's new fence posts, in bundles, rested next to the old wood.

She'd worked each night of the week to dismantle the old shed. The supporting posts she pulled out with her tractor, then filled in the holes with pounded rock dust.

At five-thirty Saturday morning, June 19, she fed the new mares, as well as Tomahawk, Poptart, and Gin Fizz. Her tea steamed from the small slit in her carrying cup as she put it down on the desk in the tack room. The mice, sound asleep behind the tack trunk, didn't stir.

Harry's favorite time, early morning, was shared by Mrs. Murphy and Tucker. Pewter liked breakfast, but she wasn't by nature an early riser. Today she awoke, ate, then curled up on the kitchen chair, her tail covering her nose.

"Mrs. Murphy! What a good girl you are." Harry held up a dead mouse.

"Thank you." Mrs. Murphy had caught a field mouse and put it on the tack-room desk.

Harry didn't know where the mouse came from, but she believed her barn was being expertly patrolled.

Harry placed the mouse on the floor. She'd take it outside and bury it as soon as she checked her barn list. Each evening, her last chore in the barn was making tomorrow's list. A big notepad with different colors of paper sat on the left-hand back corner. Each day she pulled off a different color; today's was neon yellow. That way she wouldn't confuse her chores. It irritated her to carry one day's chores to the next day. She felt she had failed or, worse, had been idle.

"Idle hands do the devil's work." This phrase looped through her head regularly, for she had heard it since childhood from her grandparents and her parents.

"Hmm." Mrs. Murphy read the list with Harry as she was sitting in Harry's lap. *"You'd better stake out the outside wall of your shed before you start digging new post holes."*

Tucker guarded the dead mouse. *"We should put this under Pewter's chair, then listen to her fib about how she killed it. She can tell stories."*

"She's an honest cat until it comes to hunting. Even a fisherman can't keep up with her lies." Mrs. Murphy laughed, the distinctive odor of dark tea curling into her nostrils.

Harry's list ran in two parallel columns. The left-hand column was the chores she needed to accomplish. The right-hand column was the calls she needed to make.

"All right, let's go stake this thing."

"She listened." Tucker's ears pricked up.

"Luck, plus it's the obvious thing to do."

Harry scooped up the mouse, buried it under the big lilac bush. Since it was a little mouse this took two minutes. Then she

grabbed a ball of chalk-impregnated orange twine out of the truck. She'd bought
the twine at the building-supply store. She
had enough odd wood bits to make stakes.

She walked over to the site. "All right,
you two, the trick is to double the size of
the old shed and enclose ten feet by
twenty feet for tools. I want a workbench, a
band saw, and Peg-Board, too. Everything
up on the wall, and I'll put in a sturdy door
that I can lock. Might as well do it right.
And I've still got three huge bays, so I can
put the dually and horse trailer in the shed
with my tractor. Guess I can put the old
Ford truck in, too, but it's so handy to have
that truck by the back door. Oh, this is exciting. And a standing seam tin roof, yes."

She'd totaled up her sums and knew she
could afford it, because Tazio, as clever as
she was brilliant—the two qualities being
unrelated—had been squirreling away
odds and ends from her other jobs.

Harry would need to pay for the roof,
gutters, and downspouts, but other than
that, she and Tazio had scavenged the
other materials, including two windows for
the toolroom/workroom.

At eight in the morning, Tazio, Cooper,

Blair, and Paul showed up to help. Susan came around ten with a cooler full of fried chicken, macaroni salad, sandwiches, cookies, and a second cooler with drinks. Fair was on call that weekend, so he couldn't be there.

Butterflies floated overhead. Robins sang as goldfinches and cardinals darted from tree limb to tree limb. The noisy bluejay contented himself by squawking at Pewter, who, now wide awake, was watching the workers from the open door of the hayloft.

"I will kill that bird if it's the last thing I do," Pewter swore.

Simon, playing with a broken Pelham chain that once hung on Gin Fizz's bit, one of his many treasures, said, *"Ignore him. He's a blowhard."*

Mrs. Murphy, hidden under enormous peonies, all of them blooming late because of the unusually cool, long spring, stifled a laugh. The bluejay, intent on tormenting Pewter, swooped in front of the gray cat, then dove like a fighter jet to the lilac bush that was at the corner of the yard by the back door. The peonies, which should have been in a better line, meandered out across the lawn. Mrs. Murphy's big showy white ones were near the lilac bush.

"Stupid fat cat!" the handsome bluejay rasped, then hopped from the lilac bush to the newly mown lawn. He strutted and screamed more obscenities. He walked straight toward the white peonies, his tail feathers spread and his head high.

Like lightning, Mrs. Murphy sprang from her hiding place, one swift paw slamming onto his tail, but he was quick. He twisted and narrowly escaped, leaving Mrs. Murphy with two long blue-striped tail feathers.

"You almost got him!" Pewter, in her excitement, leaned too far out the hayloft opening and began to fall. Her sharp claws dug into the wood and she hung on, finally hauling herself up.

"Pewts, I would have broken your fall," Tucker, now looking straight up, promised.

"Thank God for claws." The gray cat breathed a long sigh.

"I'd have made a hole in the dirt," Simon said. *"My claws aren't that good."*

"Bet he doesn't come back for a while." Mrs. Murphy, fur fluffed, laughed.

"I hate that bird." Pewter stomped to the hayloft ladder, turned around, and backed

down, rung by rung. She joined Tucker and Mrs. Murphy outside. *"How's it going?"*

"Framing goes fast. Even got the roof joists up. Now, Mom had to buy those, you know. It's easier to buy them than make them. By tomorrow night, weather permitting, they'll have the siding up, T-111. Mom will put batten boards on the T-111 to make it look better. Then all that's left to do will be the sheathing on the roof. Roofer can't get here until the middle of the week. They're all pounding and talking." Tucker liked being around humans when they were happy. *"Every time Tazio drops something, Brinkley brings it to her. He's smart, that Lab, besides being big and strong."*

The three friends sauntered over. Brinkley, head in a big water bucket there just for him, enjoyed the cool water. He lifted his head up, licking his lips. *"Isn't this something?"*

"Yes. Mom's going to paint it that dark green, Charleston green. She says the dark green holds up better than black paint. She doesn't like black sheds." Tucker had covered herself in paint last time Harry painted the eaves of the barn.

"When will they break for lunch?" Pewter focused on the important stuff.

"Soon." Brinkley wagged his tail.

Blair called out from his perch to the others, "Hey, let's eat. We've been hard at it."

"Guess he heard you," Brinkley told Pewter.

"I'm sure." Pewter dashed to the cooler, which Susan was opening.

"Do you all want to eat in the kitchen?" Harry asked.

"It's so beautiful today. Let's eat right here. Our own picnic." Susan spread a tablecloth on the ground and, with help from Tazio, placed the food on it.

Outdoor work made them all very happy, Pewter especially. Soon the humans were eating and sharing tidbits with the cats and dogs.

"Coop, what's your schedule this week?" Susan asked.

"Mornings. I actually have the evenings to myself. I wish the county would hire more law-enforcement officers, though. We're all working overtime. The money's good, but I have no life. I can't believe I actually have off every evening this week. I can buy groceries. I can get my hair cut. I can mow the lawn." She grinned.

"I'll mow your lawn," Blair offered.

Cooper, who found Blair very attractive, smiled. "That's the best offer I've had in years."

"Not only will I mow it, I'll edge your walkways and whatever. Bought a new edger yesterday." He smiled.

No one said what they were thinking, which was, "How would Little Mim take this?"

Paul, next to Tazio, reached for mustard. "Harry, the mares look good."

"They've settled in. Hey, did anyone look at the Weather Channel?"

"Storms tonight," Susan succinctly answered.

"That one in the beginning of the week kind of brushed us. Thought it would be much worse. The weathermen overdo." Tazio ate a crunchy sweet gherkin.

"There will be a raindrop in Richmond. It will be two miles wide!" Susan mocked.

Harry made a mental note to ask Blair about his property when they were finished today. She didn't want anyone else to over-hear, not because she felt they would be indiscreet but because she'd promised Herb to be delicate in the matter.

They caught up on gossip, traded opinions about their favorite baseball teams.

Tazio, on her third pickle, asked, "Coop, any progress about Barry?"

Harry reached for the pickle jar.

"No. I keep hoping we'll get a break. We did do one thing, though, for which I thank Fair. He tested each of the mares to make sure they were what Barry and Sugar said they were—you know, had the correct bloodlines. And when the babies come next year, he'll test them."

"He didn't tell me." Harry was surprised.

"And?" Paul's dark eyebrows raised up.

"He called me this morning on my way over," Cooper replied. "Said they were legit."

"But wouldn't someone find out? I mean soon enough?" Blair, not a horseman, was puzzled.

"Yes. But if the paperwork were faked and, say, Person A bought a mare, he might not know he was duped until the foal was born. The owner would go to register the foal, thinking she was a granddaughter of Secretariat, and find out otherwise. Then they'd take saliva to check the DNA from the mare and discover she wasn't what the seller said she was."

"But the owner would come right back on Barry and Sugar," Harry declared.

"If they were still in town," Coop laconically replied.

"Barry wouldn't do that. Sugar neither. I can't believe they would." Paul defended them. "I'm new to Crozet, but I think they were straight up."

"They were," Harry simply responded.

"I have to track down any and every possibility."

"Do you think Barry's murder has something to do with his business, then?" Harry shrewdly asked.

"Well"—Cooper paused and held her breath, while everyone stared at her—"it might prove a fruitful avenue. He wasn't alcoholic, no drugs—maybe a joint occasionally, I heard, but a pretty clean guy. No gambling debts. His debt was on the property he rented. He'd paid for the mares outright, he and Sugar. He paid for his truck outright. He hadn't paid for the stud fees, but as I understand it those aren't due until the foal stands and nurses." Coop looked at Harry.

"Right."

"So what's left?" Tazio held up her hands, a pickle in the left one.

"Business or romance?" Coop reached for another piece of fried chicken.

"Carmen. She's got a temper but not that bad." Susan laughed.

"We'll find out. It takes time." Coop had faith in herself and in Sheriff Rick Shaw.

"I think it's connected to Mary Pat." Harry opened a can of Coke.

Everyone looked at Harry, waiting for more. She smiled and shrugged.

She decided not to say more, but she thought, Mary Pat disappeared with Ziggy Flame in 1974. Thirty years later a young man, infected with rabies, is killed. He was just starting out in the breeding business, but Barry definitely had the gift. Did he find out what happened to Ziggy Flame? Did something occur to him as he pored over bloodlines, walked St. James Farm, visited the sales? And if he found out what happened to Ziggy, surely Mary Pat's killer would be in Ziggy Flame's shadow.

28

Silvery mist enveloped the sleeping countryside. A faint gray light on the eastern horizon announced dawn, dragging in its wake a new day, bright as a freshly minted copper penny. Church bells would not call the faithful to service for hours on this Sunday morning.

Alicia Palmer learned to awaken before dawn when she lived with Mary Pat, who was a happy early riser. This chore became a habit, one that served her well in her glory days in Hollywood, where she'd be ensconced in the makeup chair at five-thirty in the morning.

Fence lines hugged rolling terrain and rambling roses spilled over road banks as Alicia walked down the long curving drive toward the graceful brick pillars, whose twelve-foot wrought-iron gates stood open.

If Alicia reversed her walk, the drive, lined with majestic pin oaks, would fork, one half twisting toward the outbuildings and barns. The other half of the Y, the left prong, swung to the main house.

Alicia stopped at the juncture of the Y, the house and barns enshrouded in mist. Although beautiful, a ghostly aura permeated St. James: it was never the same without Mary Pat.

The cool tang of the morning, of the rambling roses, filled her nostrils. She'd loved St. James as much as she'd loved Mary Pat. She'd been young here, full of energy, pride, and naïveté. She wondered that she could ever have been that young, and yet here she was standing at her favorite spot, standing where she stood at age twenty-five. What a trickster time is.

Tears filled Alicia's luminous eyes. She leaned against the white fence and thought if she closed her eyes Ziggy Flame would gallop over to her. Ziggy, being surprisingly tractable for a stallion, favored Alicia.

The untractable creature was Mary Pat,

a woman who lived at full blast. During her life Alicia had met the rich and powerful of Hollywood and, by extension, the political hangers-on eager for vote magnets, yet none of them ever measured up to Mary Pat. The sheer raw energy of her could become an irritant as people tried to keep up physically and intellectually.

Alicia realized early on she could keep up physically but not intellectually. She didn't mind. She'd never thought of herself as particularly bright, but she was sensitive.

"A thorn was given me in the flesh," Alicia mouthed the words from Second Corinthians, Chapter 12, Verse 7.

Miranda had quoted the Scripture to her in relation to the Japanese beetles currently invading her garden.

Alicia felt that the thorn in her flesh was the memory of Mary Pat. If she'd been more attentive, if she'd been less ambitious, she knew in her heart all would have been well. She felt a vague and growing guilt. If she'd stayed, she believed, Mary Pat would never have been killed. She left for her screen test and returned to desolation and accusation.

She could prove nothing. Not her innocence nor lack of complicity. She had only her own sensitivity for a guide, that same sensitivity that had made her one of the best actresses of her generation. The star part of her life meant nothing to her. Being a fine actress meant something.

Nostalgia overwhelmed her. A slash of pink illuminated the eastern sky. Mary Pat used to say, "Live each day as though it were your last."

Echoes from the past seemed louder in the fog. Alicia felt the fog would lift in all respects.

29

While everyone else returned to work on Monday, Fair Haristeen, who'd been on call during the weekend, was still working. Fortunately, he loved his work, but this afternoon he was tired.

Priscilla Freidberg and her daughter, Dharam, had saved a lovely thoroughbred mare from the killers. So many good animals wound up on the knacker's wagon to be hauled to the slaughterhouse because people could no longer afford them if they couldn't run. Thoroughbred, standardbred, and quarter-horse racing, while exciting, led to heartbreak back at the shed row. Horses were run too young in America, the fault of punitive taxes and rising prices. Few could afford to keep a horse until three to run him. The youngsters would go out as two-year-olds. The people in Washington, responsible for much of this, would then turn around and consider passing legislation to protect the animals at the end of their careers. If they'd considered how very different and difficult raising stock was, this would never happen in the first place. The suffering should be laid at Congress's door.

Fair, like most large-animal practitioners, honed his contempt for government over the years. What would a bunch of urban politicos know about country life? Nor did they care. The votes were in the big cities.

The rescued mare suffered a high bowed tendon, which turnout in the pasture would cure in six months or more. A low bow usually had a better prognosis, but this mare would be fine. Bowed tendons occur on the back side of a horse's foreleg: Hemorrhage and inflammation cause swelling and adhesions to develop between the tendon and its sheath. The swelling is visible to the human eye and warm to the touch.

"Pasture rest. She'll be fine in six months. Call me back then, just before you start her in work."

People like Priscilla and Dharam saved what animals they could working with thoroughbred-rescue operations. This mare, a typey bay who could have stepped out of a George Stubbs's painting, might have been a touch slow on the track, plus she bowed in heavy going, but she had a winning attitude.

"Dr. Haristeen, I'm thinking about vet school after I graduate," Dharam said.

"You see wonderful things and terrible things in this business. And you see wonderful and terrible people, but all in all, I wouldn't trade one minute of my life as a vet. Not one." He cleared his throat and turned as the white Jeep with the county seal drove down the gravel drive. "Well, maybe this one." He sighed. "Better go get your paperwork. All your rabies paperwork, Priscilla. Jerome is on a major tear."

Without a word, Priscilla dashed into the small office in the barn as her daughter's eyebrows raised. The sight of Jerome slamming the door of the county car provoked no comment. They'd talk plenty after he left.

"Jerome, I can't get away from you." Fair

smiled, as he'd encountered Jerome twice over the weekend.

It seemed Jerome wasn't taking the weekend off.

"Fair, had a thought since yesterday."

"Only one?" Fair's lips curled slightly.

Jerome ignored this and asked, "Could you lie about giving rabies shots?"

This took Fair by surprise, so he thought a moment. "Sure. But what would be the point?"

"Money."

"Money. How could I make money faking the paperwork?"

"Easy. You don't put out for the vaccine. You'd pocket the cash for the paperwork, right? How would your patient know whether they were actually getting the vaccine or just a placebo?"

"Hopefully by my reputation," Fair replied evenly.

"Oh, I don't mean you personally. But it's possible?"

"It's possible, but first let me explain that even the small-animal veterinarians aren't getting rich off rabies shots. An equine vet pays two dollars per large animal dose. They pay for the syringe and needles. The first shot usually costs the customer about fifteen dollars, here in central Virginia. Figure in the gas cost to drive to the various farms, too. Don't forget taxes. Even if a vet managed to give one hundred rabies shots a week, which is extremely doubtful, he'd pocket seven hundred fifty dollars at best. Only a fool would risk his practice for a piddling sum like that. And more to the point, Jerome, I think I can speak for every veterinarian in Virginia. Rabies is a matter of public health, human health, not just cats, dogs, horses, cattle. Who would be that irresponsible? That would be criminal."

Jerome scuffed the dirt with his boot. "Well, Fair, I'm heading that way. This is criminal."

"What do you mean?"

"Barry and Sugar. What if a doctor gave them a shot of live virus, not killed?"

Fair's eyes widened. "That's monstrous."

"All a doctor or some smart person would have to do is put saliva from a rabid animal into a syringe and shoot it into someone, not even into their bloodstream.

I've been doing my reading. Just shoot it into the muscle. It would get to the nerve endings soon enough and start that long journey to the brain."

Fair shook his head. "The victims would remember getting a shot."

"Barry couldn't tell anyone anything. As for Sugar, his mind was going, wasn't it? And it's not like he would have known. He might have thought he was getting a flu shot or that Lyme-disease shot that's questionable. Some say it works and some say it don't. Bill Langston, Hayden McIntire, a nurse friend—anyone could give a flu shot."

Dharam and Priscilla walked over. "Jerome, I believe you want our rabies certificates."

Jerome grunted. "Thanks." He rifled through the sheets of paper. "What about your cats and dogs?"

"Uh, I've got those up at the house. I'll be right back." Priscilla knew from her friends that Jerome was being a stickler about all this.

"I'll get it, Mom."

"We'll both go." Priscilla had noted the

intense conversation between the two men.

Jerome returned to his subject. "The other thing about a needle. If those guys thought they were getting a flu shot, by the time the rabies showed up there's no needle mark. Slick."

"Tell you what. Why don't you come to my office Wednesday? Let's sit down and go over this and I'll help you. I'm not saying your thesis is wrong. I suppose it could be done. Have you asked other vets?"

"Every single one I see."

"Well, what have you heard?"

"Like you, they wondered about getting a live virus, but when I talked about saliva they listened. No one outright said it wouldn't work, although everyone thought it was"—he paused—"far-fetched."

"I guess what keeps crossing my mind is, why?"

"That's easy. Rabies is one hundred percent fatal."

"I know that." Fair tried not to be irritated. "But surely there are easier ways to kill someone, if we even knew that those two men were killed. There's no reason to think Sugar was murdered."

"You don't know that."

"You're right, I don't," Fair conceded.

"See, what I think is that this is a fine way to get rid of someone. They wouldn't know what hit them and they'd never think of their flu shot or whatever carrying rabies. They'd die long after their shot."

"Jesus, it'd be a lot more humane to pull the trigger." Fair whistled.

"This ain't about being humane."

"No, no, it isn't." Fair watched the two tall women, folders in hands, emerge from the back door of the house. "Now you've got me wondering. Well, look, I'll see you Wednesday and that will give me time to make a couple of calls. My old professor at Auburn ought to have some thoughts about this."

"Talked to Hayden McIntire, Bill Langston, Tavener, Dr. Flynn, Dr. Cowles, all the vets. Kinda got them interested, too." Jerome puffed out his chest. "And Sheriff Shaw. See, Fair, I see the bottom of the barrel, a lot. I know how those people think."

"People who mistreat animals aren't necessarily killers. I know they're the bottom of the barrel, but killers, I don't know."

"People who disrespect living things or disrespect the law, I know how they think. We got a situation here." Jerome's eyes blazed.

30

Tuesday after work, Harry nimbly walked along the spine of her new shed roof. Fair, Blair, Paul, Susan, Tazio, and BoomBoom, who was able to help today, stuck to their promise to help. The T-111 siding with batten added for looks had yet to be painted, and it emitted a fresh lumber odor. Harry had splurged on a standing seam tin roof. Mrs. Murphy trotted behind Harry, since she wasn't afraid of heights either.

Tazio, Paul, Blair, and Susan taped the seams of the Sheetrock inside Harry's workroom. She'd put in insulation and a small gas flame stove that looked just like a wood-burning fireplace, which she carefully vented. Harry wanted to experiment in the coming winter to see if gas heat was effective and if it was cheaper. She was very interested in the cost of operating the stove. If it worked she might put one in her bedroom, since that side of the house was bitterly cold in wintertime. Also, if the power cut out, she'd still have heat.

Paul couldn't live without music. His boom box played Latino tunes. Harry almost always worked in silence so she could listen to every animal around her, the wind come up, whatever, but she found she liked Paul's music. And she liked Paul.

Tucker sprang to her feet, followed by Brinkley. They ran down the drive.

"Intruder!" Tucker announced.

Brinkley asked, *"How do you know it's an intruder?"*

"I don't, but I have to do my job, you know."

Pewter, who had joined Mrs. Murphy on the roof, observed the Lab's one stride to Tucker's three. She started to giggle.

Mrs. Murphy's eyes followed Pewter's gaze and she giggled, too. *"Let's just say that Tucker can turn inside Brinkley. You've got to give her that."*

"I do," Pewter replied. *"Here comes*

Tavener. It's about time he buys himself a new truck."

Equine and cattle vets could easily rack up forty thousand miles a year in Virginia making calls. A very good vet, which Tavener was, would cover his own county and adjoining counties, plus he would be called out of state for special consulting jobs. On any given day Tavener or Fair might find themselves down at Blacksburg at Virginia Tech or up at Leesburg at the Marion duPont Scott Equine Center, two outstanding hospital facilities.

Tavener's Ford, a 1996 diesel engine, labored with over 320,000 miles on the speedometer. Strong as a work truck is, sooner or later the owner is going to pour money into brakes, clutch cables, maybe even a replaced piston. Tavener wasn't cheap, but he'd get attached to a vehicle and then complain bitterly if he had to adjust to a new one, because there was always something different. He did not regard items like air bags or wishbone suspension as improvements.

The two dogs stopped as the truck pulled up to the shed.

Tucker, wishing to teach the young Lab,

who had just turned a year old, said, *"Never take your eyes off the human until your human indicates it's okay."*

"But it's Tavener."

"That doesn't matter, Brinkley. The only people you don't guard are family members or best, best friends. For instance, I wouldn't stare down Susan. But I even follow BoomBoom until Harry says 'Hello' or something. A dog can't be too careful. And you have to remember—I know I keep repeating this to you—human senses are dull. It's not just their eyes or nose, but they shut down their feelings. They miss so much."

"That doesn't make much sense." The yellow Lab wagged his tail as Tavener smiled at them.

"Don't tell me you're going to break a sweat." Fair, who'd just come up on the roof, laughed as he looked down at his colleague.

"You're right." Tavener laughed, too.

"There's room up here on the roof. I don't want you to feel lonesome down there. I'm checking the crimping on the seams," Harry called to him as the other people stuck their heads out of the work-room to greet the genial vet.

"Okay, now we can tag along." Tucker bounced up to Tavener, who scratched her ears.

"Keeping everyone in line, Tucker?" Tavener sternly regarded her.

"Indeed."

"Me, too." Brinkley offered a paw.

"Dog's are so-o-o obsequious." Pewter sniffed.

"They can't help it, Pewter. They're pack animals. So are humans. It's why they get along like they do," Mrs. Murphy sagely noted.

Pewter shrugged, a thinly disguised air of superiority. *"Well, not everyone can be a cat."*

"Hey, look at that." Mrs. Murphy quickly walked to the edge of the roof, turned around, and backed down the ladder.

Tavener had lifted from the back of his truck a long, thin package wrapped in butcher paper. A verdigris pole could be seen sticking out from the bottom.

Harry hurried down the ladder, Pewter perched on her shoulders. Pewter could back down a ladder if she had to; she did it in the barn often enough, but that ladder was nailed to the wall. Under these circumstances, hitching a ride with Harry was preferable.

"Harry, you need this." Tavener beamed as he handed her the package.

She knelt down, carefully placing it on the grass, and the others gathered around. Fair finally climbed off the roof to join in.

"Oh, Tavener. This is just about perfect." Harry stood up and hugged him.

"*A cat weather vane!*" Mrs. Murphy thought this an excellent present.

The hunt horses, curious, watched from the paddock.

Gin Fizz said, *"Don't get the big head, pussycats."*

"You have your weather vane on the barn," Pewter sang out. *"We do just as much work in the barn as anyone."*

"Pewter, how can you lie like that and keep a straight face?" Tomahawk sounded stentorian.

The other horses laughed, including the broodmares who had come up from the adjoining paddock.

"What about me?" Tucker cocked her head. *"I protect every animal on this farm."*

"You're right." Brinkley was very sympathetic.

Tavener, as if understanding, opened the passenger door to his truck and lifted out a three-by-three-foot hand-painted sign. Against a Charleston green background was Tucker's head, a beautiful likeness. A thin red and gold pinstripe border was painted one inch from the edge of the sign. And underneath Tucker's likeness, neatly lettered in Roman bold, was, DEATH FROM THE ANKLES DOWN!

Harry laughed so hard, Fair had to catch her under the armpits before she fell over.

"Wherever . . . ?" BoomBoom fell in love with the sign.

"Tree Street Signs over in Stuart's Draft. Course, there's Burruss in Charlottesville. Those are the two best, but I've grown fond of the group over in Stuart's Draft. I couldn't resist! Harry, you need to warn any newcomer of your security system." He laughed heartily.

"We've got to get one for Herb for his anniversary." Susan clapped her hands together. "How about his two cats with halos over their heads?"

"Susan, do you think all the parishioners will like that?" Tazio wondered.

"Oh, look, if you're going to be a Lutheran you might as well have a sense of humor. Anyone who tries to understand centuries of dogma better get a grip," Susan forthrightly replied.

Paul laughed and shrugged. "I'm Catholic."

"And whatever Little Mim is at the moment, I am. We're leaning toward refurbished Episcopalianism." Blair admired the sign. "Harry, do you want this hanging as a sign by the back door, or do you want it on the side of the house by the back door?"

"Hanging." She couldn't get over how delightful these gifts were. She hugged Tavener again, giving him a big kiss on the cheek.

"Luckily, we've got a four-by-four left over. Bet I can build you a pretty signpost in no time," Fair volunteered.

"How about a Coke or a beer or something?" Harry offered Tavener.

"Beer. You wouldn't have any St. Pauli Girl in there, would you?"

Susan handed him one. "You know, you and I ought to buy stock in the brewery."

"Good idea." Tavener took a deep pull. "I came bearing gifts, but I came with a mission. Alicia and I have been talking." Tavener paused for a moment. "Alicia and Big Mim have agreed. Oh, Herb has agreed. And Harry, finding the ring started all of this, really. Got me to thinking. What would Mary Pat have loved best? So many things crossed my mind, but you know, I hit on the right one. I hit on the thing that would have made her so proud. If all of us put in some money, whatever you can afford, we could create a scholarship in Mary Pat's name to be awarded each year to a senior graduating from Holy Cross and going on to college. Mim says she knows how to set it up so our money will make money in the stock market. This way we only have to give once." He held up his hand. "She swears she knows how to do this. But I want all of us who benefited from Mary Pat's kindness to pitch in."

"That's all of Crozet." Susan smiled. "Ned and I will certainly be part of it."

The others agreed, even Paul and Tazio.

"But you all never knew her," Harry said.

"We can give a little something," Paul said. "A scholarship, that's special." He asked Tavener, "What would the student have to do?"

"Oh, not so much *do* but *be*. A leader. A good student, maybe not the best student but good. I was thinking maybe it would be a young person who was planning a career in the equine industry."

"She'd love that," Harry enthused.

Pewter had heard enough about all this. *"Let's put the weather vane on the shed."*

No one paid much mind.

"Sit on the weather vane," Mrs. Murphy counseled.

Pewter, with much ceremony, plopped on the pretty metal cat.

Harry reached down and picked her up, making a large groaning noise that Pewter did not find amusing.

Fair lifted up the weather vane. "I'm going to put this right up."

"Told you," Mrs. Murphy bragged.

"Before you get back up on the ladder, Jerome been bugging you, too?" asked Tavener.

"I can't turn around without bumping into him." Fair laughed. "I could kill him."

"Me, too, and not feel a twinge of guilt. He overstepped the line. He called the

Centers for Disease Control in Atlanta, and in the process of asking for information about rabies, where had it shown up this spring and so forth, he apparently told them we have a human epidemic."

"What?" Fair's jaw dropped.

"Bill Langston called me and said his phone has been ringing off the hook."

"What does it mean exactly?" Paul inquired. "That he called the Centers for Disease Control?"

"For one thing, the state veterinarian will be here tomorrow." Tavener sighed. "A good man, but we're all busy as can be and he's going to want to see each of us. And for another thing, the head of Public Health will get his butt over from Richmond, and might I remind you this is an election year. He'll chew out the county health officials, all of whom properly did their jobs. God only knows what will happen if some genius candidate gets hold of this. Remember years ago"—he directed this to Harry, Fair, Susan, and Boom-Boom—"when old Richard Deavers went crackers? For you all"—he indicated Blair, Tazio, and Paul—"Richard Deavers had money, and when he lost his mind he decided that humans were abusing animals because they didn't wear clothes. They were ashamed of their nakedness just like we were when expelled from the Garden of Eden. Anyway, to make a long story short, he must have spent hundreds of thousands of dollars trying to get legislation passed that would force us to put clothes on cats, dogs, horses, cattle, and so on. Some people believed him. Some of them put a new twist on it: nakedness encouraged human immorality. My God, what a mess. We finally voted it down as a state—not local, mind you, but state—referendum. Well, we could be in for something that ridiculous if Jerome Stoltfus isn't sat down hard."

31

No!" Harry uttered the forbidden word through clenched teeth. "No, I won't do it."

Southerners are taught from infancy a variety of ways to decline without saying no outright. It's considered bad manners to be so blunt. Furthermore, anyone who forces you into a true D no—a true D being a Southern expression that means the ultimate—is forever despised by you. They should know better. If they're a Northerner, who prizes directness, they are doubly despised, first because they pushed you and second because they lack all subtlety and don't appreciate same.

Miranda's eyes about popped from her head. Her hand flew to her mouth.

"Now, Harry, you can understand that

these are unusual circumstances." Pug Harper's voice remained genial.

Having heard the no, Pug, born and bred in Albemarle County, knew he had mortally offended one of his best people.

Jerome Stoltfus knew it also, but he didn't care. "I spent this whole Wednesday morning with the state veterinarian and people from the Health Department. Can't be having pets in public places."

Pug wanted to smash Jerome. "Harry, this will all calm down. Just for the next few weeks."

Jerome flared up. "Few weeks, hell. Animals got no place in a federal building. Says neither rain, nor sleet, nor snow or whatever will keep you from your appointed rounds. Doesn't say anything about cats and dogs. From the looks of it, that fat gray thing couldn't even get to the corner, much less your appointed rounds."

"I resent that!" Pewter spat.

Mrs. Murphy, sitting next to Pewter in the mail cart, concurred. *"Jerome, we can scratch your eyes out before you know what hit you."*

"And I can bite you until you bleed!"

Tucker, standing foursquare in front of Harry, meant every word.

"That dog's growling at me. That dog's vicious. I can impound Tucker, you know."

"For Christ's sake, Jerome," Pug, at the end of his rope, hissed, "there has never been a vicious Pembroke corgi in the history of man!"

This stopped Jerome for a moment.

"Pug, I like you. I think you are a fine postmaster, and the volume of mail in this county has tripled in the last five years. You've done a wonderful job coping with that, plus the federal rules, which would stop Einstein. But I am not removing Mrs. Murphy, Pewter, and Tucker from the post office. I mean it." Harry put her hands on her hips.

"Then I'll write you a citation." Jerome smacked his hands together.

"Will you kindly shut up!" Pug raised his voice. "Harry, Richmond's in an uproar. The damned media will get their teeth into the story. Crozet, Rabies Capital of America." He sighed.

"I gave Jerome my paperwork. Dr. Shulman can vouch for the splendid health of my family. I won't do it."

"I can put you in jail. I can impound your animals. You have contempt for public health. For the public good." Jerome was on a roll.

Pug wheeled on him, but Miranda intervened. "This is dicey. We can all see that, but, Pug," she lowered her voice, "you are going to muster out these two little kitties and this adorable and very helpful puppy when the new building is completed, aren't you?"

Pug blanched. "Now, I didn't say that but, well, there will be a new set of workers, you know, and if Harry brings her animals they'll want to bring theirs. It will be like a zoo."

"It's against the law." Jerome, not necessarily relishing Harry's discomfort, finally was in a position of some power. It went right to his head.

Harry, in control of herself, said quite calmly, "Pug, I guess I knew this was coming."

"But that won't be for at least seven months, given building delays—you know how that is—a year. But for now, take these guys home, will you?"

"For good." Jerome snapped his lips shut, the lower one slightly jutting outward.

Harry looked at Miranda, whose eyes brimmed with sympathy, then she turned back to Pug. "I'm afraid you're going to have to run the P.O. today. I quit."

"Me, too." Miranda scooped up Pewter as Harry picked up Mrs. Murphy.

Tucker, thrilled, strutted in front of the humans as they walked out the back door.

"Aren't you going to fire her?" Jerome prodded.

"Fire her? She just quit, you complete and utter asshole!" Pug clenched his fists. He wanted to smash in Jerome's face.

Jerome took a step backward. "She'll be crawling back. She'll be here tomorrow. She has to work for a living. What would she do without the post office?"

"You don't know Harry very well, do you?" The square-built man jammed his hands in his pockets. "She won't be back. She won't ask for her job back, and you just cost me one of my very best people. She's never late for work. She's never even missed a day's work, and neither has Miranda. You don't find people like that every day."

Jerome shrugged. "She was breaking the rules."

"We've got too many rules in this damned country, and you know why, Jerome? So assholes like you can get a job enforcing them. God knows, no one else would hire your sorry ass. Now, if you need your mail, pick it up. Otherwise, get out of my sight before I lose all semblance of restraint."

Jerome skedaddled out the front door.

Harry slid behind the wheel of her truck, parked at the rear of the small brick building.

"Move over," Miranda ordered her.

"Why?"

"I'm driving."

"Why?"

"You're too upset to drive. I don't want you to have an accident. Go on, move over."

It wasn't until that exact moment that Harry realized how much Miranda loved her. She burst into tears.

"Ah, Mom, it will be okay." Mrs. Murphy, on her hind paws, put her front paws on Harry's shoulders.

Pewter licked Harry's left hand, while Tucker licked her right hand.

"Home?"

"Fair's."

Miranda turned over the old 1978 Ford, the V-8 engine rumbling deep, pleasing notes. The old pickup was running on its eleventh set of tires, fourth set of brakes, third clutch cable, and a brand-new exhaust and muffler. Ran like a top.

Within ten minutes, Miranda pulled into Haristeen Equine Clinic.

Harry noticed a white truck with the state emblem on the side. "Miranda, I think the state vet is here. I'd better not bother him."

Just then the state vet, a tall man, not much more than thirty-four, ambled out and climbed into his truck.

When he drove off, Harry and Miranda walked into the clinic, and Harry no sooner saw Fair than she started bawling.

"Skeezits, what's wrong?" Fair hurried over to her, calling Harry by an old nickname, wrapping his strong arms around her.

"*Quit,*" Pewter succinctly said.

Miranda spoke since Harry couldn't at

that moment. "Oh, Fair, that Jerome Stolt-fus has opened Pandora's box. What a mess. He's got everyone in an uproar, and Pug Harper came into the post office with Jerome. He told Harry the kitties and doggy had to go. For a time. But then I asked him if that wasn't really going to be permanent when the new building was up. He said as much."

"I won't work without my babies," Harry wailed.

"Are we babies?" Tucker thought for a moment.

"Tucker, she's upset. We're her partners and friends," Mrs. Murphy reasonably said.

"I won't. I quit. I can't live like that, Fair. I know millions of people get up, go to offices, sit in front of computer screens, but I've only got this one life and it may be kind of a small life but, still, it's my life. I'm not living like that. I want to be with my animals and I want"—she caught her breath, then said with vigor—"to be outside. Working in the post office was too much inside as it was."

"I understand." He held her tight. "Miranda, what about you?"

Alma, Fair's secretary, discreetly stayed behind the reception desk.

"I quit, too." Miranda smiled broadly. "Times are changing."

"Guess they always were. I mean, I guess someone thought that in fifth century B.C." Harry was recovering.

Alma softly inquired, "Mrs. Haristeen, could I fetch you some water or coffee?"

"Alma." Harry wiped her eyes. "I would love a Co-Cola. I think I cried myself into dehydration."

"Come on, let's sit down." Fair propelled her to the sofa.

Miranda followed.

"You've got patients." Harry felt guilty.

"My patients are in good shape today." He sat next to her as Alma handed her an ice-cold Coke and a glass of ice.

She returned to give Miranda one and then Fair.

"Thank you, honey." Miranda poured the bubbling liquid over the ice cubes, which crackled in the glass.

"I'll wring his neck. I mean it. I will cut him off at the knees!" Harry was returning to form.

"I'll snap off his fingers." Tucker puffed out her white chest.

"Jerome or Pug?" Fair smiled.

"Jerome."

"You'll have to take a number and stand in line. You should have heard Tavener on the phone about an hour ago. And you know how Tavener can talk. I think he'll put a contract out on Jerome. Said he wasn't worth going to jail over but he needs killing just the same." Fair laughed.

Harry took a deep breath. "Miranda, I'm sorry I got you into this."

"Actually, you didn't. I've seen enough of the post office. George was frugal. He left me enough to garden and put gas in the car, visit my sister once a year. It was time for a change."

A wave of fear washed over Harry. "Oh, my God, I've got four mares to feed plus my guys."

"Half those mares are mine. Now, look, don't worry and don't do anything rash. Everything's going to work out."

"I'm not going back."

"I didn't say that you were. And," he smiled, "there will be four well-bred yearlings to go to the sales next year, God willing. Everything's going to be all right."

"God bless Sugar Thierry." Miranda sighed.

"What was going on with Tavener?" Harry's curiosity flooded back, pushing out her upset.

"Media. As the senior vet, the television crews from Channel Twenty-nine, Six, and even one from D.C. have camped out on his doorstep. After leaving him, they plagued Hayden and Bill. The problem with TV is they can edit out the important material and go for the jugular. Tavener, Hayden, and Bill aren't going to fan the flames of panic. People will go out and shoot any stray animal they see and, for all I know, one another. I know everyone's been reasonable and responsible, but it scares me how it will come out on the tube."

"Aren't you due for another rabies shot?" Miranda asked Harry.

"Next week." Harry finished off her Coke, the caffeine and sugar improving her mood. "Fair, thanks. I'm sorry to barge in. Thanks, Alma," she called to her.

"No problem." Alma stood up from behind the reception desk.

"Think you'll help out Pug?" Fair cleared his throat.

"Well, it's never good to storm off like that. I should give notice but I can't take the kids. So I'll call him. I can give him some names and—well, he has them, anyway, people who can fill in. But I'm not going in."

"Okay." Fair nodded.

"And I won't, either," agreed Miranda. "All the years I gave that post office. George was named postmaster in 1962. And you know, I enjoyed it and I was so glad to come back in when Harry took over after George's death. But I meant it when I said times are changing, and I suppose every person has to decide whether to change with the times or not." She placed her glass on the coaster. "It's time for me to do something different. I'm like Harry: I think things are too overregulated. When you think of the time we all waste on nonproductive labor, it's amazing anything of significance ever gets accomplished."

"Amen," Alma called from behind the desk.

"Honey, I'll come over after work tonight. I'll bring sushi," Fair told Harry.

"Hooray!" Pewter leapt up on the coffee table and turned a circle.

"Okay." Harry brightened.

Miranda drove Harry to her farm, then stayed there to garden while Harry painted her shed. She'd built scaffolding, which speeded the process since she could walk from end to end at the top. The bottom half she could paint while standing on the ground. She liked painting, because she saw an instant result. This instant result was gray since she was methodically putting on primer.

"Harry, your phone is off the hook in the tack room, it's ringing so much." Miranda called out from the rose beds.

"I know. I'll call everyone later. Needed to think. Oh, by the by, as soon as you're ready let me run you home."

"In good time."

Susan, BoomBoom, Tazio, Little Mim, Big Mim, and even Aunt Tally, furious at not reaching Harry by phone, all came down the drive within the next hour.

After recounting events, listening to everyone's ideas and opinions—all favorable to her, which was gratifying—she was alone. Susan drove Miranda back home.

The quiet slap of the paintbrush underscored the fact that she was unemployed, in her late thirties, no prospects in sight, and bills to pay. She'd graduated from Smith College with a degree in Art History and fell into the job as a postmistress the summer after graduation. George Hogendobber had died of a heart attack and Harry took the job to fill in. She never dreamed she'd stay behind the counter of the small post office in small Crozet. Not that she was heading for New York City and wealth, but with her education it seemed natural that she'd go on, get a doctorate, and teach at one of the wonderful universities within driving range: Sweet Briar, Mary Baldwin, the University of Virginia, or even Hollins, which was down in Roanoke. Randolph-Macon was in Lynchburg. There were many possibilities and Harry excelled in her studies.

The first year passed and she settled into the job. She liked being at the hub of events. They might be events such as hail peppering BoomBoom's barn roof or a new restaurant opening at the corner, but she liked knowing the news. She'd even gotten to the point where she read the papers, watched the nightly news, but came to the conclusion that where you live is what's real. Not that she didn't care about what happened in other parts, but she lived in Crozet, and if she was going to do any good in this world it would be in Crozet, Virginia.

Now what?

32

Fair called Jerome Stoltfus, who was shadowing the state veterinarian.

"Animal control," Jerome barked into his cell phone, as he drove the *exact* speed limit. Jerome was that kind of guy.

"It's Fair Haristeen."

"Now, don't you jump down my throat because Harry went postal." He chuckled at his little joke. "Those critters don't belong there, anyway, and she'll think things over and be back at work Monday. I give her Thursday and Friday to mull it over."

Fair cleared his throat. "Harry usually takes a long time to make a decision. When she makes one quickly, uh, I'd watch out. And you ought to know by now, Jerome, whether she makes a decision slowly or quickly, she won't back down. Not ever."

"We'll see." Then a flash of illumination changed Jerome's tone. "But you were married to her, so I guess you know. I was fixing to call you, but this has been intense. Today has been intense. Can we change our get-together?"

As this was why Fair was calling Jerome, he was relieved. "Sure. Any night after five. I'm usually at the clinic until six."

"How about Monday?"

"Fine."

"I've been talking to a lot of doctors. You start listening to those guys and it's a wonder anyone is healthy. Sure are a lot of ways to get sick."

"Seems to be."

"I've been looking up stuff on the Internet. Cave climbers, what do you call them . . . ?" he asked.

"Spelunkers."

"The Internet site on rabies said those people get rabies inoculations."

"That's very interesting."

"Said that when you've got an enclosed place with little ventilation and thousands upon thousands of bats that have been living there since B.C., well, you might can inhale rabies."

"Inhale it?" Fair tried not to sound incredulous.

"That's what I read." Jerome was not repeating exactly what he read, but he felt he was close enough.

"Jerome, I'd steer clear of Harry for a week or two." Fair changed the subject.

"She was wrong."

"That's not the point." Fair didn't think Harry was wrong, but no need to argue with someone as bullheaded as Jerome. "She's upset. She loves her animals the way people love their children. Take my advice and leave her alone."

Jerome slowed for a sharp curve. "Well, if you ask me, animals are more faithful than people, so I guess I can't blame her."

"Thanks." Fair hung up.

It then occurred to Jerome that the reason Harry threw Fair out a few years ago was because he'd cheated on her. The story was that he'd cheated more than once, just went through a wild phase, but Fair swore he did not cheat, if you will, until they had separated, which was when he started seeing BoomBoom.

Fair dialed the offices of McIntire and Langston. The receptionist put him straight through to Bill.

They discussed what Jerome had just told Fair.

"So it really is possible?" Fair asked.

"No. I don't think so. I don't think there have been any inhalation cases ever reported, but there are droplets of saliva—tiny, microscopic droplets—in infested caves."

"You breathe the aerosolized virus?"

Bill answered, "Yes."

"Do you have any knowledge of Barry or Sugar visiting these caves?"

"No. Well, let me amend that. There is nothing in either of their medical records requesting the inoculation. But you all would know if they were spelunkers." Bill, being new to the area, deferred to Fair. "The reason those guys get the shots is because there are so many thousands of bats. It's insurance in case someone gets bitten. And I haven't heard or read of any cases."

"As far as I know, neither Barry nor Sugar so much as set foot in a cave."

"Both of their rabies types were of the

silver-haired-bat variety. Makes sense in the absence of trauma. A tiny, tiny wound."

"Sorry to be slow here, Bill, but let me go back to climbing around caves for a moment. In your opinion, if I go into such a place, what are my chances of being bitten?"

"Let me answer that this way. If you go walking in the woods, what are your chances of being bitten by a rabid raccoon? It's about the same."

"I see. Thanks, Bill, I know you've been besieged today. That damned Jerome."

"Someone ought to tape his mouth shut with duct tape. I have some right here in the office." Bill's tenor deepened. "Along with all this excitement, the place has been buzzing about Harry and Miranda quitting."

"They did. And Jerome provoked it. I think Pug would have found a solution, at least until the new P.O. is built. I guess we forget that he has to answer to Washington."

"Luckily I only have to answer to God," Bill wryly replied.

After Fair hung up the phone, Alma popped into his office. "Doc, BoomBoom. Says Keepsake has a bad discharge."

"Tell her I'll be right over."

BoomBoom's barn, an elegant four-stall affair with a brand-new standing seam copper roof, was nestled under large locust trees. Fair was her regular vet, although she often spoke to Tavener. If Fair was out of town, which was rare, Tavener would take care of BoomBoom. As Boom-Boom felt she utilized Tavener's specialized knowledge, she always sent a sumptuous Christmas gift as a thank-you.

Fair cleaned up Keepsake, checked her with ultrasound to be sure.

"Well, she's bred."

"The lady or the tiger? A mule or a horse?"

"You'll know around the first of April." He bent over to pick up his clipboard, which rested on a tack trunk in BoomBoom's colors, magenta and gold.

"Does she have venereal disease?" BoomBoom, a good horsewoman, knew venereal diseases could be passed from stallion to mare and vice versa.

"No. She had a small tear here on the outside of her vagina and it got infected. She's a fine, healthy mare. To be on the safe side, give her SMZ and just swab her in the mornings and the evenings. Keep it clean. The flies are the main problem."

BoomBoom tolerated bugs, as she had no choice. "I looked her over when she came on back. I didn't see any blood."

"You know horses. They find more ways to injure themselves. She could have gotten caught up in thorns. Who knows, but she'll be fine."

Fair wrote up the call, walked to his truck, and pulled out a jar of SMZ since BoomBoom had only a few left. Most horsemen keep antibiotics in the barn, as well as some tranquilizers. If an animal is hurt, one often needs to keep them quiet, depending on the injury; hence the tranquilizer.

"Pug Harper couldn't find his ass with both hands." BoomBoom laughed. "You should have seen him trying to tend to the P.O." BoomBoom, knowing Harry, cut to the chase. "Does she know what she's going to do? When we all paid her a call, she seemed fine. You know, I think this is the best thing to happen to her. She needs something that will use her mind. She's way too bright to be filling mail slots."

"You're right." Fair washed his hands in the barn sink.

BoomBoom handed him a towel. "This is your chance. She's been more affectionate around you. She spends more time with you. Go for it."

He dried his hands, exhaled deeply. "Do you really think so?"

"She needs you."

"She won't marry me because she's out of a job. She has too much pride."

"She needs you." BoomBoom restated the obvious. "She needs your strength, comfort, thoughts about her future. It's not about money. We all know she won't take a nickel. That's her fatal flaw. She has to learn to receive. When she called for help on the shed, I thought that was a huge breakthrough."

He considered this as he folded the towel, placing it on the rack. "Guess it was."

"She's changing." BoomBoom smiled. "We're all changing. That's life."

"Boom, there are people in this county who haven't had a new thought in thirty years and don't want one."

"And we might pass and repass them,

but we aren't spending time with them, are we? You have to grow. It's life's imperative. Grow or die. Harry's growing. This is the best thing that's happened to her. Make it the best thing that's happened to you."

"Sometimes you surprise me."

"Sometimes I surprise myself." The beautiful blonde laughed. "Fair, I care about you. And for all of my strained relationship with Harry, which improved so much after we were trapped last winter down at U-Hall," she said, "I care about her. We've been together since we were children, all of us, and we'll be together when we're old like Miranda, Big Mim, Jim, Tracy. I'm coming to grips with the fact that we're a generation. It's kind of like being in a regiment."

He laughed. "Yeah, it is."

"You and I had a lot of fun together, but it was the wrong time. And you know the truth?" Her eyebrows raised. "I'm a consumer when it comes to men. Good as you are, well, I'm not going to settle down, and I think that shocked you. You weren't ready to settle down, anyway. We're pushed into it by society. No one should ever think about starting a relationship until one year after a divorce, I swear."

"Do you think you'll ever marry again?"

"When Kelly died, I mourned him. But you know the truth? The truth I never told anyone? If he'd lived I would have divorced him, the controlling son of a bitch." She said this without rancor. "I don't want any man telling me what to do."

"Neither does Harry."

"You don't tell her what to do, you suggest. You know how to handle Harry, when you think about it."

He laughed. "I think she knows how to handle me. A lot of times she knows what I'm going to do before I do it."

"Listen to me, as an old friend, this is your chance."

He leaned down—although not very far, because BoomBoom was six feet tall and he was six five—and kissed her on the cheek. "You're a special lady."

33

Blood was lightly splattered over the windshield of the white Jeep.

When Deputy Cooper arrived, the motor was still running.

Jerome Stoltfus slumped to the side of the steering wheel. He had been shot in the back of the head, the bullet exiting through his forehead and out the front windshield.

Cynthia double-checked her watch. Ten twenty-one P.M., Wednesday night, June 23. She pulled on thin latex gloves and felt for a pulse in Jerome's neck. None, which she expected. The body was cool but not yet cold.

She peeled off the gloves, walked over to Little Mim. "You okay?"

"Yes." Little Mim's face was bone white.

"Excuse me while I call Rick. Then I'll ask you a few questions and you can go home."

"Coop, you do whatever you have to do," Little Mim, who was shocked but in control, replied.

Cooper punched in to the dispatcher. "Get me the sheriff. Wake him up if he's asleep."

Within minutes she heard the familiar voice. "Better be good."

"Jerome Stoltfus. Shot through the back of the head. Yellow Mountain Road, about two miles from the entrance to Rose Hill."

"Be right there."

Cooper returned to Little Mim. "Did you see any other cars?"

"No. Nothing. I was coming back from Aunt Tally's and I noticed the Jeep pulled off the road. I slowed because I knew it was Animal Control, and I wondered if Jerome was picking up an injured animal since I couldn't see him. So I pulled up behind and walked to the embankment, but I still didn't see him. That's when I looked in the car. And that's when I called the sheriff's department. I knew he was dead the second I saw him."

"It's a shock to see someone like that." Cooper was genuinely sympathetic.

"Yes, it is," Little Mim answered slowly, "but what went through my head was, 'Who got him first?' I mean, everyone was furious with him."

34

Coroner Tom Yancy bent over Jerome Stoltfus at twelve-thirty Thursday morning.

He had gotten out of bed and rushed down to meet Sheriff Shaw. The two men had worked together for over fifteen years. If Rick called him at midnight it was important.

Wearing a lab coat, Rick observed closely as Yancy inspected the wound.

"A great deal of damage to the skull." He pointed to what was left of Jerome's face on the right side. "See the angle? The gun was held in the right hand, placed snug against the base of the skull—look at these powder burns—and fired upward at this angle. The bullet emerged above the right eye and pretty much took out that side of the head. Death was instantaneous. Did you find the bullet? Large-enough caliber to do this—thirty-eight, forty-five more likely."

"No. Cooper's back where Jerome was found. Wasn't on the hood of the car or in front of it. She's good. If it's there, she'll find it."

"Hmm."

Rick nodded, as he knew what Yancy was thinking. "Our perp could have picked it up. It's a possibility."

"Mm-hmm. He'd be a lucky devil, but he's been lucky so far."

"Guess you're thinking what I'm thinking."

"Guess I am."

Rick slapped his hand against his thigh. "Damn. Damn! Yancy, I don't know any more than when I started investigating Barry's death."

"You know more about rabies. I'll send in brain tissue to Richmond on Jerome, by the way."

"Christ, if he tests positive for rabies I suppose we'll have to barricade the town."

"People tend toward the irrational."

Yancy carefully picked up a bone fragment with tweezers as Jerome's hand twitched.

"I hate that," Rick said ruefully.

"I've had them sit bolt upright." Yancy laughed.

"You and I get to see what nobody else wants to."

"The human body is like a map. If you know how to read it, you'll find your destination." Yancy peered at the shattered skull. "Let's keep his head just the way it is until Jason can take photographs tomorrow. Okay by you?"

"Of course."

"Want to stay for the rest of his autopsy?"

"Sure. You got out of bed for this. The least I can do is keep you company."

"You added a little excitement to my life."

"Are you being humorous?"

"I'm a laugh a minute." Yancy put down the long stainless-steel tweezers. "I've cut open two young men and now Jerome. He's young, too, although there was something odd about Jerome. He always seemed like an old man who would wear cardigans."

"Yeah."

"Now, Sugar and Barry worked together. One was clearly murdered. The other could have picked up the disease at the same location. What I'm saying is the vector of infection was the silver-haired bat, and it's not a far putt to consider they both may have been bitten in the barn or somewhere on that farm or some farm they visited together. But Jerome—well, I'd say this is getting very interesting."

"Went over every building at St. James with a fine-tooth comb. Yancy, nothing. Nada. Zero."

"Have you asked yourself what Barry and Jerome had in common?"

"I have."

"And?"

"I think Jerome was figuring out how Barry and Sugar contracted rabies. I don't know if he figured out what it was that made Barry dangerous to someone, unless it was *about* rabies."

Both men looked down at the mortal remains of Jerome Stoltfus.

"Better hope he kept good notes."

"Our computer wiz is in Jerome's office

right now. His logbook was on the seat of the car."

Yancy pulled the sheet over Jerome, the blood seeping through it the minute it touched Jerome's broken face. "Funny thing is, you know the killer knows that. You'd better believe he flipped through that logbook."

"He couldn't get to the computer." Rick paused. "Well, I take that back. I don't know who walks in and out of Jerome's office, and I don't know what Jerome put on his computer."

"Did you send someone to his house?"

"Yes."

"You've covered the bases."

Rick spoke to the corpse. "Jerome, we underestimated you."

35

At six Thursday morning the phone rang in the tack room. Harry had already brought the three hunters in so they could eat peacefully in their stalls. She was heading out to the barn to check on the broodmares when the phone called her back.

"Hello."

"Harry," Susan breathlessly said, "Jerome Stoltfus was shot to death on Yellow Mountain Road."

"You're kidding." Harry didn't believe it, but, then again, so much was happening that was out of kilter.

Mrs. Murphy, Pewter, and Tucker, hearing the change in Harry's voice, trotted into the tack room to listen.

"I'm not kidding. Little Mim found him last night."

"Good God." Harry, who had been leaning over the desk, dropped into the old wooden office chair. "How'd you find out?"

"Little Mim called Ned when she left the scene. She wanted to know since she found the body what might be expected of her legally. Just her testimony, of course, but Little Mim's careful—more careful than I perhaps realized. And then she wanted to ask his advice on how to handle this at the next town-council meeting. She and Ned have become political cronies even though they're from different parties."

"Why didn't you call me?" A flare of anger escaped Harry.

"Because it was late and you were asleep. Don't get testy," her best friend said frankly.

"Anyone caught?"

"No."

"Damn." She grabbed a pencil and began doodling on a notepad. "I can't pretend I'll miss him. He was insufferable."

"True, but we could count on our fingers and toes the number of insufferable people we know. We don't kill them."

"I know that," Harry snapped, irritated at Susan's moralizing. "And I know something else. If Jerome was killed he must have found out something about Barry's death or about this rabies stuff. If Jerome had uncovered the link concerning the rabies infection, why would anyone kill him over that? You'd think the whole county would thank him. No, he dug up something out at a farm call or poring over paperwork. God, if only I had an idea, even a shadow of an idea."

"The sheriff and Cooper no doubt feel the same way. On the surface of it, it's crazy."

"Most things appear that way until you find the connection. There has to be a connection between Barry's murder and Jerome's."

"What crossed my mind is, what if Jerome had rabies, too."

"Susan, don't say that. Really."

"I know." And Susan did understand the potential for panic. "Are you all right?"

"Sure. Why wouldn't I be?"

"You're not on your way to work, that's why."

"Oh. I forgot about that. The news." She

rapped the eraser end of the pencil against the tablet. "I suppose if I think about it, I'll—oh, I don't know. It doesn't seem real yet."

"Did you know that Miranda already has seventy-two signatures on the petition Ned drew up concerning Mrs. Murphy, Tucker, and Pewter?"

"No."

"Miranda gets things done. Of course, it doesn't matter now. Her goal was five hundred signatures."

Harry laughed. "We don't have that many postboxes in the post office."

"She was ready to walk the streets." Susan sighed. "Harry, I wish I knew what was going on. It's a bad time."

"You're safe."

"How do I know?"

"Because I told you so."

"Do you know something I don't?" Susan asked, a note of suspicion in her voice.

"No, but it's logical. You aren't involved in outdoor work, breeding horses, animal control. You're not in danger from silver-haired bats—if any of us is—and I don't think you're in danger of knowing whatever

Jerome knew or someone thought he knew."

"You're right, but I still feel terrible."

"I do, too." Harry glanced down at Mary Pat's ring on her right pinky. The Episcopal shield, inscription underneath, glowed. "It's funny. I'm staring at Mary Pat's ring, and I feel like it's bringing me luck even though right now doesn't seem a propitious time."

"I hope so."

After Harry hung up the phone it rang again almost immediately.

"Harry, this is Pug Harper."

Mrs. Murphy and Pewter, now on the desk, strained to listen.

"Good morning, Pug."

"I don't know if you've heard of the terrible circumstances of Jerome Stoltfus's death. It was on the early-edition news."

"Susan Tucker just told me. I don't know the details."

"Nor do I. But this does change things. I will look the other way if you want to come back to work."

"Pug, that's very kind of you." She took a deep breath, then plunged ahead. "And it might work for a while. But who's to say the next animal-control officer won't barge into the post office and order me to remove the cats and dog? And really, Pug, when that new building goes up, everything changes. I know that Amy Wade can handle it. She's the best of the temps, and now that her kids are in school, I bet she'd be happy for the job."

"Why don't you take the weekend to think it over?" He hoped she'd change her mind.

"I made up my mind. For the record, you're a good postmaster, and I've enjoyed all my years on the job."

"Thank you." Pug hated to lose Mary Minor Haristeen. "Look, if you do have a change of heart, you call me."

"I will."

As she placed the phone back in its cradle, the cats cheered, *"Hooray!"*

"You'll find something better. You might even make more money," Tucker, ever the optimist, prophesied.

She smiled at the animals, then frowned slightly. "Gang, Jerome Stoltfus is deader than a doornail."

"Goody." Pewter licked her lips, her pink tongue in sharp contrast to her luxurious dark gray fur.

"Pewter, that's not very Christian." Tucker didn't like Jerome one bit but thought it better not to cheer his demise.

"And you ate communion wafers." Mrs. Murphy referred to an episode where, together with the Rev. Jones's cats, Cazenovia and Elocution, they had opened the closet containing the communion wafers. The four cats and dog demolished boxes of the round, white, thin wafers.

Harry dialed Miranda, who said she was just getting ready to call Harry.

"What in the world is going on?" Miranda fretted.

"I guess if we knew that, someone would be behind bars," Harry replied. "Did Pug Harper call you?"

"No. He'd call you first."

"Well, he did, but I declined to return. He even said I could bring the kids, but, you know, in the long run it wouldn't have worked out, so why not just get on with it, whatever it is."

"You're right. But it's going to seem awfully strange not walking across the alley in the morning. How will you live without my orange-glazed cinnamon buns?"

"Drive into town."

"Or I'll drive out there," Miranda offered.

"Thanks for getting so many signatures so fast. Susan told me."

"You'll be happy to know that everyone is on your side."

"Really?"

"People think highly of you and, of course, they adore Mrs. Murphy, Pewter, and Tucker."

"That makes me feel good. I"—Harry, about to get emotional, stopped herself— "I'm grateful. By the way, I told Pug that Amy Wade would do a great job. I think everyone will work out at the post office. What I'm worried about is rabies. Or whatever is going on."

"Me, too. When I heard about Jerome I thought of First Peter, Chapter Four, Verse Fifteen; 'But let none of you suffer as a murderer, or a thief, or a wrongdoer, or a mischief-maker.' And Jerome suffered being none of those things. He let a little power go to his head, but he wasn't a murderer or a thief. And really, all he was trying to do, apart from be important for the first time in his life, was protect the public good."

"You're right. Maybe I'll drive down to the sheriff's office and—"

Miranda interrupted her. "Harry, you'll give Rick a fit. He'll think you're criticizing the way he's handling this."

"Yeah, you're right." Harry paused. "I didn't think of that."

"Why don't you call Cooper? If you have an idea or whatever, call her. I would imagine right now that Rick is under a lot of pressure."

"You bet he is."

Later that morning, as Harry scrubbed out the large outdoor water troughs, the soft breeze rustled the early green leaves, the light color beautiful against the robin's egg blue sky. As her wet hand caught the sunlight, the ring glistened intensely.

"That's it, you know?" Harry spoke to Tucker, at her heels. "Someone is shielded by money, power, or position. If only I knew what was at stake."

36

The deep golden rays of the late-afternoon sun drenched the racing barns at St. James Farm. All the outbuildings on the property were painted crisp white. The eaves, the doors, and the window frames all shone bright white. On the middle of each post of the shed row barns, Mary Pat's racing colors gleamed.

Alicia Palmer, Aunt Tally, and Harry stood at the training track, the racing barns behind them.

Harry had called Cooper, who suggested if she wanted to help, she should go over to St. James and go through the barns one more time and look around. Since Harry was a horsewoman and

Cooper wasn't, Cooper was sincere in her request.

Aunt Tally happened to be visiting Alicia when Harry arrived.

While the humans walked out to the deep grassy center oval of the track, Mrs. Murphy, Pewter, and Tucker inspected the last of the racing barns.

"Everyone has trooped through here." Tucker sniffed. *"Raccoons, possums, foxes, mice by the busload, and, ah, yes,"* she closed her yes and inhaled, *"bobcat."*

Overhead, the barn swallows, always correctly dressed, their wings sweeping back as beautifully as a dark blue morning coat, complained, *"Out of our barns. You're a threat to our children."*

"I'll eat your children," Pewter ferociously replied. *"They'll be brunch, just like Tostitos. Those little birdy bones will crunch like corn chips."*

"MAMA!" Thirty little babies squealed throughout the barn, sending their parents darting and bombing the three animals on the ground.

"Bother." Mrs. Murphy swatted at one bold fellow. *"Tucker, do you think the ani-*

mals were here when Sugar and Barry were here?"

Tucker's luminous brown eyes opened wider. "That scent's gone. I can still smell the boys, mostly on the old shirts in the tack room, a wipe-down cloth here and there. Human oil will stay on cloth for quite a while. But the pad scents," she shook her head, "gone. These tracks"—she meant scent tracks—"are within the last three days."

"The grain's still in the feed room. That's why you've got all this traffic. Harry should take the grain," Pewter suggested.

"You're right," Mrs. Murphy agreed. "But even when Barry and Sugar were alive, I bet the foxes came in. Maybe not everybody else, but you know how opportunistic foxes are."

"MAMA!" the babes squealed from deep in their well-built nests.

Another barn swallow swooped so close, the air brushed against Pewter's fur.

"We aren't going to eat your children," Mrs. Murphy called out. "Pewter's a comedian."

"I am not," Pewter hissed, voice low.

"Pewter, even if you killed one, you're

too lazy to tear off the feathers. Remember when the pileated woodpecker died outside the back door? You didn't pull out one feather."

"That was different. He was already dead. The thrill of the kill gives me energy."

Mrs. Murphy and Tucker looked at each other but said nothing. Then Mrs. Murphy asked Tucker, *"Bats?"*

The corgi shook her head. *"No."*

Pewter, nose still out of joint, complained, *"Why defer to Tucker? Cat noses are as good as dog noses, but we don't work for humans the way dogs do, so no one really notices. You'll never get a cat to dig up truffles. Only dogs and pigs do that."*

The sleek tiger cat knew her sense of smell was acute but she thought Tucker's nose a tiny bit better. Plus, Tucker used her nose before her eyes, whereas Mrs. Murphy used her eyes before her nose.

"Get out!" Two barn swallows headed straight for the three animals, then sheered off at the last second, one turning left, one right.

"Truce!" Mrs. Murphy meowed while the baby birds shrieked.

The swallows perched on the edge of

their nests, some in the rafters, and one defiant male sat on the floor right in front of them, just out of paw's reach.

He spoke. *"I don't mind barn cats, but you two aren't barn cats. How do I know you won't do us harm?"*

Tucker lay down, resting her head on her paws so she was eye level with the swallow. *"You have my word, and even though you may not believe it, these are honorable cats."*

"Don't be gulled, Madison," another swallow warned. *"All cats are killers."*

Pewter puffed out her considerable chest. *"Of course we're killers, but what makes you think I'd waste my time on you? Why, you aren't even big enough for an hors d'oeuvre."*

"Daddy, get off the floor!" Madison's children were hysterical.

Mrs. Murphy thought the best course was flattery. *"Madison, my gray friend is a good hunter."* She bit her lip for a second. What a terrible fib. *"But we're here on a peaceful mission, and all we want to know is, have bats ever lived in here?"*

Madison hopped from one foot to the other. *"No. The bats live out in the huge old* conifers. *Might be some up at the big house, but I don't think so. The humans swept through here looking for them, too.*"

"*Ever see any sick ones outside?*" Tucker inquired.

"*No, but we keep different hours, you know. We swallows work during the day, and the bats work at night. The humans, silly beings, drive the bats outside, but between the bats and ourselves, we keep this place insect-free. Well, almost.*" His russet and buff chest plumage expanded. Madison was quite handsome.

"*They are stupid. They don't like vultures. Can you imagine what the earth would be like without vultures? Piles of dead things, kind of like piles of cars that never rust. No room for the rest of us!*" Madison's mate, Thelma, called out. She was keeping a sharp eye on her husband. That Pewter bragged too much, and if she even moved a muscle, Thelma would go for the eyes.

"*If a plague swept through the bats, you'd know, wouldn't you?*" Mrs. Murphy tried to keep to business.

"*Sure. Their corpses would be under the conifers,*" Madison replied. "*There's no ra-*

bies here. We've heard all about it, of course, and I swear upon my tail feathers: no rabies."

Mrs. Murphy, her voice musical and low, said, *"I think the rabies is a diversion."*

"How can it be a diversion when two men had it and maybe even Jerome, too? I mean, he might test positive." Tucker thought Mrs. Murphy totally wrong.

"What exactly do you mean, Murph?" Pewter's curiosity was aroused.

"Rabies is a dreadful disease, a horrible, horrible death. It's bound to cause violent reactions among the humans, right?" Everyone nodded in agreement, including Madison. *"Well, I think Barry was supposed to die of rabies, not from a torn throat. Somehow, Barry became too threatening or something and the killer couldn't wait. I am convinced both Barry and Sugar were purposely infected. Cat intuition but, nonetheless, we have to take the rabies seriously. After all, we're all susceptible to the virus. If it turns out this was the work of silver-haired bats, then we can expect the raccoons, skunks, and other groundlings to start dying from it. It won't just stay with the*

bats. And as far as I know, that hasn't happened."

"Not around here," Madison avowed, as the other swallows chimed in.

"It's possible Barry infected Sugar. Dumb things happen. I mean, he could have bitten him. It's possible." Mrs. Murphy was thinking out loud.

"Barry was dangerous but Sugar wasn't?" Tucker sat up, which made Madison hop backward. "But Sugar still had rabies."

"That's what I'm saying. Barry could have given it to Sugar. Terrible luck. I know it sounds funny to say Barry may have bitten Sugar, but what if they were play-fighting or something? Dumb things happen."

"Or they both could have been deliberately infected and, somehow in the time it takes to die from rabies—one to three months, that's what the humans have been saying—" Pewter was getting excited now, "Barry became more of a nuisance or got closer. I think that's what happened, and I think that whatever this is about has to do with St. James."

"Oh, no," the swallows said in chorus.

Madison said quite firmly, *"There's nothing here. Nothing out of the way; I mean, Barry and Sugar bred broodmares, trained horses, took in lay-ups. People came through—customers, vets, friends—but it was all business. I never even heard an argument, except with Carmen."* He asked his friends, *"Did any of you?"*

"No," they answered in unison.

Madison hopped one step closer. *"I can appreciate that you're curious. Cats are notoriously curious. I'm sure you'd like to figure this out, but all your thoughts, if you'll pardon me, seem convoluted."*

"They are," Mrs. Murphy warmly agreed with him. *"Because we don't know what this is about. Once we understand the motive, this will be crystal clear and simple."*

Thelma flew down next to Madison.

"Mama!" Their children really squealed now.

"Hush," Thelma commanded. She looked the three groundlings in the eye. *"There is one other thing. The girlfriend, Carmen. She was sleeping with both of them."*

"Aha!" Pewter smiled.

"Barry and Carmen had broken up," Tucker said.

"Oh, they'd break up and get back to-gether, and even when they'd break up, she'd sleep with him." Thelma shrugged.

"Did each man know about the other?" Tucker thought Carmen's schedule de-manding.

"Sugar knew about Barry, of course, but Barry didn't know about Sugar," Thelma, her eyes bright and black, responded. *"Didn't last long with Sugar, though. That Carmen is a no-good tart, if you ask me."*

Up at the racetrack, Alicia pointed out to Aunt Tally and Harry where Ziggy Flame's paddock used to be. After Ziggy disap-peared and Mary Pat never came home, over the years the five-board paddock fell apart. As no other stallions came to St. James, there was no reason to build a stal-lion paddock.

"You have a good memory," Aunt Tally said.

"It seems like yesterday. It's odd. Time plays tricks on you." Alicia folded her arms across her chest. "Harry, you're too young to understand."

"I know it's flying by." Harry smiled.

"I walked out the other morning in the heavy fog. At first I couldn't breathe for the emotions, but now," Alicia looked around at the estate, each building laid out with care, everything aesthetically pleasing, "I love it all over again."

"You were hurt." Aunt Tally, as always, cut straight to the bone. "No wonder your inspection visits were short."

"Bad enough we didn't know where Mary Pat and Ziggy were. Worse to be the prime suspect. The whispers, the cold shoulders." She stared out across the infield. "All those people silently disapproving of our relationship could use this as an excuse to be ugly. While Mary Pat was alive I was protected by her aura, her wealth. When she disappeared, the ugliness was unveiled. The people who were good to me were Harry's mother and father, Miranda and George, Tally, Mim, and Jim. And that was it."

"They certainly ate crow when they found out you'd inherited the kit and kaboodle. Course, that took a year. Mary Pat had to be declared legally dead. It was complicated, but you emerged the winner." Aunt Tally relished the tale. "What really shocked them was when they found out she'd adopted you. Smart, that Mary Pat.

Very smart. It was the only way she could legally protect you. Did you know you'd been adopted?"

"Yes." Alicia closed her eyes for a moment. "Since gay people couldn't get married, they had to find ways to protect one another. By adopting me, Mary Pat made it very difficult for someone to contest the will. Also, if she'd been critically ill, I would have been able to visit her in the hospital as next of kin. Heterosexuals don't realize how many barriers there are for gay people in situations like hospitalization. It's better now in some places where domestic partnership is recognized by the state, but when we were together it was still the Dark Ages. I live a marvelous life because of Mary Pat, but I'd give back every penny to see her walk out from those racing barns. You can't compare money with life, you just can't. And I know you know that, Aunt Tally."

"Speaking of eating crow." Harry's eyes narrowed, for bounding toward them were the three animals, with Pewter carrying feathers in her mouth.

Before leaving the barn, Pewter asked the swallows if they'd houseclean. She wanted some nice long tail feathers or wing feathers.

They complied, and she picked them up only to race out of the barn, followed by Mrs. Murphy and Tucker.

"She is the biggest fake in the world," Mrs. Murphy spat.

Tucker, running alongside the tiger cat, said, *"They'll never believe her."*

"She's killed a bird." Aunt Tally rapped her cane on the ground.

"Pewter, how could you?" Harry disapproved.

Pewter, upon reaching Harry, dropped the feathers and rubbed against Harry's leg. *"I am a mighty hunter."*

"Gag me." Mrs. Murphy sat on the feathers for spite.

37

What do you make of it?" Cooper leaned toward Fair's computer screen.

Fair examined the latest data on reported rabies cases, nonhuman, in Virginia. "That we are, fortunately, in a valley of the rabies cycle."

Cynthia Cooper had brought over Jerome's computer discs, his handwritten notes, plus a detailed U.S. Geographical Survey topographical map he'd had for the St. James area, since that's where the rabies seemed to have broken out.

It was seven-thirty in the evening, and long, late rays of sun were slanting over meadows outside.

"Being at the bottom of the trough

makes it unlikely for humans to be exposed?" Cooper asked.

"In theory, yes, but we know there's always a pool of the rabies virus in existence. It never goes away. It flares up, then subsides."

"Hmm, nothing new here. Go to his suspect file."

Fair clicked, bringing up Jerome's icons, while at the bottom of the screen a bikini-clad woman walked across with a sign over her head reading "Suspects."

Laughing, Fair said, "Jerome was more of a computer nerd than I would have thought."

"I just saw the nerd." Cooper felt guilty.

"Here we are." Fair opened the file and beheld photos of a raccoon, a skunk, a possum, a bat, a cow, and a horse. "And he had a sense of humor."

"I never was witness to it. When's the last time you treated a horse for rabies?"

"Never. I've given the shots. But there was a case years ago in Greene County."

She waved her hand. "I know. I was hoping we'd find something new."

"But your people have been over this."

"They aren't veterinarians."

"What else is on here that you want me to examine?"

"Jerome never used your services, did he?"

"Cooper, Jerome didn't know one end of a horse from the other."

"Well, look at this." She reached across Fair's broad chest, took the mouse, moved it, clicked, and brought up another file.

"I'll be." Fair read out the list of Ziggy Flame's progeny. "He traced all of Ziggy's descendants. He must have had help from the Jockey Club."

"My question is, why would he be interested?"

"I don't know."

"And it's curious that neither Barry nor Sugar, although in the breeding business, had these records."

"Not so curious, Coop. A stallion like Ziggy would have had great influence had he lived long enough, but Ziggy only covered mares for three years. His percentage of stakes winners was, according to this"— Fair scrolled back to the beginning of Ziggy's data on progeny—"seventeen percent. If he'd been in service longer he'd have gotten better and better mares. And seventeen percent is a terrific stat."

"What happened to the horses he sired that didn't go to the track? Can we find them?"

"Only if the owners registered them with the Jockey Club. If someone buys a horse that, for whatever reason, isn't destined for flat racing or chasing, they often don't register the foal."

"But for every foal registered, the Jockey Club will have records?"

"You'd better believe it. The American records go back to 1873, and the English Jockey Club records go back to 1791."

"Forgive me if I ask stupid questions, but I really know nothing about how this works. Wouldn't you register every thoroughbred born?"

"No." He leaned back in his office chair. "Registration is the responsibility of the owner. A breeder only goes through the process if they're going to keep the foal or if, thinking the colt or filly will bring a bigger price as a two-year-old, they decide to hold it. Usually they don't, for the simple reason that it's expensive. Breeding is a numbers game. You've got to put a lot of foals on the ground and select. Most of the big breeding farms will stand four or more stallions. In the old days a farm could afford to stand ten or even twenty, but escalating taxes and costs have put a stop to that. One result is, fewer and fewer stallions get the good mares. People can't afford to take a chance on an unproven stud. And given the laws of unintended consequences, we're narrowing the gene pool, which I think is pretty awful."

Cooper ran her fingers through her blond hair. "I take a mare to a stallion. I register the offspring."

"Right."

"What about in-house breeding?"

"Again, it depends on how deep someone's pockets are. Most of the big farms will breed some of their own mares to some of their own stallions or to someone else's stallions." He swiveled to face Cooper. "You see, breeding is both a science and an art. On paper I can be a genius. What actually gets delivered usually proves that I am a mere mortal."

"But you think Ziggy was good?"

His blue eyes lit up. "Coop, Ziggy was a star. He had bone, drive, brains. His stride was long and fluid. His heart girth was deep so he probably had a big heart, which means he could pump more blood throughout his body, oxygenate himself. It improves athletic performance. He had large nostrils and could suck that air right into his huge lungs. Ziggy had it all, except that he was a chestnut, a bright, gleaming red fellow."

"What's that got to do with it?"

"Oh, some people are prejudiced against chestnuts. There's an old saying among foxhunters that a red mare won't hunt. I've never found it to be true. For instance, Federico Tesio, the great Italian master of matings, believed that grays were—well, mutants; they were weaker. The Aga Khan, another great breeder, thought the opposite. And he bred great grays." Fair shrugged. "I think because there's so much at stake, both money and emotion, people cling to their prejudices. A prejudice is kind of like a rabbit's foot. You squeeze it real hard and hope you'll have some luck."

"I never thought of it that way." Cooper smiled.

"Horsemen are the most opinionated lot.

I've gone to vet school, specialized in re-
productive medicine, have a pretty good
track record, but I can go to a barn and
have someone standing there without a
high-school diploma swearing to me that
Hershey bars will bring on his mare's heat."
Fair held up his hand. "You can't believe
some of the stuff I see and hear. And fads.
The horse world, like any other, goes
through fad spasms. Remember the Horse
Whisperer?"

"Yes."

"Monty Roberts is an extraordinary man.
He gives lectures to ordinary people. One
lecture, they think they can do what he
does. Not so much old horsemen—I don't
mean age, but people who grew up with
horses—but the new people. One of these
new guys, a rich lawyer from Washington,
said to me, 'I whisper. My horse doesn't listen.' Actually, I apologize, Coop, this is a
lot more than you need to know, and I'm
going off on a tangent." He blushed.

"Not at all. I see similar behavior but in
different circumstances. Very often I'll be
questioning a witness to a crime or an accident and they will have a fact wrong—
say, the color of the victim's shirt. Even if

you show them the shirt, they'll cling to their perception. It's a way the mind protects itself."

"So who can you rely on?"

Cooper shrugged. "Who knows? But the more training you have in observation, the more reliable you are."

"Yes." Fair turned his eyes back to the screen. "I wish I knew what Jerome was putting together. Do you know why he was out on Yellow Mountain Road at night?"

"No."

"Big horse farms on Yellow Mountain Road." Fair ran his fingers through his blond, close-cropped hair.

"That's the only thing I've come up with, but what would he see at night? Maybe he was driving around to order his thoughts. I do that."

"Maybe, but Jerome strikes me as having had a mission."

"The one tenuous link I have is Mary Pat's notebook. Remember, we found it in Barry's possessions?"

"Right. Did Jerome read it? I know you have it down at the office, but if he was as determined as I think, he would have wanted to read it."

"He did. That might be what set him on his search for Ziggy's children and by now grandchildren and great-grandchildren. What happened to the thoroughbreds that didn't race?" She paused a second. "By the by, I read Mary Pat's notebook and didn't understand a thing. It's all Greek to me. Anyway, back to the thoroughbred that didn't race."

"Like any other animal, some died young. Not many, but some might have had colic or a birth defect or run through a fence in a thunderstorm. Those that survived—the great number—usually wound up as show hunters or event horses or, if they were very lucky," he smiled broadly, "foxhunters."

"Now, Fair, what's so special about that?"

"Their owners love them and they get to spend the fall out in the countryside with other horses. What a life!"

"You know, it sounds pretty good to me." She returned to the screen. "Keep going."

He scrolled down. "Ah."

On the screen were the names of other horses born the same year as Ziggy Flame.

Those that had glorious careers on the racetrack appeared first, followed by those having glorious careers at stud. Sometimes the two overlapped, but often they did not. Ack Ack, Arts and Letters, Majestic Prince, and Shuree were all born the same year as Ziggy Flame: 1966.

"What?"

He pointed to the screen. "Ziggy's sire was Tom Fool, an outstanding horse. You'll find that blood in good pedigrees today."

"Two stood in Kentucky."

Fair added, "One in Maryland—a full brother, born a year later, 1967." He rubbed his chin; a blond stubble rasped his palm. "Mary Pat bred that same mare back to Tom Fool the year after Ziggy. She didn't yet know Ziggy would be so good, but it's quite common for a breeder to send a mare back to the same stallion two years in a row." He paused, thought long and hard, then shook his head. "Rabies and Ziggy Flame."

"It cost Jerome his life. He made the connection we're missing." Cooper, patient, knew she had to keep digging.

"Harry called me late this afternoon. She, Alicia, and Aunt Tally were at St. James. It's a long shot, but tomorrow let's go back there."

Cooper smiled. "What are we looking for?"

"Ziggy. An echo."

38

Friday morning, nine-thirty, on June 25, Tazio Chappars opened the door of Carmen Gamble's shop. She needed a quick trim, as she had to make a presentation to a client at one in the afternoon. Brinkley followed on her heels.

Toby, the receptionist, looked up. "Oh, Tazio, Carmen called from the airport. She's on her way to Bermuda. Her aunt is very sick."

"I didn't know she had an aunt in Bermuda."

"Me, neither, but I know you need your haircut, and Cindy Green said she'd be glad to do it."

Cindy Green, twirling her scissors, called out, "Showtime!"

Toby whispered, "Brinkley, I've got a cookie."

Brinkley's ears perked up.

Tazio was right. Carmen didn't have an aunt in Bermuda.

39

Potlicker Creek flowed the four and a half miles from St. James to Harry's farm. Along the way it widened, as other small creeks fed into it, until finally it spilled into the Mechums River.

The waters, clear and cool, had been favored by the native population. Although the English had settled the eastern and central parts of Albemarle County before the Revolutionary War, only a handful ventured this far west, thanks to the vigilance and ferocity of the Monacans.

Once Cornwallis surrendered at Yorktown, the mood of the now-independent Americans swung upward and westward. Crushing war debts drove some far past the boundaries of Anglo civilization. Others knew fortunes would be made if they could only figure out how to get their produce and products to burgeoning cities and towns back east.

Potlicker Creek, not being a mighty river, offered little in the way of transportation. But those who settled at the base of the Blue Ridge Mountains discovered that the crystal creek water made soft whiskey or clear spirits, if that was your preference.

A tangle of footpaths leading back to the stills tucked in the hollows crisscrossed the creek along its course. The revenue man had tried to tame the distillers. More than one never made it back home. Finally, the government ignored the distillers until the upheavals of the Great Depression.

During that time, families along the Appalachian Chain were removed, bought out, or forced out to make way for the explosion of public works designed to revive the economy as well as to stave off revolt. Along the top of the Blue Ridge Mountains the Skyline Drive was built, in use to this day, as a monument to Franklin D. Roosevelt's vision and a sorrow to those families forced to leave home.

The moonshine men became ever more

adept at hiding or moving. Potlicker Creek would see a still erected for a season then moved deeper into a sheltering mountain crevice. As Albemarle County became more and more desirable, the distillers took their trade to Nelson County, meeting stout resistance from those Nelson County men already in the business.

Harry, Fair, Alicia, and Aunt Tally, who was making a habit of visiting Alicia, stood at a narrow crossing of Potlicker Creek a mile behind the training track at St. James. The slick slide along the creek bank bore testimony to the work of muskrats, an animal as industrious as the beaver.

Along the creek, mountain laurel and blackberries spilled over one another. A canopy of various oaks, hickories, maples, and black walnuts added to the cool stillness of the morning.

Indomitable as she was, Aunt Tally couldn't walk far on the uneven ground, slick with dew. Alicia, driving Big Mim's second vehicle, a Land Cruiser—on loan so Alicia could see if she liked it—rolled along until the farm road played out near Potlicker Creek. The short walk to the creek took ten minutes, with Fair clearing away the low brush with a machete. Aunt Tally refused an arm under her elbow, gamely stepping forward with the help of her cane.

"High winds." Aunt Tally pointed to a tulip poplar broken in half across the creek. "Must have been that storm firing through here two weeks ago."

"When Mary Pat was alive she had the men keep the trails cleared. Remember, she had trails on both sides of the creek?" Alicia said.

"Used to have wonderful hunts up here. Picnics, too. When I was a little girl, Sharkey Southwell kept a big still not four hundred yards east of here. Then he got religion and that was the end of the still. It was also the end of Sharkey's easy money. He became a roofer after that," Aunt Tally grumbled. "Sharkey added a few blackberries to his waters. In those days you could take your pick: blackberries, cherries, and, oh, the apple brandy. You never tasted anything so good in your life. Only one place makes apple brandy anymore. Down in Covesville. Legal, too. Never tastes as good when it's legal." She laughed, a dry laugh.

"Alicia, aren't there high pastures back there?" Fair inquired.

"Yes, St. James goes to the top of the mountain. There are hundreds of acres of summer pastures, which we used for the cattle. Every May we'd drive them up, bringing them back in September. Royal Orchard still has high pastures." Alicia mentioned a farm atop a spur of the Blue Ridge that ran east–west along Route 64. "Once Mary Pat was gone, I sold the cattle, and there wasn't a reason to keep up the pastures. Also, the cost of labor kept going up." She paused a moment. "I'm glad I kept St. James. You know, those three years I had with Mary Pat taught me to love central Virginia."

"Mary Pat's up there, close by." Mrs. Murphy remembered what the fox had told her.

"Hush. Alicia was extra kind letting you tag along," Harry admonished her.

"Did the fox say the high meadows?" Tucker asked.

"Yes. At least, that's the story foxes have passed down. Her ring traveled a long way, didn't it?" Mrs. Murphy looked up at Mary Pat's ring on Harry's finger.

"If Mary Pat or what's left of her is up there under a cairn of stone, Ziggy's up there, too," Pewter said.

"No." Mrs. Murphy was putting the pieces of this strange puzzle together, but she was missing some large ones. *"I think the killer, when all was safe, brought Ziggy down and got him out of here."*

"He'd never stay up there by himself. He would jump those fences. Stallions need high, high fences, and those were cattle pastures," Pewter sensibly replied.

"Whoever killed Mary Pat knew horses. That's why he kept Ziggy. He or she would have been smart enough to take a mare up there to keep him company if Ziggy had to stay up there for a while. I don't know if this was a crime of passion or a crime of money, but whoever did it has kept it covered up for thirty years. Until now." Mrs. Murphy wanted to get up to the high meadows. They'd be overgrown, but who knows what she might find? Her senses and sensibility were superior to the human variety.

"How does Barry fit in?" Pewter, frustrated at not understanding, growled.

"He rented the stables. He may have

gone up to those meadows. It'd be a stiff hike but fun. Maybe it got him to thinking. But he did have Mary Pat's breeding notes. He clearly was working toward something. And he was found two miles downstream. That part brings up questions."

"Mrs. Murphy, it would take a Hercules to carry a man like Barry two miles downstream." Pewter was right.

"Whoever killed him threw him in an SUV or the back of a truck and drove on the road. Regular road. Turned up an old farm road, came to the stream; there are old trails. He could have made it without too much effort. Then he picked up the body and walked downstream. He or she didn't need to walk miles. It was a good plan. Few people come up to Potlicker Creek," Tucker, voice low, said, her ears forward.

"Why didn't the sheriff figure that out?" Pewter played devil's advocate.

"Oh, I think he did, but too late. Too late," Mrs. Murphy replied.

"What do you mean?" Tucker walked to the edge of the creek. The bank was steep.

"Rick was thorough. They combed the banks of this creek for miles in both directions, but by the time it occurred to him to *come up the unused roads leading in, it was too late. And remember, whoever did this was smart enough not to pick a road that would come straight up to the creek. So walking along the creek wouldn't get you any tire tracks. And it rained a few days after we found Barry. There's luck involved in crime detection, not just science and observation. Rick has had bad luck. We've got to get up to those high meadows."* Mrs. Murphy, deep in thought, peered down at the muskrat slide.

"Murphy, there's rabies here. At St. James." Pewter sat down. *"And for all you know it's sweeping down from those high meadows. I'm not going up there."*

"Don't be a chicken. You have your rabies shot." Tucker pushed through the blackberries to a clear space on the bank. She peered over the side, seeing the opening to the muskrat den.

"I'm not a chicken. I'm cautious, that's all. Anyway, how do you think you're going to get up there? If you run away now, Harry will never take you out again." Pewter puffed out her chest, secure in her conviction.

"Harry will get up there. I bet you one

catnip sockie." Mrs. Murphy's green eyes twinkled.

The plump gray cat considered this. *"I'm not taking that bet."*

The three animals laughed.

Tucker addressed Mrs. Murphy. *"You know, you said this was a crime of passion or money. If Alicia is the killer it would be both."*

Pewter perked right up. *"She came back to see the ring. Aha! I knew it."*

"You two." Mrs. Murphy shook her head. *"And where was Alicia when Barry was killed?"*

"Barry has nothing to do with this." Pewter didn't like to be refuted. *"I believe Carmen Gamble killed him. Or Sugar. But Carmen was in the middle of it."*

"Well, if it's Carmen, Harry sees her often enough, and if it's Alicia, our dear human is standing right next to her." Tucker marveled at Harry's ability to land in the middle of danger.

40

Rick hung up the phone. "Jerome didn't have rabies."

Cooper, at her desk, cheered. "Thank God."

Rick celebrated by lighting up a Camel. He'd returned to his favorite brand after trying others. Two blue plumes escaped his nostrils. "If those tests had come back positive, we'd be answering the calls of people shooting one another's dogs and cats and then one another. Thank God for small favors."

It was a very small favor, indeed.

41

Black clouds, their undersides limned with darkest silver, began peeking over the tops of the Blue Ridge Mountains. The temperature dropped. The wind rustled the tops of the trees, sending a few leaves flying.

Mrs. Murphy, awakened by a persistent whippoorwill, jumped off the bed. Tucker snorted as she was stretched on the rug, but she didn't waken. Pewter, as usual, was dead to the world and draped over Harry's head.

As the tiger padded through the kitchen, the old railroad clock's black hands announced three forty-five. The short pendulum with the gold disc at the end swung monotonously to and fro. Seconds and minutes ticked away, but Mrs. Murphy rarely worried about time. She thought of it as a human invention. They drove themselves crazy with clocks, phones, machines. She thought time was an illusion and age a conceit. A cat lives every moment intensely. Pewter slept intensely. Mrs. Murphy brushed through the animal door intensely. Alive, alert, in the present, whiskers forward, that's the way to live.

She scampered to the barn just as the owl flew through the opened hayloft door.

"Hoo, hoo-hoo."

Mrs. Murphy climbed the ladder to the hayloft. Simon, sound asleep in his nest, clutched the broken Pelham curb chain, his prized possession. Simon wanted shiny things. A broken curb chain was as good as a Tiffany diamond to him.

Flatface the owl bent over from her large nest in the cupola, climbed to the side, opened her wings, and effortlessly floated down, landing exactly in front of the cat.

"Good evening," Mrs. Murphy greeted her.

"And a good evening it's been, Mrs. Murphy. Hunting's good before a storm, and how is it that I so often have the plea-

sure of your company as the old barometer is dropping?"

"You know, I never thought of that. I think it wakes me up, although tonight that whip-poorwill did the job. I was going to go to the edge of the woods to give him a piece of my mind. Have you ever noticed when the moonlight strikes their eyes just right, they are ruby red?"

"So they are. I personally don't under-stand ground nesters. Why on earth, for-give the pun," she hooted, "would any self-respecting bird want to sit in the dirt or leaves or a bunch of twigs? Even a silly house dog can eat them."

"Better not let Tucker hear you say that."

"Tucker is the exception that proves the rule. And Tazio's Lab is all right," Flatface conceded.

"The ground nesters rely on camou-flage," Mrs. Murphy, her own stripes a good cover, replied.

"That's like humans relying on prayer. Work then pray, I say. It's blasphemy that they believe the Almighty is a human. I try to overlook this offense and their stupidity. We all know the Great Omnipotent Owl watches over us all."

"Doesn't seem to be watching over this part of Virginia right now," Mrs. Murphy wryly commented. She wasn't going to get drawn into a religious discussion, since she devoutly believed spiritual life was guided by a heavenly cat of epic proportion.

"Why, things are wonderful. I haven't had such good hunting in years. Years." She fluffed out her large chest, then turned her head almost upside down.

"It makes me dizzy when you do that."

"Hoo hoo-hoo, ha." The big bird righted her head.

"You're right, hunting is superb, but I was thinking about the human deaths, murders."

"Oh, that? I did ask my friends if they'd heard of rabies over the mountains. Word came back: 'No.' I just haven't seen you to tell you."

"Thank you for asking around."

Simon rolled over in his sleep.

Flatface observed him sternly. *"He's supposed to be a nocturnal animal. Lazy sod."*

The whippoorwill sang out again just as the first raindrops splattered on the roof.

"Simon tries, but he doesn't get any fur-

ther than the feed room. He picks up under the horse buckets, I'll give him credit for that. He keeps things tidy. Then he gets full and goes to sleep." Mrs. Murphy laughed at the funny-looking possum, a very sweet soul.

"Oh, he doesn't content himself with the feed room and the leavings under the horse buckets. He opens that desk drawer every night for candy. It's a wonder he has a tooth in his head. Really, that's one of the marvelous aspects of having a beak: no tooth decay."

"Lucky. I had my teeth cleaned in December. I hate it, but Harry drags me down to Dr. Shulman and they both tell me how good it is for my health. And Pewter screams the entire way. She always knows when it's a vet trip. What a baby."

"That cat has such a high opinion of herself."

"The best—you'll love this: We were at St. James and Pewter convinced the barn swallows to throw down tail feathers. She picked them up and ran to the humans. Disgraceful."

The owl's golden eyes glittered as she laughed. *"And they believed her?"*

"That's the terrible part, they did!"

"Even Harry?" Flatface asked.

"Even Harry."

"I thought she had more sense than that. I heard she left the post office. How's she doing?"

"Mmm, her attention is focused on the murders. I don't know what she'll be like once she can think about her future."

42

I wondered when you would show up."
Amy Wade smiled, her light-brown eyes
merry. "I thought you were mad at me."

Izzy Stoltfus usually worked Saturday
mornings, but she was so undone by
Jerome's murder she had taken a leave of
absence. Amy Wade filled in while Pug
Harper frantically searched for a permanent Saturday employee.

"No. Just busy and thinking." Harry was
so used to taking her mail home, she'd forgotten her mailbox key ring. "Forgot my
key. Will you hand me my mail?"

"You know, there's a rule that we're not
supposed to do that, but it sure seems silly
here in Crozet." She slipped her hand into

Harry's mailbox, retrieving mail and magazines.

"Mom, your key is with your truck keys," Mrs. Murphy reminded her, wondering if Harry would run out in the rain to fetch it should she remember in the first place.

Tavener, Alicia, and Aunt Tally all came in together.

"Hey!" Tavener beamed at Harry. "It's not the same without you." He quickly spoke to Amy. "But you're doing a good job."

"Harry left big sneakers to fill." Amy smiled.

"Has Miranda been in at all?" Aunt Tally shook her umbrella as it continued to rain, soaking and steady.

"To pick up her mail and chat," Amy answered.

"Bills." Tavener grimaced.

"Where's Herb?" Harry inquired. "I haven't seen him for two days."

"Buying a new refrigerator," Amy informed her. "He's paralyzed by the options."

"They're as expensive as an old Datsun." Aunt Tally giggled as she tossed her junk mail in the trash.

"Don't forget, we're planning a big do for

July seventeenth. It's Herb's thirtieth anniversary." Harry suffered a moment of panic because she hadn't yet contacted a band and the good ones booked far in advance.

"He came to St. Luke's just as I left for Los Angeles." Alicia knew little of the Reverend Jones but liked what she did know.

"Alicia, those were sad circumstances, made all the more dolorous by your vacating central Virginia." Tavener propped one elbow on the counter. "Just think of the trouble we could have roused up had you stayed."

"There's still time!" Aunt Tally cracked.

"Miranda!" The cats and dog ran to Miranda, who entered through the front door.

"My little animals." She knelt down for hugs and kisses.

"Where's your beau?" Tavener liked Tracy Raz.

"My beau has been traveling throughout the South. Today he's in Nashville."

"Why?"

"Visiting friends. His expressed reason is

he wants to look at small-town development."

"Nashville isn't a small town." Tavener laughed.

"No, but he wants to study Franklin, Tennessee. Tracy has this wonderful vision for Crozet. Ever since he bought the old bank building he's wanted to create a town square and who knows what else. I'll be glad when he returns."

"Absence makes the heart grow fonder," Alicia said.

"Bull. Absence makes the eye wander." Aunt Tally rapped her cane on the floor for emphasis.

The door pushed open. Toby from Carmen's salon, Shear Heaven, said with a wrinkled brow, "We don't know where Carmen is. I called her sister for a phone number in Bermuda, because we're almost out of shampoo, and her sister said they had no relatives in Bermuda. Where's Carmen?"

Aunt Tally rapped her cane on the floor. "Hiding out. She knows more than she's telling."

Tavener put his arm around Toby's shoulders. "Don't worry. Carmen is just having one of her bad hair days." He smiled at his little joke, then turned his attention to Aunt Tally. "What could Carmen possibly know?"

"She spent a lot of time out at St. James, Tavener. She's not a dumb girl. She might have picked something up, listened to the boys and just put two and two together."

Tavener laughed. He didn't want to offend the nonagenarian, but he said, "With all due respect, she's off on a toot or she's found a hot date. We're all a little on edge. Much as I loathed Jerome, his death was a shock. Like I said, we're all on edge, but Carmen has nothing to worry about."

Aunt Tally simply replied, "I hope you're right."

43

Dew glistened on mountain laurel, cock-spur hawthorns, spruces, pines, hickories, oaks, and maples. The once-pristine high meadows, now overrun with Virginia creeper, thorns, and baby cedars, still afforded a sweeping view of the lands unfurling to the east. The soil remained damp from recent rains.

Harry's eyes swept over these high acres—elevation about 1,500 feet above sea level—and she figured she could bring them back to good pasture with three years of hard work. While burning enriches the soil, she would never burn this high—too much wind, which shifted constantly. She'd have to rent a bulldozer, knock off the underbrush, carefully rolling it in large piles. Many small burrowing creatures would be thrilled with that. Then she'd fertilize and seed for three years running. The third summer, she'd bring stock back up here for the grass; roots should be strong by then.

She loved pasture management—indeed, any type of agricultural pursuit, just seeing these old high acres of Mary Pat's set her to dreaming.

At eight-thirty in the morning, the light flooded over the trees, shrubs, and vines. A purple finch darted from one shrub to another as a kestrel soared overhead. Industrious spiders, lumbering beetles, and shimmering butterflies added to the activities of the meadow. A deep, narrow creek carried the mountain runoff down to Potlicker Creek.

Harry, Fair, Susan, and Cooper, using old topographical maps, divided the large acreage into manageable one-hundred-acre units. Each would take a corner of one unit and work inward. Given the heavy underbrush in parts, this took perseverance, good boots, and liberal applications of insect repellent.

They'd started at seven this Sunday

morning. Being country people, that seemed like a late hour. Harry's relentless curiosity had gotten the better of her and she roped in her friends to make the trek up to the meadow.

Fair drove his truck, followed by Harry in her 1978 Ford. They made it to a small turnaround about a quarter of a mile from the high pastures. Together with Mrs. Murphy, Pewter, and Tucker, they packed in the last quarter mile.

As the humans slowly moved along, the animals stayed together, walking along the westernmost outside stone wall.

"A good stone fence lasts for centuries. Needs a tap or two." Mrs. Murphy, like Harry, appreciated value for work and effort.

"Aren't many people who can build a stone fence. Takes a good eye and a strong back." Tucker closed her eyes as she pushed through thorns. *"And who can afford it?"*

"Mom could do it—the work, I mean." Mrs. Murphy stopped to sniff where a long-tailed mouse had scurried into a crevice. *"Cootie,"* she insulted the mouse.

"Domesticated twit," came the saucy reply.

"Did you hear that?" Mrs. Murphy stuck her paw into the crevice.

Pewter joined her. *"Mice go to school to learn how to insult cats."*

"Leave it. We've got a lot to cover." Tucker, nose to the ground, pressed on.

"You're lucky I have obligations." Mrs. Murphy whapped at the stones, then left the unperturbed mouse, who stuck his head out of his refuge to see the two cats, tails high, moving down the stone line.

"Boy, that gray one is really fat." He giggled as his friend came out from his nest in the stone fence.

"I heard that." Pewter whirled around and in two pounces almost caught the smart-mouth.

"Pewter," Tucker chided.

"Almost!" the gray called out triumphantly. *"A split second earlier and I'd be enjoying mouse tartare."*

The two mice, who had repaired to the same nest, huddled together until Pewter rejoined her companions.

The younger mouse said, *"Amazing how fat creatures are light on their paws."*

The cats and corgi scrambled over tumbled gray stones as a flash of blue, a skink, sped along the tops.

"It was nice of Cooper to come along, given that she worked late last night." Tucker liked Cynthia very much and thought she should have a corgi.

"Susan fixed lunch. Wonder when the humans will take lunch break?" Pewter hoped a chicken sandwich had been made all for her, no sharing with Mrs. Murphy and Tucker.

"If we do find Mary Pat or some sort of evidence, Cooper needs to be here," Mrs. Murphy sagely noted, ignoring Pewter's focus on food.

"Harry won't screw it up," Pewter said.

"No, but—well, better that she's here." The tiger cat stopped, lifted her head, inhaling the tart odor of deer.

Pewter turned left at the corner, now moving along the southernmost wall.

Mrs. Murphy stopped, sitting on top of a flat stone. *"Let's take a quick breather. This stuff is tough going. So much has grown over the stone. You know, it's wasteful to let a pasture go. Really."*

"Mmm." Pewter sat next to her as

Tucker climbed up on top where stones had fallen away, giving her an easier climb.

Tucker watched Susan, carrying a long thick stick, swat at underbrush as she fought her way through. *"Well, if no one renting the stables was using this pasture, I guess it cost too much in time and labor to keep it up."*

"Or the farm manager was lazy." Pewter noticed a high cloud shaped like an arrowhead move eastward.

"Or the worker was in on it and didn't want people coming up here," Mrs. Murphy said. *"Marshall Kressenberg was a groom here when Mary Pat disappeared. He moved to Maryland and has had such success breeding and raising thoroughbreds. That was before our time. If we'd been here and could have smelled him, we'd know."* She knew she could smell fear, and she believed she could smell guilt.

Both Pewter and Tucker looked at her. *"That's a thought."*

"According to Cooper—at least what I've been able to overhear these last four weeks—the prime suspect was Alicia, but they didn't have enough evidence to

charge her. She wasn't here on the exact day Mary Pat disappeared. Everyone else who worked at St. James or who was in-volved with Mary Pat in one way or the other checked out. Police figured she was missing a minimum of twenty-four hours before she was reported missing by Kressenberg. Well, if Alicia and Marshall were covering for each other, that would work. Alicia's in L.A. Her alibi is airtight. Marshall reports Mary Pat's disappearance late, a day later." Mrs. Murphy had given the matter a great deal of thought.

"That doesn't have anything to do with Barry. At least that's one murder out of the way." Pewter batted at a bright yellow milk butterfly.

"I think Barry figured out Mary Pat's murder or was close to figuring it out." Mrs. Murphy's beautiful green eyes opened wider. *"And as for Carmen, I think you are right. She's guilty. I don't think she killed him, but she's guilty. She did something or said something that exposed him. Think about it."*

Pewter began to feel uneasy.

"Harry found him. Okay, that was fate or bad luck, I reckon, but as usual she's put-

ting her foot right in it. She's got no business up here." Tucker fretted over her human's boundless and dangerous curiosity.

Pewter took a deep breath, scanning down the long length of this southernmost fence. *"Didn't the fox give you any direction?"*

"No. She said it was a story passed along. Nobody knew any more, but she reported that Mary Pat hadn't been buried deep enough under some stones. Some creature managed to get her hand and part of an arm. At least that's what she'd heard. But she also said there were human remains that had never been found all over the county, some going back before the Revolutionary War."

Tucker looked at Mrs. Murphy. *"That's comforting."*

They laughed, got up, and started moving again along the stone wall. By the time they reached the easternmost corner, the humans were working in their second quadrant.

"Break time." Pewter sat down.

"A corner would be a logical place, wouldn't it?" Tucker said. *"Easy to remember."* The corgi used her front paw to wipe

away a cobweb that dangled from her eyebrows. *"In case the killer wanted to come back."*

"Gross." Pewter made a face.

"Maybe it would be easier to dig under a corner, because the stones wouldn't give way as easily. Maybe. I don't know that. Of course, some kind of marker like a huge tree is a possibility, too," Mrs. Murphy said.

"But the fox said stones?" Tucker's ears drooped for a second as her tone was questioning.

"Yes, she did," Mrs. Murphy answered.

Tucker carefully inspected the inside of the corner and the outside. *"Woodchucks used to be here."* She squeezed down in the hole, then backed out. *"It's promising. I'll dig a little. You two move up the wall."*

"I can dig," Pewter offered.

"Not as fast as I can. I can ruin a rose garden in fifteen minutes." Tucker smiled, then ducked back into the hole, digging her way down to the nesting area.

"Come on, Pewter." Mrs. Murphy moved off.

Twenty minutes later a dirty Tucker, with a heavy bone resembling a femur in her mouth, triumphantly raced on top of the wall, leaping over fallen branches and thick entwining vines to reach the cats.

"Tucker!" Mrs. Murphy shouted with excitement.

"Let's take this over to them." Tucker, who had dropped the bone for the cats to inspect, picked it up again.

"First let's see if we can get them here. Then you can lead them straight to the spot," Pewter suggested. *"And we won't have to go back and forth through the underbrush."*

The three meowed, yowled, barked, and whined. Eventually Harry made her way over, thinking someone had cornered a snake or upturned a tortoise.

Upon seeing the bone she gasped, then put both fingers in her mouth and whistled.

Fair, Susan, and Cooper hacked their way toward her from their separate directions.

Upon seeing the whitened long fragment, Cooper immediately called Rick on her cell phone.

44

The sweet smell of honeysuckle filled the late-afternoon air. Midsummer could fall anywhere between June twenty-first and June twenty-third, but Harry celebrated the entire week right up to July, since she loved the festivals and myths surrounding the longest day of the year.

However, this last Sunday in June she was anything but celebratory. That morning, as soon as Cooper called Rick regarding the long bone proudly displayed by Tucker, part of her was thrilled that this might be one of Mary Pat's bones and part of her was sickened. The idea that the vivacious Mary Pat was killed, then dragged to a lonely grave undiscovered until now, made her sad, far sadder than she could have imagined.

Cooper, to protect Harry, Fair, and Susan, waited for Rick Shaw. When he arrived she asked Harry to direct Tucker to lead Cooper to the spot. But both Cooper and Rick sent the three humans partway down from the meadows. The two law-enforcement officers didn't want any of them to know the exact spot if more bones were buried there. Why take the chance that Harry, Susan, or Fair might slip, say something to the wrong person?

Once Tucker took Cooper and Rick to the site, Cooper walked the corgi down to Harry, ordering all of them to go home.

Fair promised he'd visit Harry tonight after he checked pedigrees on his computer. He said he had an idea. Before leaving he also asked Rick to call him at the clinic should the sheriff find the remains of Ziggy Flame, as well.

Rick promised he would but cautioned them all not to jump to conclusions. One bone that looked like a femur did not constitute the solution to the disposition of Mary Pat Reines's remains. Nor were they even sure the bone was human. Rick especially cautioned Harry, who was known to jump the gun.

Harry, as always, sought solace in hard work. She was installing large rectangular trellises reaching from the ground to the roofline of her new shed. Her tools already hung neatly inside. The old but serviceable 1958 John Deere tractor rested inside, the manure spreader hooked up to the PTO. Her two-horse trailer was now sheltered along with the big Ford F350 dually that pulled it. Only the 1978 Ford endured the elements. That venerable machine remained parked near the back door. That way, should it rain, she could make a dash for it.

As she worked, she talked to her animals. Tucker would get up each time Harry took more than three steps. The cats reposed in the shade of the long barn overhang, but they could hear everything Harry said to them. Matilda, the four-foot-long black snake, hung from a huge old walnut tree in the back lawn. Her hunting radius started on the paddock by the western side of the barn, and over the summer she would make a big counterclockwise circle until, by fall, she was back at the barn, where she would hibernate throughout winter. Matilda evidenced no fear of the cats, dog, or Harry. Being a reptile, she rarely conversed with the mammals, but she kept one glittering eye on them always. Pewter bragged too much about her hunting prowess, and Matilda was determined to give the gray blowhard a vicious bite she would never forget if the fat kitty so much as looked cross-eyed at her.

"I just painted that eave." Harry squinted up as she carefully placed the trellis straight against the outside wall.

A thin powder of sawdust spiraled out of a perfectly round hole, where a carpenter bee had already made an impressive home for herself and her offspring.

"Can't keep up with them. They're as industrious as beavers," Tucker sympathized.

Carpenter bees really didn't do damage, but the sight of those round holes in overhangs, eaves, and doorjambs offended human aesthetics. Some people worried that the large flying bombers, often mistaken for bumblebees, would sting them, but the carpenter bee with its smooth black bottom wasn't a stinger.

"Beavers built another dam on the creek. Low down this time. I walked over there last night," Mrs. Murphy informed them.

"Good. That will give us a good pond." Tucker, wary of beavers, appreciated their engineering skills.

Anyway, who could afford to dig out a pond these days? The beavers really were doing them a favor.

Harry walked back to the barn, shaded her eyes with her hand, checked to make certain she'd lined up the trellis perfectly. She had. She walked back, climbed the ladder next to the trellis. Gently she tapped in long thin nails to secure the top. Then she climbed down and nailed in the bottom. She subsequently put in a row of nails across the middle.

"There."

"Perfect." Pewter, considering herself an expert on all things demanding a critical eye, praised her human.

"Now the big question. Do I plant climbing roses, clematis, or morning glories?"

"Morning glories are running wild over the back pastures. I say roses. That will bring out all the bees. I like to hear them," Tucker suggested.

"I vote for that." Mrs. Murphy half-dozed. *"Plant the clematis around the lamppost by the back walkway."*

"Clematis has those big showy flowers. Purple. Hmm, maybe white. Of course, I could do both purple and white." Harry paced along the building. "I'll do that on the lamppost. If I put out climbing roses the fragrance will be spectacular, plus I think the clematis will go better on the back there because I've got the ivy lining the walkway. That's it." She walked inside, plucked a shovel off the wall, and began digging a bed for the rosebushes. The good soil would be enriched from the compost heap.

Yesterday she'd bought rosebushes and clematis starters at the big nursery, Eltzroth, on Route 29 south of Charlottesville.

Just as she pulled the last of the soil over the roots, the low motor rumble of Miranda's Ford Falcon alerted Tucker.

"Miranda!" Tucker recognized the sound of all of Harry's friends' vehicles.

"We know that." The cats could identify the sounds, too.

"That looks good. Roses are so tough." Miranda, large basket in both hands, kicked the car door shut. "Thank you for calling me about your adventure this morning. I thought you might need refreshment and"—she smiled—"conversation."

Wiping her hands on her jeans, Harry kissed Miranda on the cheek. "I'm so glad to see you."

"Well, come on. Let's take a tea break. It's almost teatime. Where would you like to eat? Kitchen? Screened-in porch? Back-yard?"

"Let's go in the kitchen. It's nice and cool inside."

Harry took the basket from Miranda and the two women made their way to the kitchen slowly, for Miranda had to stop and admire Harry's flowers. The animals shot ahead of them. Pewter knew something good in that basket had her name on it.

Once the iced tea was poured and the herbed turkey sandwiches—along with extra turkey for the cats and dog—served, the two women sat down.

"Tucker found a bone." Harry jumped right in.

"That's what you said." Miranda pushed over a jar of her homemade herbed mayonnaise should Harry want more.

"Did I?"

"When you called." Miranda shook her head.

"I'm getting forgetful." Harry frowned.

Miranda reassured her. "You have a lot on your mind and it's a good mind. Don't worry, you're not losing your memory."

Mrs. Murphy stoutly spoke up. *"I worked hard this morning. More food, please."*

"Here, Murphy." Harry gave her another morsel of turkey.

"Big Mim's calling a gathering. She wants everyone at her house tomorrow evening."

"About this?"

"No. Mim's too smart to be that obvious. We are all to get there at six to go over details for Herb's anniversary. He'll come over at seven-thirty. You know Mim. She'll find out as much as she can this way. It will appear spontaneous."

"I don't think Big Mim ever had a spontaneous moment."

"Before you were born." Miranda winked.

"Is that what happens, Miranda? I mean, as we go along in life there's no time to be free, to just pick up and go."

"And where would you go?"

Harry laughed. "I don't know." She dropped more turkey for each critter, then grew serious. "I know that bone was Mary Pat's. I just know it."

"My grace is sufficient for thee: for my strength is made perfect in weakness." Miranda quoted Second Corinthians, Chapter 12, Verse 9.

"What made you think of that?"

"I don't know. It popped into my head. Happens to me a lot. Eventually I figure it out." She dabbed the napkin at the corners of her mouth, light-pink lipstick transferring to the napkin. "I trust in the Good Lord's messages."

"Which reminds me, how was church today?"

"Wonderful, even if Ruthie Dalsky did forget her robe. She never sings off-key, so what's a choir robe compared to that?" The ice cubes tinkled as she lifted the tall glass. "Harry, I think the Good Lord brought Alicia back for a reason and I think she'll stay. She'll move back."

"You think she killed Mary Pat and will come to get justice?"

"No. I don't know what I think. It's a feeling."

"Well," Harry exhaled, "my feeling is, whatever my pets found will be in Tuesday's newspaper."

"Did you see anything?"

"No."

"I helped," Pewter boasted.

"Eat your turkey, turkey." Mrs. Murphy tapped her with her right paw.

"If they find Ziggy Flame it will be a different—mmm, not a solution to all this, exactly, but a different take than if they don't. Because if Ziggy isn't up there with Mary Pat, then I believe she was killed because of him." Harry thought out loud.

"Isn't it you who says people are killed for love or money—not horses?"

"Ziggy, at the time of Mary Pat's death, was just proving himself at stud. Had he lived he would have been worth a fortune. It's funny, Miranda, I feel like I'm walking in a fog and I can see shapes up ahead but I can't quite make out what they are. I know I'm getting closer. I know that if Mary Pat is up there, more than her bones will be pried loose. Someone is going to break."

"It takes them longer, but they do figure things out," Pewter said between chews.

"We haven't figured it out yet, Pewts. We

just know that the murders are related." Mrs. Murphy reached up, her claws digging into the tablecloth.

"Murphy!" Harry rapped her paw but gave her another piece of turkey nonetheless. Then she gave Pewter and Tucker a piece, as well.

"If that is Mary Pat, someone is going to be pretty darn nervous," Tucker said.

While Harry and Miranda visited with each other, Fair was glued to his computer. What he was finding was extremely interesting, and he kicked himself for not thinking of it earlier.

45

Newcomers to the country take some time to adjust to the pace of life. It's not so much that it's slower but that it often begins before sunup. If a person's work is physical—like that of a farmer, a carpenter, a stone mason—folks from the North may think such a worker is lazy. Instead of working fast, the Southern worker keeps a slower but steady pace. It's not until the Northerner labors in the heat that he or she can appreciate the wisdom of this approach.

Blair Bainbridge, when he first moved to Crozet from New York City, suffered the normal prejudices about Virginians. Being a gentleman, he kept them to himself. As years passed, he began to understand that people worked very hard but they didn't make a show about it. He also began to understand that showing off your knowledge was not a good thing. The point was to bring people together, to be inclusive, not to set yourself above others. Even Mim Sanburne, for all her imperiousness, rarely tried to make someone else look stupid. As for Little Mim, her graciousness in the face of unpleasantness astonished him. In fact, the worse it got, the more gracious Little Mim became. That this was the ultimate social revenge had not yet occurred to him. Nor had it occurred to him that if he married Little Mim, there would still be things the family would never say in front of him. This was not because Mim, Jim, or Little Mim disdained Blair but rather because it took twenty years, at least, to comprehend the mere basics of manners and mores of Dixie. Just as aristocrats in old France had learned from birth how to move, how to address people, the various courtesies, and, above all, their own genealogy, so, too, did Southerners, regardless of station. It was bred in the bone.

Harry at six in the morning was inspecting the new beaver dam. She didn't want to disturb their work, but if she ever could, she'd like to build a pond on this site with a small spillway below to the creek. Nature leeched out some of the water, but the beavers constructed a formidable dam, their lodges dotting the rough pond created by their effort. A blue heron and a green kingfisher worked the waters.

Green kingfishers are native to southern Texas and the tropics, not Virginia, but there was a beauty right on Harry's farm. No doubt the shining fellow hadn't read the *National Audubon Society Field Guide to North American Birds*.

On seeing the green kingfisher, his white collar immaculate, Harry made a mental note to call Nancy King, a friend who was an avid bird-watcher.

Insects buzzed around, squirrels romped, a doe with twin fawns raised her head from grazing to observe Harry and her companions. The doe often jumped into the large paddocks to graze with the horses. Sugar and Barry's mares chatted contentedly under wide spreading oaks.

Crossing below the beaver dam, Harry scrambled up the creek bed. Trotting to the three-board fence line between her property and Blair's, she put one hand on the top board and vaulted over, thrilled that she could do it. She'd been good at gymnastics in school.

Pewter scooted underneath. Mrs. Murphy, pretending to be one of the hunters, leapt between the lower board and the second board in the fence. Tucker, like Pewter, squeezed under.

They walked to the top of a low rise midway between the property line and Blair's lovely farmhouse. The old Jones family graveyard, neatly set off by a wrought-iron fence with a curly filigree above the gate, promised peace when the end came. Bryson Jones, Herb's impractical but beloved uncle, rested here, along with all the Joneses through the mid–eighteenth century. The married daughters over the centuries rested here, too. Surnames of Lamont, Taliaferro—pronounced Tolliver—and Sessoms slept with the Joneses. Sessoms is a Cherokee name, and the marriage of a Jones daughter to a Sessoms in the late eighteenth century became a cherished family story.

Leaning against a spectacular oak, Harry thought about three of her contemporaries gone to eternal rest—Barry, Sugar, and Jerome. She didn't like to dwell on her own demise, but under the circumstances it was hard not to think about it.

"Tucker, ever notice that skulls are grinning?"

"Can't say that I've thought about it," the corgi replied seriously, the slanting rays of the early sun burnishing her coat red-gold.

"Don't," Pewter, sitting on a flat long slab, said. *"Morbid."*

Just then a fat caterpillar, green with spiky outgrowths, traversed over her tail, all those caterpillar feet in her fur. Pewter jumped straight up, flipping the caterpillar onto another flat slab tombstone.

Harry, Mrs. Murphy, and Tucker laughed.

"Mighty Puss!" Murphy mocked her.

"Oh, shut up." Pewter turned her back on them all, picked up her tail, and licked the fur back down.

The sky, a brilliant blue, promised a spectacular day.

Harry exhaled through her nose. "Up and at 'em."

"Is she going to cut hay today?" Tucker wondered.

"Think so, but at the moment," Mrs.

Murphy paused as Harry opened the gate and headed toward Blair's, *"she's going to pay a social call. Pewter, are you coming?"*

"No, I'm going to stay here and commune with nature," came the haughty reply.

"Oh, I thought the caterpillar was more nature than you could handle." The tiger bounded out of the graveyard along with Tucker.

"I'll show them. Bunch of snots. I'm not afraid of a caterpillar. It felt creepy, that's all. Too many chubby legs, and there's sticky stuff on the feet. O-o-o." She wrinkled her nose as she turned to watch her family skip toward the farmhouse.

Her nemesis, the bluejay, zoomed into the oak, shrieked, squawked, shook the branches, and then, conceit to the max, floated down to perch on top of a vertical tombstone not four feet from Pewter, who was nursing her pride.

"Where'd you put the caterpillar, idiot cat?"

Pewter's pupils widened. *"What are you doing here?"*

"Looking at your sorry self," the jay whistled.

"I'm not sorry. I'm sitting here amongst the dead, which provokes me to philosophical musings." She wished that the hateful bird were even six inches closer. She knew she'd nab him for sure then.

"Don't make me regurgitate!" The bluejay's topknot stood straight up as he laughed, which sounded like *"queedle, queedle,"* the little happy sound jays make.

"Actually, I didn't think your range would be this far. There's plenty to eat at our place."

"I fly from one state to the other if I feel like it. Bluejays migrate, you know. Life's too good here, so I stay. Course, right now it's getting a little exciting, what with Tucker finding Mary Pat's thigh bone. All the wild animals and birds are talking about it."

"I helped, you know." Pewter puffed out her chest, as did the jay. They looked like odd mirrors of each other.

"Queedle, queedle," the jay's beak clacked.

"I did!"

"Pewter, you'd run the other way if you saw a dead anything."

"Bull! I picked up a dead pileated woodpecker, and I've seen plenty of dead old

things." She stopped for a moment as she inched a tad closer. *"The smell. Hate the smell. Tucker, of course, loves it, but dogs are—well, I don't have to explain."*

As birds have a sharp sense of smell, the jay shrugged. *"Doesn't bother me one way or t'other. I'm not a carrion eater so I don't much care, but the crows, now, they'll tell you that the eyes and the tongue are the greatest delicacy. Whenever a large mammal dies, they hurry to get there before the buzzards."* He slicked down his handsome crest for a moment. *"I love acorns and seeds. I bury them, you know."*

"You don't remember where you buried them."

He cocked his head. *"Sometimes I do forget. Tell you what, whoever planted Mary Pat up there on that high ridge didn't forget."*

"Don't know if it's Mary Pat for sure." Pewter scooted a tiny bit closer.

"It is. We birds can get the word out faster than you guys. And I'll tell you something else, fatty: No Ziggy Flame up there. I bet you Ziggy was right under the human noses all the time."

A thin tongue of breeze licked the distinctive pin-oak leaves.

"That was before my time, but everyone says that Ziggy was charismatic and bright, a bright chestnut. I don't think anyone could hide him. Not for long. He wasn't under their noses." Pewter refuted the jay.

"You know, if you fly over those high pastures there are old trails, and some will take you east, some west. But the most interesting one, considering what's going on, is the one that will take you right down into Greenwood and Route 250. Whoever killed Mary Pat could have hidden Ziggy, then walked him down to Greenwood, loaded him on a trailer, and been out of town before you can say 'caterpillar.' "

"Guess that's one of the reasons—the disappearance of Ziggy Flame—that Alicia wasn't as solid a suspect as the cops hoped she was." Pewter swished her tail. Since the caterpillar had crawled on it, she felt like other things were crawling over her. *"I mean, the woman inherited everything but a couple of broodmares. Ziggy Flame was hers. Why steal him?"*

The jay gurgled, then spoke clearly. *"Throw everyone off the track."*

"Do you think Alicia Palmer killed Mary Pat?"

He shrugged, fluffed out his feathers. *"I don't know Alicia, but one human's pretty much like any other. They're killers by nature."*

Pewter didn't dispute this. The human predatory drive seemed out of proportion to their needs. *"Harry's different."*

The bluejay liked to needle Pewter, but Harry did seem closer to animals than most humans. He decided not to disparage Pewter's favorite human. He watched as Blair opened the back door of his farmhouse. *"Aren't you going to join them?"*

"No."

"What if a whole bag of tent caterpillars fell on you?"

Pewter shuddered. *"Ugh."* Then she leapt at the bluejay, who simply flew straight up, circled, and dive-bombed her.

"Fat cat!"

"I will get you," Pewter spat as he circled her one more time, then sped away.

Harry, like the Sanburnes, recognized that Blair was from other parts. But much as it cut against the grain, she decided to come straight to the point with him. This denied her the pleasure of coming to the point by those decreasing concentric circles that gathered in a wealth of information. That information might appear extraneous, but in good time it was always money in the bank. The other reason she shied away from this was she would go straight to the point only with a dear friend. Such communication was a sign of love and respect. Much as she liked Blair, he wasn't as close to Harry as Susan, Miranda, or Herb.

After Harry and Blair exchanged ideas about Carmen's disappearance, the strange events going on, Amy Wade's settling in at the post office, and other sundry things, Harry thought she might as well get to it.

"More tea?" Blair offered.

"No, thank you. I've overstayed my welcome as it is. I know you've got a lot to do."

"Not as much as you." He smiled.

"The shed is wonderful. I can't thank you enough for your help, and the fence posts are a godsend."

"Harry, you've bailed me out of so many things. If it weren't for you, I don't think my cattle would be looking as good as they do."

"Oh, Blair, you would have learned sooner or later."

Harry had built him a cattle chute, which made worming, giving shots, and tagging so much easier. Blair had been trying to catch his cattle one by one in the field.

"I hope you will forgive me for being direct."

He leaned forward, his sensitive eyes welcoming. "You know I think it saves time." Saving time is quite a virtue among Northerners.

"That it does. As you know, this is the old Jones place, and you've done a beautiful job restoring the cemetery. Herb can't keep up with that and his duties, too."

"Thank you."

"Actually, I should tell you that he and I have spoken and he's asked me to broach this subject." She took a deep breath. "Blair, should you sell this place for any reason, Herbie and I would like to buy it together. We'd work with you any way we can because, as you know, neither one of us is exactly cash heavy."

A broad smile crossed Blair's face, a

face instantly recognizable to anyone who read magazines or looked through clothing catalogs. "No kidding."

"We celebrate his thirty years at St. Luke's next month on the seventeenth. I reckon he'll retire sometime in the next ten years, maybe even the next five. He'd like to live in the farmhouse. And I'd like to farm the bottomland."

"I see. Is the next question about my intentions regarding Little Mim?" Blair, in his sweet way, tried to be Southern by saying intentions.

"Actually, no." Harry exhaled, relieved that she had spoken about the land. "I don't think that's my business."

"Harry, you really are different, you know that?"

"No."

"Trust me. You are. You are the strangest combination of curiosity and rectitude. You can't resist being a detective, but you don't want to pry into someone's personal life."

She flashed her crooked smile. "If I thought you were a murderer, I'd pry."

"Oh, Harry." He tapped the table with his knife. "I didn't want to fall in love with Little Mim. I thought she was just another spoiled, empty, rich snob, but I was wrong. She's not. And becoming vice-mayor has brought her out of herself and out from under her mother's shadow. She's a remarkable lady."

"She is." Harry, while not feeling especially close to Little Mim, could appreciate her good qualities.

"Aunt Tally is for me. Jim and I get along great, but the mother—oh, she's not thrilled about my line of work, and she thinks I'll fall prey to temptation. All those female models. Since most of them are anorexic or bulimic, I'm not attracted one bit!" He laughed.

"Big Mim's much better about you than she used to be."

"I guess. I do wonder how much longer I can model. I think I'm about due for a big life change."

"Me, too."

"Well, you've already started on yours. It's weird to go into the post office and not see you."

"Weird for me, too. I don't know what comes next. I have to sift through dreams and reality."

"Your dream?"

"To farm."

"The reality?" His eyebrows raised.

"You can't make a thin dime."

"Bet if you found the right crop or crops you could."

"That's one of the things I have to think about. Like ginseng—it's a good cash crop. Soybeans can be, too. All kinds of things are going through my head, although I'm caught up in what's been happening around here."

"I guess we all are in one way or another." He laid his knife across his plate. "Harry, I promise you I will give you and Herb first option, should I sell. And I will be as fair as I can."

"Thank you."

"Do you want to tell Herb or should I?"

"I will, since he spoke to me in confidence. Which means we should keep this between ourselves," she said warmly. "If you do sell this wonderful old place, I hope you don't leave Crozet. I've grown to like you very much. We all have."

"Thank you. I feel the same way about you. If I move from here it will be to Dalmally or—and this is my hope—over to Rose Hill. Aunt Tally could use us over

there, and Little Mim would be a tiny bit far-
ther away from her mother."

"I hope you don't expect Aunt Tally not
to meddle." Harry laughed.

"No, but she's not as bad."

As Harry walked out the back door to
leave, she and Blair shook hands on the
first-option deal. A piece of paper was only
as good as the person who signed it. A
handshake staked your reputation on it.

46

Using the Jockey Club software, Fair spent all night checking every registered offspring of Ziggy Flame, those horses born between 1971 and 1974. Then he checked their offspring. He did the same for Ziggy's full brother standing in Maryland. Ziggy Dark Star had a great career at stud. The printout of his offspring was almost book-length.

This only covered horses registered with the Jockey Club. During Ziggy Flame's brief career, he'd also produced hunters and foxhunters from non-black-type mares. Mary Pat generously allowed good horsemen who were not in the race game to breed to her rising star. Big Mim benefited from this generosity and was riding a third-generation hunter with Ziggy Flame blood, as was Harry. Her Tomahawk had Ziggy blood, since his grandfather, Flaming Tomahawk, came from one of Big Mim's best mares.

As hunters and foxhunters have no central registry such as the Jockey Club, there was no way Fair could get statistics on those horses. While Ziggy's brother may have been bred to non-black-type mares in the beginning of his stud career, he proved a powerful sire so early that the chances of him covering a less than stellar mare were thin. His stud fee had been seventy-five thousand dollars, payable when the foal stood and nursed, as is the custom. Show-ring people and foxhunters were shut off from that blood.

As Fair feverishly worked, he thought about the limitations of equine breeding. In America, it's every man (or woman) for himself. There is, as yet, no sense of genetic capital, no commitment to improving bloodstock nationwide. This translates into money and brains or both. Those with the big bucks have access to the best thoroughbred blood. Those without have to be highly intelligent and figure out a way to tap into those bloodlines through a sister, brother, or offspring of a great horse. These horses might never have raced or they retired early with an injury, therefore their get—the term for offspring—would bring little at the yearling sales. But it's the get of these horses that make the great eventers, jumpers, hunters, and foxhunters. The people who own them, if professional horsemen, have spent their lives combing the back pastures of the large breeding farms, haunting the smaller sales, traveling from Maryland to Oklahoma to Ocala to New York, always searching. Others would select a few well-made mares and start a small broodmare band, as Barry Monteith and Sugar Thierry had done. They would then find that half-brother to Lord At War or Pleasant Colony, breed their mare, and pray.

Fair had intended to have dinner with Harry but was so caught up in his research, he canceled. She understood, as he told her what he was looking for and why. Since he had been so attentive of late, she knew he had to be totally wrapped up in his research. Rather than be put out, she was excited he was working late. She wanted to see the results.

It was now nine o'clock, Monday morning, June 28. Fair carried a banker's box filled with printout sheets to Deputy Cynthia Cooper and Sheriff Rick Shaw.

"Can you condense this?" Rick lifted the white lid off the box.

"More or less." The tall veterinarian appreciated how well organized and sparse the county sheriff's headquarters were. Rick ran a tight ship.

"Fair, sit down. Can I get you coffee or a Coke or anything? A doughnut. Rick's big on Krispy Kremes."

Fair waved off Cooper's offer. "Caffeine to the max. I stayed up until four-thirty this morning."

"It must be good." Rick smiled as he dropped into his chair, which he pulled out to face Fair.

"I think it is. I wanted to see if there was consistency in the offspring of Ziggy Flame. The Jockey Club has his records concerning registered breedings. His first year he was bred to fifteen mares. This only counts horses registered with the Jockey

Club; remember, no records for the others unless Mary Pat left them."

"She did." Cooper told him. "That's in the notebook we found in Barry Monteith's effects."

"May I see them later? It'd be good if I could take them home."

"We can do that." Rick nodded, thankful that Fair, a specialist in equine reproduction, wanted to study the notebooks.

"Ziggy's second year he bred twenty-two mares, and the last year he bred thirty-one. Those are pretty good numbers for a stallion in central Virginia. Ten or fifteen would have been more usual. Granted, Mary Pat had fabulous connections, one being Paul Mellon, one of the best breeders America has seen. So she had a wider cast to her net than most people starting out with an unproven stallion but one who had a good racing career."

"What were you looking for?" Rick's eyebrows knitted together.

"Sorry, I got off the point, didn't I?"

"That's all right."

"I was looking for color. Ziggy was a flaming chestnut, hence his name. Color in horses is complicated. But I was looking for percentages. You see, a chestnut stallion bred to a chestnut mare means one hundred percent of the offspring will be chestnut. So all of Ziggy's offspring bred to chestnut mares must be chestnut. On the cover letter there, I've broken down the colors of his offspring according to the color of the mare he bred."

"Great." Cooper smiled.

"Okay, I'm a little dense here. All I know about horses is they eat while I sleep. Why is this important?" Rick reached for his cigarette pack.

"This is why." Fair handed him the stats for Ziggy Dark Star, Flame's full brother, a bay—which is a dark brown horse with a black mane and tail—born in 1967. Ziggy Dark Star's lip tattoo started with a W. "This horse, a full brother to Flame, was a bay. But look at the number of chestnut offspring each time Dark Star was bred to a chestnut mare."

"Same percent as Ziggy Flame," Rick read the cover letter.

"Yes." Fair was jubilant. "If he were bay, there would be more color variation in the offspring."

"And you're sure a bay stallion wouldn't

produce this same percent of chestnut fillies and colts?" Cooper was fascinated.

"That's why I've brought you the box. There's the printout of every mare bred to Ziggy Flame and Ziggy Dark Star. Her age, her breeding, her color, the color of her offspring, her own breeding, the color of her progenitors. And everything is broken down in the cover letter, but all the research is in that box."

Rick handed the cover letter to Cooper, who scanned it. "Fair, what you're telling me is that Ziggy Dark Star is, or I should say was because he died in 1999 at the ripe old age of thirty-two—"

Fair interrupted. "Thirty-three. The papers for Ziggy Dark Star say he was born in 1967, but Flame was born in 1966. He was thirty-three."

"Ziggy Dark Star was Ziggy Flame!" Cooper couldn't believe it.

"Wait a minute. How could the owner . . . uh"—Rick grabbed the paper back from Cooper—"Marshall Kressenberg . . . turn a chestnut horse into a bay?"

"By getting up in the middle of the night and periodically dying the horse." Fair crossed his heavily muscled arms over his broad chest. Working with animals weighing over a thousand pounds made the strong vet even stronger.

"That's fantastic." Rick shook his head.

"For seventy-five thousand a pop, you could do it. You would happily do it. That stallion was covering thirty-five to forty-five mares a year in his prime. Do the math. But also in the box are a few articles about Marshall that I thought might convince you."

Cooper reached down and pulled out copies of articles appearing in *The Blood-Horse* and *Thoroughbred Times*, the grand publications of the thoroughbred industry. "There are a lot of them."

"All of them mention how fanatical Marshall was in his care of the stallion. How only he would handle him and so on. I expect he used dye. But I'm telling you, I stake my reputation on it, Ziggy Dark Star was Ziggy Flame. Apart from color, consider the lip tattoo. The Jockey Club in 1945 began requiring all racehorses to be tattooed on the inner lip. So the first letter in 1945 was A, followed by a series of numbers. Every twenty-six years the letters repeat. The letter for 1966—Ziggy Flame's birth—was V. The letter of Ziggy Dark Star, supposedly born in 1967, was W. That would be so easy, changing V to W."

For a moment all three sat and stared at one another, then Rick struck a match on his thumb, lighting up his unfiltered Camel. "Wonder how close Jerome came to knowing this? He read Mary Pat's notes, which might have gotten him to thinking about more than rabies. My guess is he was pretty close to figuring out that this murder, Barry's murder, had something to do with money, real money, and breeding."

"I don't know if he approached it from the color standpoint, but he knew enough, he was getting hot. In a million years I would have never credited Jerome Stoltfus with that kind of"—Fair didn't want to be unkind, so he didn't say "intelligence"—"research ability."

Cooper, mind in high gear, rubbed her forehead with her finger. "Barry? Does Carmen know? She's kept a tight lip, which is highly unusual for her."

Fair's eyebrows turned upward. "I thought Carmen had disappeared, sort of."

"Sort of." Rick's tone of voice indicated

no more information would be forthcoming on that subject.

Fair, uncharacteristically, pushed. "Is she all right?"

Rick, voice low, said, "I can't talk to you about Carmen, but she's healthy and she's safe."

"Okay." Fair sheepishly grinned. "She's such a character, you know, I really don't want harm to come to her."

"If she'd pick her boyfriends with a little more care, I don't think it will," Cooper deadpanned.

"Makes me wonder if that notebook is all Mary Pat left. What if there was something . . . incriminating—to the killer, I mean," Rick changed the subject.

"What's staggering about this is the profit. The horse was an active breeder almost up until the end. Take an average of forty mares a year and seventy-five thousand dollars a pop, and you come out with seventy-five million dollars over Ziggy's breeding career. And what did it cost to keep him in high style? For his twenty-five years in Maryland, let's say that Marshall Kressenberg spared no expense. Obviously, the last years would be more expensive. Let's say he averaged twenty thousand a year keeping Ziggy in the pink and a few thousand a year in glossy ads in the thoroughbred publications. Marshall, at best, spent about five hundred thousand dollars on the stallion over a twenty-five-year period. Think of the phenomenal profit. Seventy-five million! I'd say that's a major motive for murder." Fair's deep voice rose upward.

"When you hit it, you hit it big." Cooper whistled.

"And Ziggy's sons are doing well at stud. Marshall has Ziggy Bright Star, Ziggy Silent Star. The guy is raking in more money than we can count. No wonder he has horses running and we see his silks on the televised races. This is just amazing," Fair said.

Rick drew a deep drag. "Okay, the money is big, but who knew that this stallion would have such a great career?"

"By his third year at St. James, his first crop were on the track. They were doing pretty good. An experienced horseman would start looking at this guy. Obviously, no one could have foreseen what an incredible sire he would become, but even assuming he would be, say, a B– sire as opposed to an A+, the owner could ask about ten or fifteen thousand per mare. Enough to pay off the farm over time." Fair rested his case. "And we all know that Marshall Kressenberg worked as an exercise rider and groom for Mary Pat. He, even then, was enough of a horseman to see that Ziggy was special, very special."

"He took a hell of a chance killing her for a horse." Rick stubbed out his cigarette.

"People have killed for less," Cooper wisely said.

Rick stood up to stretch. His back ached. "All right, Fair, I'm interested. I can't arrest Mr. Kressenberg, but I can pay him a call. The first thing I want to know is, who have you told?"

"Harry."

"God." Rick sat back down.

"She won't tell." Rick defended his ex-wife.

"She may not tell, but I bet she's halfway to Carroll County, Maryland, by now."

"No, she's not. I made her swear to stay here."

"Her nosiness will lead her somewhere. That woman has an unerring instinct for trouble." Rick fumed. "Well, Fair, she's your problem. The first thing I want to do is to talk to the sheriff up there in Carroll County. The second thing I want to do is batten down the hatches for tomorrow. The feeding frenzy will be worse than it has been."

Cooper noticed Fair's quizzical expression, so she told him, "The news about Carmen's disappearance will be in the papers and on TV, too. There will be all manner of speculation and bull. And we all know rabies will come up. Is Carmen dead in a ditch of rabies? Jeez." She rolled her eyes.

"If you two go up to Westminster"—Fair named the town in Carroll County where Marshall Kressenberg had his farm—"I'd like to go. I think I can be helpful."

"Of course. And you've already been helpful. I need more, Fair, more to convict this guy if he's our man, but this is the first real break we've had."

"Did you find more bones up on those high meadows?" Fair inquired.

"Uh—yes, but not many. We did find part of a jaw. That will be a big help. I should have a positive I.D. soon."

"I guess we all believe it's Mary Pat."

Fair rose. "What a mess this is. What a sad, tangled mess. Oh, before I forget, in the box are the names, addresses, phone numbers, and e-mails of those folks in our own county who breed for the track—in case you want to check who has sent mares up to Carroll County."

"Thank you." Cooper was overwhelmed by the amount of research Fair had done.

Rick walked Fair to the door, clapped him on the back. "Harry's rubbed off on you, old buddy. Now I've got two amateurs to deal with. Thanks, though."

Fair blushed. "Keep it to yourself."

47

While Rick called the Carroll County sheriff, Coop drove over to Dalmally Farm. Rick had given her permission to visit Big Mim, a pipeline to high rollers like Marshall Kressenberg. She found the always immaculately attired older woman standing in a paddock, watching Paul de Silva jog a promising two-year-old filly, Violet Hill.

"Tracks okay." Big Mim observed the fluid-moving youngster as she came straight toward her then straight away. "All right, let me see her from the side."

Paul jogged her up and back so Big Mim could watch both the animal's left and right sides. Violet Hill was by an Argentinean stallion, Wolf, out of one of Mim's good mares, Fanny Hill, and was not intended for the thoroughbred sales. This one Mim wanted to keep for herself to foxhunt and maybe go to a few hunter shows.

The slender, petite woman liked a horse that was forward, that would step out and was, above all, brave. This blood-bay filly, her mane and tail glossy black, just might be the ticket.

"Again, Mrs. Sanburne?" A sweating Paul held the cotton lead rope in his right hand.

"No, you'll melt." She laughed, then turned as she heard Cooper walking toward her. Violet Hill pricked her ears and nickered, as well. "Hello, Coop, what do you think of my girl?"

"What a beautiful color. I don't think I've ever seen a horse that color."

"Blood bay. You don't see many of them, really." Big Mim trod through the grass to meet the deputy at the fence.

Violet Hill enjoyed human company. She wanted to join the two women. Paul led her over so Cooper could admire her and pet her.

"She's a ham." Paul tickled her muzzle.

"I have presence. I'm not a ham," Violet Hill replied.

The humans laughed, although they had no idea what Violet had just said.

"She likes her treats. Would you like to see anyone else today, madam?" Paul, obeying equine etiquette, deferred to the animal's owner and his boss.

"No, thank you. Violet shines like patent leather. You're doing a good job, Paul."

"Thank you, Mrs. Sanburne. Oh, is it convenient for Tazio to come by at four to walk the stable site?"

"You know what, tell her to come at five-thirty if she doesn't mind. Then she can just stay for the meeting about Herb's party. Otherwise she'd have to go back and forth."

"Very good." His Spanish accent sounded melodic.

"Going to heat up even more today." Big Mim, like all country people, paid attention to the weather. "It's actually pleasant now if you're not jogging horses. Would you like to sit?" She indicated a wrought-iron bench, two seats, and a wrought-iron table under the old walnut tree near the barn.

As they sat down Cooper quietly said, "I wanted you to know that half an hour ago Doctors Sandra and Nelson Yarborough identified the bit of jawbone we found with the molars still intact as belonging to Mary Pat Reines."

Big Mim closed her eyes for a moment. "God rest her soul. I don't suppose you know how she died."

"No."

"Poor Mary Pat." She folded her hands together. "Harry finding the ring was the beginning of what I hope will be resolution."

"Is that a nice way of saying we should find the killer and convict him?" Cooper ruefully smiled.

"Yes. Forgive me, would you like a refreshment?"

"No. I'm also here to ask your help."

These magic words enlivened Big Mim. "Of course."

"How well do you know Marshall Kressenberg?"

"I've known him since he was an exercise rider for Mary Pat. I know him through the horse business."

"Tell me about him."

"He left after Mary Pat disappeared. I don't remember exactly when. Perhaps a few weeks after she disappeared. It was all

too depressing. He got a job in Maryland—
a better job, as he moved up to apprentice
trainer. He found Ziggy's full brother, who
due to injury had not raced. Marshall, who
paid attention to Mary Pat's program,
tracked down the horse. He borrowed to
the hilt and bought the stallion from Old
Wampum Farm in Kentucky. That's how he
started his own business. The rest, they
say, is history. Tavener never forgave himself for not locating and buying Ziggy Dark
Star himself. But he had sense enough to
purchase a small share. He knew Mary Pat
had bred back her mare the year after
Ziggy Flame was born. She took the mare
back to Tom Fool, so Tavener knew Ziggy
had a full brother. Lost opportunities. We all
have our share of those."

"Perhaps not so lucrative." Cooper
watched a buck-moth caterpillar crawl
along a limb, followed by others. They
seemed to be gregarious creatures. "Do
you consider Marshall a friend?"

Big Mim thought a moment. "No. A business associate. We have a good relationship. As I said, he's a good horseman and
I appreciate that. He has good manners, is
pleasant company."

"Anything else you can think to tell me?"

She paused. "Well, he's hardworking. He always says he's lucky, he had good advice early. Studied Mary Pat's organization. Hung out with Humphrey Finney, the auctioneer. He tried to learn from the best. He married a lovely girl, a St. Mary's County girl, I believe, and they have four children. Also, he gives generously to various charities, and his wife heads the Heart Fund in Carroll County."

"How much business do you do with him?"

"Not too much, Cooper. He's strictly a flat-racing man, and I'm a 'chaser,' if you will. Occasionally I'll run a horse on turf or dirt, but my real love is steeplechasing and foxhunting, of course. I don't think I've bought more than two mares from him over the years. I liked their conformation, the bloodlines. I see him at the sales, at the Preakness, and occasionally when he comes back here to Albemarle County."

"You never took a mare to Ziggy Dark Star?"

"No, no. That would have been foolish."

"Why?"

"Seventy-five thousand dollars for a

season to Ziggy Dark Star. For what I do that would be throwing money away. You see, dear, I can go to the 'two-year-olds in training and up' sales—meaning older horses—and find a well-bred horse who isn't fast enough on the flat track for a reasonable amount of money. I can turn those into steeplechasers. Or I can breed one of my mares to a good stallion who isn't as expensive. I have always liked doing business with Payson Stud in Lexington, Kentucky. I've had wonderful luck crossing my mares to St. Jovite, Lac Ouimet, Salem Drive. Granted, St. Jovite is a little pricey for my purposes, but he's a marvelous animal, just marvelous." Big Mim loved studying bloodlines, watching horses move, run over fences, or walk around the paddock. She possessed a razor-sharp eye.

"I'm totally ignorant. I don't see steeplechasers in your barn."

"They're with a trainer in Pennsylvania. I like him and I like the way he brings along my horses. There's no point in my building a track, hiring a trainer, the whole nine yards. This works better, and when the horses retire, I bring them home and Paul will turn them into foxhunters."

"How do you know they can do that?"

"Steeplechasing grew out of foxhunting. I know the horses can jump. What Paul has to do is let them mellow out, if you will, teach them to go in company, and we have to acquaint them with hounds. He's a good man with foals, too. I'm quite pleased with him, and I think he's going to work out."

"Do you think Marshall Kressenberg was capable of murdering Mary Pat and stealing Ziggy Flame?"

This took Big Mim by surprise. She sat up straighter. "Why, I don't know. I never thought of such a thing. I—I don't know."

"Do you think Alicia Palmer capable of the crime?"

"Never." She was vehement. "She loved Mary Pat."

"Lovers routinely kill each other."

"No."

"She became rich beyond most people's wildest dreams," Cooper probed.

"No."

"What if she made a deal with Marshall? He kills Mary Pat and she gives him Ziggy Flame."

"No. Absolutely not. Alicia's a heart person, not a money person. You don't know her."

"No, I don't, but she certainly had a crystal-clear motive. And you are her friend. One can be blinded by friendship."

"Cooper, I'm not even blind to my own children's faults. I'm not that kind of person. I'm not a subjective person. It causes my family some distress. It's one of the reasons my son, Stafford, moved to New York. He says I was never a warm, loving mother."

"I'm sorry. I don't mean to upset you, but we've had a break in the Mary Pat case. I have to ask difficult questions. What do you think about Ziggy Flame and Ziggy Dark Star being the same horse?"

"Ziggy Flame was a chestnut. Ziggy Dark Star was a bay. A horse of a different color," she wryly commented. "Are you sure you're on the right track?"

"Marshall could have dyed the horse."

"Good Lord!" This had never occurred to Big Mim.

"We've combed all the articles about Marshall, and each one says only he handled the stallion. This was presented as fanatical devotion. It was, but perhaps for the wrong reason."

The queen of Crozet, speechless for a moment, opened her left hand, her large engagement diamond catching a ray of light. "Oh, Cooper, never, never would I have thought of such a thing. It's horrible. It's too horrible."

"Clever. And he's gotten away with it—or they've gotten away with it, if Alicia is involved—for thirty years."

"Cooper, I know, know in my heart of hearts that Alicia could never do such a thing."

"I know, but none of us thought of Ziggy Dark Star being Ziggy Flame, either."

Big Mim leaned back in the chair, the wrought iron hard against her back. "Does Marshall have any kind of criminal record?"

"Rick checked. Speeding tickets. Other than that, clean as a whistle."

"I see." Big Mim paused. "Are you going to question him?"

"Yes."

"Might I make a suggestion?"

"Please. You know so much more about people than I do." Cooper meant this sincerely.

Big Mim smiled. "Sometimes I do. Sometimes I don't. It would seem to me inevitable that Marshall Kressenberg will find out about Mary Pat. It will be in the news tomorrow, right?"

Cooper nodded, then grimaced. "Along with the story that Carmen Gamble is nowhere to be found."

Big Mim, wise in the ways of Sheriff Shaw, and picking up the lack of urgency in Cooper's voice concerning Carmen, simply replied, "Carmen will appear in good time, hair the latest cut, nails polished, lipstick bright."

"Let's hope so." Cooper smiled. "What's your idea about Marshall?"

"If you question him, he'll be defensive, alert, whatever. However, if we have a ceremony for Mary Pat, bury her remains, and Marshall is invited, then perhaps you can spring a trap."

"What if he doesn't want to come down?" Cooper asked.

"Let me take care of that. I'm going to present this as a gathering of all who loved her and worked for her. We put her to rest at last. Just let me handle it. Herb can conduct the actual service, and the burial will be at St. James, with Alicia's permission."

"Don't tell Alicia—about Marshall, I mean."

"I won't. Have you told Alicia yet about Mary Pat?" Big Mim folded her hands together.

"I have not. I was going to her after seeing you."

"Allow me to go with you."

"All right."

By the time they reached the large, varnished front door with the pineapple knocker at St. James's main house, Cooper was curious as to what Alicia's reaction would be. Big Mim had enlarged on her idea for a trap on the drive over. That was on Cooper's mind, too.

A housekeeper led them to Alicia on the screened-in porch.

Big Mim broke the news.

Alicia took it calmly until Mim hugged her, then she broke down with racking sobs.

She tore Cooper's heart out, except in the back of the young deputy's mind was the nagging fact that Alicia was one of the greatest actresses of her generation.

48

With effort, Big Mim and Little Mim steered the gathering to the business at hand. Shrewdly, Big Mim opened the interior doors to the huge flagstone-floor porch. As the meeting commenced, everyone could see out onto the porch, where Mim's staff, under the able direction of Gretchen Robb, placed dishes on the two tables. Seeing the dazzling repast awaiting them, everyone wanted to finish in a hurry.

During the meeting the bar was open. Given the heat, most people stuck to mint juleps, gin rickeys, and Tom Collinses, with the occasional martini. Fair and Tavener quaffed delicious ice-cold water. Harry, Miranda, and Tazio stuck to iced tea, a slip of mint floating on top.

"We've got the band?" Mim looked over her reading glasses at Harry.

"We do."

"How much?" Tavener, also peering over his reading glasses, inquired genially. "Do I need to sell another horse?"

This was greeted with laughter.

"You'll be fine, Tavener." Harry flipped open her notebook to read off the figures. "Okay. One thousand two hundred dollars for the band, plus gas because they're driving from Harrisonburg. That's five players, three sets. Pretty good, I think."

"Me, too." BoomBoom, accustomed to organizing events herself, nodded.

"Any discussion?" As there wasn't a peep, the elegant Mim pressed on. "Flowers?"

Susan stood up, a habit from school.

"And now she will recite the Pledge of Allegiance to the Flag." Harry giggled.

"At least I remember it," Susan shot back, all in good humor. "Each table will have a small vase of multicolored baby roses. All flowers have been donated by Fair Haristeen."

Everyone clapped as Fair acknowledged their praise.

"Susan, what about the tables? What

did you all decide?" Mim tapped her clipboard with the eraser end of her yellow
pencil.

"BoomBoom and I settled on small seat-
ings of eight. That means we have—wait a
minute." She flipped over a page. "Twenty
tables, but if we need to, we can add two
more. Dave's Rent-All has the tables. They
will set up and will also have tablecloths.
We picked white. It will set off the colored
roses and the beautiful program Miranda
has designed." Susan sat down.

Miranda, who was Big Mim's age, said in
her rich, honeyed voice, "Are you ready for
me, Miss Big?" She was the only person in
the room who could call Mim that, except
for Aunt Tally, who could call her much
worse.

"I am, Cuddles."

This brought howls of laughter from the
group, since Cuddles was Miranda's nickname in high school and somehow didn't
fit her at all.

As the group hurried to finish, Paul de
Silva, freshly showered, tiptoed in the back
door. He lived in one of the small, charming
dependencies on the estate. He lost no op-

portunity to show up at any social get-together where Tazio might appear.

Miranda explained that the program would be printed and bound, which thrilled everyone as this would cut down on speeches, the bane of any celebration.

Big Mim was already addressing that subject. "Since the printed program has testimonials—including, you will note, one from each pastor of each denomination in Crozet—we have trimmed the celebration speeches. My husband, the mayor," she nodded toward Jim, who beamed back, "and Herb will have to say something, of course. I think we'll set a record. Only two speeches."

"Another sermon?" Tazio winked.

"The last thing to die on the Reverend Jones will be his mouth," Aunt Tally cracked.

Without further ado the meeting broke up, perfect timing because Herb was just motoring down the driveway. While he knew there would be a party, Big Mim didn't want him to know all the particulars, which was fine by Herb. There had to be some surprises.

"Preacher approaching," Gretchen called out.

"Look holy." Big Mim clapped her hands together.

By the time Herb passed through the front door, the assembled, all standing, were chatting amiably and waiting anxiously for the dinner bells to be struck.

Gretchen, who loved this part of her job, ceremoniously glided through the living room, striking three small hanging bells that she carried before her. The bells were suspended in a small frame, which was light and easy to carry. It was a bit like a glockenspiel without the flat bars.

"Dinner is served." Gretchen hit the low note, the middle note, the high note. "Dinner is served."

"I dare you to come out with a tuba," Aunt Tally said as Gretchen walked by.

"I don't have the wind for it, but you do." Gretchen winked at the nonagenarian.

"I'll get you for that." The old lady, now on the arm of Fair, who had come alongside her, moved toward the porch.

Once they'd served themselves and seated themselves—this was as informal as Big Mim got—the volume increased.

Harry, Miranda, Susan, Tazio, Fair, Herb, and Paul sat at one table. Behind them were Tavener and Aunt Tally, whom Tavener begged to sit with him. Naturally, Fair protested, and Tally was in heaven. Little Mim sat with her great-aunt, as did Blair. BoomBoom and Bill Langston were at that table, too.

"Where's Alicia?" Aunt Tally wondered loudly.

"Home. She said she couldn't face a big group of people just yet." Little Mim had called Alicia per her mother's instructions.

"Surely she knew Mary Pat was dead," Aunt Tally bluntly said.

"Knowing and *knowing* are two different things," Bill Langston replied.

"Piffle." Aunt Tally speared cold asparagus, fresh from the garden.

"Now, now, she's a very sensitive woman. She's an artist." Tavener made certain Aunt Tally's glass was filled.

"She had the most to gain. Everyone here knows that." Aunt Tally adored Alicia, but that never prevented her from exercising her relentless logic.

Tavener's face flushed for a moment.

"She didn't. Now, you know that. She didn't kill Mary Pat."

"Didn't say that she did." The old lady's eyes glittered. "I just wanted to see you leap to her defense yet again. All you men were and probably still are wildly in love with Alicia. Everyone over forty, anyway. Everyone who remembers."

"I loved Mary Pat," Tavener quietly slipped this in, "which isn't to say Alicia isn't lovable or that you aren't right per usual, Tally."

"We're all in love with you." Fair leaned back from his table and winked at Aunt Tally.

"Liar!" The old lady was jubilant.

Herb stood up, lifting his glass. "Age cannot wither her nor custom stale her infinite variety. Tally Urquhart!"

Everyone stood, toasting the grand old lady of Crozet.

She nodded in recognition, then said, "I commend your good taste."

Laughing, they all sat down.

Paul had a hard time not staring at Tazio, who, while being friendly to him, wasn't exactly flirting. She liked him well enough, though. The other women could tell.

Meanwhile, Bill Langston drooled over BoomBoom. She was used to it.

Herb, taking all this in, chuckled in a low voice. "Ah, yes, another successful Virginia party."

"Haven't had a fistfight yet." Fair picked up the thread of conversation.

"I remember when you and Blair got into it at a summer party," Herb replied. "Should we line up for good seats?"

"Oh." Fair blushed deeply, the red going right up to the blond roots on his forelock. "I—well, he was courting Harry. Lost my temper. Jealous."

"Oh, honey, he wasn't courting me. He was being neighborly." Harry smiled, as this was three years ago.

"Wish I'd seen it." Tazio thought the herbed cold salmon was delicious.

Fair cleared his throat. "According to Aunt Tally, at a successful Virginia party: someone has to fall in love, someone has to leave in tears, someone has to have a physical fight, someone has to be very young, someone has to be very old, and all must have a sense of humor."

"You're just trying to shift the burden off

yourself." Susan smiled at Fair, a valued friend.

"Actually, we haven't had too many fist-fights lately," Miranda noted. "As for the falling in love, we're doing quite well on that front."

"Was Tavener in love with Alicia or Mary Pat?" Tazio whispered, not really believing Tavener's gallant declaration concerning Mary Pat.

Miranda firmly said, "He was in love with Mary Pat. You never knew her. She was incredibly charismatic."

"But she was—what, some fifteen years older than he was." Tazio's voice rose slightly.

Tavener said, "You never knew Mary Pat."

Tazio apologized, "Sorry, Tavener, really. I was being nosy."

He reached behind Aunt Tally's chair, touching Tazio's shoulder. "Being human. And this is Crozet. We're all rummaging around in one another's business."

"I'd like some." Aunt Tally tapped her glass with her knife.

"What?" Tavener was ready to rise and fetch her whatever she desired.

"Scandal. Then you could rummage around in my business."

"Would you be my date at—you know." Tavener cut his eyes toward Herb. "We could start a scandal."

"Goody." She clapped her hands like a child, while Little Mim looked at her mother, who glanced heavenward.

Keeping up with Tally Urquhart was a full-time job.

The room buzzed with chatter.

Fair, half-turned in his chair, spoke to Tavener. "I've been thinking about this rabies thing."

Tavener tipped his chin up for a second. "Get ready for hell week. Buzzards will be all over us again tomorrow."

"What's on your agenda tomorrow?"

"Vet a purchase for Orsinis . . . umm, have to check my book. Why?"

"I have no desire to talk to the media. Do you?"

"No."

"Why don't we meet at St. James, the stables? That's the epicenter of this earthquake."

"Hell, Fair, the media will be crawling over that place. And another thing, the health department was there, the sheriff's department, you name it, they've gone over that place with a fine-tooth comb. Even the state vet was there, and nada." He threw up his hands.

"Alicia will bar the media. She's hired security. I've spoken to her."

"Fair, I don't know what we can do."

"Two things: We can look again ourselves, without other people around. And we can escape the media."

"Umm, that's a thought."

"Can you make it by noon?"

"Uh, yes, I'll be at the Orsinis first thing. Yeah, I can do it. If nothing else we'll enjoy the view."

Herb, having finished his main course, was visiting tables. On his way back to his table, he stopped at Aunt Tally's.

"We're planning a service for Mary Pat. Mim's in charge."

"She runs the world." Aunt Tally was ready for dessert.

"Oh," Tavener and Blair both said at once.

"We've just been discussing it. You haven't been left out," Herb's deep voice reassured them. "Little Mim, I think your mother has put you in charge of the phone calls."

"Okay." Little Mim, who often rankled at doing her mother's bidding, didn't mind this chore.

"We're inviting anyone who ever worked with Mary Pat, friends from afar. You know, we never really had a formal service."

"Well, we never really knew." Tavener sighed.

"When will you be doing this?" Boom-Boom inquired.

"July third, Saturday. It's a big weekend, of course, but we're hoping people can make it." He rested his hand on Aunt Tally's shoulder for a moment.

When Harry arrived home at nine-thirty that evening, she found one smashed lamp on the bedroom floor, along with her formerly clean and folded laundry. Two cats, disgruntled at having been left behind, had misbehaved. They hid in the barn until they thought she would be asleep. Boldly, they sauntered into the house, lights out, at eleven. They hopped on the bed and, that fast, Harry grabbed them.

"Caught you! Thought I was asleep, didn't you?"

"She made me do it," Pewter wailed.

"You are disgusting!" Mrs. Murphy growled.

Harry clicked on her flashlight, hidden under the pillow. "I am looking at two bad pussycats."

"Tucker, you could have warned us, you suck-up," Mrs. Murphy, tail still fluffed out, grumbled.

The dog was laughing too hard to reply.

"No catnip for a week. All my laundry, and I'd just washed it, too."

"We didn't get it dirty," Pewter defended herself.

"Holes in my red T-shirt. My fave," Harry complained with feeling.

"That was an accident," Mrs. Murphy explained. *"I dug in too deep when I threw it off the bed."*

"HA!" Pewter shook herself after Harry let her go.

"I mean it, no catnip for a week, and I might not take you in the truck with me. Now I have to buy a new lamp. My fourth new lamp this year since you routinely smash them. You know how I hate to spend money."

Catching and scaring her cats energized

Harry. She couldn't sleep. She grabbed a book, read a few lines, then laughed. She laughed harder and harder. "Scared the poop out of you two."

Indignant, the two felines thumped out of the room and repaired to their bowl of crunchies in the kitchen, where Pewter proceeded to bite the tips off the little Xs of dry cat food.

"Eat the whole thing, Pewter. I'm not eating what you drop back in the bowl," Mrs. Murphy said, wrinkling her nose.

"It's like biting the little ends off pretzels. Tastes the best." Pewter half-closed her chartreuse eyes.

"Selfish pig."

"You are jus-s-s-t perfect." She drew out the *s-s-t.*

Mrs. Murphy, furious at being outsmarted by a human, jumped up on the counter and sat in the window behind the kitchen sink. She could see the barn, the new shed, and the nearest paddocks. *"Pewter, has it occurred to you that Marshall Kressenberg may not be the killer? Mother's getting herself all fired up over this and she might be wrong. Dead wrong."*

"He's in on it. Harry called Old Wampum Farm and asked if they'd fax the record of Ziggy Dark Star's sale to Fair at the clinic. They had no such record." Pewter brushed the tidbits of food off her whiskers.

"I know. The old man who supposedly sold the horse died in 1984. The subsequent owners say they don't have adequate records. He wasn't much of a record keeper. I reckon he was either in on it or Marshall paid him off. But what if there's more than one—killer, I mean?"

"Harry's thought of that." Pewter, full, felt better.

"Yes, but she's prepared for the wrong one." Mrs. Murphy sighed. *"She trapped us, but a human is much larger than we are. I'd feel better if I knew just what she was up to or what Big Mim had said to her. She isn't going to hold down this killer."*

"You worry too much," Pewter flippantly said, but Mrs. Murphy's words had their effect. *"What can we do?"*

49

The early-morning news carried the story of Carmen Gamble's disappearance, along with footage of the sign at St. James Farm and the Shear Heaven beauty salon.

By eight o'clock the only people in Albemarle County not informed of this latest development were either dead themselves or about to be. And if any of those hovering at death's door happened to revive, the clarion of democracy—the free press—would make certain they were aware of this latest bizarre event in Crozet. The whole rabies story was pumped up and rehashed, as well.

By nine o'clock, eleven stray dogs had been shot and killed by citizens convinced that panting equaled frothing at the mouth.

Feral cats, being smaller, hid in outbuildings and barns. They escaped the vigilance of alert suburbanites living in the new developments that had sprung up in Crozet. Cats with human companions hid, too.

Harry and Miranda showed up at the post office to help Amy Wade, who would be swamped not with mail but with the media, citizens, and every crackpot in western Albemarle County. If no one else will listen to you, the poor soul behind the postal counter must.

Amy nearly cried when they came through the front door. The three of them knocked the mail out in forty-five minutes.

Wisely, Harry had left her cohorts at home.

Since the post office is a federal building, the doors cannot be locked against citizens. When the TV van with the antennae on top drove up, all three women groaned.

A reporter, hair perfectly cut and wearing tan pants, a navy blazer, a blue shirt, and red, white, and blue tie, sailed through the door. Cords trailed behind him, kind of like a Portuguese man-of-war jellyfish.

"I am here in the Crozet Post Office, a

small, tidy building in this nondescript town." He walked over to the counter as the cameraman walked in front of him, then swung behind for the reaction shot of Harry, Miranda, and Amy. The reaction shot suggested someone was flatulent.

The reporter's cue cards were held up by an assistant behind the long-suffering cameraman. Now he lifted one with Harry's name on it.

"The postmistress is Mary Minor Haristeen." He then looked to see which one was Harry.

"I'm no longer the postmistress. That office belongs to Mrs. Amy Wade," Harry said levelly.

"Ah, which of you is Mrs. Wade?"

"I am." The dark-haired, pretty young woman with the merry freckles smiled.

"In a small town the post office is one of the nerve centers. What's the feeling here in Crozet about this unprecedented epidemic of rabies?"

"Two cases don't constitute an epidemic," Harry tartly replied.

"And those two young men knew each other. They were in business together," Miranda chimed in.

"We don't think that's an epidemic. We think it's rotten bad luck." Amy finally wedged a sentence in.

"Are you aware that stray dogs have been shot throughout Crozet this morning? People are taking this seriously," the reporter intoned, voice low for emphasis.

"Idiots!" Harry exclaimed.

"Why do you say that, uh, Mrs. Haristeen?"

"The incidence of rabies among cats and dogs is practically negligible thanks to vaccination. And if you'd done your homework, you would know the strain of rabies that killed Barry and Sugar was that of the silver-haired bat."

He ignored that, saying in a louder voice, "How do you know Carmen Gamble isn't dead of rabies? Perhaps her body is in the woods."

Before Harry could erupt—and she was close to it—the door opened and Fair and Tavener pushed through the cables, assistants, and hangers-on valiantly trying to get their faces on camera.

"Didn't I just see you two?" The reporter blinked.

"You did. We couldn't even get through

St. James's front gate. There were more reporters and cameras than at White House conferences." Tavener, face ruddy with anger, barked, "Pack up and go back from whence you came. All you're doing is creating panic, injuring innocent animals, and getting in the way. This is my post office. I have a postbox, and I'd like to get to it." Tavener brushed by an assistant.

"Me, too," Fair echoed Tavener.

The cameraman tilted the camera upward to capture Fair, tall and imposing.

The reporter bore down on Harry. "You resigned your position because of your animals, didn't you, Mrs. Haristeen?"

"No, not exactly." Harry leaned over the counter.

"But it is a fact that you brought two cats and a dog to work even after the rabies cases were diagnosed."

"They have their shots and so do I." She bared her teeth as though fangs, which made Miranda laugh.

"Harry, you know that's what will be on the news," Miranda said.

"I don't give a damn." Harry defiantly grinned.

"Shots or no shots, don't you think the

sight of those animals might frighten people? It's against the law to bring pets to a federal building unless they're seeing-eye dogs." The reporter at least knew that much.

"This is Crozet." Amy Wade shrugged.

"But under the circumstances such behavior seems if not irresponsible then insensitive." The reporter—delighted for the footage, something a little different than the other stations covering the news—kept at Harry. He looked up suddenly, aware that a very tall, powerfully built blond man was staring down at him.

"Leave her alone," Fair flatly said.

The reporter stood his ground. "And who are you?"

"Dr. Pharamond Haristeen."

"I see." The reporter smiled weakly.

Tavener stepped up next to the reporter. "And I'm Dr. Tavener Heyward. We're both veterinarians. Since your camera is running, let me state unequivocally that there is no danger to citizens of Albemarle County or the state of Virginia from cats and dogs. Furthermore, there is slim danger from the silver-haired bat—scientific name, *Lasionycteris noctivagans*. Both Dr.

Haristeen and myself have thoroughly inspected the barns at St. James. The health
department has crawled through the attics
of the main house and all the dependencies. There is no evidence of rabies
there."

"How can you tell?" The reporter asked
a reasonable question.

"No carcasses," Tavener replied.

"If there is rabies in the bat population,
you'll find a disproportionate amount of
dead bats. And we didn't. We found a few
deceased bats, we took tissue samples.
No rabies. This is a strange and upsetting
case—the deaths of Barry Monteith and
Sugar Thierry—but there is no proof that
rabies is sweeping through the bat population, or through other reservoirs of the
virus, such as raccoons or skunks."

"Then how did these two men die from
rabies?" The reporter leaned forward, mike
thrusting close to Tavener. "And there is a
young woman missing who was close to
the men. It may all be related!"

"We don't know." Tavener sounded professional and at ease before the camera.
"My guess—and it is only a guess—is that
one or both of the men, while traveling to

other barns and to other states, may have been bitten by a bat at one of those locations. The bite is almost always painless and the mark quite tiny. It's possible they never knew."

"I'd certainly know if a bat bit me." The reporter sounded disbelieving and a trifle boastful.

"Not if you were asleep." Fair put him in his place.

"What *about* Carmen Gamble?" the reporter prodded.

"We're hoping she'll show up. Carmen is—well, mercurial."

"She often traveled with Barry Monteith. They were dating," Harry piped up.

"Isn't it true that if there were a rabies epidemic in Crozet, the town would lose tourist money? Like the seaside town in *Jaws*?" The reporter sounded aggressive and smart.

His audience would just eat this up.

"No. The money doesn't stop here. It goes straight to Charlottesville." Tavener walked back to the table to sort his mail.

Fair leaned against the counter. "Crozet is just Crozet. Nothing pretty about us but beautiful country and great people."

"Great people? The animal-control officer is shot dead. Two other men are dead. Doesn't sound like too many great people to me. Jerome Stoltfus, former county animal-control officer, may have held the key to the rabies epidemic!" The reporter really didn't know when to stop, trusting his editor to put together the footage he was churning out. "And weren't the remains of Mary Pat Reines, a leading citizen and wealthy woman who disappeared in 1974, just uncovered? Great people? Crozet is becoming the murder capital of Virginia!"

"Do you know any place on earth where there hasn't been a murder?" Miranda was irritated but covering it.

"That's not the point," the reporter snapped, not really angry but putting on a show for the camera.

"We'll see." Tavener tucked his mail under his arm. "Boy, why don't you run along?"

"Uh, before I go . . ." The reporter checked his name cards, handed him by the assistant. "Haristeen. Are you two related?"

"Married," Miranda called out.

"Were," Harry corrected her.

"Will be again!" Fair grinned from ear to ear, brimming with bravado, but, then again, faint heart ne'er won fair lady.

As Tavener ushered, pushed, propelled the gaggle of unwanted media people out, shutting the door behind them, Harry punched Fair in the arm. "Who says?"

"I says," Fair, uncharacteristically, bragged.

"The woman has to give her consent. Otherwise there's an ugly word for it." Harry replied in a light tone.

"Foolish. The word is foolish." Fair smiled. "Miranda, Tavener, Amy, you heard it here first. I want this woman to be my wedded wife, again. And I'll keep asking her until she says yes."

"God." Harry covered her eyes.

"Give the man points for perseverance." Tavener laughed.

"And good looks." Amy winked.

"And love." Miranda adored the big vet.

"Harry, take your time." Fair squeezed her hand.

"Oh, hell, she's had three years of you pursuing her. The first year after the divorce you were worthless. The last three you've been assiduously courting her." Tavener slapped his mail on the counter for emphasis. "Say yes and be done with it, Harry."

"You two made a great team when you were married," Amy Wade said encouragingly.

Fair leaned down and kissed Harry. "You're outnumbered."

Harry, embarrassed but secretly thrilled, murmured, "Let me think about it. I won't take three more years."

"Heart. Not head." Miranda smiled.

Tavener walked to the front door, where the sight of the reporter bagging people on their way to the post office infuriated him. "I have half a mind to tell that jerk I'll show him where Mary Pat was found."

"Why?" Fair asked.

"Because I'll haul him up to those high meadows, to the corner of the stone wall, turn around, and leave him there. Let him find his way down in the dark." He slapped the mail against his leg, opened the door, and called over his shoulder, "Harry, he's a great vet and a good man. Say yes."

50

The uproar over rabies and Carmen's disappearance continued through the rest of Tuesday and Wednesday. By Thursday, July 1, Rick Shaw, Jim Sanburne, and Tavener Heyward made public appeals for people to calm down.

Not only were people shooting animals, they were shooting one another. This, as much as a desire to restore public confidence, prompted the televised appeal.

Shootings occurred in Brown's Cove, Boonesville, and Sugar Hollow, places where impulsive action independent of law enforcement was not unknown; but they were also happening in tony locations like Ednam Forest and Farmington Country Club.

One person would fire at another's dog and pretty soon it would erupt into the gunfight at the OK Corral. Rick and Cooper were exhausted. So were the veterinarians in town, who had to patch up the animals while Bill Langston and Hayden McIntire patched up the people.

The lawyers would reap the benefits of this disorder. Of course, if it kept up, the undertakers would experience a blip in profits, as well.

Everyone with a grain of sense kept their pets out of the public eye. But dogs especially can foil human intentions. Digging under fences or climbing over them caused many a problem.

Both Rick and Cooper were praying the upcoming Fourth of July weekend would find people focusing on their parties. Hopefully this scare would die down.

Big Mim spent Tuesday and Wednesday with Alicia since St. James was under siege. When the reporters packed up and left the front gate, Mim thought it safe to leave.

Harry and Miranda finished up Tuesday working with Amy Wade. Wednesday, both women stayed in their respective homes.

Thursday afternoon, Cooper drove out to Harry's farm. She'd put in so much overtime that Rick gave her the afternoon off. She brought wonderful sandwiches from Bodo's, a bagel place in town. No sooner had Harry set the picnic table outside than Fair came down the drive with sandwiches from the service station at the intersection of Route 250 and Miller School Road.

"Jackpot." Pewter licked her lips.

"How do you know she won't put some in the fridge?" Tucker hoped Pewter was right, though.

"Look adorable. Show lots of tummy." Mrs. Murphy opened her mouth slightly, inhaling the delicious aroma of sliced turkey, ham, and roast beef.

"Good idea." Pewter ran across the lawn to the picnic table.

Harry and Cooper brought out drinks and condiments from the kitchen while Fair placed three plates and utensils on the oilcloth tablecloth.

The three humans sat down to eat. Harry cut the sandwiches in quarters. That way everyone could have a little bit of everything.

"I'm starved." Harry bit into a turkey

sandwich in which she had placed crisp pickles.

"How can you eat pickles like that? You didn't even slice them lengthwise." Cooper, working on roast beef sliced paper-thin, marveled.

"I've known Harry to open a jar of sweet gherkins and demolish the contents in less than fifteen minutes."

Harry, mouth full, shook her head. "No." She swallowed, then said, "Takes twenty minutes."

"I am so hungry I feel faint." Pewter hit the pathetic note.

"Me, too." Tucker tried looking terribly sad.

"Well, I'm here for whatever you'll give me," Mrs. Murphy flatly stated.

"Oh, for God's sake." Harry tore off a bit of turkey and fed it to Pewter. She was rewarded with purrs so loud they sounded like a feline diesel engine.

Fair and Cooper followed suit, so Mrs. Murphy and Tucker were happily engaged, too.

The food revived Cooper. She really had been tired. "Oh, that's good. I'll try some ham now." Harry handed her the plate with the sandwiches piled on it. "Thank you." She grabbed the mustard jar, slathering the tangy condiment on the rye bread. "I've been on the force for thirteen years, since college graduation, and, guys, I have never, ever been through what I've been through the last two days. People are totally irrational about their animals."

"Tell me." Fair reached into a bowl of Utz potato chips.

"I'm not," Harry fibbed.

Everyone, animals included, laughed at her.

"I thought people were blind about their children. They're worse about their pets!" Cooper took some potato chips, as well. "Rick has smoked more from Tuesday morning to this afternoon than the whole month of June put together. Chain smoking."

"All it does is divert us from what's important," Fair added.

"That thought has occurred to me." Cooper put her sandwich quarter on the plate for a moment; she'd been gesticulating with it in her hand. The animals were ready for something to fall out of it. "Well, here's news, too. Haven't had time to tell you. I've been too busy eating. Actually, all of us were hungry." She noted the refilled plates. "The news is that Marshall Kressenberg isn't coming to the service Saturday. He's in Ireland. His secretary said he left on a horse-buying trip. I don't believe it, but we'll get him. Don't worry."

"He did it?" Fair thought a pickle would be delicious. Harry glared at him when he picked up the jar. "Don't worry. I'll leave plenty for you."

"Good." Harry fed Mrs. Murphy a piece of roast beef. This was her third sandwich quarter and Mrs. Murphy's second.

Cooper said without hesitation, "Oh, yeah. We have to prove it, but he's our man."

"Well, it occurred to me that Ziggy Dark Star's tattoo could tell the tale. We didn't discuss that," Harry said.

"Fair did," Cooper replied.

"You did?" Harry's voice rose at the end of the question.

"I did."

"Was there a Ziggy Dark Star?" Harry was puzzled.

"No. I expect Ulysses Malone, the owner of Old Wampum Farm, was paid off. He bought Ziggy Flame's mother in the dispersal sale in 1974. And he bought the foal born in 1967, the result of Mary Pat's breeding back Ziggy Flame's mother to Tom Fool. But before he could register that colt, it ran through a board fence in a thunderstorm and killed itself. Now, there would be no reason to register the death with the Jockey Club, since the colt hadn't been registered yet in the first place. He hushed it up because he didn't want people to think he didn't take proper care of his horses. He also fired his farm manager."

"Marshall would know the letter sequence. He altered the tattoo." Cooper was still hungry.

"Wait. Let me get this straight. Ulysses Malone and Marshall Kressenberg create an imaginary horse, send in the paperwork and the blood work to the Jockey Club, and are issued a tattoo number starting with a W for 1967?" Harry couldn't believe the simplicity yet daring of the plan.

"They sent in Ziggy Flame's blood," Fair said.

"But what about Ziggy's tattoo?" Harry, irritated that she hadn't thought of this, questioned.

"First off, how many people do you know who have a mare to breed who are going to walk up to a stallion and hold his upper lip?" Fair replied. "And V is easy to turn to W. Who would suspect anything?"

"You've got a point there." Harry nodded. "I've been around horses all my life and I'm real, real careful around stallions."

"We do know that Ulysses Malone died a wealthy man. He'd made the money through breeding. His business took off in the late 1970s," Cooper said. "I expect he was given a share in Ziggy Flame rather than being paid a lump sum. Safer, plus there was the potential for long-term profits, which, luckily for him, materialized." Cooper had learned a lot about the breeding industry because of this case. "When Mary Pat's broodmares were dispersed, he bought the mare who was Flame's dam. He had the reputation of getting bargains at dispersal sales. She produced a few more foals, too, before she died at age twenty-three."

"My horses have tattoos. Why didn't I think of this earlier?" Harry, distressed at her oversight, complained.

"Lot going on," Cooper laconically responded.

"Too much upheaval." Pewter batted a piece of rye bread. Bread was okay, but meat was better.

Harry turned to Fair. "You didn't say anything to me?"

"When have I had time? Or you?"

"Well, when did you figure this out?"

"Over the weekend. When I did all the bloodline and color research. I told you about most of that, but the tattoo slipped my mind, really." Fair apologized. "And one other thing I haven't had time to tell you. I've only told Rick and Cooper.

"I read Mary Pat's notes. This was the book that Barry found and probably read. She used a kind of shorthand.

"Once you get used to Mary Pat's system you can figure it out easily enough.

"Mary Pat suspected the nick between her mare and Tom Fool blood would be golden. She jotted it down. Of course, she died before she could have been sure just how good their cross was, but even the late foals that old Malone got out of the mare did very well at the sales and track."

"Barry must have figured this out." Harry

rubbed her chin. "The real question is what in God's name did Barry do with this information? Jeez, I must be slipping!" Harry said worriedly. "I didn't even badger you to read Mary Pat's notes."

"You've been more rattled than you realize." Cooper took the bull by the horns. "The whole post-office business is upsetting. I mean, Har, even if you were ready to leave, to move on, it would have been nice if you could have done it your way. Pug Harper—well, it was really Jerome—pushed you."

"But I thought I was okay," Harry plaintively said.

"Honey, you are okay." Fair soothingly draped his arm around her shoulders, pulling her close. She kept her hand on the pickle jar, however. "It's just your way. Everyone who loves you knows that. You aren't a person who shows much emotion. It kind of works on you from within."

"Meaning, I don't know what's going on?" She thought a minute. "I guess that's kind of true. If it's outside me, I can figure it out. If it's inside me, it takes a long time."

"Breakthrough." Tucker smiled.

"It's a pity she's not a cat," Pewter

mused. *"Life would be so much more clear for her."*

Mrs. Murphy climbed up on the plank seat. She snuggled next to Harry. *"Her eyesight would be better, anyway."*

"Okay, I missed the tattoo. Signs point to Marshall Kressenberg's having something to do with Mary Pat's death. There are a lot of blank spaces, though, lot of loose ends."

Cooper leaned her elbows on the table. "Once we get our hands on Kressenberg, I think those ends will get tied up."

"So the rabies is just that. Not connected?" Fair asked.

"Certainly seems to be the case. Except we have the murder of Jerome Stoltfus hanging over our heads. Marshall, I hope, will spill the beans on who killed Jerome. I'm thinking that somehow, in Jerome's mania to find the cause of the rabies case, he found damning evidence against Marshall Kressenberg. Jerome figured out that Ziggy Flame was Ziggy Dark Star. Jerome proved much more resourceful than we ever imagined. He'd started doing color research."

"I'll be," Harry sighed. "And you're sure Alicia doesn't have a hand in this?"

"No, I'm not sure." The tall, blond woman folded her hands together over her plate. "But Alicia Palmer hasn't cracked over all these years."

"Neither has Marshall Kressenberg," Fair responded.

"But she had all the money in the world. Why help him?" Harry wondered.

"Because she wanted the fortune. She didn't want to wait until Mary Pat died an old lady and she herself would be much older. She wanted to be her own woman. As long as Mary Pat lived, Alicia would have to dance to her tune. As it was, they fought over Alicia's desire for an acting career." Cooper had seen a lot of mischief over inheritances.

The three humans and three animals sat quietly for a minute or two.

Fair rose, walked to his truck. He held up a white paper bag. "Chocolate chip cookies!"

"Hooray!" Harry clapped her hands.

"It's not that exciting," Pewter grumbled.

"Chocolate is the human version of fresh

mouse." Mrs. Murphy closed her eyes, swaying slightly.

"Or marrow bones." Tucker, full, rested her head on her paws.

"So we're not out of the woods yet?" Harry returned to the subject at hand. "There might be an accomplice or two?"

"Yes," Cooper simply replied.

"I've had my head in the sand. Wonder what else I've missed. Maybe I missed something that would help. I'm upset. At the risk of bragging on myself, I'm usually pretty sharp about details, people, clues. At least I think I am."

"Harry, you are. You are." Cooper smiled. "But you are going through a big life change."

"You mean I have to find a job?" Harry laughed.

"A career. Something you love." Fair put in his two cents.

"Kind of a muddle right now."

"Honey, this has all happened fast. Give yourself the summer to think things through and explore options. Everything will be fine."

"When you say it, I believe it. When I'm home alone, doubt creeps in." She sighed.

Fair resisted the obvious riposte that she shouldn't be home alone, he should be with her.

It was true. Harry was rattled. Her mind was clouded by quitting, by questions about her future. She was also rattled, although happy, because she realized she did love Fair. This was a quiet, growing realization, and she'd address it when all this settled down. She knew she ran away from emotion, but she swore to herself she wouldn't do that about Fair and she'd sit down to talk to him. She gave herself an August 1 deadline. She was again in love with him.

Had Harry been on course, she would have realized she had been given a clue Tuesday, a disturbing and dangerous clue.

51

A soft rain pattered down Saturday, July 3. Tiny drumbeats resounded throughout central Virginia as leaves bowed then bounced back with each raindrop.

The service for Mary Pat Reines was held at eleven-thirty A.M. at St. Luke's. The simple interior of the old eighteenth-century church invited all who stepped inside to consider the spiritual side of life. For those aesthetically attuned, the clean lines, crisp whiteness of the walls, dark forest-green long cushions on the original maple pews, and deep pure colors of the stained-glass windows made sitting in St. Luke's a visual delight.

A balcony along the back wall also contained the organ. The long pipes, looking

golden, were in the walls behind the front of the church. St. Luke's couldn't afford to purchase an organ until the boom years under James Monroe's presidency. The one they bought had to have been the best, because it was still in use today.

The church was full but the balcony held only the organist, Merilee Kursinski, and her assistant, the ever-jolly Meredith Mc-Laughlin. Elocution and Cazenovia, Herb's cats, sat on a front balcony pew, as did Mrs. Murphy, Pewter, and Tucker. The Reverend Jones loved animals, taking St. Francis as a personal saint, so if the balcony was not in use, he thought a small four-footed congregation was in order. For Herb, all souls, including his beloved cats, were equal before God. Although at times he wasn't so certain about Elocution, given her tendency to desecrate communion wafers. She had been the one who led Cazenovia, Mrs. Murphy, Pewter, and Tucker into this misdeed during the winter, causing no end of trouble when communion Sunday came due. Poor Herb opened the closet door only to discover the tattered remains of the communion boxes.

Telltale kitty-fang marks pointed to the culprits.

Down below, the front pew contained Alicia Palmer, Tavener Heyward by her side, the elder Sanburnes, and Aunt Tally. Immediately behind them sat Harry and Fair, Miranda—alone since Tracy Raz was still out of town—Susan and Ned Tucker, Little Mim Sanburne, and Blair Bainbridge.

BoomBoom, Tazio Chappars, Paul de Silva, Amy Wade, and Bill Langston sat in the third pew.

Many of Mary Pat's friends—the older generation—had passed on. Those in the church knew her, but most were from younger generations, such as Harry, Fair, and Susan, who were still in grade school when Mary Pat disappeared.

When Herb entered from behind the lectern, he wore his full robes of office, an impressive sight. The green of the Trinity surplice contrasted with the black of his robes. With his deep Orson Welles voice, blue-gray eyes, and silver-gray hair, Herb exuded authority and something quite special: compassion.

"I am the resurrection and the life, saith the Lord: He that believeth in me, though

he were dead, yet shall he live: and whoso-
ever liveth and believeth in me, shall never
die.

"I know that my redeemer liveth, and
that he shall stand at the latter day upon
the earth: and though this body be de-
stroyed, yet shall I see God: whom I shall
see for myself, and mine eyes shall behold,
and not as a stranger.

"We brought nothing into this world, and
it is certain we can carry nothing out. The
Lord gave, and the Lord hath taken away;
blessed be the name of the Lord."

Outside, Cooper heard the organ, then
the voices of the congregation as they
sang. Although little of Mary Pat had been
recovered, that little was to be interred at
the family cemetery back at St. James.
Cooper was the escort and would drive in
the front of the hearse.

Although she didn't like funerals, she did
like driving the big Harley-Davidson motorcycle, which she'd parked under a tree.
She put plastic over the seat due to the
rain. Although not part of the motorcycle
patrol, Rick allowed her to pull funeral duty
so she could ride the Hog. One of the ad-
vantages of being part of a small force was

she wasn't hemmed in by so many restrictions.

She leaned against the hearse to chat with the driver and assistant, who held a huge golf umbrella. A large casket was not in order. Alicia requested the bones be cremated, so a beautiful small casket, two feet square, contained Mary Pat's ashes.

This small, elegant mahogany casket reposed on a plinth in the center front of the church, below and between the lectern and the pulpit.

The service, somber yet beautiful, concluded. Tavener and Fair acted as pallbearers. Each gentleman took one of the curving brass handles. Going before everyone, they carried Mary Pat out of the church.

They placed the mahogany casket in the back of the hearse, then each waited for the lady he was escorting.

Fair stood out in the light rain as people filed by. Harry, two kitties and one doggy in tow, slipped out the back door of the church. Her high heels sank in the thick, sodden grass.

"Damn. These things are worthless." She pulled her feet up high with each step.

"I heard that," BoomBoom half-whispered.

Harry turned around. "Why'd you come out the back?"

"Stopped at the bathroom." BoomBoom reached over and took Pewter, whom Harry was carrying like a loaf of bread.

"She's heavy." Harry smiled.

"She is." BoomBoom bent over in jest. "Hard to carry two cats at once."

Harry and BoomBoom put the animals in Fair's truck. Harry hurried to Fair as fast as she could in her heels. "Sorry it took me so long."

"That's okay. Had a chance to see everyone."

They climbed into the truck and drove out to St. James for the graveside ceremony.

The graveyard was high behind the main house. One could see the back of the house, some of the barns, and the training track from the location. The graveyard, surrounded by trees, did not attract attention when one was at the house or the barns.

A small, square canvas tent had been erected over the grave, which the gravediggers had mistakenly made full size.

People gathered under the tent. Others stood outside, their colorful umbrellas adding festive color to the dolorous occasion.

Herb stood at the head of the grave. Alicia stood, although there were chairs, to his right. Tavener was next to Alicia. Harry was next to Tavener. Fair was next to her.

Across from the grave stood all the Sanburnes. Aunt Tally, cane in hand, rested on a chair.

Mrs. Murphy, Pewter, and Tucker sat under the huge black gum tree at the back of the graveyard. Although only thirty yards away, no one noticed them. Harry had given them a lecture on being very, very quiet.

"Why does it always rain at funerals?" Pewter whispered.

"To irritate you," Mrs. Murphy replied.

"Did you know there's a gravestone where Stonewall Jackson's arm is buried near Chancellorsville?" Tucker informed them. *"There's not much left of Mary Pat. A couple old bones. They should give them to me. I'd bury them."*

"You're terrible." Pewter giggled softly.

"Well, I ask you, what good does burying

bodies and bones in a casket do? Nothing. All that protein goes to waste." Tucker kept her voice low. "And what carrion eaters don't use will enrich the soil."

"Spoken like a true dog." Mrs. Murphy wrinkled her nose.

"Bodies spread diseases, especially if they get in the water supply. That's why humans bury their dead," Pewter resolutely stated.

Tucker cocked her head. "All they have to do is find a place far away from water, put the bodies there, and vultures, dogs, and bugs will do the rest. It's not right to waste resources."

"You'll eat anything." Mrs. Murphy rolled her eyes.

"If it doesn't eat me first," Tucker whispered, a little too loudly.

A few raindrops slipped through the leafy canopy, dribbling on Pewter's gray fur, which she had groomed to perfection. "Bother. Why are they taking so long? Herb said words at the church. That ought to be good enough."

"Have to do the ashes to ashes, dust to dust." Tucker stood up for a better look, but she beheld only legs and shoes.

"Humans have to talk. Jibber jabber." Another cascade of droplets dotted Pewter's fur.

"I've noticed how silent you are," Mrs. Murphy commented.

Pewter, crabby, removed herself to a place under the black gum where the leaf cover was thicker and where she was away from Mrs. Murphy and Tucker. This placed her on the opposite side of the grave from them.

At the grave site, Herb prayed before the final blessing. "O Lord Jesus Christ, who by thy death didst take away the sting of death; Grant unto us thy servants so to follow in faith where thou hast led the way, that we may at length fall asleep peacefully in thee—"

Harry, while listening to the prayer, saw Carmen Gamble step out of a squad car, high heels first, dressed in black. No one else saw her, as all were focused on the graveside service. Slowly Carmen began to walk up the rise to the site. She cast her eyes up toward the ridge, toward the high pasture where these whitened bones had been found. Harry remembered Tucker with the thigh bone, and then it hit her: She didn't know where the other bones were found, because she, Fair, and Susan had been sent back when Rick arrived. Tavener had said at the post office, "At the corner of the stone wall." She blinked, tensed, then shouted, "You! Tavener, you killed Mary Pat!"

The shock of Harry Haristeen disrupting a sacred moment was quickly replaced by the sight of Tavener Heyward pushing Harry into the grave, then jumping in after her. With his right hand he pulled a small, flat handgun from his inside coat pocket and put it to her temple as he collared her, his left arm around her throat.

"Everyone get out of here!" Tavener bellowed. *"Now!"*

Fair moved toward the edge of the grave. "Let her go. Take me."

"Get out, Fair, *out*, or I will shoot her right now. After all, she's in the grave," he snarled.

"So are you," Harry choked out.

Tavener jerked his left arm harder so she couldn't speak. "One, two, when I get to three, this nosy bitch will be dead unless all of you run—and I mean fly—down to the house."

Alicia paused as she backed away. "You'll go to hell for this."

"I'll have lots of company," Tavener coolly replied.

Mrs. Murphy had climbed the tree on hearing the first commotion. *"Pewter, stay on your side! Tucker, come with me. We're going to the grave site."* The tiger cat had also seen Carmen Gamble walking up the hill.

"Why?" Pewter was still mad at the tiger cat.

Mrs. Murphy didn't even back down the tree. She leapt off the branch. *"No time to explain."*

Pewter overcame her pique. Something important was happening. She needed to be there.

Since the humans were slipping and sliding down to the house, the animals didn't have to navigate through them. Within seconds both Tucker and Pewter saw Harry in the grave, gun to her temple.

Mrs. Murphy and Tucker moved up behind Tavener. Pewter headed straight for him.

Tavener loosened his grip on Harry, who gasped for breath as she tried to step back, staggered, took another small step back. He noticed the gray cat barreling for him but thought nothing of it. He didn't hear Mrs. Murphy and Tucker behind him, because Harry made harsh rasping noises as she gratefully sucked in air.

Without conferring with one another, each of Harry's friends knew what she had to do.

Pewter soared off the edge of the grave site. Mrs. Murphy did the same from the back. Tucker, paws spread out, legs stiff and straight, slid down.

Pewter hit Tavener on the chest before he had time to react. He pointed his gun away from Harry's head to shoot the brave gray kitty, but Mrs. Murphy landed on his head, claws sinking in his face. Harry, using her high heels, stepped on his foot with all her weight.

Tucker, now in the pit, ran at him as hard as she could in such a shortened space. She slammed into the back of his knees. He buckled. His rib cage hit Mary Pat's casket edge. Harry heard the crack.

Harry leapt on him, grabbing his right wrist, while he clawed at her with his left hand.

Tucker immediately bit Tavener's left hand. The intrepid corgi wouldn't let go.

Mrs. Murphy and Pewter, clawing and biting his face and neck, spattered blood everywhere.

Cooper, using trees and shrubs as cover, was sneaking up from the house. She saw her chance. Sprinting to the grave, she trained her service revolver on Tavener. "Harry, I've got him."

"Not until I get the gun, you don't," Harry hoarsely replied, fighting like mad to break his fingers.

Blood flew everywhere. From Tavener's face, from his left hand, from Harry's face where he'd managed to dig his nails into her flesh.

Fair, running harder than he'd ever run in his life, reached the edge of the grave and launched himself in. He closed both huge hands around Tavener's right hand, then snapped Tavener's arm over his knee. The gun fell to the ground when the forearm broke like a matchstick.

Harry, exhausted, rolled back against the edge of the grave. Fair picked up the gun, tossing it to Cooper.

Harry reached for her cats and dog. She

couldn't speak. Fair understood and lifted out Tucker, then gently placed Mrs. Murphy in Harry's arms while he held Pewter.

Tavener moaned, struggled to his feet. Fair placed Pewter on the edge of the grave, walked over, and kicked Tavener so hard he went down face-first, spitting teeth.

"I'll kill you!"

"Fair, leave him," Cooper firmly commanded.

Fair, eyes wild, advanced on Tavener.

Harry managed to choke out, "Don't," as she put Mrs. Murphy at the grave's edge and climbed out herself.

"Come on, Fair. Think of the legal fees," Cooper sarcastically said, while the animals looked on.

With tremendous effort, Fair backed away. He was shaking so hard that Mrs. Murphy was afraid he'd come apart at the seams.

Bill Langston, Blair Bainbridge, and Paul de Silva were next on the scene. Paul and Bill jumped into the grave.

Blair stood over Tavener just in case. Cooper, immobile, never took her gun off him.

Fair swung out of the grave, then broke down, sobbing, "I thought I'd lost you," as Harry put her arms around him.

Tucker leaned against Fair's leg as Pewter rubbed his other leg. Mrs. Murphy rubbed against Harry's leg.

Pewter walked to the grave, looked down at the crumpled Tavener. *"Humans are no match for cats,"* she taunted him, then thought a moment and added, *"and corgis."*

It was then that the stunned humans, coming back together, saw Carmen Gamble in their midst, shaking a fist at Tavener.

"Scum!" Carmen spat.

52

Multicolored Japanese lanterns waved over the quad at St. Luke's Church on July 17. The thirtieth anniversary of the Reverend Herbert C. Jones's ministry brought out everyone to honor the good man. Given the recent events, it felt like a new beginning. Better times were ahead.

Herb had been given many presents, but his favorite was the big hand-painted sign of Cazenovia and Elocution with halos over their heads.

Speeches made—Herb's being particularly touching—the celebrants settled into wonderful food, ice-cold drinks, and spicy conversation.

Mrs. Murphy, Elocution, Pewter, and Cazenovia lazed on the podium now that the humans had vacated it. The cats liked being above everyone.

Tucker remained at Harry's round table, along with Fair, Susan and Ned, Cooper and Miranda, Paul de Silva and Tazio Chappars. Since Brinkley remained at the table, too, Tucker enjoyed some bracing dog talk. Carmen managed to sit through the speeches, but the minute they were over she was table-hopping.

Big Mim, Jim, Aunt Tally, Alicia, Little Mim, Blair, and Herb sat at the table next to Harry's. These tables were up front by the podium.

The recent uproar dominated conversation.

"Rick is really good. He could be police chief in a big city if he wanted to." Cooper praised her boss, also at the party. "For five days we couldn't crack Tavener. He wouldn't open his mouth. You know how Rick finally cracked him?"

"No," everyone replied.

"He brought in a photograph of Tavener's mother. All he said was, 'She didn't raise you to kill people.' That did it. He gushed like a fountain."

The people at Herb's table pulled their chairs closer to listen.

"So he, not Marshall Kressenberg, killed Mary Pat?" Big Mim inquired.

Cooper nodded affirmatively. "He was in love with her. He told the truth about that. He begged her and begged her, and one evening he grabbed her down at the barns. He thought no one was around. He was wrong. He kissed her and she pushed him away. He grabbed her again; she hit him. He lost it and strangled her. Marshall Kressenberg, who had been up in the hayloft, witnessed the whole thing."

"He could have helped her!" Alicia was aghast.

"Chicken." Cooper shrugged. "Or maybe he saw his chance. We'll know his side of the story when we extradite him back to the States."

"And then they dragged her up to the high pastures?" Harry felt so sorry for Mary Pat.

"Threw her in the pickup truck. It rained that night, washing out their tracks. They buried her at the corner of the stone wall. Then Tavener had the bright idea to bring up Ziggy Flame. They'd be missing together. While Tavener walked up Ziggy Flame, Marshall walked up a mare so Ziggy wouldn't jump out of the pasture. Since Tavener was Mary Pat's vet and Marshall worked at the barns, no one doubted their word about the number of mares on the farm. They thought only Ziggy was missing. Also, mares were going in and out of St. James daily to be bred. That part was easy."

"When did they move Ziggy to Maryland?"

"When Marshall left. Tavener dyed him. Showed Marshall how to do it. Tavener falsified all the papers."

"And made a fortune." Fair knew Tavener had done these terrible things, but he couldn't reconcile this behavior with the colleague he'd worked with and liked for years.

"Why kill Barry and—maybe I'm jumping the gun—Sugar?"

Everyone leaned forward, quiet.

"Barry found both Mary Pat's diary and her breeding notes. She'd hidden them behind a loose board in the tack room at the biggest barn. Why we'll never know, except that she really didn't have much privacy, I suppose. Servants everywhere. I don't know. Do you?" Cooper looked at Alicia.

"She probably wanted her breeding notes at the barn. That's where she did her work. And the diary, maybe she didn't want me to find it. I don't think the servants snooped, but I did." Alicia cast her eyes downward.

"Barry read the notes and the diaries. He put two and two together, since there were many references to Tavener's declarations of love and his desires to go into the thoroughbred business with Mary Pat. Tavener managed to find the diary in Barry's things. He burned it as soon as he got his hands on it, but he couldn't find Mary Pat's breeding notes with Barry's stuff. Barry did a better job of hiding those, probably because they meant more to him."

"But what about the rabies? People have been crazy about that. Did the men really have it?" Blair asked.

"That's the terrible part." Cooper looked toward Blair. "Tavener gave it to Barry and Sugar. Barry had been blackmailing him. Maybe graymailing is a better word, because Tavener confessed that Barry didn't make threats. Suggestions, not threats. Lots of business suggestions. Then Tavener would come through with the money. Barry put most of it in the business. We think he kept some for himself—he bought a new truck, anyway. Sugar, who kept the books, didn't know where this money was coming from, and he finally got mad enough at Barry that Barry just said he had something on Tavener. We don't know if he told Sugar everything, but Tavener wasn't taking any chances. Even if Barry hadn't told Sugar, it was possible Sugar might figure out some things in time."

"How?" Aunt Tally simply asked.

"Shots. He told the guys he'd give them their rabies vaccine free. It's expensive and anyone who works with animals for a living ought to have it. He gave them a live virus, not a killed one. And since it generally takes so long to develop, they felt fine."

"I'd like to add here that veterinarians do not usually work on humans," Fair mentioned.

"No, but you can if you have to. Vets work with humans during emergencies," Big Mim said.

"You'd think Barry would be suspicious."

Aunt Tally said, sharp as a tack about Barry. "After all, Tavener was forking over money to him."

"Tavener acted like their best friend. He did a lot of work gratis. I know Fair did, too. Tavener gave them all their equine medications for free. He said that took discipline. He had to act as though he was enthusiastic about their business, liked them, acted like a mentor."

Susan observed the loudly dressed Carmen. "And she was in danger, too?"

"A slip of the tongue." Cooper smiled. "She mentioned to Tavener when he was in her shop that Barry showed her the diaries. When Jerome was killed it slowly dawned on her that, with Barry's nosing around, this might have something to do with the horses."

"And?" Harry tapped the edge of her glass.

"I took her to my house and told her not to show her face. The hardest part was cleaning up after Ruffie since he couldn't go outside." Cooper laughed. "The hardest part for Carmen was knowing her family and the gang at work had to be frantic."

"So you were on to Tavener?" Fair was still surprised at the turn of events.

"Mmm, getting close, but Rick and I just didn't have enough."

"But why didn't Tavener wait for the rabies to kill Barry?" Harry asked.

"Barry pushed too hard. Tavener said Barry wanted an extra hundred thousand dollars to buy more broodmares. So Tavener asked Barry to meet him down past St. James's entrance gates. He told Barry not to tell Sugar if Sugar was there. As it turned out, Sugar was in town.

"So Barry met him, and as Tavener wrote out the check he offered Barry a drink from his flask. Loaded with Quaaludes and bourbon."

"What would he have done if Barry hadn't taken a drink?" Fair wondered.

"Shot him, I guess. But Barry did take a drink. They chatted. When Barry started to fade out, Tavener drove down the road, turned up one of the farm paths. He stopped, hauled out Barry, and carried him to the creek, then walked downstream until his strength gave out. He dumped him, slashed up his throat with a serrated knife. He did a pretty good job of mimicking an animal bite, but Tavener overlooked the fact that the lack of saliva would be a tip-off that this wasn't a natural death. So he felt safe. He thought he'd be able to pull off Sugar's murder, too, and close the door forever on this. Harry found Barry shortly thereafter."

"Luckily, I didn't see Tavener, or he would have slashed my throat." Harry breathed a sigh of relief.

"Barry was young and strong. He lasted longer than most people." Cooper rested her hand on the table edge.

"The ring?" Alicia asked.

Cooper shrugged. "He swears neither he nor Barry had it."

"Fate," Big Mim said.

"And Jerome?" Little Mim, who'd found Jerome, would not soon forget.

"Tavener lured Jerome out. Given Jerome's ego and excitement, that was easy. He told him he could show him how to collect the live rabies virus. He said he'd just found an injured animal by the road, which he believed was rabid."

"Jerome didn't suspect Tavener?" Fair thought Jerome wouldn't have trusted Tavener at this point.

"Jerome, like us at the time, was focusing on Marshall Kressenberg. Tavener had been helpful; none of us suspected anyone so close to our community. Jerome didn't, either. And Jerome's curiosity got the better of him. He wanted to see Tavener collect the live virus. He'd told Tavener and others how someone could be killed, remember?"

"Flu shots." Fair exhaled.

"Told me. Questioned medical people," Bill Langston added.

"Poor Jerome. He couldn't resist showing off what he knew." Susan pitied him.

"Well, they met on the road. Jerome didn't have time to get out of the car. Tavener shot him with a gun bought at a gun show, a used gun. No papers. Then he disposed of it. He was bold and arrogant. He still thought he could get away with it."

"He was clever." Alicia's eyebrows came together in disgust.

"Clever, and he relied on being a pillar of the community," Cooper said. "He was protected by position. In fact, if Barry hadn't found Mary Pat's diary and breeding notes, none of this would have happened."

"Curiosity killed the cat," Little Mim said.

"Two cats, Barry and Jerome. It seems to me like Sugar paid for Barry and Jerome's curiosity."

"Thank God for my two cats!" Harry beamed. "And Tucker. Or else I think curiosity would have gotten this cat"—she pointed to herself—"too."

"You're very lucky." Alicia smiled. "Mary Pat's ring protected you. She wanted us to find her. I really believe that and now she's at peace."

"I believe that, too," Cooper said surprisingly. "But because of one man's lust and greed, four people are resting—we hope—in peace but long before their time."

"But it was their time." Paul, usually quiet, spoke up. "When the Lord wants you, it's your time, no matter how it looks to us."

"I'm sure you're right," Tazio smiled, "but it's all sordid and shocking."

"Dreadful," Big Mim pronounced judgment.

"Do not think to repay evil for evil, wait for the Lord to deliver you." Miranda quoted from Proverbs, Chapter 20, Verse 22.

"I'm supposed to be the Bible-quoter here," Herb teased.

"Well, nobody does it better than you." Miranda raised her glass to Herb.

They toasted the good reverend and switched to happier subjects.

Harry, who rarely drank, sipped champagne in honor of Herb. Her normally sharp senses had been dulled by her own predicament. She felt if she were on top of her game she would have somehow figured out Tavener was in on this. She figured it out at the end and nearly got shot for it. She couldn't control her impulses. She blurted out everything at the grave site, heedless of the consequences.

She would give her future some hard, clear thought. She hated being muddled. But whenever she'd think about what she wanted to do, all that came to mind was a big question mark.

Harry thought to herself, what was the Bible quote that Miranda would say on the days when Miranda's arthritis kicked up? "Strengthen the weak hands, and make firm the feeble knees." Ah, yes. Well, perhaps the Good Lord would strengthen her weak mind.

She slipped her hand through Fair's and

watched the fireflies come out to compete with the Japanese lanterns.

On the dais, the cats, filled with delicious food, observed the humans.

"Do you ever get tired of Herb's sermons?" Pewter asked Elocution and Cazenovia.

"No. We like to help him." Elocution lay on her side, her tail lazily waving to and fro.

"He gives good sermons, but all this life-after-death stuff—I don't know," Pewter said.

"I believe in life before death." Mrs. Murphy smiled.

Dear Reader,

I've had my rabies shots, my annual FVR-CP shots, which cover just about everything a kitty can get. I endure worming once a month. Large ugh. My teeth are good.

I mention this because much of this book is about health.

Pewter also gets all her shots and is a big weenie about it. The dogs, on the other hand, are pretty good.

I hope you've taken care of your shots and teeth and whatever a human needs to do. Expensive though it is, it's still not as expensive as being sick.

As I've gone along with this series I've found that I truly love the characters. Funny, isn't it? I mean I even like the corgi and, well, dogs are okay but a cat can't be but so close to them. They're just so slavish! If I have to admit it, I like the dogs here at home, a motley crew of rescue mixes as well as Mother's foxhounds, her pride and joy.

Now, I adore the horses but cats and horses have a special friendship.

Whoever you are reading this, I hope you have an animal in your life that you can tell *everything* to and know it won't go any further. We make the best friends—just be sure we get our shots, okay?

Always and ever,

Sneaky Pie